HOME OF THE BRAVE

J. N. CHANEY
RICK PARTLOW

LAS VEGAS, NV

1st Edition

CONNECT WITH J.N. CHANEY

Don't miss out on these exclusive perks:

- Instant access to free short stories from series like *Backyard Starship*, *Sentenced to War,* and more.
- Receive email updates for new releases and other news.
- Get notified when we run special deals on books and audiobooks.

So, what are you waiting for? Enter your email address at the link below to stay in the loop.

https://www.jnchaney.com/taken-to-the-stars-subscribe

CONNECT WITH RICK PARTLOW

Check out his website

https://rickpartlow.com

Connect on Facebook

https://www.facebook.com/DutyHonorPlanet

Follow him on Amazon

https://www.amazon.com/Rick-Partlow/e/B00B1GNL4E/

JOIN THE CONVERSATION

Join the conversation and get updates on new and upcoming releases in the awesomely active **Facebook group**, "JN Chaney's Renegade Readers."

This is a hotspot where readers come together and share their lives and interests, discuss the series, and speak directly to J.N. Chaney and his co-authors.

facebook.com/groups/jnchaneyreaders

CONTENTS

1

Snow whipped at the cockpit viewscreen as the north wind wrestled with me for control of the lander, and I wondered if this was such a good idea.

"Isn't this thing supposed to have anti-gravity or something?" I asked through clenched teeth, pushing the controls downward despite the stomach-dropping feeling of going over the first dip of a rollercoaster.

"You've been flying landers for two years now," Valentine McKee reminded from the copilot's seat beside me, "and you still don't know how they work? It's not anti-gravity, it's gravity-*resist*. There's a difference."

"And the difference is, this snowstorm is kicking our ass."

I checked the altimeter, which now looked a lot more like the ones on airplanes since I'd reconfigured the controls to suit me. The reading there was the only indication I had that we were less than a thousand feet up. Everything on the optical cameras was flat black, and even the sensors that worked on principles I wouldn't have understood if my major in college had been physics and not history showed nothing within miles of us.

"You could have let *me* fly the lander," Giblet commented, arms crossed, his expression sullen. Well, as sullen as his bird-like face got.

When I'd first met Gib and was absorbed with the alienness of everything around me, I'd put a little too much emphasis on his avian features. And they were there, to be sure. His hair was feathery and a fine down of it covered his whole body, and put together with his narrow face, aquiline nose, and the vertical pupils of his eyes, it painted a clear picture of the bird DNA mixed with his human genes. Maybe that DNA was what made him our best pilot or maybe it was just his innate confidence. But that confidence could also make him a huge pain in the ass.

"How are we even gonna find the LZ in this storm?" Dani Campling asked, sounding even tenser than I was.

I don't know, maybe I would have been tense, too, if I was sitting in the second row, helpless and at the mercy of someone else's piloting skills in a mess like this. But Dani wasn't the nervous type. She'd been a deputy sheriff in rural Ohio before she'd joined our merry little band and while I'd been shanghaied into this whole thing by a scheming robot, she'd volunteered, eager for the sort of adventure that got her shot at. I wondered if her discomfort was because of the flight or the company. Her relationship with Giblet had been…tricky…ever since Tamura's death.

Giblet had fallen head over heels for her, but she'd chosen the Kamerian pilot over him. Gib hadn't taken that well and while he'd backed off after Tamura had died, which was a lot more sensitive than I'd given him credit for, Dani still seemed uncomfortable around him. And it was a small cockpit.

"There's still a big red dot on the navigation screen showing us where we have to go," I explained as patiently as I could muster under the current stress. "And the altimeter will tell me when we're about to land. The only trick is not letting this damned wind push us too far off course."

"Why doesn't it have an autopilot?" Dani snapped, shaking her head. "Most commercial airplanes on Earth have autopilot systems that can land by themselves and they don't even have this gravity-resist stuff." She threw up her hands in exasperation. "I mean, our boss is a damned AI, for God's sake!"

"Lenny isn't our boss," Val said, an edge to his voice that demonstrated what a sore spot that was for him.

And maybe for me, too. Lenny had engineered all this, his plans going back over two centuries, had snatched Val, Laranna, Giblet, and me out of our lives and away from our friends and families and thrown us at the wall to see if we stuck. He'd owned up to it and put everything in our hands from now on, but that couldn't quite undo all that had been done.

Anyway, I knew the answer to this one.

"We don't have auto-landing systems for the same reason that we don't have robots like Lenny running around with guns like the…what did you call them from that TV show you like?"

"Toasters," Dani supplied.

"Yeah." The controls bucked and tossed again, and my knuckles went white as I gripped the steering yoke for dear life. "They don't trust thinking machines much out here and after what happened to us, I don't know that I blame them. Anyway, it's computer-assisted…you know. Fly-by-wire, sort of."

Not enough. And as the turbulence grew worse the closer we got to the ground, I found myself wishing for a galaxy that wasn't so damned paranoid.

"Two hundred feet," Val told me. I nodded sharply and throttled down the landing jets.

One last gust of wind battered the lander and then the details of our landing site rushed up at me, finally revealed through the blowing snow. A flat, inviting field, brown and dead where it wasn't already covered with snow, the grass of summer long gone. Netting flapped in the wind in front of the metal stands, empty parking lots, the whole thing surrounded by tall trees, some evergreen, some having dropped their leaves a couple months ago.

Then the landing gear touched and we lurched forward as the treads sank to the limits of their hydraulics before springing back up.

"We're down," I sighed, yanking the quick-release for my seat restraints.

"Crappy landing," Giblet murmured, rising from his seat. "I could have done better."

"Yeah, we all know what a great pilot you are, Gib," Dani said, glaring at the Varnell. "You don't have to keep reminding us of it every single time someone else is at the controls."

He sniffed, then zipped up the jacket we'd fabricated for him back on the *Liberator* and pulled the hood up, disguising his features.

"By the way, these clothes are ridiculous."

"You'd rather advertise to everyone what you are?" Dani wondered, fists on her hips. "We picked out our clothes because they fit in, not so you could feel fashionable."

Val ignored the two of them and I wished I could so easily. I felt for Gib, knowing what unrequited love was like, though mine had been requited a little sooner rather than later, and since he was my best friend, it hurt even more. But we had a job to do and my immediate concern was that he'd let his feelings get in the way of it.

Val squeezed out of the cockpit to the utility bay, slapping the control to open the hatch. I squinted in anticipation of the wind-blown snow, but it wasn't as bad down here as it had been in the air and only a few wisps of white wafted in past the overpressure of the cockpit.

"What did you call this place again?" Giblet asked, pushing past Val to stick his head out the door.

"A little league baseball field," I supplied. "Kids play ball here in the summer, but it's closed for the season."

Giblet cocked an eyebrow at me and sneered.

"No, dumbass, the name of the *city*."

"Oh. Arlington. Arlington, Virginia. It's just outside the capital city of my country, Washington, D.C. Most people who work in the government live out here."

"The ones who can afford it," Dani added, grabbing a jacket

out of the equipment locker and pulling it on over her shoulder holster.

The guns worried me, though I carried one myself beneath my fur-lined bomber jacket. If we got caught with them, we'd be up shit creek…but then, if we got stopped by the cops and they found Giblet, illegally carrying a concealed weapon would be the least of our worries.

"Even if this *baseball field* is closed," Gib said skeptically, hesitating over the unfamiliar words, "are you sure the camouflage will be enough to keep them from finding the lander?"

I hopped down the short set of steps from the hatch to the ground, my boots sinking an inch into the snow cover. No lights glowed from the metal poles at the edge of the baseball field, the only illumination coming from the streetlights a few hundred yards away. No danger anyone would see the lander tonight. Hell, I wasn't sure *we* could find it again. But the storm wouldn't last forever and in daylight…

"Let's turn it on and find out," I said. "Everyone come on out so we can button this thing up."

Giblet hung back, gazing at the snow with obvious distaste, but eventually, he followed the others and touched the control on the fuselage to close the hatch behind them. It folded up into the silver of the lander, snow fountaining off the edges before the door disappeared into the polished surface.

"Activate the camo," I told him. Gib nodded and traced a line down a strip beside the hatch control.

The edges of the lander crackled as if with a static charge from the storm and then…the entire thing disappeared. Well, not *really*. As advanced as the technology Lenny had brought with him was, even it couldn't manage true invisibility. Instead, as I understood it, cameras all over the surface projected the images from the opposite sides, creating the illusion that the craft wasn't there. Incredibly effective at night, it remained to be seen how well it would work in broad daylight, but we couldn't stick around to find out.

I grunted in satisfaction, then shuddered as snow went down my collar, reminding me to pull out the knit cap Dani had commissioned from the fabricators back on the ship and put it on. It wasn't incredibly cold, maybe thirty degrees, but the dampness and the wind cut through me, and Giblet already shivered beneath his jacket, used to warmer climes. Val, the old cowboy, faced the north wind with an equanimity I strived to match.

"That'll have to do," I decided. "Dani, is your…cellular phone working?"

I always wanted to call the thing a *car phone*, because those were the only mobile phones I'd seen before I left Earth back in 1987. The idea that they were half the width of a deck of cards now was mind-boggling in ways that hyperspace travel and pulse guns weren't. Those were alien gadgets, but these science-fiction hand computer things were something that had happened back home while I was in stasis.

"Should be," she confirmed, pulling the device out and powering it up. "I mean, as long as no one's closed my checking account, my phone bill is set up for auto-pay and I sure haven't been spending money on anything else." Dani snorted. "Thank

God I didn't have a shared account with anyone, at least not since I broke up with Randy."

The screen lit up with the image of a kitten rolling around in a basket of yarn and Dani pumped a fist in triumph.

"Yes! Got four bars even! Hold on, let me get us an Uber."

"What the hell's an Uber again?" Val mumbled, eyes scanning the end of the parking lot like a hawk looking for voles in the grass.

"It's like a taxi, right?" I asked Dani, still not a hundred percent sure about that.

"What's a taxi?" Val asked, glaring at me.

"A car's on its way," Dani told us, grinning as she read from the screen. "It's a white Honda CRV," she added. "He's less than five minutes away."

"I'm just gonna assume anyone who pulls up here during this storm is gonna be for us," I told her, heading for the parking lot, hoping the movement would warm me up enough that I wouldn't catch pneumonia before the Honda got here.

It didn't even take five minutes, as it turned out, and a Honda CRV turned out to be something like a station wagon that had been put through a trash compactor. Or maybe I'm being unfair just because a lot of what Dani's generation call an SUV look just like ugly station wagons to me. The guy driving the car matched it perfectly as far as I was concerned, just as short and compacted and stuffed-looking, though that might have been the impossibly puffy coat he wore, like the temperatures were thirty degrees colder and this was the freaking Arctic circle. Between the Michelin-Man jacket, the trapper hat, and his ridiculous, bushy beard, the guy could have stepped out of some commercial for frozen dinners.

"Hi," he said with a smile, his passenger's side window opening just a few inches, as if he was afraid rolling it all the way down would cause his car to freeze over. "I'm Darrell. Are you Dani Campling?"

"That's me," Dani said, smiling brightly enough to keep the guy distracted.

Dani got into the front seat with Darrell, making small talk while us three piled into the back. Gib scooted all the way behind the driver so he wouldn't be visible in the rear-view mirror.

"So, that's a fancy area you guys want to go to," Darrell continued his spiel as he pulled away from the curb. These new cars were quiet, at least, though that meant the driver seemed to feel the need to fill the gap with his voice. "Lotsa rich DC fat cats live there."

"That's the idea," I murmured, not caring if he heard me.

"How'd you all wind up in the parking lot of the ball field anyways?" Darrell went on. He shook his head and the flaps of his overly warm hat waggled like a hound dog's ears. "It's some nasty weather out here to be walking around! I almost didn't work today, but I like, need the money, y'know?"

"It's where our ride dropped us," Dani told him, honest but not completely so. "It couldn't go any farther."

Well, it could *have*. If I'd had my way, it would have. But no commander ignores the recommendations of his experts and Dani was as much of an expert as we had on modern-day Earth. What I knew about it was nearly as useless as Val's experiences back in the 1870s, and the only reason he'd come instead of Laranna was that he was human…and that had been a near thing.

"So, you a Commanders fan?" Darrell asked, changing gears. I frowned, not knowing what a commander was in this context but also not willing to reveal my ignorance of everything past the release of *Predator*.

"Bengals fan," Dani corrected him, and I intuited that the Commanders was a football team. Maybe Virginia had their own team now? I thought everyone from northern Virginia was a Redskins fan.

"Aw, man, I feel bad for Joe Burrow. He keeps getting hurt just when it looks like it's going to be his year."

"I feel worse for us," she shot back. "At least he gets paid millions of dollars. All we get is the shaft."

Millions of dollars? Jeez, NFL salaries had gone up a lot since I left.

The two of them kept chattering about football players whose names I didn't recognize and I pretty much tuned them out, staring at the snow and trying to see something of the buildings beyond it. I'd never been to Virginia, though I'd visited DC once with my parents. Hell, we might have come through Arlington, but I didn't remember a thing about the trip other than seeing the Washington Monument and the Lincoln Memorial. The part of Arlington we were in was definitely upscale, full of large houses and small yards, and every one of them looked a lot like the rest, as if the cookie-cutter subdivisions I hated as a kid had suddenly become the in thing.

I don't know how the driver told one of them from another in this storm, but it might have been his phone. He had it mounted on a plastic holder attached by a suction cup to the window and it looked as if it was mapping the way. I didn't know they could do that, too, but hell, there didn't seem to be much they *couldn't* do. I didn't like much of what I'd seen of the 2020s the last time we'd visited, but I really wanted a cell phone, and I was pissed they didn't work in space.

"Your destination is on the right," the phone's mapping system advised and Darrell pulled over to the sidewalk in front of a two-story house, its slate-gray paint nearly lost in the snow.

"Here you go!" he said, grinning at Dani like a man who'd come to believe in love at first sight. "Hope you have a nice stay in Arlington!"

"Thanks, Darrell," she said, keeping his eyes on her while Gib slid out the side and turned away, his hood still low over his face. "Drive safe."

"You certainly had him eating out of your hand," Giblet commented dryly as the Honda pulled away from the curb. "You seem to have that effect on men."

"You'd rather he took a good look at you and drove screaming off the side of the road?" Dani asked, her smile unpleasant.

"Enough," I snapped, stepping between them and heading up the walk to the front steps.

The porch light was on but none of the interior lights and I hoped we hadn't come too early, that he wasn't out watching a late movie or something. Only one way to find out. I touched the doorbell. It rang inside, a light, playful tone, and I waited.

A light came on and floorboards creaked. My heart beat faster, my breath coming short and irrational fear nearly had me turning to run down the block in an absurd game of ding-dong-ditch. I squared my shoulders and set my feet. It was too late to run.

The door opened and an old man stepped up. Okay, so he wasn't *old* old, not like Poppa Chuck. Just older than I ever thought I'd be, sixty years old if I'd calculated right. Lines cutting into that once jolly, rounded face, lines of pain and sorrow, laughter and joy, a lifetime that I had yet to experience because I'd been snatched out of it. The beard was new, white as snow. Gray hair had always come early to the Barnaby family.

"Hi, George," I said, blinking back what must have been melting snow in my eyes. "It's been a long time."

His eyes went wide, his face slack in disbelief and he stammered the only thing he could say.

"Charlie?"

2

"No," Dani insisted, slamming her palm on the table. "It's not a good idea."

"Maybe not," I admitted, "but it's the only one I have that makes any sense." I stood from the galley table and spread my hands, looking around at the others.

Laranna, Val, Mallarna, Constantine, Giblet and, of course, Lenny. The silvery robot might have officially given leadership of the resistance over to me, but that didn't mean he was out of the planning room. Or, in this case, the lunchroom. It had become sort of a tradition now to do our planning in the *Liberator*'s galley, because I hated the operations room.

"What's our second choice?" I asked. "What do we do if we don't go to Earth for help?" I shook my head. "Someone tell me because I'm not getting anything else. We've asked for help from everyone, and everyone who will has already given it. The only ones who have what we need won't give it up because they think they need their ships and their armies to defend themselves against the Anguilar. We've begged, borrowed and stolen everything we can and it's not enough."

"We have the fighters," Gib reminded me. "They're more powerful than anything anyone else has...except the Anguilar."

"Yeah, but that's a big exception," Laranna agreed, standing beside me, hand on my shoulder. "We've got twenty fighters, five Liberator ships, and about fifteen thousand ground troops, and that's enough to turn back any attack, but it's not enough to go on the offensive. If we can't get more ships, we need more people, more weapons. Does anyone else know where we can get them?"

"Not Earth," Dani said. "Look, I told you, things are screwed up back home. I mean like on the brink of disaster screwed up. All it'll take is one spark to send it over the edge. I'm talking World War Three, civil wars, everything falling apart. It's bad and if aliens show up, it could make it so much worse."

"Then we have to pull everyone back to Sanctuary," I told her. "That's it, no trying to free other worlds held by the Anguilar. No island-hopping, no long strikes into the heart of the empire, nothing. We defend what we have because that's all we can do... and we let them have Earth, because we can't defend it from them without the help and support of the people who live there."

"I'm not giving up hope of freeing Copperell," Val said, glaring at Dani. "I can't go back to Brandy and tell her that we're never going to do anything to help her people."

"I wouldn't allow it," Laranna declared. "I won't let all those billions of people suffer the same fate that Strada did. I won't let them be slaves to the empire." She shrugged, her resolve softening. "But if you're right, Dani, we have to approach this carefully."

"We can't go in half-cocked," Val agreed. "We need your help with this, Miss Campling."

Dani squeezed her eyes shut, rubbing a hand over her face.

"Fine. But we have to do it small, careful. We can't take an army down there. Me, you, Charlie, Val."

"And what about me?" Constantine wondered, the first time he'd spoken up the entire meeting. And it was true, he *was* human. Sort of…he'd had modifications to let him live for centuries, since the Middle Ages. The problem was, he *looked* like he'd just stepped out of the Middle Ages, and often acted like it.

"Val's bad enough," Dani said, not trying to spare either of their feelings. "He can halfway pretend he's from the modern day." She motioned at Constantine's plain, brown cassock. "You're not even close."

"We're gonna need one more," I said, fighting down the irritation rising at the entire argument. I wanted to tell Dani that she signed up for the duration and that meant going along with the plan no matter what she thought of it, but I suppressed the urge. "We need a…well, an *alien*."

"I'll go," Laranna offered as if it was obvious. "I can tell them about Strada."

"I don't think that would be the right way to go," I said, carefully because Laranna wasn't someone it was wise to piss off even for people who didn't sleep beside her. She looked at me sharply but gave me the chance to explain. "You look too…human." I laughed at her outraged expression. "Hey, I'm not complaining, I love the way you look. But it would be too easy for them to dismiss you as just a woman wearing body paint or something."

"Or with skin tattoos," Dani added. "He's right. We need someone who looks more…different."

I looked around the room, settled on Mallarna for a moment.

"I'll go if you need me," she offered, waving a hand, though she sounded uncertain about it.

"No," Dani said, and I thought I might have seen a little bit of a shudder go through her. "No offense, Mallarna, but they're going to take one look at you and run away screaming. Not that I think you're horrible looking but people on Earth get freaked out by big insects, and you're going to look like a big insect to them."

"I am *not* an insect," Mallarna objected, her eyes flaring.

"And you're not a field operative, either," I reminded her.

"It's not just that they'll be scared," Dani pointed out. "The ones who aren't scared will wind up wanting to dissect you. We need something in-between. Something different but not *too* different."

"Then I have to go," Giblet said.

I stared at him, and I wasn't the only one.

"Yeah, yeah," he said, waving the looks away, "I know, I'm volunteering. Don't have a damned heart attack."

"He *would* be perfect for this," Val said, shrugging. "I mean, I never once felt scared looking at his scrawny, feathery ass."

"Same to you, hairball," Gib shot back at him.

Dani snorted a derisive laugh.

"You must be joking. Talking about getting dissected! All Gib has to do is open his mouth and he'll piss everyone off enough that they won't bother killing him first before they start cutting him up."

Gib glared at her, eyes narrowing and, sensing a coming explosion, I stepped in, literally and figuratively, putting myself between the two of them and coming to Gib's defense.

"The Varnell," I reminded Dani, "have some pretty impressive powers of persuasion. Something about pheromones and voice modulation, I think, but I've seen it in action. If our aim is to convince people to help us, Gib is the guy for it. He could sell ice to Eskimos."

"Inuit," Dani corrected me and I blinked, shaking my head. "People keep telling me that, but I've never seen it. As far as I can tell, Giblet's biggest strengths are flying a fighter and being an obnoxious asshole."

I expected Gib to explode, but what actually happened was far more worrying. Giblet's expression shifted, as if he'd pulled a mask over his features, something I'd seen before but not recently. The Varnell smiled broadly, an old friend laughing with me at the bar after we'd shared a few beers and told stories about the good times. Warm, fuzzy feelings filled my head, squeezing out all the anxiety and anger.

"Danielle Elizabeth Campling," Gib said in a gently chiding tone, a mother warmly correcting her young child, "you've got to learn to stop judging people by their appearances. After all, don't you always talk about how tired you got of other cops judging you by your appearance?"

Dani frowned deeply, not with the disdain her expression had held a moment before but something more thoughtful.

"Well, yeah," she admitted, pushing a strand of red hair out of her face. "It got frustrating, them thinking I was brainless just because I didn't look like a member of the Russian Olympic women's weightlifting team."

Gib's chuckle was honest, genuine, as if he truly appreciated her humor.

"Of course! And it's not like it's your fault that you're a beautiful woman. It shouldn't take away at all from the fact that you're also courageous, capable, confident…"

Dani flushed, her light complexion reddening with embarrassment, but also with obvious pleasure at the compliment.

"I wish more men understood me like you do," she admitted, and I found myself nodding. But inside, horror crept up from my gut, cold tendrils traveling up to my chest, the internal knowledge of what was happening that couldn't quite make it through to my conscious mind. If Dani felt any of that, it certainly didn't show on her face. "It's been rough, and I have to admit, that's one of the reasons I was ready to leave."

"I understand, I really do," Gib assured her, putting a hand on her arm. Dani smiled and covered the hand with her own. "And if I might be so bold, while you're obviously a beautiful woman, your appearance is the least of your attractive qualities. You're one of the more intelligent sentients I've ever encountered and the fact that you're absolutely fearless in combat drives me to distraction sometimes." He leaned in closer, the soft, downy hair of his face teasing at her skin. "I would consider myself perhaps the luckiest man on this ship if you'd consent to dine alone with me tomorrow. It'd be nice to just talk and get to know one another better."

Dani was already nodding eagerly before he even finished the question.

"I'd like that," she said. "I'd like that a lot. Maybe in my cabin?"

Gib took his hand off her arm and his face shifted again, reality snapping back to coherence, losing the dull haze that had fallen over it.

"All right," he said, the gentle, wooing tone disappearing from his voice. "Everyone satisfied?" Gib cocked an eyebrow at Dani. She looked confused, as if she'd just woken from a dream.

"What?" she stuttered, looking between Gib and the rest of us. "What the hell just happened?"

"Giblet," Laranna snapped, glowering at the Varnell, "that wasn't nice."

"Maybe not," he admitted easily, "but it was necessary." His expression hardened and he glared back at her, at the rest of us. "All of you seem to forget exactly why my people are shot on sight by the Anguilar, why we've been driven out of every *civilized* system over the last few centuries." He touched a hand to his chest, shaking his head. "It's my fault, really. I've stopped myself from using the full extent of my abilities out of…concern as to how you would all see me if I did." Gib pulled his chair back out and sat down again. "I suppose I thought you'd think better of me if you just considered me a good pilot."

"Are you telling me," Dani asked, still standing, staring at

Giblet with a fire that would have melted steel burning behind her eyes, her face flushing again but this time not from pleased embarrassment, "that all that was just you using your…mojo or whatever?"

Gib cocked his head to the side and rolled his eyes.

"Come on, Dani, be honest. Would you have ever agreed to have dinner alone with me in your cabin if I hadn't been using my…*mojo* on you?"

The words should have been scornful, given the question, but instead, there was a hint of sadness behind them. Dani opened her mouth in what I expected would be a harsh retort…then closed it. When she spoke again, her tone was quiet, lacking her earlier outrage.

"Maybe," she said, and if someone had hit Giblet between the eyes with a sledgehammer, he wouldn't have looked any more stunned. "It'd be nice to be asked."

Resolve firmed in Giblet's face.

"All right, I'm asking. Would you have dinner with me?"

Dani's expression was unreadable.

"Yes."

I closed my mouth before something could fly into it and I wasn't the only one. I believe I could have knocked Laranna over with a feather.

"I hate to interrupt this fascinating conversation," Lenny said, and if a robot could plant his tongue in his cheek, Lenny did. "But we've yet to decide on a plan. This is your decision, of course, and I would not tell you which route to take, but when I made my many visits to your planet, Charlie, among my primary goals was to avoid discovery. I considered this vital both to ensure that I had as little impact as possible upon your development as a society and to avoid disrupting your independent technological progress. After all, if you'd had proof of the existence of gravity-resist and faster-than-light travel, you might have spent decades trying to perfect them rather than proceeding on your own path."

"And?" I prompted, making a get-along-with-it gesture. The AI robot had been alive—if that was the word for it—for thousands of years, maybe tens of thousands, and in all that time, he still hadn't learned the value of getting to the point.

"I believe your desire to involve the humans of Earth is justified," he concluded. "I'd hoped to leave them undisturbed for another century or two, but their development in isolation may provide something valuable to our efforts." Lenny gestured to Dani. "However, Deputy Campling's point is not without merit. This must be done carefully, tactfully."

"Well, you got the wrong crew for *that*," Val cracked. Of all of us, he seemed the least affected by the idea of going back to Earth, probably because, for him, it was as much an alien planet now as Strada or Copperell.

"This concern for disrupting their society seems misplaced to me," Mallarna said, regarding the rest of us with obvious skepticism. "My world was obliterated, Copperell has been enslaved for over a century, Strada was under the heel of the Anguilar for decades. That is the fate which awaits the Earthers if the empire comes for them and I don't think anything we could do would cause nearly that amount of disruption."

"True," I acknowledged, "but we don't need to get off on the wrong foot. We should take an unarmed lander for our…whatever, diplomatic mission with me, Dani, Val and Gib, but we need armed backup ready. Lenny, do you think a Vanguard could fly patrol in high orbit without being noticed?"

"By the detection devices your world has available? Almost certainly. The only way it would be seen is if someone happened to be looking up through a telescope."

"And even then," Dani put in, "they'd probably think it was a satellite."

"I'll fly overwatch," Laranna offered immediately. "Keep your comms online and I can be down in a few minutes if you need me."

"The *Liberator* should stay out in translunar orbit," I told Lenny. "Keep the Moon between Earth and your position."

"Where do we land?" Dani asked. "Who do we talk to?"

"In the movies," I said with a chuckle, "aliens always land on the White House lawn. That doesn't seem like a bad idea. It's public, so there'd probably be TV cameras reporting it and they couldn't bury it and pretend it never happened."

I mean, I wasn't sure if I believed in all that Area 51 and Roswell stuff, but knowing that UFOs and aliens were real, I couldn't rule out that the government already knew about the aliens and were covering it up. Dani was already shaking her head.

"That'd be a disaster. We should do this quietly, give the government a chance to break the news slowly. People are panicky, like cornered animals. The ones who even believe it's real will use the excuse to riot, to burn everything down. And most won't believe it's real. Even if you took them up for a ride in space, they'd think it was all a *gummint* plan to fool them into paying more taxes and fighting another war."

Laranna eyed the woman doubtfully.

"You certainly have a low opinion of your own people."

"Only because I know them," Dani shot back. "We need to find someone we can trust and approach them quietly, carefully."

"Well, that's a problem," I allowed, "since I don't know anyone who's in a position to do that. Do you?"

"My uncle is an alderman in Chicago," she offered with a shrug.

I scowled and closed my eyes, racking my brain. The problem was, everyone I knew who was important, my dad's friends, even the high-ranking officers I'd met through ROTC would all be retired or dead by now. Thirty-seven years was a long time. I squinted at the germ of an idea gleaming at the back of my mind.

"I wish we had access to that internet you always talk about," I muttered. "I need to look something up."

"Well," Lenny said, motioning expansively, "when we were in Earth orbit trying to locate the transponder to take us to the Kamerian weapons cache, I took the liberty of downloading your internet, as you call it. It seemed like a good source of intelligence."

Dani blinked, staring at him like he was a nine-foot-tall metal robot with Michael Keaton's face.

"You downloaded the *internet*?"

"All the data I could easily access," Lenny confirmed, shrugging as if it was no big deal.

"All right, Lenny," I said, not belaboring the point any further, "look up George Barnaby. Born 1965. If you can, find out what he's doing now."

"Your friend, George?" Laranna asked, eyes going wide. I'd told her about him, of course. I'd told her everything.

"He wanted to go career Army," I said with a shrug. "His family was rich, influential. Maybe he dropped out of all that and sold life insurance, but knowing George's dad…"

"I've found him," Lenny said.

An image appeared on the holographic display, a three-dimensional representation of a two-dimensional picture, pulled from the…well, whatever this world wide web thing was. I didn't recognize the picture at first, without context, just a middle-aged man, or on that line between middle-aged and old. Maybe sixty. That made sense.

"George Anthony Barnaby, graduated the University of South Florida in 1987," Lenny read off. "Four years in the US Army, then back to college for a master's degree from Georgetown. Back to the Army, where he spent a career working in the Pentagon, retired as a brigadier general and is now…a deputy national security advisor to the President of the United States."

"Way to go, George," I murmured. I nodded to Dani. "There you go. We have a contact. Lenny, find us an address."

I turned to the others, laughing.

"We're going to D.C."

3

"This is impossible," George Barnaby declared, shaking his head violently, like he was trying to clear away a hallucination. He backed away a step from the open door. "Impossible!"

His mouth worked but no words came out and I understood. He couldn't enunciate it, but I could imagine his thoughts readily enough. Impossible that I could be on his doorstep more than thirty-five years later, looking nearly the same as I had that night in 1987.

"I know it's crazy, George," I said, taking a step inside, across the threshold like a vampire invited into his home. "But it's me and I can explain."

"Your shoes!" he said quickly, pointing at my Nikes.

"Yeah, the shoes!" I nodded, brightening. "You noticed that. They don't make these anymore, do they? I bet they haven't since the eighties…"

"Wipe off your shoes before you come in!" George snapped, shaking his head.

The man was, I sensed, not handling this well. I paused to scrape the snow and mud off my Nikes on the mat before stepping forward again. I spoke quickly, sensing that the man was about five seconds from calling the cops. Or running screaming out into the snow.

"George, it *is* me. It's Charlie Travers. The last time I saw you was the day before graduation. We'd gone to see *Predator* and you kept repeating that line by Arnold…*get to da choppah*. You dropped me off in your Camaro because I was too poor to buy my own car…dropped me off at DeLuca's Pizza where I lived in that little apartment on the second floor. We were talking about how you were going to take Lorna to see it before you got shipped off to your officer's basic course and I said something whiny about how you were reminding me that I didn't get active duty and also that my girlfriend had just broken up with me." His eyes went wide and I knew I was getting to him, but I had to put the final nail in it. "The last thing I said to you was that I'd have plenty of time to think about what I was going to do with my life while I was at field artillery officer's basic course. And that I'd see you tomorrow."

George stopped backing away, his face gone pale, and a tear trickled down his cheek.

"I never told anyone that," he insisted. "Not Lorna, not the police when they came asking about you a couple months later. Not even your parents when they called me to see if I knew anything."

Then he screeched and tried to run past me into the snow.

"Son of a bitch!" I blurted, grabbing him around the waist, ducking my head to avoid the wild haymakers he was throwing.

"You're a ghost!" he shrieked, legs pumping as he tried to power his way past me. "You're a damned ghost! Get away from me!"

It felt like bullying an old man, but I didn't have any choice since he was about to run out into the street and probably get the cops called on him for being nuts. With a heave that came clear down from my knees, I picked George up and ran back into the living room, tossing him down on the first piece of furniture we came to, an expensive-looking leather couch. The breath went out of him in a gasp and I stood, pinning him to the tasteful red cushion with a palm on his chest.

"Calm the hell down, George. I'm not a ghost, I'm not a clone and I'm not a Commie spy. It's me, Charlie, and there's a perfectly logical explanation for why I'm not sixty years old."

The door slammed shut and George started like a deer in the headlights. I glared back at Val and the cowboy shrugged.

"Snow was getting inside," was all he said.

"Who the hell are these people?" George demanded. "What are they doing in my house?" His eyes fixed on me again and he pushed my hand away, sitting up. "What are *you* doing in my house and why are you still twenty-three years old?"

"Technically, if we're going by biological age," I told him, shrugging, "then I'm twenty-five. It's been about two years since I came out of the stasis pod."

"Stasis pod?" George repeated. "What the hell's a stasis pod? It sounds like science fiction."

Grinning, I sat down on the couch beside him and motioned for Giblet to come into the living room. It was a very tastefully appointed room, the walls decorated by what I took for family photos plus a few paintings. Whales, mostly.

"George," I told him, "I disappeared off the face of the Earth thirty-seven years ago, left everything behind except what I was wearing on my back, and now I'm showing up at your door not looking like I've aged a day. If someone gave you that set of incontrovertible, inarguable facts, what would you say the likeliest possibility was?"

I nodded to Giblet and he tossed his hood back and leaned down over George with a broad smile.

"Hey there, bud. Name's Giblet. Nice to meet you."

George, of course, fainted.

"Aliens," George muttered, shaking hands turning his coffee mug into a wave pool. "Goddamned aliens." His blue eyes flickered toward me. "And you were *abducted*, like something from that stupid TV show on the History Channel."

I took a sip of my own coffee and nodded. It sucked, but seeing as how we were uninvited guests and Dani had appropriated his coffee machine to fix it for us, I didn't complain.

"I don't know what a History channel is, but it sounds cool. Yeah, though. I was abducted by an artificial intelligence. A robot from another galaxy. We call him Lenny. That's not his real name, obviously, but I had to call him something."

The recliner shifted under my weight again, sloshing the coffee, and I cursed softly, set my feet flat on the hardwood floor.

"And you…" George peered at Val, licking his lips as if his mouth had gone dry. "You're from…the old west?"

"I never thought of it as old," Val admitted. "It was just *now*. But yeah, I s'ppose I was in the west. Texas is still west, though not as west as California."

Dani snorted a laugh.

"Nowadays, California is more *to the left* than to the west."

"Valentine was taken from Earth in 1873," I repeated, trying to be patient, knowing this was going to take some time. I mean, it hadn't taken that much time for me, but I'd been thrown into the fire head-first, confronted with a starship full of aliens who wanted to kill me. "He spent nearly 150 years in stasis. Gib and I only slept for thirty-five."

George studiously avoided looking at Giblet just yet, as if he knew he couldn't handle it. Instead, he spoke to Dani.

"And you…your name is Dani?"

"Dani Campling," she agreed.

"When are you from? Did you get…abducted by the robot, too?"

Dani had been in the middle of a sip of her coffee and she choked at the question, ready to spit it out in a gush of laughter.

"No one abducted *me*, General Barnaby. These two jokers…" She toasted Val and me with her mug. "…got caught digging up an artifact at the Serpent Mound and I arrested them. Then a bunch of alien bounty hunters blasted their way into my substation and the next thing you know, I'm on a starship heading to some unknown, forgotten weapons cache to steal a bunch of space fighters for a war I didn't even know was going on."

"The Serpent Mound is in Ohio," I supplied for George, "near where I used to live. There was a transponder buried there during the last war, showing the way to the weapons depot. That's why I came back to Earth a few months ago."

"They followed you?" He'd asked the question before, been answered before, but again, patience.

"They followed the signal from the transponder," I corrected him. "They knew we'd be looking for it and they got to it before we did so they could set a trap for us."

"The Aguilar?" George attempted.

"Anguilar," I corrected him. "They're sort of scavengers. Exiles from another galaxy who specialize in stripping systems of their resources and moving on. But when they reached our galaxy, they caught it just after a huge civil war and decided it was ripe for the conquering. They hired the bounty hunters to come after us, here and on the planet with the weapons cache."

"We obviously made it out alive," Giblet added, seeming to revel in George's discomfort at his presence…and his existence.

George squeezed his eyes shut for a moment, and when he opened them, he finally focused on Gib.

"Can I…touch your…feathers?"

"Only if you buy me dinner first," Gib shot back, then glanced meaningfully at Dani in a way that made me blink in confusion.

I wasn't sure if they'd actually gone through with that date and if anyone else was, they hadn't shared. Dani's expression was so flatly neutral that I knew it had to be on purpose.

"Naw, I'm just kidding," Gib went on, then leaned closer to George, gesturing at his face invitingly. "I know, I know, Charlie explained it. You're gonna think this is makeup or something."

George's hand shook as he hesitantly reached out and took a strand of feathery hair between thumb and forefinger and pulled gently. Then harder.

"Ow!" Giblet complained, yanking away. "I said you could touch it, not rip my freaking hair out!"

"Sorry!" George looked at the strand of hair in his hand and quickly let it drop to the floor. "How…how did you learn English?"

"It wasn't easy," Gib told him. "Especially with the translator!"

"There's this…goo," I explained, "that you get put in your ear and it translates what everyone else says, so no one has to learn another language. But since we have three people now who speak English and are in command positions, a bunch of the others elected to learn the language in case we ever needed to come back here." I rolled my eyes. "It's a hell of a lot easier than college French was because there's a computer learning program that can teach you the stuff in your sleep, but he's right. With the translation gunk in my head, I couldn't tell him if he was making a mistake. I had to go through Lenny." I nodded to Giblet. "Go ahead and say something in your own language."

"Your friend here looks like a piece of chewed leather."

Gib smirked. When he spoke, all I heard was English but from the confused look on George's face, the real words had come through. I didn't bother chiding him for the insult. It was hard enough for me to get used to this old man being George. He seemed more…frightened than George had ever been.

"Okay," George said, setting his mug down on the table and clasping his hands together. It was chilly enough in the living room that my bomber jacket still felt comfortable but sweat trickled down George's forehead. "Let's say I believe you about all this. I'm not sure I do, but I can't figure out a better explanation. What do you want from me? Or did you just drop by to say hi and let me know you haven't been dead all these years?"

"We need your help. And you need ours. The Anguilar are coming here. I don't know when, but they know this is my home planet, thanks to that bounty hunter, and I've hurt them enough that they want to hurt me."

George looked at me for a second, then burst out laughing.

"You?" He shook his head. "Charlie Travers, the kid who couldn't even get active duty in the Army? You're some kind of big-time rebel leader now, fighting aliens?"

I'd been patient, but now he was pushing past the edge of my patience and it was all I could do not to snap back at him.

"Maybe us humans are just better at war than anyone else," I offered. "I'm not trying to pretend I'm some kind of Che Guevera or something…"

"Well, *that's* a relief," Dani interrupted, "since he was a murdering, racist piece of shit."

"…but together," I went on, glaring her to silence, "we've

been able to strike some pretty serious blows against the Anguilar. Maybe it's not me, maybe it's just the people we've brought into the movement, but the Anguilar sure as hell *blame* me. The upshot is, they're coming here and you need to get ready for them. I'm here to help you with the technology you can use to defend this planet, and to see if you'd be willing to put some troops and supplies into the fight in return."

"What kind of technology?" he asked, his ears perking up like a cat who just heard the can opener.

"As much as you can produce," I said. "I mean, we can show you the specs for things like hyperdrives and gravity-resist, but you don't have the industrial base to make it yet. But there are things that Lenny told me about that you *can* start producing almost immediately. High-temperature superconductors, though I barely understand what those are, if I'm being honest. Fusion reactors that can provide all the power for the entire nation with just seawater. Fabricators that can manufacture just about anything with just the right raw materials. Hell, you could put together a space shuttle with a couple of the bigger models."

"We don't use space shuttles anymore," Dani murmured and this time, I rolled my eyes at her for interrupting the sales pitch.

"The point is, this is tech that can revolutionize everything. Anyone who has it will be the top dog on this planet…and before long, in this *solar system*. You can bring in raw materials from the asteroid belt and there won't be any shortages of anything." And we were getting damned close to the end of my science and engineering knowledge. "I should have brought Mallarna," I lamented. "She could have given you the facts and figures better.

But she's like, half an insect and I figured we'd be better off with mostly humans this trip."

"Insect?" George asked, then shook the question away. "Okay, I get you. But do you have any proof? Did you bring anything you can show people?"

I thought about showing him my handgun but decided it might just get him scared again.

"We came down here on a lander," I offered, against my better judgment. I hated giving away our ride, but then, there were more of them up on the *Liberator*, and they were just a phone call away. "It's hidden but I'll show it to them if we get a chance to talk to your bosses. I doubt they can reverse-engineer it, but they're welcome to try."

George nodded slowly, eyes unfocused, thoughtful.

"I have to make a call," he said, pushing up from the sofa. Dani moved to block his way, but I waved her off.

"Either we trust him or we don't," I told her. "Go ahead, George."

Dani cast a doubtful look at me, but I let George leave the room. I avoided meeting the eyes of the others, instead taking my first opportunity to get a good look at the living room. At those family photos. George not too long ago, no more than five years, standing with a younger man, younger than me, at what looked like a commissioning ceremony. Another with George at a wedding, giving away the bride. His son and daughter, I assumed.

An older picture drew my eye, a family photograph in front of one of those generic, gray, photo-studio backgrounds. The son and daughter, but both in their teens, the daughter maybe eighteen, the son thirteen or fourteen, with a younger and thinner George in his Army uniform, along with his wife. She had to be in her early forties when the photo was taken but still young enough for me to recognize her.

It wasn't Lorna, his old college girlfriend. That was who I would have expected. But I knew the face well, the pale blond hair, the green eyes. It was Jill. Jill Beck, the one who got away, the girl I'd thought I loved, who'd broken up with me just before graduation. I said nothing. Even if I'd been able to find the words, what was there to say?

"I did it."

I turned at George's words as he rushed back down the hallway with his cell phone held out as evidence.

"I managed to get ahold of Mr. Donovan!" I must have been staring at him as blankly as everyone else because he immediately clarified the statement. "My boss. The President's National Security Advisor." He waved it away. "Anyway, I didn't tell him everything, but I managed to get him to agree to see you. But we have to leave now…like *right* now, because even in a snowstorm at night, the traffic in D.C. sucks dead donkey balls."

George grabbed a jacket off a rack beside the door, then snatched a set of keys from a hook on the wall beside it.

"Come on!" he urged, rattling the keys. "We can take my car!"

4

George had a nice car.

"Range Rover," he said with proprietary pride as we walked into the garage. It was built for two cars, the other space occupied by a small, two-door Audi, but George didn't look at it, motioning at the SUV instead. "I've always wanted one and I finally broke down and bought it last year." He touched a button on the key fob and the lights flashed briefly along with the unmistakable thump of the doors unlocking. "And more important for us tonight, it's four-wheel drive."

"Shotgun!" Giblet called but I blocked his way as he reached for the front passenger door handle.

"Even with that hood up," I told him, "you're not sitting up front where anyone could see you."

"That's very speciesist of you!" he objected, but I ignored him, pulling the door open and sliding in beside George.

"You're in the middle," Dani said, pushing Gib in front of her.

The doors thumped shut before George touched a button near his rearview mirror and the garage door rumbled open. Headlights illuminated wafting snow, shooting stars in the depth of the night and the Range Rover pulled onto the street, the garage closing behind us.

"It's a nice car," I allowed, running a finger over the leather dashboard. I looked across the center console at him. "So's the Audi. I thought you used to like American cars."

His laugh was a bitter snort.

"That gets complicated nowadays, Charlie. Cars supposedly American are made from parts machined in Mexico or overseas. The money goes to American corporations but half their stockholders aren't American and some of the so-called *foreign* cars have manufacturing plants inside the US. Nothing is simple anymore."

"No, I guess it isn't," I admitted. "Like for instance…how the hell did you wind up married to *Jill*?"

His eyes flickered off the road toward me and he jerked the wheel, almost running us into a car parked at the curb before he straightened it.

"Umm…that's a…that's a long story. I mean, we were both pretty devastated when you disappeared, Charlie."

"Jill?" I asked, goggling at him. "The same Jill Beck who dumped my sorry ass right before graduation was devastated when I wasn't around anymore?"

Pain tugged at the corners of his eyes, and his mouth worked soundlessly, the only noise the whoosh of the heater vents and the scratch of the tires on the residential road as we crawled down it at low, safe speeds.

"I'm sorry, Charlie. We both thought…when it started, she wasn't happy and neither was I. I'd just stayed with Lorna because my folks liked her but I was gonna break up with her once we graduated and I headed for Benning." There. I'd been looking for the George Barnaby I'd known in college and there he was, as if all those years of being a high-ranking Army officer and a bigwig in Washington had washed away and he was a kid in trouble again. "Jill and I started talking about it one night and…you know. One thing led to another."

George's eyes turned soft and liquid like a hound dog begging for scraps.

"Honest to God, Charlie, I wouldn't have done it if she hadn't sworn to me that she was planning on breaking up with you anyway. You have to believe me. I figured…I figured that once you were off in Oklahoma for field artillery training, you'd meet someone and I could break it to you gently in a few months."

"And then I disappeared," I finished for him. I wasn't angry. I should have been, but it had been thirty-seven years ago for him and if it had only been two for me, it was two years that had made everything from my life on Earth seem incredibly unimportant.

"You disappeared," he agreed, the desperation leaving him like the air from a balloon, replaced by an old despair. "And both of us felt guilty, but we…needed each other even more. We were married for thirty years."

Now it was my turn to taste despair. I knew. From the photos, I knew. Their marriage hadn't ended in divorce.

"How?" was all I asked.

"Cancer." He gasped the word out, like the mere mention of it seared his soul. "Fast. So fast. Visited the doctor for abdominal pain and then three months later, it was over. I was hoping…" His teeth clenched and I thought he fought back a sob. "I was hoping she'd get to see grandchildren before…"

I hesitated. This wasn't the same man I'd known, was a man who'd lived an entire life since then. But I put a hand on his arm, comforting.

"It's okay, George," I told him. "I'm glad you two got the time together. I'm glad you were both happy. That's all that's important to me."

George took a long, steadying breath and nodded. I couldn't blame him for being shook up. I was a ghost out of his past, a reminder of the guilt he'd felt so long ago.

"I'm married, by the way," I told him, grinning.

"Seriously?" he asked, then glanced back at Dani. "You mean, you two…?"

Dani burst out in a scornful laugh, joined by Val and Gib and I scowled at them, wondering what was so funny about that.

"No," Dani assured George. "We've barely known each other for six months."

"I'm married to…" I shrugged. "An alien."

"You mean like...*him*?" George asked, jerking a thumb back at Giblet.

This time, everyone laughed even harder. Except Giblet.

"I'll have you know," he said archly, "that Varnell women are highly thought of for their beauty. They've become queens on some worlds where there's still a monarchy."

"I'm so sure," Dani said, cocking an eyebrow at him. "Is that why you hit on everything with two legs and a pulse?"

"She's not a Varnell," I told George. "She's a Strada. I mean, she's humanoid. She looks very human except that she's kind of...green. Like the dancing girl in Star Trek. Sort of. Not *that* green..." I trailed off, shaking my head. "Forget it, she's beautiful and, frankly, deadly. A warrior among a society of warriors. She taught me everything I needed to know to survive out there."

"So, let me get this straight, Charlie," he said, sounding so much more like George. "You not only got abducted by aliens and became the leader of a bunch of aliens fighting against an evil empire, but you *also* got married to some hot, green alien chick who's a cross between the Orion slave girl from Star Trek and Red Sonja?"

"Well, when you put it that way," Dani commented from the backseat peanut gallery, "I have a hard time believing it myself... and I've *seen* it." She smacked me on the shoulder. "Hey, when you meet with the President or whoever, maybe you should leave that part out. Just stick to the whole 'hey, we got technology for you' thing and forget telling him that your wife is a hot green alien." She shrugged and eyed George. "Though she *is* hot. I'm straight and everything, but there's no mistaking that."

"I don't think you're helping," I told her.

"She's right, though," Val said, sitting back in the plush leather, arms crossed. "I mean, my wife Brandy is the most beautiful woman I've encountered and I ain't one to comment on anyone else's wife, you understand, but I'll just say there ain't many females around like Laranna and I have no clue how Charlie got so lucky."

My ears were warm and I was sure I was blushing. But George was smiling, maybe the guilt and sorrow vanished in the good humor filling the car.

"So this may be a personal question," he ventured, turning out onto a main street, out of the residential boulevard, "but can you two..." George shook his head, as if searching for the right words.

"I'm going to give you the benefit of the doubt," I told him, "and assume you're asking if we can have kids together." Because the alternative would have been just rude. "And the answer is... probably. It might take a little genetic tinkering, but the technology is there to do that if we want it."

"Do you?" he wondered. "Are you going to try?"

"I think so. Eventually. If we both survive long enough." I nodded to him. "I saw the photos of your kids. So, your son followed in your footsteps?"

"Yeah, despite my warning not to," George said with a rueful chuckle. "He's an infantry captain, but he's actually in town at the moment, visiting his fiancée. He was a company commander with the 82nd Airborne but he's about to be transferred to the 3rd Ranger Battalion."

"Wow, congratulations!" I said, impressed. It took some qualifications for an officer to get into the Ranger Bats. Or at least it had when I was dreaming of it. "You must be really proud of him."

"I'm proud of both of them," George assured me, smiling like he was basking in the warmth of a fireplace on this snowy night. "Mary's got her PhD in biochemistry and works for a pharmaceutical company. She's got a kid of her own now, a little girl. Lives in California. I don't get to see them enough."

"Grandpa," I mused, shaking my head. "Goddamn, George, I never thought of you as a grandpa."

"If I'd known how much fun it would be," he told me, "I would have had grandkids first, trust me." His smile faded away and he stared at me as if seeing me for the first time, really. "Aw, Jeez, Charlie, you know…I hadn't thought about it, really. I'd just thought of what you being gone so long meant for me. I hadn't thought about what it was like for you. Are you okay with all this? Adjusting, I mean? How much do you know, anyway?"

"A lot. Dani has told me most of it." I motioned into the back seat. "And I've watched some movies and TV shows she had on her phone. *The Lord of the Rings* is just incredible, by the way."

"Oh, my God, wait'll you see the new *Dune* movies!" he enthused, then calmed down as if remembering where he was. "But that's not quite what I meant. I meant, had you heard about your parents?"

I frowned. That was something I hadn't really *wanted* to think about and I'd much rather have discussed why the new Dune movies were so great. But I suppose it had to come out eventually, particularly since I'd sought out George.

"No," I admitted, and I hoped I didn't sound as uncomfortable as I felt. "What happened to them?"

George's face contorted like he didn't look forward to breaking the news to me, but before he could get the words out, we were very rudely interrupted. The light at the intersection was green, clearly so even through the falling snow, but the big, black SUV pulled straight out of the side street anyway, fishtailing with a screech of tires directly into our path and slamming on the brakes.

"Holy shit!" George blurted, pounding his foot into the brake pedal, throwing me hard against the seatbelt.

Accident? Just an asshole driver? The thought passed through my mind with a flash of anger at his recklessness.

"Behind us!" Giblet snapped and I twisted around in my seat at the warning.

An identical black SUV was right up on our back bumper, looming in the rear window like some predatory dinosaur cornering its prey.

"Black Suburbans," Dani said, her face gone pale. "That's government."

George stared helplessly at me as the doors of the vehicle in front flew open and a half a dozen blocky men in ill-fitting dark suits piled out, their expressions grimly identical, like they'd all been cloned off the same gene. My gun weighed a hundred pounds, pushing against my chest like a jagged reminder of the decision I had to make.

"Don't resist," I snapped as the government agents closed in on us. "Don't touch your weapons and keep your hands up. Do *not* fight them."

"I hope you know what the hell you're doing, Travers," Giblet said, shaking his head. He glared at George. "I gotta say, I don't think much of your choice in friends."

And that was the last any of us had to say about it because George hit the button to unlock the doors and the black-suited government agents yanked them open. The automatic pistol that was shoved in my face was probably no larger than a 9mm, but it yawned large enough that I could have been forgiven for thinking it was a 155mm Howitzer.

"Put your hands behind your head and don't move!" the buzzcut behind the gun yelled at me.

I said nothing. These guys looked like the type who would take any response as a challenge to their authority, so I just did as I was told and didn't even try to take off my seatbelt. My stomach twisted and tossed as he roughly pushed me back into my seat and disengaged the seatbelt, not worried about myself but scared shitless that Gib or Val would do something stupid.

"Get out!" the agent yelled at me once I was free of the safety belt.

He backed away a step, keeping his weapon trained on me and I tried to remember what little I knew about police procedure from my own day, thinking that this wasn't it. Cops would stay on the outside and order perps out of their vehicle, watching from far enough away that they could open fire without hitting each other. These guys weren't regular cops though and the fact that they were treating us like this must mean they knew there was something different about us.

"Get out and get on your knees!" he yelled again. "Don't look at me, look at the ground!"

I did it, unable to see the others but keeping my ears open. The other agents yelled the same orders at George, Val, Dani and Giblet and only George tried to answer back.

"I'm George Barnaby, deputy national security advisor to the President!" he insisted in the classic "do you know who I am?" attitude. "You can check my ID! I'm *General* George Barnaby!"

The agents didn't care, and George grunted as he was dragged out of the car. No one else drew any extra attention as I got down on my knees, the snow soaking through my pants. The same agent kept his gun trained on me while another who I could barely make out in my peripheral vision went around behind me and pulled up my jacket, patting me down.

He found the gun almost immediately, yanking it out of the shoulder holster.

"Gun!" he yelled, a hysterical screech in his tone as if he hadn't expected any of us to be armed. "He has a gun!"

"Be careful with that," I told him, trying to sound calm. "There's no safety."

"Shut up!" he snapped, patting me down even more thoroughly. "Do you have any other weapons?"

"Lockblade knife, left front pants' pocket," I told him.

It's disconcerting to have a guy stick his hand in your pants pocket but I didn't bother sharing my feelings of discomfort with him despite what Dani had told me about how touchy-feely everyone was in the 2020s, just kept my eyes downcast as he pulled the knife out.

"That's it for this one," he announced.

"We got three more guns and five knives," someone called from the other side of the vehicle, which made me feel inadequate and I wondered who'd been carrying an extra knife.

Cold metal smacked against my right wrist, and I winced as the handcuff closed tight and the agent wrenched my arm around my back, then pulled the other one to meet it. They weren't too gentle about it and my wrists and shoulders screamed at me that this wasn't their idea of a good time. I ignored them, waiting. It was gonna happen. Just a matter of when.

"What the hell?" The exclamation was a different tone from the commands screamed at us or even the warning that we were armed. It was disbelief, the discovery of something they not only hadn't expected but couldn't possibly imagine. "Is this guy wearing some kind of damned mask?" Giblet.

"Ouch!" Gib cried plaintively. "Stop trying to pull my face off, dammit!"

"Sir…I don't think this is a mask."

Silence for a long moment, just the distant rumble of cars passing by on cross-streets and the whisper of snow, and then an older, steadier voice spoke.

"Get them in the vehicles and get them out of here."

"What about General Barnaby?" another asked, a woman this time.

"Keep him here. I'll call for a separate transportation for him."

Rough hands pulled me to my feet and as I was shoved into the back seat of the massive, black SUV, I caught a fleeting glimpse of George's face. He stood, his hands not cuffed, between two of the federal agents, while a third, older man paced behind him, a cell phone held to his ear.

George saw me and blanched with the stricken expression of a guilty man found out. I didn't want to believe that he'd sold us out, tried to convince myself that it had been his boss who'd reported it. Then I was in the back of the Suburban, with Dani and Val crowded beside me and Giblet in the other vehicle, surrounded by armed agents.

Whether George had betrayed us or not, this wasn't his fault. It was mine.

5

"I WANT TO SEE MY FRIENDS," I repeated, rattling the handcuff chains that kept me secured to the metal interrogation table.

I tried to demand it, tried to be forceful, but my mouth was full of cotton and it came out a rasp. I'd lost track of how many hours I'd sat confined in this little metal room with bright lights shining off everything, but I did know they hadn't let me up from this uncomfortable metal chair to go to the bathroom and they hadn't offered me food or water.

They'd just kept asking me the same questions over and over.

"Where did you get those guns?"

The agent was too young for this, not more than a year or two older than me, and totally unable to pull off the intimidating bureaucrat image he was attempting. His haircut was as cheap as his suit and the tension beside his eyes told the story. He was out of his depth and killing time until someone with a lot more seniority got around to questioning me.

"You're not important enough for me to tell you anything significant," I said. "I want to see my friends and I want to speak to someone in authority. Someone who can make decisions."

"You don't get to make demands!" he yelled, leaning over the table at me, sticking a finger in my face. "You're up shit creek! You'll never see the sun again unless you tell us the truth!"

"Oh, yeah?" I cocked my head to the side and regarded him dubiously. "On what charge? Carrying a concealed weapon? You think that's enough to keep me in jail for the rest of my life." I snorted. "That's if you can convince a judge that it's a real gun. Or, more likely, your bosses are going to want to hang onto the gun and pretend none of this happened. Now, I'm gonna say this one more time…I want to see my friends."

His pasty face screwed up in a pout that made his overly large ears stand out even more, and I thought the throbbing vein in his temple was about to burst. But before he could launch into another tirade, the door to the interrogation room opened and the older agent I'd seen during the arrest stepped through, holding a bottle of water.

He was somewhere north of forty, though like Iowa north, not Canada. Gray at the temples, crow's feet at the eyes, but still in good shape. His suit was tailored, his haircut professional and he didn't look like a kid fresh out of college who'd never heard a shot fired in anger.

"Good morning," he said with a friendly but professional smile. He set the water bottle on the table in front of me, then made a shooing gesture at the younger man. "Hamner, go get yourself some coffee. And get me some while you're at it."

"Yes, sir," the kid said obediently, the metal legs of his chair scraping on the concrete floor.

I had no idea what this building was, I realized. On the way in, the snow had obscured any exterior signs and we'd come up in an elevator from the parking garage and then through empty back hallways. Empty made sense, given that it had been near midnight when we'd arrived and I only knew that because of a clock on the wall on the way into the interrogation room. That had been the last time I'd seen Val and Dani, though I wasn't nearly as worried about them as I was Giblet.

And Laranna. I worried that the transponder Lenny had injected under the skin of my triceps muscle wouldn't be detectable through the thick concrete and metal of the building, half because Laranna might not be able to come to our rescue because she wouldn't know where we were…and half because she might come storming down in her fighter, blowing up anything that looked threatening.

I took the water bottle, not even attempting to pretend I wasn't thirsty, and unscrewed it as best I could with my wrists cuffed together. Drinking from it was even more awkward, but I managed, and I didn't stop until half of it was gone. Then I frowned as I realized the water would make me have to pee even more. The older man sat down across from me in the recently vacated chair and crossed his legs, clasping his hands over his knee.

"I'm Special Agent James O'Brien," he said. "Tell me something…Charlie Travers, you said your name was?"

"I'll tell you something, Special Agent O'Brien," I shot back. "I've been here for at least three or four hours and I haven't had the opportunity to go to the john the whole time. I also haven't been read my rights, which means that nothing I've said so far could be used against me in a court of law even if you had anything to charge me with."

The even smile didn't falter, nor did his steady gaze.

"My apologies about the whole bathroom thing. When Hamner gets back, I'll make sure he escorts you to the men's room. As for your Miranda rights, well…I'm afraid you're in a unique position when it comes to that. Should I spell it out for you? You claim to be Charles Travers and your fingerprints are on record, so I know you're not lying about it. But the Charles Travers who matches your fingerprints was born in 1964. And you don't look nearly sixty to *me*, Charlie."

"I'm willing to explain," I began, "but it has to be to someone who can…"

"Oh, I'm not finished yet," O'Brien interrupted, chuckling. "But I'm sure you know that. Not only do you have the fingerprints—and the name—of a man born fifty-nine years ago, but you were also in the company of a man who claims to be Valentine McKee, a deputy US Marshal from Texas…in 1873. As well as Danielle Campling, up until a few months ago a sheriff's deputy in rural Ohio who disappeared after a terrorist attack on her substation."

"A terrorist attack?" I asked, laughter bursting out despite my best efforts to quell it. "Is that what they told you? Oh, jeez. I bet they scrubbed the video records, too."

O'Brien leaned forward, eyes lighting up as if I'd just tossed chum in the water in front of a great white shark.

"So, you admit to being there? To taking part in the attack?"

"I admit to being there," I agreed. "I was there when the attack happened…I was in a holding cell. Deputy Campling put me there."

"Why did she arrest you?" he asked immediately, snapping at that bait again, and I shook my head.

"Trespassing. Which you should already know, since I'm sure she filed a report." I made a gesture that was cut short by the cuffs. "Come on, you're the FBI, right? Don't tell me you don't know all this already."

"What I know is that you had with you a…" He broke off, as if he couldn't bring himself to say the words.

"Alien," I supplied. "You can admit it. It's what he is. It's where I've been, and Dani Campling, too. Why I don't look sixty years old and why Val is still alive. Where those funky-looking guns came from. I'm not hiding it, but I'm not telling *you* anything else. You know why?"

"Enlighten me, Mr. Travers." The words were frosty cold, not as if O'Brien was angry but more like he was working so hard trying to control himself that he couldn't risk showing any emotion.

"Because I know full well that I'm going to wind up repeating this a hundred times already and I'm sure as hell not going to *start* with an FBI agent who obviously doesn't even know everything that's already happened. You know I'm telling the truth about this…or at least, you know that *something* funny is going on, so don't waste any more time trying to sweat it out of me. Call your boss and he'll call *his* boss and hopefully, at some point, someone from the White House will take it all over. Because that was where we were heading when you kidnapped us." I sighed, sagging in my chair. "Well, that was where George *told* us he was taking us. For all I know, he turned us in."

My friend.

O'Brien grunted softly, as if satisfied that he'd finally come across a question he could answer.

"We had no idea you'd be with General Barnaby. We were just as surprised to find him there as he was to see us."

"Then how did you find us at all?" I asked him, feeling stupid. I'd refused to answer his questions and now I wanted him to answer mine.

By way of reply, O'Brien pulled his cell phone out of his pocket and held it up.

"Everyone uses these and doesn't think about how efficiently they can track your every movement. I'm sure Deputy Campling didn't think about that when she used her phone to order an Uber. As I said, the event at her sheriff's substation was recorded as a terrorist attack, so naturally, there was quite an interest in locating Ms. Campling."

Oh. I felt bad for doubting George. But he was probably better off away from us.

"As for your…demands," O'Brien went on, rolling his eyes at the word, "they're wasted on me. Trust me, the moment we understood that your weapons were nothing anyone had seen before and that your friend—what did you call him again?"

"His name is Giblet and he's a Varnell."

"Giblet?" His eyebrows shot up. "Isn't that a little…on the nose, perhaps?"

"It's an approximate translation."

"Well. Once we determined that your friend *Giblet* wasn't simply wearing makeup and a costume, I, as you so aptly put it, called my boss and he called his boss and I'm pretty sure it went all the way to the Attorney General's office before it ricocheted sideways to the Defense Department." He looked at the display of his phone and from what Dani had told me, I knew he was checking the time. A lot of people didn't wear watches anymore, and most of the ones who did had what she'd called *smart watches* connected to their phones. "I don't know if the entire thing has made it to the White House or even the entire way up the chain in the Pentagon, but I'm fairly certain that we won't have to wait too much longer before all this is removed from my hands entirely." The smile returned, although this time not as professional and cool as before…more genuine. "I suppose that's why we've been trying to get some answers while we can."

And now I felt kind of like a shit. I'd imagined this guy as nothing but a roadblock, like the typical federal agents I saw in movies, clueless and hopeless, bureaucratic buffoons and here this guy was reacting not too far different than I would have.

"You think this is all gonna get buried," I guessed. "That they'll haul us away and put us in some deep, dark hole and you'll never find out what happened to us, like the Ark of the Covenant at the end of Raiders."

"Top men," he agreed with a nod, and I laughed softly. I liked this guy.

"Don't," I told him. "Don't worry. For one thing, I don't intend to get buried, and I have, you might say, friends in high places. And I don't mean the White House. One of two things is going to happen here, Agent O'Brien. One, the guys in charge are going to screw this up, which is a distinct possibility given that we're talking about the federal government—no offense meant."

"None taken," he assured me with the amusement of someone who dealt with the federal bureaucracy on a daily basis.

"If that's the way it goes, well…" I sighed. "I can't abandon Earth when you all might be in danger because of me, but I won't be coming back and negotiating again. I'll do it as best I can on my own."

"And what if they don't screw it up?" O'Brien asked. "As unlikely as that might sound."

"Then you won't have to worry about dying of curiosity… because eventually, *everybody* will know." I held up my shackled wrists. "Now, while we're waiting for your boss' boss to get here… about that trip to the bathroom?"

O'Brien pulled a set of handcuff keys out of his jacket pocket and stood to unlock my restraints. Before he could get the second lock undone, the door to the interrogation room opened and a man who, if I'd been asked to judge him in one word at first glance, I would have chosen *self-important*. He was tall and slender and while O'Brien's suit was expensive and well-fitted, this man's was flashy, conspicuous consumption beyond the need for professionalism, and though I wasn't a watch guy, I recognized the Rolex.

Balding, he indulged in a blond comb-over, and I would have bet good money that he'd dyed it from gray. The ID lanyard around his neck seemed out of place, as if he were slumming here, and the disdainful look he gave O'Brien bugged me and I'd only decided I liked the special agent a few minutes ago.

"Oh, good, you're already setting him loose," the man said with a saccharine smile.

"Deputy Director Mansfield," O'Brien said, springing to his feet. By which I assumed he meant the deputy director of the entire FBI and my eyebrows shot up. That was quick.

"Hurry up, O'Brien," Mansfield urged, making a come-along gesture, "we don't have all day. These gentlemen...and lady... have important business with the President and we don't have time to wait for you."

O'Brien looked like a steer that had just received the bolt between the eyes preparatory to having its throat cut. Stunned, he finished unlocking my cuffs and even though I'd told myself I wouldn't do it, that it was cliched, I rubbed my wrists where the metal had bitten into them.

"Come along, Mr. Travers," Mansfield said. "I understand you've been treated quite poorly and I plan on allowing you to freshen up and have a proper breakfast before we take you to the White House." His grin beamed flawlessly, thanks to what must have been some very expensive dental work. "And let me offer you my sincerest apologies for not extending the grateful hand of friendship to you and your companions immediately!"

As if demonstrating what he meant, he thrust out his hand and I numbly shook it, offering a glance of helpless confusion to O'Brien. Even the best-case scenario I'd laid out for him hadn't involved quite this much bending over backwards. Then I heard the voice from the hallway and suddenly, everything made sense.

"Is everything okay, Leland?"

Smooth, soothing, filled with persuasive charm, just four words and yet I had to step out into the corridor to meet the speaker face to face. Giblet waited there with a broad grin on his face, Val and Dani trailing behind him, escorted by a man and a woman in gray and black suits, badges visible at their belts.

"Hey, Charlie," Gib said, and even through the haze of pheromones and the buzz of his hypnotic subsonics in my ears, I recognized the smug, satisfied tone in his voice. "Have these boys been giving you trouble? Sorry I didn't straighten things out sooner, but you know how it is. Had to wait until the big guns arrived before I could plead my case. But Leland here is a very intelligent, reasonable man with the good of the nation foremost on his mind…aren't you, Leland?"

"Why yes, I am," Mansfield said, just the slightest hint in the ease of the agreement in the just-barely-unfocused glint in his eyes that he'd fallen under Giblet's spell. "I've worked my whole life to prepare for an opportunity like this and I wouldn't dare let it pass by! Come, come, Mr. Travers," he said, motioning for me to follow the others. "This place is unpleasant enough when I'm forced by duty to visit here."

"Good luck, Charlie," O'Brien said, leaning against the frame of the interrogation room door.

I nodded, glancing sidelong at Gib and Deputy Director Mansfield, walking arm-in-arm through rows of staring FBI agents.

"I think I'm gonna need it."

6

It was another Chevy Suburban, but this one was a hell of a lot nicer than the last one I'd ridden in. Maybe because I wasn't handcuffed and someone had given me an egg and sausage sandwich and a cup of coffee.

"Have you ever been to the White House, Mr. Travers?" Leland Mansfield asked, looking back from the front passenger's seat. He wasn't driving, of course. Someone as important as the deputy director of the FBI wouldn't. The driver was a nondescript younger woman who looked a lot like my earliest memories of my kindergarten teacher. Of course, she'd seemed a lot older to me back then.

"No, sir," I told him, staying respectful despite the fact that he was under the influence of Giblet. "I visited D.C. once as a kid, but we didn't get to the White House. I think Carter was president at the time."

Mansfield nodded encouragement as if every word I said was the most intelligent, fascinating thing he'd ever heard, and I wondered what exactly Giblet had told him about me. I suppose I shouldn't have complained since, without Gib, we would probably have been on the way to a black site with bags over our heads.

"It's just so incredible how you and Mr. McKee jumped forward in time." He nodded at Val. "I would kill to sit down and have you tell me stories about what the old west was like."

"Killing ain't necessary," Val assured him, his expression as bemused as I felt. "I'd probably be in a talking mood if you bought me a bottle of bourbon."

"So, we're going to meet the President?" I asked, trying to drag the conversation back to important matters.

"Well, not *first*," Mansfield admitted, rolling his eyes. "I tried, believe me. I told the President's staff that this was beyond important, that it was an existential threat to the entire world, not just this country. But National Security Advisor Donovan insisted that you see him first so he could at least come up with a coherent response to present to the President before we spring you on him. Oh, he said the meeting will definitely take place," Mansfield hastened to add. "I wouldn't let him off the phone until he gave me that assurance. But President Louis is a politician, you understand. Never had a *real* job, never had to deal with a crisis like this face-to-face. Wouldn't know what to do without someone holding his hand through it."

The driver glanced aside at Mansfield with a vaguely horrified look on her face, as if she didn't know what to think about the man being so blatantly honest.

"Is General Barnaby going to be there?" I wondered. I hoped he would be so I could let him know I didn't blame him for what happened.

"I wasn't told that," Mansfield said, shrugging as if it wasn't important. "That's a White House thing. I had the devil's own time just trying to get the FBI director to patch me through to the Attorney General and then looping Mr. Donovan in on the whole thing was another gauntlet to run. In the end, I had to put Mr. Giblet here on the phone in a video call to convince them!"

I eyed Gib sharply.

"I'm glad you were able to talk them into it, *Mister* Giblet," I told him, "particularly given that it was only on video, not in person." In other words not spoken, I worried that he hadn't been able to use his pheromones at all and his subsonic modulation not to its full extent.

"I can be quite persuasive, Charlie," Gib assured me, arms crossed, sitting back in the plush, leather bucket seat like he was the king of the damned world. "Both on the phone and in person. I'm very eager to meet Mr. Donovan."

And I could take from that what I wanted. I stopped talking and took in our surroundings. Things were much different than they had been last night. The snow hadn't lasted long and it was already melting off the sidewalks, hadn't even settled on the road surface because of the heat built up the day before. Still, the white patches added a decorative touch to the office buildings lining the surface streets. Driving the interstate had been sporty, with the slush and more cars than I'd seen in my whole life. I wondered if D.C. had been like this back in my day and I just hadn't visited to notice or whether the traffic had gotten worse along with everything else.

Great. Now I sound like my dad.

It wasn't all my fault, though. A lot of the pessimism I had about the 2020s had come from Dani, and she'd lived through it. Political unrest, riots, hatred and violence against the police, a pandemic, wars, genocides, terrorist attacks… And I thought I'd had it rough just expecting a nuclear war to break out between the US and the USSR. From what Dani had told me, Russia was still causing trouble and it somehow felt like the collapse of the Soviet Union had just made them even more dangerous.

It was hard to tell just by looking at D.C., though. People walking down the sidewalks, huddled in their coats even though it had to be forty degrees out by now, cars driving along as if this was any other day. Maybe it just seemed worse to Dani because it was *her* generation, the same way mine had nightmares over nuclear war and the gas crisis and plane hijackings and the Munich Olympics massacre. Maybe everyone in every time period thought their problems were the worst ever.

I had a different perspective after the time I'd spent off Earth, after seeing what it was like to *really* be subjugated, after seeing an entire planet destroyed along with everyone on it, after seeing thousands of refugees forced to live on a secret sanctuary world because every other planet they'd called home had been captured and enslaved. There'd been, Lenny had told me, *trillions* of people in the old Coalition worlds. The civil war and the invasion of the

Anguilar had reduced the total population of the former Coalition to five hundred billion, give or take, which sounded like a lot until I divided it among hundreds of inhabited worlds.

"There it is," Mansfield announced, pointing like a kid on his first trip to Disney World. "The White House."

"It's very impressive," Giblet told him dutifully. Only someone who knew the Varnell as well as we did could have noticed the twitch at the corner of his mouth where he struggled not to bust out laughing. "I'm sure your country is very proud to have such beautiful landmarks."

"Why, thank you, Mr. Giblet. Yes, it is one of our most prized architectural achievements! If we have time, I'll take you to see all our monuments. My personal favorite is the Jefferson Memorial, but there are so many others! This is a beautiful city!"

I shared a look with Dani and she subtly rolled her eyes, careful not to let the two FBI agents in the vehicle with us see it. Mansfield sounded like a tour director for the D.C. Chamber of Commerce and knowing his position in the government and the mystified look in the eyes of the other agents, I had to think this was because of Gib's influence. I half felt bad for him and half wanted to bust out laughing. It wasn't like Gib was telling him to commit treason or anything. We were here to help.

I didn't remember seeing so much security at the White House when I'd seen it on the news back before I left, but maybe that was just part and parcel of the paranoia Dani had talked about. The gate looked like it could hold off an M1 Abrams tank and the uniformed Secret Service agents manning it were dressed in body armor and carrying some kind of weird-looking submachine guns. They stopped the SUV at a rising barricade and the driver flashed them an ID.

"Deputy FBI Director Mansfield," the older man snapped, waving his own ID at the guard. "We're expected."

The guard made a quiet call on his radio earpiece then nodded to the driver and motioned us through the gate. If he was offended by Mansfield's brusque attitude, he was professional enough not to show it. I let out a breath I hadn't been aware I was holding and we were through, heading around the drive to the rear of the building.

"If you could do us all a big favor," Mansfield said to Giblet as the vehicle pulled up to the curb, "and put up the hood of your jacket until we're in Mr. Donovan's office? We want to avoid causing undue alarm until everyone's been informed of the situation."

"Of course, Deputy Director," Gib said, concealing his features. "Anything we can do to make this easier for you."

He was pouring it on a little thick, and I thought it might be more for our benefit than Mansfield's because Dani's cheek twitched as she suppressed a laugh. I wanted to tell Gib to cool it but I didn't know if I could get away with it. I wasn't sure how exactly his mojo worked and the escorting agents might not be as mesmerized as Mansfield obviously was.

The Secret Service agents who opened the doors for us certainly weren't bedazzled and stared at us civilians with the dubious glare of men and women who didn't like having their established routine disturbed. They looked us all up and down carefully, but no one forced Gib to take off his hood or tried to get a look at his face, and I wondered if they'd been warned about it. If they had, that was more forethought and caution than I'd expected from politicians.

The Secret Service agents walked us in through an entrance I didn't recall seeing before, though I wasn't any sort of expert on the White House. It was on a small roundabout, sheltered by an overhang supported by Greek columns and I couldn't remember enough of my art history classes to tell whether they were Doric, Ionic, or Corinthian. I'd like to say that I was realistic enough to believe I'd never see the inside of the White House except on a tour, but I guess there used to be some stupid-kid part of me who imagined a ceremony with the President hanging the Medal of Honor around my neck for charging some enemy machine gun nest.

I wasn't that old, but I hoped I was old enough to understand why that had been a foolish dream even if I'd achieved my goal and become an active-duty infantry officer. Most Medals of Honor were posthumous. I still might make the posthumous thing, but the odds were, no one would ever know how I died or if they did, be around to give me a medal.

I tried not to gawk as I followed the escorts through the entrance to the West Wing, kept my eyes downcast like there was some danger that I'd run into someone like George, who recognized me from 1987. We did get stares from the passersby, but from the age and the big ID lanyards around their necks, these people were minor functionaries rather than senior staff. I couldn't resist a few looks around, of course. It was the White House. The art was tasteful and impressive, I suppose, but I couldn't have named a single painting or sculpture…at least not until we got to the West Wing lobby.

I stopped there, would have even if our escort hadn't, and stared at the painting hanging over an antique leather couch. This one I recognized. What American wouldn't?

It was *Washington Crossing the Delaware.* Not the original, of course. That was much larger than this. But it had been done by the same artists, Emanuel Leutze and Eastman Johnson. There were others there, of course. *Vernal Falls, Yosemite* and *Old Faithful Geyser in Yellowstone.* But I only spared them the barest glance, transfixed by the work of Leutze and Johnson.

"Wait here," Mansfield told us, passing by the receptionist to duck inside one of the offices there. His own agents stayed behind with our escort, and I wasn't sure who stared at us harder.

"I can't believe we're in the damned White House," Dani murmured, her shoulder touching mine as she looked at the painting. "I thought sure they'd toss us all in a cell and throw away the key."

I glared at her sidelong, then forced my face to neutrality in case anyone was watching.

"Well, you might have mentioned that before you let me go ahead with this plan of action," I whispered back.

"Like you would have backed out once you'd made your mind up." She sniffed, as much of a laugh as either of us dared. "Maybe Laranna can change your mind, but I don't have that talent."

I made a shushing gesture, afraid she'd mention Giblet or his powers of persuasion. One thing I didn't want was these people twigging to the fact that an alien was basically practicing mind-control on them. It sounded so much worse when I put it like that. Dani made a face at the gesture, probably just her general dislike of being told what to do, but she went silent and gave up pretending to be fascinated by the painting.

"You know that painting isn't historically accurate," a deep and sonorous voice from behind me stated.

I turned and found myself face to face with a stocky, broad-shouldered gentleman in a dark-gray herringbone suit that seemed to be perfectly color-coordinated to both his tie and his café-au-lait skin tone. He couldn't have been much past forty, looked about the same age as Val, and there wasn't a trace of gray in his short, tightly curled hair. Nor was there any doubt in those dark, piercing eyes, the sort of all-noticing gaze I'd seen from sergeants-major and the better colonels I'd met and maybe my third-grade homeroom teacher.

"The flag," the man expounded, gesturing. "It hadn't been adopted yet when Washington crossed the Delaware."

"I know," I replied, doing my best not to let my curiosity make me seem desperate. "But I try not to let that spoil it for me. I figure it's a painting, not a photo. It's the emotional impression the event gave to the artist and the one he wanted to create in other people who saw it."

"That's a very enlightened viewpoint for someone nearly forty years behind the times, Mr. Travers." He raised an eyebrow and offered me a hand. "Parker Donovan, National Security Advisor to the President."

His grip was firm and dry, practiced, like he was used to

pressing the flesh. Not a military man, I judged, though he had the right temperament for it, nor exactly a politician. This was Washington, so I bet lawyer.

Donovan grinned slyly.

"I can see it in your eyes, Mr. Travers," he said, raising a finger in accusation. "The assessment. Trying to figure me out. I was told you're the leader here, despite your age, and I understand now why that is." He motioned to the hallway on the left. "Please, come to my office."

Apparently, the invitation extended to all of us as well as our Secret Service escorts, though I wondered if that was Donovan's decision or theirs, because we moved as a group through the narrower, interior corridors to an office larger than my whole apartment back at DeLuca's Pizza. It was curiously devoid of decoration, spartan and bare but for a bookcase full of reference material and a single painting hanging over the mahogany desk.

"You like art, Mr. Travers?" Donovan asked me as we entered the office. "I'm not a huge fan, but this is my one indulgence."

I gave it a look, trying to be polite. Brightly colored yet also somehow stark and in-your-face, it depicted students, I supposed from the books they were carrying, all of them Black, with soldiers carrying rifles behind them.

"It's *Soldiers and Students*," he said. "Or rather, a print of it. Jacob Lawrence painted it, inspired by the Little Rock Nine, a group of Black American students who desegregated Central High School in 1957, as well as an event five years later, when angry protestors swarmed a group of US Marshals at the University of Mississippi. The US Marshals had been deployed with a mission to protect James Meredith, a Black American student as he attended what was previously an all-white university. I don't believe there were any soldiers there protecting the Little Rock Nine from protestors, but as you say, this was his attempt to convey the emotional response these events gave him."

Donovan looked back at the four of us and waved to the convenient number of chairs gathered in front of his desk. I'd expected something along the lines of the folding metal chairs my college professors kept in their offices, but these were more akin to the one my dad had kept in his study, high-backed and leather-upholstered with padded armrests.

"Please, have a seat."

"Thank you, Mr. Donovan," Giblet said, for once misreading the room as he threw back his hood, hoping, I supposed, for the shock effect. His alien features brought no more reaction from Donovan than had my appreciation of *Washington Crossing the Delaware*. "I appreciate the expeditious nature of this meeting and I very much look forward to our peoples working together to a common goal."

Pheromones practically dripped off every word and even I found myself agreeing, so no doubt Donovan would as well, but a deeply engrained annoyance accompanied that feeling since I knew what was happening. And I saw a similar expression on Donovan's face, though I wasn't sure Giblet did.

"It's certainly enlightening to discover we're not alone in this universe, Mr. Giblet," Donovan replied, though it was so carefully neutral that I had to revise my estimation of him as not a politician. Maybe not *just* a politician would have been a better description. "I doubt any of us suspected what the first alien we encountered would look like. If I may say, I find it highly unusual that you're so humanoid…as well as so obviously related to the bird species we have on this planet."

"That's a long story, sir," I told Donovan, jumping in because I was afraid of what Gib's response to that might be. "The bottom line is, all of the life native to this galaxy is related, dating back hundreds of thousands of years to a time when genetic material was taken from this world and used to seed others. Thousands of others. Maybe tens of thousands. The galaxy is full of life and all of that I've encountered is more or less humanoid."

Donovan shook his head, though I sensed it wasn't so much from negation as disbelief.

"You have to believe us, sir," Giblet added. "We have no reason to deceive you. There's nothing for us to gain from this. We're taking a huge risk, in fact, just being here. This is for your benefit. We're here because this is a matter of the continued survival of your people as an autonomous world."

"Yes, I spoke with George about what you told him," Donovan said, leaning back, elbows resting on the arms of his desk chair, fingers steepled together beneath his chin. "These *Anguilar* who you say are on their way."

"They're coming," I told him. "Don't know when, but this place is too tempting of a target. The only reason they haven't come already is that they don't know how quickly technology has progressed here and how quickly the population has exploded. From what I've been told, the last time they looked at the planet, there were less than two billion people on Earth."

"We're not coming empty-handed," Gib said. "If you spoke to General Barnaby…"

"Yes, he told me all about fusion reactors and spaceships." Donovan frowned. "I can't deny your existence, Mr. Giblet, though I'd dearly love to have some genetic samples taken to prove conclusively that you're not simply a man who's had extensive surgical procedures performed on him."

"You can take his blood," I offered. Gib scowled at the idea, and I clarified. "A small sample, I meant. We have no objection."

"We will," Donovan assured me. Gib kept frowning and I think it was more at the idea that the National Security Advisor wasn't swayed by his mind tricks nearly as much as Mansfield had been than it was at the prospect of giving up a blood sample. "But the fact remains, even if you *are* a genuine extraterrestrial, Mr. Giblet, we have no evidence that this technology you're promising to give us actually exists. And I can't take this to the President until I have some reason to believe you can deliver the goods."

I glanced back at Dani and Val and they both nodded. Now was the time.

"We have a lander," I told Donovan. "If you talked to George, then you know that already. I can take you to it. If you want, send a pilot along and I'll show him…" Dani gave me a dirty look and I sighed. "…or *her* how it works. Fly it wherever you want it."

"Maybe you could just tell us where it is," Donovan suggested, the sly edge to his voice making me distinctly uncomfortable. "Give our pilot directions on how to fly it."

"No, I'm afraid it's locked down with biometric security," Dani put in, the first time she'd spoken since we'd entered the office. "It'll only work for one of us."

I wasn't sure what biometric security was, but that might have been a damned good idea. If only we'd thought of it before this very second.

"Very well, Mr. Travers," Donovan said. "I'll call one of the backup pilots for Marine One. The rest of you," he added with a genial smile, "will, of course, be offered every amenity while you're waiting for him."

Donovan was a competent, intelligent man. But I didn't like that smile. It promised bad things.

7

I WASN'T sure why we had to take a helicopter.

Not any tiny little OH-58 Kiowa, either. This was huge, a Sikorsky Sea King, one of the helicopters they used for Marine One, and the interior looked more like a stretch limousine than any of the Hueys I'd flown in during my time in the National Guard or ROTC. Leather seats, enclosed and air conditioned, walls, even curtains across the windows.

And guards of course. You'd think I was some kind of terminator robot with a bunch of laser guns built into my arms as many guards as they'd sent on this trip. I mean, the pilot and copilot they were sending with me to learn how to fly the lander were armed, but maybe that was SOP. I had no idea. But the fire team of Marine infantry accompanying them didn't come as a set with the Sikorsky, I was pretty sure. They had some kind of carbine version of the M16 but with a lot of weird shit hanging off it and some kind of short, funky-looking rifle scope mounted on it and all I could think was that it looked heavy and I'd rather carry the old Matty Mattel.

Not to mention the body armor they wore, which had to be pretty weighty as well. It probably felt pretty good with the temps outside still hovering around freezing but I couldn't imagine wearing that stuff somewhere hot, like Florida. Or the Middle East, which was where US troops had spent a lot of years recently, according to Dani.

"Is this the ball field, sir?" the pilot, a man named Benito Gonzalez, asked. He was a captain in the Marine Corps, not much older than me, and about the same build though he looked absolutely skinny compared to the combat troops because of the lack of body armor.

I looked out the side window he'd pointed to and saw the field a few hundred feet beneath us, still coated white from last night's snow. It was colder here in Arlington than it had been in DC and the snow still hadn't melted off the sidewalks, though it was gone from the roads, either through plowing and salting or just the sun beating down on this mostly clear day.

"I think so," I said, not quite yelling because there was enough soundproofing inside this bird that the rotor and engine noise wasn't overwhelming. "I only saw it from the ground, at night, during a snowstorm, but if it's at the address Dani's phone gave us, this has to be it."

They'd at least let her have her phone back long enough to check, though they'd neglected to give any of us back our comms. Or our guns, but I hadn't really expected that.

Things had been…well, tense would have been putting it mildly.

"Why can't they come with me?" I'd demanded, staring down Donovan as we'd waited under the shade of the driveway for the helicopter to arrive.

While *I'd* waited. The others were still inside, and I hadn't been happy about it then and still wasn't now.

"There's room on the lander for all of us," I'd continued when Donovan hadn't responded immediately. He'd been talking on his cell phone but I didn't care, and I'd had the sense that he was doing it to put off talking to me. "There's no reason for them to stay behind."

"They'll be waiting for you at the hangar," Donovan had assured me, holding a hand across the speaker of his phone, the look on his sculpted face one of tightly controlled irritation. "You have to understand, Mr. Travers, if you're sincere in what you've told us, this is the most incredible opportunity that humanity has ever encountered. But if you're not, and we just walk into whatever trap you might have set, well…the only reason every man and woman in this government wouldn't be prosecuted and sent to prison for the rest of our lives would be that none of us had survived. So, no. I won't be allowing all of you to travel together in that lander for a very real worry of what you might do once you took off in it." He'd nodded out to the horizon and I'd followed the gesture to the helicopter approaching. "You'll travel with Captain Gonzalez to your lander, then fly it to the hangar at Joint Base Andrews, and your friends will be waiting for you there." He'd shaken his head like every bureaucrat I'd ever dealt with from the DMV to MEPS, each one telling me that this was just the way things were. "I'm afraid this is the way things are going to have to go if you want to work with us."

I was beginning to wonder if I did. But it was too late to back out now. I told myself that as long as Gib was back there talking their ears off, we'd be okay. Maybe this Donovan was a little more resistant than the others, but most people weren't, and all it would take was one. He'd keep the rest of them safe, and I hoped Dani and Val would keep him in line, though I hadn't had the opportunity to tell any of them that.

Donovan had rushed me outside once he'd made the call to bring in the chopper.

Get to da choppah. I wondered where George was and whether he had any clue what was being done.

Gonzalez seemed like a nice enough sort, quiet and competent, though his copilot, a first lieutenant named Bartholomew, had said not a word nor had he even bothered to look at me.

"I don't see anything down there." Gonzalez said, squinting out the window.

"You wouldn't," I told him. "It's kind of invisible. Tell the pilot to set down as far away from the dugout as he can so you don't accidentally land on it."

His eyes narrowed as if he wasn't sure if I was screwing with him, but then he got on the radio in his earpiece and spoke urgently to the pilot. The pilot must have taken his word for the invisibility of the target because the helicopter descended even faster, spiraling gently down to the open end of the field. The rotors came dangerously close to the outfield fence and I cringed, not wanting my first ride in a Sea King to be my last.

But these pilots were the ones who flew around the President of the United States and we touched down gently, with hardly a bounce.

The Marines were up first, one of them, another captain, holding a hand to keep the pilots and me in our seats while they went to the door of the helicopter. Light flooded the interior of the aircraft, harshly white as the afternoon sun reflected off the snow, and I had to squint and look away both from the glare and the wash of frigid snow kicked up by the rotors. By the time I was able to keep my eyes open, the Marines were down the steps and I slowly unstrapped from my seat, getting up and moving to where I could at least see outside.

The Marine officer stepped back up before I could get into the doorway, the muzzle of his carbine pointed in the general direction of my midsection, and I froze in place. For some reason, the barrel of a 5.56x45mm rifle firing a plain old copper-jacketed lead slug was so much scarier than the more esoteric crystalline emitter of a pulse gun, despite the fact that I knew pulse guns could do a lot more damage.

The Marine lowered the barrel and waved us toward the door.

"It's clear," he snapped. "Let's go."

"Thanks for making sure there were no deadly Little League ninja assassins out there waiting to ambush us," I told him as we passed by.

The rest of the fire team had moved to the edge of the diameter of the slowing rotors, all of them down on one knee, their weapons trained outward. My shoes sank about an inch into the snow and I looked around, struck by a sudden fear that the lander was gone, that someone had stolen it and I'd look like a total fool hunting around an empty ball field, feeling the empty air like a blind man without a cane.

I needn't have been concerned. The snow showed me the way. It had been stirred up into a temporary blizzard by the rotors and slowly, gently showered back to the field. Except where it touched the lander. There, it outlined the curved, almost saucer shape of the craft, though I couldn't blame the others for taking a moment to notice it.

"Holy shit," Bartholomew said, breaking his silence for an almost reverent profanity.

Even the Marine infantry team stood, stepping back from the apparition with eyes wide through their protective goggles. I traced a line around the spacecraft with my fingers, the surface cold and smooth beneath them, damp from the melting snow. There. It flattened out by the hatch, the barest of recesses, and the security plate was just to the left of it. At the touch of my palm, the mirror camouflage deactivated and a lot more curses joined Bartholomew's as the lander sprang into corporeality.

"Well," Gonzalez murmured, standing just behind me, "I guess no one's going to think it's a hoax now."

"I'm opening the lock," I announced loudly, not wanting to alarm the heavily armed Marines, since they seemed to take this sort of thing seriously.

"Stack on the door!" the officer ordered. I think he was a

captain, which seemed strange for a fire team, but I suppose they'd cobbled the group together from what they had on hand.

They worked together well enough, though, lining up along the side of the hatch, their weapons trained on it, preparatory to it opening and, I don't know, spewing out a stream of alien monsters.

"You know," I told them, hitting the control to open the hatch, "this is a *spaceship*. An alien spaceship. If we meant you any harm, I would have brought an armed fighter with a particle cannon that could blow up this entire ball field in one shot."

The Marine captain said nothing but I thought I detected a twitch in the muscles around his eye. Stifling a chuckle, I opened the hatch. It folded outward, turning into a set of steps and before I could make a move, Captain America charged up and into the lander, the clomp of his boots on the floor echoing through the ship. I waited as patiently as I was capable of until he returned, his carbine clutched across his chest.

"Clear," he announced, stepping out of the way.

"Yeah, what did you expect?" I wondered, heading up the stairs with Gonzalez close behind. "It's not like I didn't lock the door behind me."

I fell into the pilot's seat, ignoring the instinctive move Gonzalez's hand made toward his shoulder-holstered pistol. It was another one of those plastic things like Dani had carried as a sheriff's deputy and I didn't much care for their look compared to the old Colt forty-fives or even the Beretta 9mm's that had been new when I left.

"Are the Marines coming?" I asked, nodding back at the door.

Gonzalez settled down into the copilot's position while Bartholomew took the seat between and behind us. Him being there, just out of my line of sight, made me uncomfortable, but I doubted either of them cared.

"No, they'll head back with the Sea King," Gonzalez told me. There was something about the way he said it that I didn't like, but I didn't know him well enough to be sure I wasn't just paranoid.

Nodding, I hit the control to close the hatch and powered up the drives.

"Tell me how this thing works," Gonzalez said.

"Hell if I know how it works," I admitted, "but I can tell you how to fly it. It's a lot easier than a helicopter because I could never have learned to fly a helicopter in the time it took me to learn this thing. You hit this button for power up." I indicated the one I'd just touched. "These are basically the throttles." This time, I pointed to a series of small levers set into grooves in the console. "Everything else goes through this steering column. It moves back and forth to put the nose up or down, the whole column goes left and right to bank and you turn the wheel for right or left. Simple."

In demonstration, I gave the bird some gas and pulled back on the yoke, taking her off the ground with the barest hint of motion and none of the roar I would have expected from a helicopter or an airplane.

"There's some kind of thing they call gravity-resist involved in making her fly in an atmosphere," I explained, keeping the lander a few meters off the ground while I hunted around for the camouflage control. "Just making us invisible again," I explained. "I didn't figure you'd want people seeing a flying saucer land at Andrews Air Force Base."

"Joint Base Andrews," he corrected me automatically, then glanced over with realization in his expression. "But it wouldn't have been that when you were…"

"Taken," I supplied. "I'm sure there've been a lot of changes I haven't heard about yet." I twisted in my seat to spear Bartholomew with a glare. "You're in the navigator's seat, so make yourself useful. That console in front of you is rigged to accept longitude and latitude. If you have those for the hangar we're going to, now's the time to input them."

He looked like he wanted to say something snarky in return, but Gonzalez gave him a nod and Bartholomew pulled out a small device a little fatter than a cell phone and tapped its screen.

"That's a GPS," Gonzalez told me as I turned my attention back to the controls, taking us higher and clear of the ball field so we wouldn't get in the way of the Sea King. Its rotors had begun to turn, and I guessed it was about to take off. "Global Positioning System, based on satellites in orbit. It gives you your exact coordinates down to a few meters, anywhere you have a view of the satellites."

"That would have come in handy during some land nav tests," I said, grunting a laugh.

"You were in the military?" Gonzalez asked, eyes glued to the motions of my hands on the controls.

"I was in the Army National Guard and in ROTC while I was in college. Got commissioned and was about to walk at graduation when all this…" I spared a hand from the wheel to motion around me expansively. "…kind of happened to me."

"Where were you headed?" Gonzalez shrugged. "I mean, if you hadn't been abducted?"

"I wanted active-duty infantry," I sighed with old melancholy. "But the PMS at my university hated me and I wound up with National Guard field artillery. I was a few weeks from reporting to Ft. Sill, Oklahoma, and for that reason alone, I would rather have been kidnapped by a psychotic robot with delusions of grandeur."

Gonzalez laughed like a man familiar with the politics of college ROTC and I could have told him more stories, but I was finally getting the longitude and latitude from Bartholomew's station, the coordinates drawing a yellow line on the main screen, showing me which way to go.

"Now we just follow the yellow brick road," I told Gonzalez, pointing to the dotted line. "It's very user-friendly. Hell, I can even fly one of our starfighters and I'm pretty far from a crack pilot." Sighing, I pushed the controls to follow the indicators. "That's one of the reasons I'm here, to be honest. We have people who've trained to be warriors their whole lives, but not one of them has been trained to be a soldier. Or Marine, in your case. We have people, myself included, who have a natural talent for flying a fighter, but none who've been trained to be a combat pilot. For all that the Anguilar are undisciplined, treacherous bastards, they've at least been part of an organized military their whole lives."

"Gonna be a hard sell," Gonzalez opined, tilting his head to the side as if trying to look at the events from a different angle. "Getting not just this country but the entire world involved in a war against some weird aliens they've never met..."

"They will," I assured him and fell silent, concentrating on flying.

It was a short trip, would have been shorter if I hadn't been careful about not going supersonic. We were invisible to radar, practically invisible to visual scanning, but a sonic boom would attract attention. What had taken a couple hours by car, and half that by helicopter, was halved again in the lander, not least of which because momentum wasn't the enemy with the technology built into the little ship.

I'd never seen Andrews Air Force Base, so I didn't know if it had changed a lot since it had become *Joint Base Andrews*, but from the air, it looked a lot like every military base I'd ever seen. Lots of identically boxy administration buildings, bigger ones of sheet metal for storage, and even bigger for hangars. Runways of course, and while I counted on the collision avoidance systems to keep our shuttle from running into any of the landing aircraft, I did my best to stay out of their flight paths.

I couldn't devote my full attention to the fighters, but their lines weren't familiar to me. Dani had told me about new birds that had been adapted while I was gone but I couldn't recall the numbers or names. I'd ask Gonzalez later, after we were on the ground.

Past the main runways, well off the main roads, there was another landing zone. Not a runway, not for conventional airplanes, but more a barely paved series of pads, for helicopters or possibly VTOL jets if they had any. I couldn't be sure because there were no aircraft parked there at the moment, nothing but a few of the ubiquitous black Suburbans in the lots around the large, sheet-metal hangar. Rust marred the side facing us, evidence of disuse and abandonment, though I wondered if that was deliberate camouflage.

"Just set down as close as you can to the hangar," Gonzalez instructed, pointing out the main viewscreen. "Don't worry about bringing it inside, we can do that later since you've got that cloak of invisibility thing."

Bartholomew laughed sharply and I sensed there was a reference there that I didn't understand. I supposed I'd have to get used to that, having missed most of thirty-seven years' worth of popular culture. Hell, these guys might not even understand movie quotes from the 1980s.

On that depressing note, I feathered the throttle and gently lowered the lander onto the central pad. I wasn't sure if I'd just gotten that good at piloting the lander or if the background automation was simply programmed for softer touchdowns than the fighters, but our landing gear met the tarmac with barely a jolt.

"There you go, my jarhead friends," I said, hitting the quick-release for my seat restraints. "We hope you've enjoyed your flight with Alien Robot Airlines and that you'll keep us in mind next time for all your transportation needs…"

"Hey, Charlie," Gonzalez said, turning me back around as I was heading for the door, "one more thing."

"Yeah?" I asked.

He winced as if he were in physical pain, sighed.

"I just wanted to let you know I think you're a good guy. And I'm sorry about this."

"Sorry about *what*?" I asked instinctively before an instinct even more deeply ingrained reminded me I'd turned my back on Bartholomew.

I barely had time to raise a hand and start to turn back when something jabbed into the side of my neck. I slapped at it, brushed at a hard, plastic tube before it withdrew and I finished the turn to see Bartholomew backing away from me, one hand on his pistol, the other holding a hypodermic. I guessed they still used those.

"What the hell was *that*?" I demanded, advancing a step, fully intent on kicking the guy's ass.

Something had gone wrong with the lander's gravity control, though, because the whole thing was spinning and suddenly, the floor had an irresistible attractive force. I surrendered and it rose up to meet me.

8

I'D FULLY INTENDED to join the military from the time I was a junior in high school. Which meant I knew the regular drug tests would be coming and I hadn't done so much as smoke a joint my whole life. The upshot of all that was that I had no experience whatsoever with being under the influence of drugs.

Yet when I woke up with my head stuffed full of foam rubber and a gauzy haze across reality, somehow I knew I'd been drugged. Not whatever that asshole Bartholomew had stuck me with—that had just knocked me out. This was the good stuff, good enough that I didn't even feel the strain in my shoulders from my hands being cuffed behind my back, wasn't stressed about the implications of the fact that I'd been shackled to a chair and had a hood over my face.

"Good, you're awake."

The voice wasn't familiar, or at least I knew it wasn't Mansfield or Donovan. I hadn't figured it would be. This was dirty work and guys like that never got their hands dirty. I had, I realized, been such a patsy, though thanks to the drugs, I wasn't beating myself up over it. In fact, it was hilarious. After all this time, all I'd been through, I'd let them sucker me.

"Is something funny?" Same voice, except irritation put an edge to it. Had I been laughing? I wasn't sure.

Better laugh again, just in case.

This time, I was sure I'd been laughing and that made things feel all better somehow. He must not have agreed because a strong, cruel hand gripped me on either side of my jaw.

"I said," he growled, "is something funny?"

"You are," I replied, though it sounded muffled and distorted, which might have been a combination of the hand and the hood material over my mouth or might have been the drugs. "You're hilarious."

I wasn't sure why, except that there was something about the whole thing that was ridiculous. But that wasn't the only thing.

"And me," I admitted as the hand came free. "I'm an idiot for thinking we could ever trust you. I should have just done this without you. You're a bunch of paranoid primitives just like everyone else told me you would be. Sorry, I should say *we* are paranoid primitives. I'm one of you, though I hope to God smarter than you idiots have been."

"And your plan was what?" A rough palm pushed against my chest, sending me rocking back in the chair. It was cold, hard metal, bolted to the floor. Maybe designed for something just like this. "To pull us into your war? To drain our resources?"

"Your *resources*," I scoffed. "You're an idiot." I tossed my head, trying to shake the hood free. It wasn't on tight, but I couldn't quite manage it. "I wish I could see your face so I could laugh in it."

The hood came off in an explosion of light and I winced, slitting my eyes at the bright overhead lamps. I was inside a high-roofed building, maybe the hangar we'd landed at, but it was sectioned off by sheetrock walls into the tiny room where I was confined. Just two chairs and a table between them. I supposed the other was for the man standing in front of me.

Yeah, he was nothing like Mansfield or even…what was his name? The first FBI guy…his face swam in front of me, but his name was a butterfly fluttering just out of the reach of my drug-addled thoughts. O'Brien? Maybe that was it.

This guy was no O'Brien. He wasn't FBI, wasn't a cop of any sort, and I would have been willing to bet he wasn't military, either. Head shaved totally bald, though he should have gone ahead and gotten rid of those stupid, bushy eyebrows while he was at it. His face was soft and fleshy, but the blue eyes were as hard as steel, someone who'd done a lot of bad things in his life and was at peace with it. Not someone to screw with. Still, I was a man of my word.

I laughed in his face.

"You don't know shit about science, do you, Baldy?" I asked him. Which was kind of ironic given that I didn't know that much, either, but this part I'd had explained to me in detail. "If you have cheap space travel, you have all the resources you could ever want. Do you know how many tons of iron are in just *one* rock out in our asteroid belt?" I hoped he did because I had no idea. "Enough to supply the entire Earth's demand for a thousand years." Or something like that. I didn't remember the exact time. Not that I had a bad memory in general, but it was hard to focus when I was pumped full of whatever the hell they'd given me.

I shook my head, trying to clear it.

"And we have cheap *star* travel. We have hundreds of thousands of asteroid belts and moons and planets, all full of minerals and water and hydrogen and whatever the hell else we need. We have fusion reactors and even better than that, we have power cells that suck energy right out of another dimension. Nobody wants or needs to steal Earth's precious bodily fluids."

Okay, channeling *Dr. Strangelove* now, but this dude looked like he was on the wrong side of fifty, so maybe he'd get the reference.

I sucked in a breath, feeling light-headed, and braced for what I figured would be either a smack in the face or the hood coming back, but Baldy just smiled thinly.

"If we don't have anything you want," he asked with calm logic, "then why are these Anguilar you talked about so intent on conquering us?"

Ooh. That was a good one. I might have noticed the tactic sooner if it weren't for the chemical cocktail coursing through my veins. He wasn't stupid and he wasn't a brute, he'd just manipulated me.

"A couple reasons, my follicularly-challenged friend," I told him, chuckling mostly at my own discomfort. "First of all, even though you can get resources from space, there's one thing that's harder to get and that's food. I've been told, though I have no clue about this kind of science shit, that it's theo…therot…" I clenched my teeth and tried to concentrate enough to pronounce the word. "*Theoretically* possible to grow food in orbital farms if you brought in water and soil or some hydro…hydro…" Damned drugs. Couldn't think of the word.

"Hydroponics?" Baldy suggested and I nodded enthusiastically.

"Yeah, that. You could do it in orbit or just in deep space and grow your food there, but there's problems with that. First of all, it's expensive and requires constant maintenance, and every alien equivalent of a dollar they spend building shit like that is one they don't spend building warships. And they *are* at war…they have been for decades, ever since they invaded this galaxy. The other problem is that it's pretty vulnerable to attack. If you're counting on an orbital farm for all your food, you're gonna have to commit a bunch of ships and troops to guarding it and if you do lose it, you're screwed. You're gonna starve."

I stopped, frowning, wondering where I'd been going with all this. Don't do drugs, kids.

Oh, wait, yeah…I got it.

"So, they can't grow food in space. But they could still use that same kind of technology to grow it on a planet. Build, like… food factories where they grew nasty shit like soy paste and algae powder, which I understand from Lenny, a lot of militaries used to use back in the old days. But again, that's high maintenance. You need educated technicians and the kind of work they do on those food factories, well…they could be building weapons and ships. And again, they're big targets. Anything centralized is a target for the resistance." I grinned broadly. "That's us."

"You actually call yourself that?" he wondered, the corner of his mouth quirking up like he considered it amusing.

"*I* didn't call us that," I assured him, shaking my head but stopping quickly when the motion sent flashes of light sparking in my vision. "There was no name, really. The resistance is a description, not a name. I started calling us, not the entire movement but us the military part of it, Vanguard Wing a little while ago, after we acquired a bunch of Vanguard starfighters. They're the best weapon we have and we were trying to make them the keystone of our strategy." I winced. "It still seems a little lame, I know. But they're aliens and, except for a few who hang out with me, most of them haven't watched our TV shows or movies, so they don't know how kitschy it is."

Damn it. I'd gotten sidetracked again. Squeezing my eyes shut, I brought myself back on topic.

"But back to the point, if you'd stop trying to derail me here." I probably should have hidden my anger, but hiding anything at all was nearly impossible. My mouth just kept moving despite everything my brain tried to get it to shut up. "Farms. Food. The Anguilar need all the food they can get, not just for their own troops but to use as a weapon against their conquests, the people they rule. If they're the only food provider, it doesn't make any sense to rebel against them, right? But that's labor intensive… which is fine with them, because if there's one thing they know how to do, it's enslave people and put them to work." I shrugged. "Oh, and they do some mining on their conquered worlds, too, because even though, like I said, you can get resources from space, they figure this is cheap and easy and all it costs is the lives of some of their slaves. Mostly adult, military-aged males who refuse to sign up for their infantry to be cannon fodder."

Baldy didn't look convinced. He sat back on the edge of the table, tapping it rhythmically with his fingertips.

"You're saying they're coming here to turn us all into slaves and steal our food?" His grimace dripped skepticism. "That doesn't make any more sense than taking our mineral resources. If they control all those worlds already…just one or two should be enough to grow all the food they need."

I couldn't help it, I shook my head again despite the inner-ear distress it gave me from the narcotics.

"You don't understand. The galaxy has been at war for *centuries*. There were these guys called the Kamerians who took it over and formed the Coalition government, but they were pretty nasty—think the Romans—and there was a huge civil war that they finally lost. Everything fell apart then, and everyone was on their own. That was when the Anguilar came and took over, and *that* fight has been going on for over a hundred years. There's a few worlds, like Copperell or the other Anguilar government centers, that have a billion or more people, but most of the inhabited planets only have populations in the hundreds or even down to the tens of millions. That's not enough to farm food for a whole galaxy. How many you got here now?"

"Eight billion," Baldy told me and for the first time, I saw him swallow hard, like he'd finally believed something I'd told him.

"Eight billion," I said with a nod. "And I bet just this country grows enough food to supply most of the world if you could get it to them. All the Anguilar would have to do is put a few cruisers in orbit and threaten to blow up your cities unless you provided them food." I shrugged. "Except they're not smart enough to do that, so what they'll probably do instead is come on in and wreck everyone's military capabilities first, take out all the national governments, starting with ours, and *then* make demands. And it'll work, too, because you're all at each other's throats right now and they'll use that against you. They're good at that. That's why it took decades for anyone to organize a resistance against them, because none of the other powers trusted each other."

Baldy was silent and now that I finally had a second to think and the drugs were, apparently, beginning to wear off, I finally grasped the questions I wanted answered.

"Where are my friends?" I asked him. "Are they here? Why did you do this to us?"

I kinda knew the why already. Donovan was no fool and he'd noticed the way Mansfield had reacted to Giblet, probably noticed his own reaction and figured out what was going on. I should have known it was a danger. After all, if Gib's abilities were universal and foolproof, his people would have been ruling the galaxy, not hunted down like criminals wherever they went. But a little righteous indignation couldn't hurt. It also didn't get me anything.

"I don't make policy, Mr. Travers," Baldy told me, "I *am* policy. And I'm also not authorized to give you any information." But I could tell he wasn't comfortable with the question. Maybe I was working on his conscience, if he still had one.

"Well, you'd better find someone who *can* authorize you to give me some information," I shot back, "or I swear to God, you'll regret it."

His brow furled, scarred and lined from whatever mysterious, violent life he'd led.

"Really? You think you're in any position to make demands, Mr. Travers?"

"No, not me," I corrected him, laughing. Not because of the narcotics this time, an honest laugh. "I've screwed this up and I know it. You need to be worrying about my wife."

Baldy was clearly amused by the idea.

"Your wife? Why should we be worried about her?"

"Because she was raised from birth to be a kick-ass warrior woman," I told him. "Because for some reason, she's decided that she loves me and because anyone who gets in her way usually gets a big, sharp knife stuck right in their neck. Because she's patrolling in orbit as we speak in one of those Vanguard starfighters, waiting for me to call and tell her everything is hunky-dory. And, not least, because she's in command right now of the big, heavily armed cruiser sitting just beyond the Moon. A cruiser big enough to lay waste to an entire city in a few minutes…and then move onto the next one because nothing you have could touch it."

"You're threatening us now?" Baldy asked. "Threatening our cities? What makes you better than these Anguilar?"

"I'm not threatening anything," I clarified. My mouth was getting dry and I paused to work up some moisture. "I *can't* threaten anything because, thanks to you, I'm not in charge right now. I'm *telling* you how my wife and my friends are going to react to what you've done. I'm human. I'm an American. So are Dani and Val. That's why I brought them along. But that also means that everyone else up there, everyone making the decisions now, *isn't*. They don't owe you or the United States or Earth any loyalty."

Baldy snorted.

"And the only indication we have that any of that actually exists is your say-so. You better hope you have friends up there, Mr. Travers, because you certainly aren't making any new ones down here."

A loud knock interrupted him and I started, not having a clear idea where the door was in this room. It was, as it turned out, behind me, and it hurt pretty bad to twist around and find that out. Baldy's frown pinched his soft face into something petulant and he shoved the table backward as he pushed away from it, the metal legs scraping against the cement floor.

"What is it?" he demanded, yanking the hollow, rusted door open. "I left instructions not to be…"

His mouth snapped shut on the last word and he backed away from the door, eyes as wide as saucers.

"Get back inside and keep your hands where I can see them."

Despite the discomfort, I twisted around farther at the voice, teased by its familiarity. George Barnaby walked through the door, a wicked-looking Beretta 9mm in his hand, the muzzle pointed between Baldy's eyes.

I gawked at him, unable to speak, sure that this was a hallucination from the lingering effects of the interrogation drugs they'd given me.

"Where are the keys to his cuffs?" George demanded, gesturing at me.

"General Barnaby," Baldy said, hands raised palms outward, "you don't want to be doing this. This is going to end your career…"

"It's going to end *you*, asshole," George warned, voice raising to a bellow as he advanced a step, "unless you give me those damned keys!"

Baldy sighed and pointed to the front of his jeans.

"They're in my pants pocket." He moved his hand slowly towards it. "I have to get them out."

"No, keep your hands up and turn around," George instructed him.

Baldy sighed and turned around, hands going behind his head. George approached slowly, cautiously and pulled the government agent's tan sport coat up at the back, revealing a holster tucked into the belt on the right side, just behind his hip. George tried to yank the gun out but wound up taking the holster with it. He looked at it, brow furling in consternation, then stuck the whole thing into the pocket of his black leather coat.

"All right, *now* you can get those keys."

"There's cameras in here," Baldy warned, fishing the key ring out of his pants and holding it behind his head for George to take. "There's no way you can get away with this. There's probably Air Force SPs on their way here already."

George rolled his eyes as he took the keys, though Baldy

couldn't see it.

"You think I got a star by being stupid?"

"It's been known to happen," I mused quietly, finally finding my voice. George shot me a dirty look.

"The first thing we did was feed those cameras a loop going back fifteen minutes. No one's coming to help you until long after we're gone."

He got the cuffs off me and pulled me to my feet.

"I'm okay, George," I assured him. "I can walk."

Then I almost fell over and barely caught myself on the back of the chair.

"Yeah, you look like it." George grabbed Baldy's collar and pushed him toward the chair. "Sit down, hands behind your back." He handed me the cuffs. "Put these through the slats of the chair and make sure they're tight."

It was awful trusting of him to think I could even stay on my feet long enough to do it, but I somehow managed to squint with one eye and get a clear view of one of the many images of Baldy's hands to get those cuffs on him.

"All right," George said, grabbing my arm and leading me toward the door. "Come on, let's get your friends and get the hell out of here."

"George, how the hell did you do all this?" I asked him, following as he held the door open for me.

"I wasn't always a desk jockey, son," he said with a grin. "Follow me…infantry."

Great. Some guys just got a sports car for their mid-life crisis. Trying not to fall over, I followed him anyway.

9

THE HANGAR LOOKED nothing like a hangar, probably hadn't been one for a lot of years, given how dented and rusted some of the doors looked, how faded the paint on the walls was. I expected that. What I didn't expect was how empty the place would be.

"Where the hell is everybody?" I asked, looking up and down the long hallway as we emerged from the interrogation room. Nothing in either direction, though the entrances on both sides were invisible behind what I thought had to be some kind of security barriers. "I thought there'd be a bunch of guards…"

"Most of them went with your lander," he told me, motioning for me to follow him farther into the structure. "They loaded it up on a flatbed, covered it with a tarp and took it out of here. The rest were on their way with an ambulance to take your feathered friend Giblet to be dissected."

I stopped in my tracks and stared at him, horror creeping up into my gut.

"What?"

"Don't worry," George said, sighing and motioning urgently. "That's how we got into this place! We intercepted the ambulance on the way here…it's parked out back and the crew is locked in the cargo box of a U-Haul truck in the back lot of a truck stop off I-495." He shrugged. "It's winter and they have jackets, they'll be fine. Giblet and the others are still here…we just have to find them."

As if in demonstration, he tried another of the doors along the hallway and it opened immediately, the interior dark and deserted.

"Damn," he muttered. "Assuming they haven't heard the commotion and snuck them out of here somewhere."

Getting the idea, I rushed to the next door on the other side of the hallway, working the hatch and throwing it open. Again, nothing. This one was a storage closet, filled with old furniture and cleaning supplies…and lots of cobwebs. I half expected to find an iron maiden or a rack or some other medieval torture device, given the nature of the place.

George was about to take the next door, but I waved at him.

"Give me that gun you took off the bald guy."

He pulled out the holstered weapon, another of the plastic toys they seemed to like so much nowadays, hesitated, eyeing me doubtfully.

"Aren't you still strung out?"

"I'm fine," I insisted. "I mean, I won't be running any marathons for a couple hours, but I can think straight."

Sighing, he handed it over.

"Just don't shoot anyone unless you have to. I'm already committing treason, I'd like to avoid accessory to murder."

I grunted, shoving the holster into my jacket pocket and holding the gun low by my side. A SIG, like the one Dani had carried. I'd had the chance to take a few shots out of hers on the *Liberator*'s range and knew how to operate it. No safety, which seemed weird to me, and no hammer either. *Striker-fired*, she'd called it and if I hadn't been shooting pulse guns the last two years, I would have been pretty uncomfortable with the whole concept. This one had the same setup as hers, with an electronic sight and a tiny flashlight mounted in front of the trigger. No laser though. After watching *The Terminator*, I'd figured all the guns in the future would have sighting lasers.

I gave George a nod and he tried the next door. Locked. Which probably meant there was someone inside. I moved to one side of the door and he knocked on it sharply. The sound was hollow, foreboding. Raising the SIG to high ready, gripped in both hands, I wondered if the intelligence types inside were as pissed off at the interruption as Baldy had been. At least they answered the door more promptly.

"Is the transport here?"

I heard the voice before I saw the woman, and when I did see her, she was already in motion, lunging at George even as he pointed the Beretta her way. Right up until I put the barrel of the SIG against her temple. She froze and I got a good look at her.

Short, stocky, wearing a light jacket and jeans just like Baldy, though she was younger than him, maybe mid-thirties. Stern, businesslike, even with a gun to her head.

"Don't make a sound," I warned her, grabbing her arm and pushing her back inside. "Put your hands behind your head and back up slowly."

"You, too!" George ordered, his gun trained on the second agent in the room, younger than Baldy and the stern woman, muscles straining against his jacket like someone who spent a lot of time in the gym. "Keep your hands away from your sides and get on your knees! Do it now!"

These guys didn't try arguing or reasoning their way out of it the way Baldy had, just did as they were told…or that was what I thought they were going to do. They both assumed the position, hands behind their heads and I let my gaze flicker to the back of the room. Dani and Val were there, in chairs like the one I'd sat on, hands cuffed behind their backs, ankles secured by chains. There was a nasty bruise across the side of Val's face that looked suspiciously like a rifle butt and dried blood under Dani's nose, but otherwise, they looked okay.

One other figure sat on the floor, huddled against the far wall, trussed up like a Thanksgiving turkey with flex ties, a black hood pulled over his head.

"You guys all right?" I asked.

"I think Gib is unconscious," Dani said, her features twisted with rage as she struggled against her cuffs. "They gave him some kind of drug after they gagged him and put a hood over his head. I'm not sure if he's breathing."

"Shit," I murmured, taking a step toward the prone Varnell.

That was when the big guy made his move. I suppose I should have expected it. He was young, strong, with hair a little too blond and a little too long, noticeable in a profession where it probably paid not to be noticed. He lunged at George, and probably would have reached the Beretta before George could fire it… but I was still pretty young myself and, even more importantly, I'd been fighting for my life the last two years. I could have shot him, maybe should have, but I went from instinct and slammed the butt of the gun down on the side of his neck as he passed.

The big guy grunted and went down, eyes rolling back in his head, not quite unconscious but stunned. The woman took advantage of the distraction and brushed back her jacket, reaching for the gun she carried in the identical place Baldy had stashed his, just behind her hip. I'd expected it though, and I left the big guy for George. For all that I'd spent the last two years fighting beside a badass female, old instincts kept me from hitting a woman, but old training gave me an alternative.

Falling to a knee, I swept my free leg back in an arc that took her at the ankles and chopped her legs from under her. Technically, it wasn't *me* who knocked the wind out of her, it was the floor, and when she hit between her shoulder blades with a pained expulsion of breath, the gun she hadn't fully gotten a grip on clattered away, plastic on cement.

"Get his gun," I warned George, gesturing at the big guy, who was beginning to stir.

George looked shocked, as though he hadn't expected anyone to resist, but he did as I said and patted the big guy down, pulling away yet another of the identical compact SIGs. I grabbed the woman's pistol and regarded it with skepticism.

"I figure we almost have enough of these things to open up an exotic gun shop on one of the pirate enclaves." I nodded to the female agent. "Give me the keys to those cuffs."

"I can't," she hissed, rolling onto her side, wincing at the pain in her back. "I'd wind up in a cell right next to you in some black site in Eastern Europe."

"The keys are in that muscle-bound asshole's right jacket pocket," Dani provided and George nodded, rummaging through the big man's pockets.

The big, blond agent came back to coherence in the middle of it, shaking his head, eyes focusing sharply as he tried to turn over. I stepped on his wrist and held it down, pointing one gun at him and the other at the woman.

"Relax," I told them both. "We really don't want to shoot anyone, but given how you've treated my friends and me, I'm not going to lose sleep over it if I have to put a bullet in someone's kneecap to keep them too busy writhing around in pain to cause me trouble."

It was an empty threat. I was a good shot, but I would never have taken the chance on hitting something as small as a kneecap. If one of them attacked again, I'd have to fire center-mass, just like I'd been taught. It worked though, and the big, blond bruiser settled down until George found the keys and tossed them to me.

This would be the tricky part, getting the others free while keeping an eye on both the agents. Speed was the key, I decided, so I tucked one of the guns in my pocket and grabbed Dani by the arm, pulling her to her feet and working the key in her cuffs one-handed while I kept the SIG trained on the female agent with the other. The key scraped all around the lock and I cursed softly.

"If you weren't married," Dani murmured, "I could make all kinds of off-color jokes right now about whether you needed me to help you fit it in."

My ears got hot with embarrassment, but I got the cuffs unlocked, then pressed the key into Dani's hand and turned my full attention back to the prisoners.

"Get Val free first," I warned her, "then both of you check on Gib. And give me the restraints. We need to get these two tied up quick."

Dani, lacking the need to split her attention, got herself and Val free of their shackles in seconds, then tossed the cuffs and leg restraints at my feet while she hurried to Gib. I took care of the female first because she was the smarter of the two agents and worried me the most. At least she was smart enough not to try anything with a gun to her head and putting the cuffs on one-handed was a lot easier than trying to take them off. The leg restraints were trickier since I'd never even seen them before, but I was able to set the gun down and use both hands for that now that she was at least cuffed.

"Here." I shoved the other cuffs at George and pulled the second pistol again, holding both of them against the blond guy's head. "Don't move," I told him quietly. "I can't miss with both of them."

Once George had the man trussed up nicely, I jogged to the

back of the room where Dani and Val had Giblet sitting up, the hood pulled off. Dani worked on pulling off the gag while Val unlocked the metal cuffs. But that left the plastic ties. I turned back to George.

"You got a pocketknife?"

"What am I?" he demanded, fishing a lockblade out of his pocket. "A civilian?"

"I would never say that about you, bud," I assured him, grabbing the knife and tossing it to Val.

"Gib, are you okay?" Dani asked, finally pulling the knot of the gag loose and pulling the wadded cloth out of Gib's mouth. "Come on, say something!"

Gib's eyelids fluttered and a spasm of coughs racked his body just as Val got the last of the plastic ties cut off his arms and legs. Dani cradled the Varnell in her arms, relief making her shoulders sag.

"Thank God," she sighed. "I thought you were dead."

"Naw," Gib said, slurring the words a little. "Those damned monkeys didn't even give me the *good* drugs." His eyes flickered open and he looked up at Dani's face. "You know, if I'd known you were into gags and handcuffs, I would have asked you to dinner sooner."

"I should have known you'd find a way to ruin this moment," Dani said, pushing him off her and standing with a look of disgust.

"Hey, come on!" Gib protested, holding his head. "I've been drugged!"

"You need to learn when to shut up, old buddy," I advised,

offering him a hand.

"I don't know if even nearly getting dissected is enough to teach him *that* lesson," Dani said.

"We need to get going," George said, looking back and forth between us and the door. "We caught them when their guard was down but we're running out of time. We need to get to the vehicle while we can still get out the gate."

I passed one of the SIGs off to Dani.

"Try not to shoot anyone. I know you think they deserve it but most of them are just doing their job."

She grunted noncommittally and checked the gun's load.

"Let's go."

"You won't get away," the big, blond muscle-head insisted, thrashing where he was cuffed hand and foot on the floor. "You should just give up now."

"Oh, brilliant!" Gib said, spreading his hands like he'd just received a revelation. "That's a wonderful idea! I'll just surrender so you can cut me into little pieces!" Snarling, he hauled back and kicked the agent in the side. "That's for hitting Dani, you piece of shit!"

"Come on, Gib," I said, grabbing him by the arm and guiding him out the door.

Still no one else in the hallway and why should there be? As far as they were concerned, their people were interrogating me and keeping Gib under wraps until the transport got here and until then, I imagined their highest priority was to make sure as few people as possible knew any of this had happened. I didn't know how they planned to keep Mansfield and the other FBI agents quiet, but maybe threats of relocation or prosecution under the National Security Act or some such thing could do it. For those who didn't bend, well…who would believe them with no proof?

I let George take the lead and he took us…well, hell, I wasn't sure if it was toward the front or the back of the hangar because I'd been unconscious when they'd brought me in. We finally reached the ceiling-to-floor metal wall that I'd taken for some kind of security barrier and I suppose I'd been right since there was a guard station there, enclosed in what was likely bulletproof glass, watching over a single entrance, metal double doors that looked newer and in better repair than anything else I'd seen in the hangar.

But the door to the guard shack hung open and inside, a senior NCO in what I assumed was a set of Air Force utilities—either that or they were selling tie-dye BDUs now—lay trussed up with duct tape, a fury and frustration in his eyes that I could relate to, given that I'd felt the same way just a few minutes ago.

The security doors weren't open, though, and George went straight to the booth, stepping over the taped-up guard to smack a palm down on a round, red button there. A buzzer sounded and the doors unlocked with an audible metallic click.

"Quick, get through!" George yelled. "Then hold the door for me! We only got ten seconds before it sets off an alarm with base security!"

Great. I grabbed the handle and yanked one of the doors aside, waving the others through. George had already leapt out of the guard shack and nearly tripped over his own feet when he tried to cut like an NFL defensive back and head for the exit. I counted the seconds down in my head and had just reached eight when George got to the door. I pushed him through then slipped out myself and pulled it shut behind us. It slammed shut and I took a deep breath, falling back against it.

We were in what used to be the real entrance to the hangar, with the main doors shut tight, the only light coming from a few bare bulbs overhead. But a smaller side entrance stood open, revealing the blackness of full night without…and a tall man in what I took for the modern version of Army BDUs standing in it, a carbine tucked against his hip. A baby-faced softness rounded the edges of the soldier's face, but his eyes were clear and calm, like someone used to danger. Dani raised her handgun, taking up a firing stance, but George already had a hand up, stepping in front of her.

"No, it's okay, he's with us!"

I looked between the two of them, then spotted the captain's bars and infantry emblem on the chest of the younger man's uniform…and *Barnaby* on his name tape.

"Your son?" I asked George, shaking my head. "You brought your son into *this*?"

"I didn't give him a choice," the soldier said, smiling thinly. He motioned through the open door at an ambulance. Not a military ambulance, just Kern County according to the letters emblazoned on its side, and not a new one at that, not from the scrapes and worn paint. "Get in the back, all of you. There's no security going out of the base but if anyone gets the word that something's up at the hangar, they'll shut down the exits."

He threw the back doors of the vehicle open and Val clambered in immediately, the cowboy never one to look a gift horse in the mouth. He reached back and offered a hand to Giblet and despite their earlier friction, Dani helped support him from the back as he climbed inside. George and his son reached in behind them and pulled out a pair of jackets—Kern County EMS uniform jackets.

"You're going to ride up front, George?" I asked.

"Well, they know all of you," he said, hesitating while his son donned his own jacket.

"And they won't know the Deputy National Security Advisor?" I asked him, shaking my head. "Put Val up front. Dani's face and mine are in databases but his isn't."

"I'll do it," Val said, hopping out of the ambulance. "Not much of one for sitting in the back, anyway."

George sighed and handed off the jacket, pulling himself into the rear compartment. I was about to join him when his son stopped me, offering a hand.

"I've heard a lot about you," he said as I shook it. "Thought I should introduce myself. Captain Charles Barnaby." He grinned. "But you can call me Charlie."

10

I DIDN'T REALIZE I'd been holding my breath until we passed through the front gate and I let it out. I couldn't see much of the windshield, not through the tiny gap between the gear cabinets, but it looked like we were passing through a town. Which town, I couldn't even have said, knowing next to nothing about Maryland or Virginia.

No police lights, no helicopters, no black Suburbans.

"I think we're good," Charlie Barnaby called back after a few minutes.

George settled back onto one of the gurneys and slipped his Beretta's safety back into the on position. I didn't have that luxury but I still had the holster we'd taken and I slid the gun into it and tucked it into my belt around back, the way I'd seen the agents carry it.

"George, I will be forever grateful to you for getting us out of there," I told him, "so don't take this as any doubt in your plan, but where the hell are we going?"

"Someplace you never heard of," he told me. "Culpeper. Southwest of here. Little rural town. Jill..." A spasm of pain passed across his face. "Jill's family owns land out here. It's in her brother's name now that her father died, but he's never there. Has no interest in farm life so he always let her stay there and do her painting and gardening. Once she passed, he told me that I could use it as a vacation home. I'm hoping..." George sighed. "I'm hoping no one will be able to put the pieces together and figure out my connection to it."

"Why did you do it?" Dani asked. I looked over at her at the same time as Charlie, but she didn't flinch away from the attention. Giblet sat beside her, leaning against her shoulder, and she didn't push him away. "Why'd you do it, General Barnaby?" she repeated. "Why'd you help us? It's going to end your career and probably land you in jail."

"Yeah, it probably will," he admitted. "But once I understood what they were going to do to you..." George licked his lips as if his mouth had gone dry. "I talked to contacts I had in the Pentagon, and the ones who admitted to knowing anything about it would only tell me that the whole thing was going to get buried. And I knew what that meant. I guess before, I didn't actually accept that you were really the Charlie I knew. But once I did, I couldn't let this happen to you. Jill wouldn't have wanted it. Unfortunately, Charlie dropped by when I was in the middle of planning all this and refused to let me go alone."

"I'm sorry, George," I told him, putting a hand on his arm. "I didn't mean for this to happen to either of you. And uh…Charlie?" I didn't finish the question, but I didn't have to.

"Yeah. Jill and I…well, for all that we both felt like we betrayed you, we both loved you. And when we found out we were having a boy, we both thought Charles would be a good name."

I opened my mouth, closed it again, not sure what to say. It was an honor, but it also made me feel guilty as hell since I hadn't actually died and worse, hadn't experienced all those intervening years the way they had.

"How far away is this Culpeper place?" I asked instead.

"An hour and a half if we were going straight there. But we have to dump this vehicle and I don't want to be on the interstate, so it'll be more like two and a half." He nodded ahead. "We stashed my son's SUV halfway between on a county road."

"You really knew Charlie before?" Gib asked. "Back here when he was just a kid?"

"He's still just a kid," George snorted. "As much of a kid as I was at twenty-five." He frowned. "It *is* twenty-five, right?"

"I guess," I said with a shrug. "I haven't really been able to keep track of it since I left. I mean, I know it's been about two years, but I wouldn't have been able to tell you what month it was, much less the date."

"Charlie ain't no kid," Gib said, shaking his head. "I wouldn't have risked my life following his orders a dozen times now if he was. And we wouldn't have hamstrung the Anguilar Empire so bad they're willing to risk everything just to come after this place to get back at him. Charlie has freed *worlds* from slavery, old buddy George." Gib put mockery into the last three words. More than usual. "He infiltrated one of the Imperial Headquarters cities, stole their secrets, drop-kicked one of their generals in the chest and got back out again. He led us onto a planet-destroyer and blew the thing up before the Anguilar could use it against another rebellious world. So thanks for keeping me from getting carved up into pieces, I appreciate the hell out of it, but you have a long way to go before you can call him *just a kid.*"

My ears burned so fiercely I thought they had to be practically glowing, and I couldn't meet Gib's eyes, much less George's. But I had to say *something.*

"I didn't do any of that alone, Gib. All you guys were right there beside me, putting your lives on the line as much as I did."

"Yeah," Dani agreed, her smile showing some malicious enjoyment of my embarrassment. "That's why they call it being a leader."

"The thing is," Gib went on, still addressing George, "Lenny—he's that robot that snatched us all and put us in stasis on his zoo ship—he says he picked us all for a reason. That he had predictive algorithms and historical precedence and all kinds of happy horse crap that said we were the right people for the job. And he picked Charlie to be the leader." Giblet raised a hand palm up. "Of course, he was right. So, I wondered…could you tell back then? Could you see anything different about him?"

"I'm right here," I muttered. I felt like they were talking about me like I was the subject of some student's history essay.

"No," George admitted. "I mean, I never thought Charlie…" He coughed and looked me in the eye. "That is, I never thought *you* were any more of a natural leader than any of the rest of the guys in ROTC. Well, I mean, the *good* ones, not the dirtbags. Then again, that might have been because Colonel Danberg hated your guts and never gave you the opportunity to lead anything larger than a squad."

"Who's Colonel Danberg?" Dani asked.

"Professor of Military Science," I explained. "Basically, the officer in charge of our college ROTC cadre. The guy who can make your life miserable if he doesn't like you."

"And why did he hate you?"

"God knows," I sighed.

"I know." George scowled, staring at the shifting, swaying floor of the ambulance. "After you…disappeared…I kind of got pissed off, blamed him for what happened. I guess maybe I blamed him so I wouldn't have to blame myself. I went to his office and got in his face, asked him what he had against you, why he'd sabotaged your career."

"What did he say?" I couldn't help blurting out the question. All this water under the bridge, all I'd gone through, and I still couldn't help but wonder.

"He wasn't the least bit sorry, that's for sure. He told me that story you always repeated, about our first FTX. When we went out to Ocala National Forest and you were the platoon sergeant for the defensive position. You argued with him about putting down concertina wire in that stand of grass that jutted into our defensive lines because you were afraid the Op-For would sneak right through it and flank us. But he wouldn't let you do it because you couldn't see it from our position and doctrine was to never set up obstacles you couldn't keep under direct observation."

"Yeah," I said, anger rising even after all this time as I remembered the incident. "He chewed my ass about it…and then the op-for did just what I said, snuck up through the high grass and we got our butts kicked."

"And Danberg said," George went on, "that doctrine was there for a reason. That he'd known leaders like you in Vietnam and they always did great in combat, but they couldn't be peace-time leaders because they didn't understand that the military has to go by the book in peacetime to maintain discipline. And we weren't at war. Not a hot war, anyway."

I leaned back against the cold metal of the cabinets built into the interior wall.

"Well, at least now I know the reason. It was a stupid reason, but I guess it's at least something other than the fact he thought I was a shitbird."

"Maybe he was right," Dani ventured and when I shot her a glare, she went on unapologetically. "After all, you stepped right into a war out there. And like this Danberg said, you're thriving. What d'you think is gonna happen when the war ends? Are you still going to want to run the military? Or would you rather ride off into the sunset? Go raise kids with Laranna?"

"It's different out there," I insisted, maybe a little peevishly. "I could have made it work. I could have adjusted."

"Probably," George acknowledged, putting up a hand in surrender. "But I'm talking to you now as someone who made a thirty-year career of the Army, and I can tell you that you would never have been happy with things the way they were. You probably would've got out right after your commitment was up, maybe gone over to the Gulf in '91 if you were in the right unit." He shrugged. "I did. Only enemy I saw were the ones surrendering and you probably would have had it the same way. I didn't see real combat until I went over to Iraq as a colonel. That was fifteen years in."

"You're probably right." It took a lot to admit that, particularly given that it wasn't nearly as long ago for me and not nearly as easy trying to be objective about it. "It doesn't matter. I'm where I belong." I motioned around, not at the ambulance but at everything. "This isn't really my home anymore. If it ever was." A thought struck me and guilt stabbed into my chest. "By the way, George, I owe you an apology. When we got pulled over, I thought at first that you turned us in. I should have known better. I guess it was right after you told me about you and Jill and I wasn't really thinking straight."

"I don't blame you. To be honest, I was thinking it was my fault, too, that Mr. Donovan had stabbed me in the back, and I'd been a fool to trust him." George sniffed a humorless laugh. "Of course, as things turned out, I was."

"What are you going to do now, General?" Dani asked him. "You can't go back."

"Yeah, Baldy back in my cell recognized you," I agreed. "Maybe your son could get away with it if no one recognized him, but…they'll throw you in a hole and forget where they put the hole."

"Would it surprise you to know," George asked with a thin smile, "that I haven't thought that far ahead?"

"Now you sound like the George Barnaby I used to know." I wanted to laugh, but it wasn't funny. I'd ruined his life by coming to his door last night. "You could come with us," I offered, suddenly inspired. "I mean, it wouldn't be a posh Arlington suburb, but we got a world called Sanctuary…well, we got a city there and some farms around it and it's just beautiful. River valley, mountains, woods. And God knows, we could use a general or two because while a lot of us have combat experience, we're pretty thin on the ground for leadership experience. How the hell do you think an ROTC grad who hadn't even made it to OBC yet wound up in charge?" I pointed at the cab. "Val up there, his wife Brandy is our chief intelligence officer and she was basically a waitress on an Anguilar-occupied world. She just happens to be incredibly smart and knows how to make connections. With your career, everything you've learned over the years, you could really help us out."

George sat back, a stunned expression on his face erasing the years for a moment and reminding me of the first time he'd asked Lorna out and she'd shocked him by saying yes.

"I hadn't even considered that." He looked lost in the thought for a second, but then shook himself like a dog shaking off water and sagged back down into depression. "But no, there's no way I could leave my kids, my granddaughter. Not after what your parents went through…" George winced, realizing what he'd said.

"What did they go through?" I asked, remembering our

earlier conversation that had been cut short by the FBI. "What happened to them?"

George was silent for long enough that I thought he wasn't going to answer the question, and I was about to repeat it when he finally looked me in the eye and spoke.

"I know you and they didn't get along very well. That they were hard on you." The careful way he worded it made me think he didn't agree, and I tamped down the anger roiling in my gut before it could make its way to my big mouth.

"Neither one of them gave a shit about me or my life. They never came to a single game or track meet, never once showed the slightest bit of interest in any plans I had for the future and when I turned eighteen, it was 'so long, have a good life but have it somewhere else.' They had the money for vacations to Europe and Hawaii every year after I left, but never enough to help me afford a real apartment or God forbid, a car!"

Damn. Hadn't been able to keep all that anger down, after all. I settled back and shrugged as if it didn't mean anything.

"Neither of them came to my commissioning and I doubt they would have been at the graduation, if I hadn't gotten snapped up by Lenny the day before it happened."

"They did come," George corrected me, quiet, soft. "That's how I first found out you were missing, when they couldn't find you."

I stared at him, realized my mouth was hanging open and snapped it shut.

"They never stopped looking for you," he went on, staring through the wall of the ambulance at something decades away.

"Even called me every few weeks just to make sure you hadn't contacted me. They tried calling Jill, too…until they figured out she and I were together, and then they stopped and I didn't hear from them again for a while."

George swallowed hard, and I sensed he didn't want to say the next part. I didn't much want to hear it.

"They both passed away just about twenty years ago now. Car accident. They were on their way to Minnesota in mid-January because someone had seen one of the posters they kept putting out about you being missing, and thought they saw you in St. Paul."

I'd been shot. I'd been beat up. I'd been burned. Had my ribs broken more than once. Nothing had hurt worse than those words. Nothing else had made me want to curl up into a ball and cry like a baby. I didn't, but it was a near thing. I couldn't speak, couldn't move, for fear of losing control and breaking down in front of the others.

It was one thing to find out I was wrong about my parents. That probably happens to a lot of people as they get older. Things change and they understand where their mom and dad were coming from back when it seemed like things had been bad. It was another to find out that not only had I been wrong about them, but they'd died while I was in stasis and I wouldn't have had the chance to make things right even if I'd made that phone call the second I landed back on Earth outside DeLuca's Pizza.

"I'm sorry," George said, sounding utterly miserable. "I wish they were still around. I know they would have been happy just to know you're still alive."

That wasn't making it better, but I just nodded. It wasn't his fault. This time, it wasn't even mine. It was just how things had turned out. Sometimes, life just sucked.

"It's okay," I said, finally, my voice a hoarse whisper. "I had to find out somehow. Better from you than that bald butthole in the interrogation room throwing it in my face."

"Stop it," Dani snapped, and I looked up in surprise at her sharp tone. "Stop blaming yourself. It was their fault." She held up a hand to forestall my objection. "Sure, maybe that was just how they were, maybe they were old-fashioned, but if you're telling yourself you blew the chance to make things right with them, you didn't. *They* did. They had the first twenty-three years of your life to get to know their son and if it took you disappearing off the face of the Earth for them to realize it, that's on them, not you." Dani looked like she was getting wound up and I thought she might take all of it out on me before she fixed George with a glare just as fierce. "And you. What good do you think you're going to do your kids or your granddaughter in jail? You come with us, you can come back and visit them whenever you have the time…probably just as often as you do now. So stop being a damned martyr. I'm not gonna be the reason you wound up spending the rest of your life behind bars."

"Yes, ma'am," George said, wide-eyed, maybe not agreeing with her argument but smart enough not to contradict her.

Giblet smiled broadly and slipped an arm around Dani's shoulder which, to my shock, she didn't immediately push away.

"And this," he said, "is why I love her."

11

"I CAN'T SEE A DAMNED THING."

Leaning forward in the front passenger's seat, I tried to follow the path of the Toyota's high-beams, but even those only illuminated a couple dozen yards of the dirt road ahead of us and nothing at all past the steep ditches on either side. I didn't see any way two cars could drive past each other on this road and hoped I wouldn't have to see it demonstrated.

"It's okay," Charlie Barnaby assured me, his grin as confident as I would have expected from an Army Ranger. "I've been driving this road since I was fourteen. I could do it with the lights off…and I have."

"I'm sure I don't know anything about that," George said archly from the seat behind us.

The Toyota Sequoia was aptly named, since it seemed about as large as a redwood and had third row seating, something I hadn't seen except in station wagons. I hadn't asked the younger Barnaby why he needed a vehicle large enough to transport a little league baseball team because I thought it would have seemed ungrateful under the circumstances. I'd been happy enough to leave the ambulance when we'd pulled off on a side road and dumped the thing for the waiting SUV. I was sure the authorities would be looking for it by now, and for George.

I just prayed that the murky ownership of the farm property would throw them off as long as he thought. I certainly couldn't have found it even in daylight after all the turns onto unmarked dirt roads we'd taken.

"Mom knew," Charlie said. "But she figured you'd just get upset if you found out about the bonfires over behind the Kowalsky place."

"Let me guess," I said. "Forty-four ounce convenience store cups with Kool-Aid and rum?"

"And red solo cups with cheap beer," he agreed, laughing. "I had my friend Dan as the designated dweeb, though. He'd come along and try to hit on girls but he didn't drink."

"Yeah, your father was that for me," I confided, pretending to whisper it.

"I heard that, young man," George said in a mock growl.

"Which young man are you talking to?" The question brought a general wave of laughter, not that it was incredibly funny. We'd been as tense as a guitar string for nearly three hours and now we were all pretty strung out from exhaustion and post-adrenaline rush. And of course, in my case and Giblet's, *actually* strung out from the after-effects of the drugs.

"Here we are," Charlie announced, braking nearly to a stop, then taking a left turn at a mailbox.

If the road had been narrow, the driveway was barely wide enough to allow the Sequoia to make it through. But at least now the lights had something to show us. I'd expected something like Poppa Chuck's old farm, but this place was more like a vacation home. The house didn't look weather-beaten and workaday, it had been remodeled and not that long ago. The barn had been left to go to seed but the trees had been trimmed and although the grass was dead with winter, it had been mowed before its death.

"Do you still have the garage door opener?" George asked as his son pulled the Toyota around to the back of the house. "I'm afraid I left mine back in the Range Rover."

"No," Charlie tsked, "but I have the app on my phone, you old fossil."

The phone was in the center console and he tapped the screen, scrolling through menus as he drove, which made me more nervous the closer we came to the closed garage door. Then again, it wasn't *my* car. One last tap and the right-hand garage door opened, lights coming on inside and out.

"I'm *not* a fossil," George whined. "I was the one who programmed the VCR for Grandma and Grandpa."

"And what the hell is a VCR?" Charlie asked, guiding the SUV into the garage. It was big, bigger than the garage on our house back in the day. Everything seemed to be bigger now. Even the problems.

The Ford pickup that took up the other half of the garage

was certainly bigger than the ones I remembered before I was taken, with a full back seat that looked just as roomy as the Sequoia's. Not new, though, not from the dings and dents in the fenders.

"Don't sass me, Captain. You know damn well what a VCR is. We had one until you were eight years old." He shrugged. "I *still* have it, somewhere. The attic maybe."

The car stopped and Charlie Barnaby shifted to park, shut it off.

"Oh, I remember all right, Dad," he said, opening his door. "I used to watch Pokémon videos on it." He touched a button on the wall and the garage door motor rumbled its way down.

For some ridiculous, irrational reason, I felt a profound relief when it clunked shut, as if we were finally safe.

"Let me out of this damned thing," Giblet said, pushing at the back of the second row of seats before Val and George could even get through the doors. "If we drive in this thing again, I am *not* sitting back here."

"Yeah, why don't you drive next time?" I suggested as sarcastically as I could muster while George unlocked the inner garage door. "That way when a cop sees you, maybe he'll be so convinced he's nuts that he won't bother to pull us over."

"Okay, everyone come on in," George said, reaching through the door to switch on a light inside the house. "I know you must need rest. There are four bedrooms, take whichever ones you want and get some sleep. Or if you're hungry, there's food in the kitchen. I can heat something up for you quick, if you like."

"You have any peanut butter?" Gib asked. "I'm not big on

human food, but Charlie had the ship's kitchen make some peanut butter once and I could just kill for a peanut butter sandwich."

"I'll take care of it for you," Dani said. "I'm not much of a cook, but I think I can manage peanut butter and bread."

"I'm gonna get some damn sleep," Val declared, brushing past them.

"Dad," Charlie said, leaning into the cargo compartment of the Toyota and pulling out his rifle, "I'm going to take a walk around the perimeter and make sure everything's secure."

"Did you bring night vision?" George asked him as the younger man opened the side door out of the garage.

"Naw. But I know this place well enough not to need it."

He disappeared into the night, and I followed George into the house.

It was rustic, I suppose, though in a tasteful way, the walls of the living room decorated by naturalist paintings, landscapes, a few animals and birds. I recognized the style.

"Those are Jill's," I said. "She used to draw pictures like that in her sketchbook."

"They are." George gazed at them with pride and possibly a little melancholy. "She would come here and paint and the best of them she'd sell, but the ones I liked, she would put up here." He blinked, rubbed at something in his eye. "So, Charlie…I know they took your gear but there's got to be some way you can contact your people, get them to come pick you up."

"Probably," I said, touching my arm where the transponder was just below the skin. "But our situation hasn't changed. For all that Dani was handing out invitations to skip out of town, the problem is, the Anguilar are still coming. I don't know when, but I can't think it's going to be long. I still need to find a way to get Earth ready for them."

"We're not going to be able to get the administration to listen," George warned. "They've convinced themselves that you're a threat…not you personally but the existence of aliens, the idea that people might find out about them. They think it would change everything and they're right about that." He sighed, leaning against the back of a brown, leather couch. "Make no mistake, Charlie, it *will* change it all. I mean, if we'd detected some radio signal from a far-off star that said there was intelligent life, it would throw a big monkey wrench into the works on a philosophical level, but it wouldn't really change the way we all lived. But you're talking about dumping an entire new reality on everyone's head. Not just that there's a bunch of different civilizations out there but that there's a war going on and we're all about to get pulled into it. People are going to panic."

"What's our alternative plan, then?" I asked him. "I was willing to try to keep this quiet. I thought maybe we could do it on the down-low, like a covert operation. But if you're right, that's not going to happen. They won't let it. We might have to go public."

"How the hell do you plan on doing that?" George demanded. "It's not like you can book an interview on *60 Minutes*."

And that was a good question. What the hell did I know about it?

"Maybe…" I shook my head, sat on the arm of the couch. "Maybe we could contact the AP, get it on their wire."

"Oh, for God's sake."

I twisted around at the invective, saw Dani walking out of the kitchen. Giblet was back there, sitting at the table, wolfing down a sandwich. Dani glared at me, her arms crossed.

"Both of you geezers, young and old, act like it's still the damned Twentieth Century."

"Hey now, let's not get nasty," George grumbled, frowning. "It's bad enough pushing sixty without you and my son constantly rubbing it in my face."

"Then stop acting like it. The AP…" She rolled her eyes at me. "…is nothing but a bunch of stringers across the world who send reports to a central clearinghouse computer system. They're worthless and no one pays any attention to them anyway."

"So, what, then?" I asked her, spreading my hands. "You know this place better than I do. How do we let people know what's really going on?"

"You need someone with an audience," she said. "Someone who can't be shut up. You need videos on the internet that people will copy faster than they can be taken down, and that means you need someone people would notice if they're censored."

"That sounds good and all," George said, "but who? Who's big enough that would even give us the time of day? I mean, it's not just a matter of finding someone famous, they also have to be crazy enough to listen to your story."

"That leaves one person I can think of," Dani said. "Bill Cordova."

George groaned, rubbing at his temples with the heels of his hands.

"Seriously? Look at the crackpots he has on his show…people who believe in absolute bullshit like the lost continent of Atlantis and…" His mouth snapped shut.

"You were gonna say 'flying saucers,' weren't you?" Dani asked, mouth twisting in a wry smile. "But yeah, that's why he's perfect. He'll listen if we show him Giblet. He'll put us on his YouTube show and his podcast and hell, I think he's on a bunch of other platforms, too. There's no way the government can take it down."

"And how do you plan on getting in to see him?"

I hadn't heard the door to the garage opening but then, Charlie Barnaby was a Ranger. His carbine was slung across his chest, mud coating the sides of his boots from where he'd done his check of the property. Charlie shut the door behind him and looked at all of us questioningly.

"Well? How do you plan on getting him to interview you? You can't just call him, you know? All our phones are probably being monitored." He pulled his out and waggled it around. "Not this one. I bought it at Wal-Mart with cash and loaded it with a card I also bought with cash."

"You did all that today?" I asked, blinking in disbelief.

"No, I always keep a burner phone," he said with a chuckle. "I'm just paranoid. But we can't use this one, either, not without alerting the government. They may not be tracing this phone, but they're definitely tracing Cordova. Especially since he's had people like that ex-NSA guy on, spilling state secrets."

"He's right," George agreed. "Any way we contact Cordova, all we're doing is warning the government what we're planning."

"Well…" Dani tilted her head to the side. "I do know where his studio is located."

George and Charlie both stared at her in amusement.

"I was driving through there last year," she said, shrugging it off. "Thought I'd check out the neighborhood. And I know when he records his shows because he has a live chat on his website. We could just…show up."

"Where is it?" I asked, feeling lost. "Where's his studio?"

"Chattanooga," Dani told me. "Tennessee," she added, and I sighed.

"Yeah, thanks, I'm from the 1980s, not the 1680s, I know where Chattanooga is."

"Hell," George commented with a derisive snort, "the way kids today are educated, you probably know more about geography than half of Cordova's listeners."

"Please, Dad," Charlie said, shaking his head as he walked to the kitchen and retrieved a beer from the refrigerator, "let's not do the whole 'back in my day' thing right now. It's hard enough wrapping my head around the idea that the guy I'm named after is actually still younger than I am."

"Hey, at least you got named after the guy who freed a couple planets," I told him. "Most people just get named after some uncle who was a plumber."

"All right," George said, though I didn't know if he was

addressing the complaint about his nostalgia or Dani's plan. "You've got the phone, son. How far is Chattanooga from here if we avoid the interstates?"

Charlie operated the phone one handed, downing a long swig of some German beer with the other.

"Almost twelve hours," he said.

"And what day is it?" Dani asked, spreading her hands helplessly when Charlie offered her a bemused glance. "Sorry, I live in space most of the time. It's hard to keep track."

"Wednesday," George supplied.

"He tapes on Friday morning. Which means we have to leave no later than tomorrow, unless you want to wait a whole week."

"In that case, we're all gonna need sleep," I said. I ran a tongue over my teeth. "And toothbrushes. You got any spares laying around?" I asked George. I was actually a little hungry, but I couldn't bring myself to eat anything until I got rid of the mangy cat that had crawled into my mouth and died.

"We always keep a few extras in the bathrooms," he told me. "Y'all might want to take advantage of the showers, too…and between my spare clothes, Charlie's, and my daughter Mary's, there's gotta be enough for you to find some fresh gear. After that, y'all split the bedrooms amongst yourselves. I'll sleep out here on the couch."

"I'll take the first shift on guard duty," Charlie Barnaby volunteered. "Who wants me to wake them up in three hours?"

I was about to reluctantly volunteer. Three hours wasn't much but Charlie had also driven this whole way and he deserved to get some sleep. But Dani raised a hand before I could.

"I'll take next," she said. Charlie gave her a nod.

"Which room you gonna be in?" he asked. "So I don't wind up waking everyone else while I'm trying to find you."

By way of answer, Dani went to the kitchen table, grabbed Giblet by the hand and pulled him into the hallway, pushed one of the bedroom doors open and shoved him in ahead of her. The Varnell said nothing, his eyes wide.

"This one."

The door closed and I gaped at it, speechless. George looked between the door and me, his expression as confused as I felt.

"How does that even work…" he began, but then shook his head, waving a hand in negation. "You know what, never mind. I don't even want to know."

12

"I GOTTA ADMIT," I said around a mouthful of cinnamon pop tart, "I don't get this whole podcast thing."

Dani sighed, took a sip of her instant coffee.

"What's not to get? You had radio talk shows back then. This is just like that except instead of going out on a radio station, you just upload the audio files to a server and people can download or stream it."

"Yeah, I understand that part," I acknowledged. "I mean, it's kind of strange that you're doing this without anyone asking for it…kind of like those people playing the guitar on the street with the case open, begging for money."

"That's so going to get you canceled," Charlie said, laughing softly.

The kitchen table was barely big enough for all six of us, and that was only after we'd dragged in a couple of chairs from the dining room. It would have felt silly sitting at that huge dining room table eating stale pop tarts and frozen microwave burritos, though. Well, George, Dani and Val were eating the burritos. I wouldn't touch the things with a ten-foot pole, particularly not when we were about to take a twelve-hour road trip. I was even being careful with the half cup of coffee I'd accepted.

I didn't know what being canceled meant and I didn't feel like derailing my train of thought by asking, so I just pressed on.

"But I still kind of understand that. I mean, I knew a guy who wrote a book and had a thousand copies printed up and he sold them out of the trunk of his car. I guess that's even easier when everything is…digital? Is that the right word?'

"You have no idea," George lamented.

"What I *don't* understand is how people make money at it. Are there commercials, like on radio?"

"Sometimes," Dani said. "A lot of the bigger shows have sponsors, too. They don't have full-blown commercials, but they mention them a few times a show. It's complicated and I'm not an expert. The bottom line is, Cordova has the largest audience of any podcast or YouTube channel in the world, at least ten million people per episode. Mostly because he doesn't talk down to his audience and he approaches even weird subjects with an open mind."

"*Too* open," George put in, starting to sound like one of the two old hecklers in the balcony on *The Muppet Show*. "I remember when he used to be a Moon landing denier."

"He changed his mind," Dani insisted. "He's not a scientist, but once he had a few on who explained to him why the Moon landings couldn't have been faked, he changed his position."

"There's people who don't believe we landed on the Moon?" I asked, disbelief drawing the question up an octave at the end.

"There are people who believe the damned Earth is flat, Charlie," George confided.

His son glanced at him as if unused to his father referring to anyone else by that name, but said nothing. I felt weird enough wearing his old clothes without also stealing his name. Val fit better into George's wardrobe and had taken a pair of work jeans and a flannel shirt, while Dani had borrowed Mary's old clothes. Gib, unfortunately, was not built like any of them but had, at least, taken an old Lynyrd Skynyrd concert T-shirt that George had acquired as a young teenager and kept for sentimental reasons.

"That's the problem with the digital age," George went on, waving the remnants of his burrito like it was a laser pointer. "Whatever crackpot thing you believe, you can immediately find thousands, or tens of thousands of other crackpots out there who believe the same thing and you can surround yourself in a bubble of lunacy until you don't understand how crazy you sound."

"And here we go again," Charlie murmured. "Come on, Dad, we're not going back to an analog world, no matter how awesome you think the eighties were."

Charlie, despite his youth, looked a lot more like his father this morning, the tension and the lack of sleep dragging at both of them. George's features sagged under the stress, like he might melt away if the pressure went any higher. By contrast, Val looked as even-keeled as ever, eyes sharp and alert, while Dani and Gib seemed…almost chipper. They weren't talking much to each other and honestly, Gib was talking hardly at all, which was not like him. He just sat there, picked at his cherry pop tart, and smiled a lot.

I checked the clock on the stove, wishing I had a wristwatch or a cell phone…or really wishing I had my comm back and could explain what was happening to Laranna. It was almost eight in the morning, though the dull, gray light filtering in through the blinds promised an overcast day.

"We need to get going," I said.

"I'll get the Toyota warmed up," Charlie said, standing.

"Wait," I told him. I hadn't been looking forward to this part, but I'd come to the decision last night while trying to sleep. "I think it might be better if we go alone. Just the four of us."

"What?" George snapped, rocking back as if I'd slapped him. "Why the hell would you do that?"

"Because I've already screwed up your life," I said, "and I don't want to do the same for Charlie here. And I know if you go with us, he'll insist on coming with you."

"You're damned right I will," Charlie said. I might not have been the greatest at reading people, but I got the sense he was relieved at my proclamation, that he hadn't been looking forward to getting into this any deeper and had been hoping his dad would stop before it was too late. He'd never say it, though, that much I was sure of.

"How the hell are you going to get there, then?" George demanded.

"The pickup," his son suggested so quickly that I knew he'd been thinking about it, too. "It's registered to Uncle Pete. It wouldn't trace back to us. It gets crappy gas mileage, but I could stop by the ATM on the way out of town and grab some money out of my account for you to fuel up, get some food."

"You won't be able to get a hotel room," George warned, though the note of acceptance in the words told me that he'd warmed up to the idea enough to at least consider it. "You'll get there tonight if you leave now. You'd have to park in a rest stop or a truck stop or something to kill time if the guy records late morning like you said."

"Yeah, we could push it back a few hours," I agreed, "but I like leaving some cushion in the schedule, just in case. And the truth is, the farther away we are from DC, the better. They'll be hunting for us but they won't be looking in Tennessee."

"I'll find the keys to the truck," Charlie said. "And while I'm at it, I'll check the oil and the fluids."

He seemed eager to be away from the table, probably not wanting to give his father a chance to argue against the idea.

"What if you get pulled over?" George asked. "None of you have a license."

"I do," Dani said, then shrugged. "I mean, my license is still good, but my wallet is somewhere either in the FBI building in Arlington or at Andrews."

"And if you had it with you, you'd get arrested even quicker. If Charlie was with you…"

"They have our descriptions," I reminded him. "All that would do is make sure Charlie gets in trouble, too. We'll just have to drive carefully, stay at the speed limit and not get pulled over."

"What about the guns?" George asked. "Are you going to take them with you?"

"Damn straight we are!" Giblet said immediately, and I nearly echoed him before Dani voiced the doubt nagging at the back of my thoughts.

"If we take them," she said, putting a hand on Gib's arm, "we're kind of making a decision. So far, we haven't actually hurt anyone. I think we need to talk about what we're going to do if they catch up to us again."

"I want this to work," Val put in. "And even though it's been a long spell since I was employed by the government of these here United States as a marshal, I'd hate to have to shoot someone doing their duty."

"It wouldn't be one of my favorite things, either," Gib cut in, "but you know what I'd like even less? Getting dissected and studied under a microscope. There's no way in hell I'm letting myself get taken by those assholes again." He shook his head, his jaw set like he was about to go into combat. "If you won't shoot 'em, give me a gun and I'll go down fighting instead."

"It won't come to that," I promised him, though how I could be sure, I wasn't ready to explain. "But here's what we'll do. We're taking the guns with us for now. If we get pulled over by the cops, I'm going to dig this transponder out of my arm and push the panic button."

"How are you gonna do *that*?" Dani asked, a horrified expression on her face as she rubbed at her own arm.

"Painfully, I imagine." I looked aside at George. "I need a replacement pocketknife if you have one. But if we make it to this podcaster's studio and he agrees to interview us, then we'll have some leverage and they won't be able to disappear us without anyone knowing. At some point, we have to be ready to negotiate, trust them. Once they have no choice but to work with us. But I give you my word, Gib, I'll put a bullet in anyone who tries to hurt you."

He met my eyes for a long few seconds before finally nodding.

"Anyone else, I might have my doubts," he admitted, "but you've never lied to me, Charlie."

"*Anyone* else?" Dani asked, glaring at him, maybe just teasing or maybe not.

"It's…a figure of speech."

She responded with an unconvinced grunt and Gib looked as if he might try again but the garage door opened, and Charlie held out a keychain.

"Found them," he announced. "She's gassed up and, as far as I can tell, she had her oil changed about 3,000 miles ago. You should grab a few bottles of water out of the kitchen to take with you. The less you have to show your faces, the better. Hats, too. There're some baseball caps in the closet in the bedroom on the left. I used to collect them from every city we visited."

"I'll get 'em," Dani volunteered.

"Wear them whenever you're out of the car," Charlie advised. "Oh, and you…" He nodded to Gib, handed him a pair of cheap sunglasses. "Wear these, too. And the hood. And slouch down a lot."

"Thanks," Gib told him, obviously controlling his inherent snark as he took the shades and tried them on. He grinned crookedly. "Gosh, you all look less horrible through these."

"Is that what you think about *all* humans?" Dani asked, emerging out of the hallway with her hands full of ball caps. Gib winced, snatching off the glasses just in time to catch the cap she threw underhand at him.

He looked at it, saw the mouse-eared emblem and grimaced.

"Gib," I told him, "take it from a happily married man and don't say a damned word."

"I'm…" He looked between Dani and me and got up from his chair. "I'm going to go get some of that bottled water."

"He's learning," Dani said, throwing me a hat emblazoned with Utah's Landscape Arch, then settling a Grand Canyon collector's cap over her red hair. "I thought I saw some crackers in there. I'll grab those and the peanut butter. It's one of the few things that can keep him quiet."

Charlie handed me the keys.

"I'm gonna go find you a pocketknife," he announced.

Val headed out to the garage, which left just George and me at the table. The—the *old man*, I came to realize, for that was what he was—couldn't meet my eyes for a moment, as if he was ashamed at accepting my decision to leave without him so easily.

"You've done more than I had a right to ask of you, George," I assured him. "I will forever be grateful for you getting us out of there, and if there's anything I can do to help you, I will. If all this goes to shit, if there's no way we can work with the US government, that offer still goes. You can come with us. I know

I've made it sound like it's a nightmare out there, a war-torn hellscape, but it's really not. I've seen some beautiful places, places that haven't been touched by civilization, human or otherwise. I've met some incredible people who I'd give my life for, and who'd give their lives for me." I grinned. "And I'd really like you to meet my wife. I've told her a lot about you."

"She's actually…green?" he asked, and the face he made brought an involuntary guffaw.

"Sort of. You'll see. I'll tell you what. Stay here as long as you feel safe, give this all some time to shake out. Whatever you do, George, do *not* go all noble and turn yourself in. If things go good, I'll make a deal for you. If they go bad, I'll come back here and get you. Hell, I'll land right out there…" I pointed to the front door. "…in the damned yard and drop the ramp."

"Thanks, Charlie," he said, offering me a hand. I made a face at it and pulled him into a hug.

I hadn't been much of a hugger back before, but figuring out that every time you said goodbye to your friends could be the last time had converted me.

"You know," he said, holding me out at arm's length like I was a long-lost son, "through all these years, besides Jill…you've always been the best friend I ever had."

"Same here," I told him.

Well, I amended silently as Gib hauled a case of water past us out to the garage, the best *human* friend. But some things just didn't need to be said.

13

"THERE's so many more cars on the road than I remember," I said, trying not to grind my teeth.

It was tough. We weren't on the interstate, thank God, but it seemed like every lane was packed and everyone was going ten miles an hour over the limit. It didn't make any sense, given that I was used to flying starships, but sixty miles an hour seemed ridiculously fast when there were cars close enough that I could have reached out the window of the pickup and touched them.

The pickup was another problem. The thing was *huge*, which I'd known in my head just looking at it, but I hadn't realized how much more difficult it would be to drive the thing than a regular car. It filled up the lane and the damned hood was so high that I could barely see the tail lights of the cars in front of me.

At least there was no snow on this road. I had absolutely zero experience driving in snow. Honestly, I had nearly zero experience driving, period. I hadn't driven a car in two subjective years and the last time and the only vehicle I'd driven regularly had been George's Camaro. This damned pickup was *not* any sort of sports car.

"Look out!" Dani said, pointing to the left.

A moron in what was, apparently, the most recent version of the Dodge Charger darted out of his lane without signaling and without worrying about the gigantic pickup truck beside him and I jerked the wheel to the right as I braked, sending up a spray of gravel from the breakdown lane. The pickup jolted as we hit a bump and I pulled it back into the lane, laying on the horn. In the back seat, Gib stirred from his nap and looked around, his sunglasses flashing in the rearview mirror, then put his head back down and began to snore gently. Val's eyes were closed as well, but he sat up straight and I couldn't tell if he was asleep or just trying very hard to ignore the chaos all around us.

"Is *everyone* in this decade a freaking suicidal idiot?" I asked no one in particular. Then I sighed, took in a deep breath and half-turned to Dani in the front passenger's seat. "Where the hell are we, anyway?"

One of the first stops we'd made once we got out of Culpeper was at a Wal-Mart, where Dani had pulled her hat low and borrowed Gib's sunglasses to go inside and use some of the thousand dollars in cash Charlie Barnaby had given us to buy the cheapest cell phone that would meet our needs and a plastic card with an activation code on it. She'd also picked up a six-pack of Diet Cokes, a handful of Payday bars, and a bag of Doritos that had served as lunch, but right now, I was more interested in the map on that cell phone.

"Almost to Roanoke," she said, then leaned over to check the dashboard readouts. "We're about half a tank down. Tell you what, why don't you pull over at the next gas station and I'll take over?"

"Sure thing," I agreed way too readily.

"You don't much like driving, do you?" Dani asked, chuckling.

"I never owned a car. Not that I didn't want to, but I couldn't afford it. My first job, I took a bike to work and back every day, rain or shine." I shrugged. "I used to think that was why Jill broke up with me."

"And now you know it was just because she was cheating on you with your best friend."

I didn't want to look away from the road, but the instinct was involuntary and when I looked back, the brake lights on that same stupid Charger lit up and I had to slam my foot down to keep from rear-ending him.

"It wasn't like that," I told her. "You heard what George said. She wasn't happy with us and George was gonna break up with Lorna. It just happened."

"Yeah, I heard what George said." Dani shrugged. "And I know what he did for us. He's a good guy. But tell me something, if you hadn't found Laranna, if you weren't happy, and you came here and found out about George and Jill…you'd be really pissed off, right?"

"Probably," I admitted. "For a while. But that was also a long time ago."

"For everyone else," she agreed. "But not for you."

"You *trying* to get him pissed off?" Gib asked, though he didn't move from his recumbent position, and I couldn't see if his eyes were open. "He's already doing his best to run into one of these insane metal cages on wheels, you know. Maybe we should let the poor man concentrate on driving."

"Maybe the topic makes *you* uncomfortable," Dani said, staring out the window.

"Why the hell would it?" Giblet sat up now, leaning forward over the center console. "Charlie's my best friend, so unless you and him have been getting busy behind my back, why would the topic make me uncomfortable?"

"You know why." Dani's lips pressed together tightly and I thought she wouldn't say more, but then she blurted it out. "Because of Tamura."

Gib took off the sunglasses and met her eyes and I wanted to yell at him to put them back on, particularly if he was going to make himself visible through the windshield, but I sensed this was one of those arguments I'd be better not getting involved in.

"Tamura's dead," he said flatly. "I'm sorry he got killed but he wasn't my friend and he wasn't my *boyfriend*, either, so why should I think about him at all, much less be angry about him."

"Because you think I chose him over you. I can tell you still think about it. I could tell last night."

"Oh, really?" Gib's eyebrows shot up. "You're telling me that after just a few months, you can read Varnell body language well enough to know what I was thinking last night?"

"Y'know," Val said, eyes still closed, "I ain't no relationship expert or nothin' but maybe this is a conversation y'all should be having in private."

"I don't know why," Dani said. "You're both two of our closest friends and you've both been married a while now, happily I assume."

"Well, aside from the fact that I keep running off to other planets trying to get myself killed, yeah, mostly."

"Then you tell me," Dani said, pointing a finger at Giblet although she was presumably talking to Val and me, "how can you build a solid relationship when one person resents the other because she rejected him in the past?"

"I don't resent you, dammit!" Giblet said, throwing up his hands. Then he shrugged and chuckled and made an even bigger mistake. "Well, except for the part where your advice to Charlie almost got me sliced into pieces by quack doctors on this backwards planet."

"*My* advice?" Dani repeated, her face going almost as red as her hair, as if steam was about to come shooting out of her ears like in the old cartoons I watched when I was a kid. "Now you're blaming this on *me*?"

"Well, if I recall correctly, my dear," Giblet said, not giving an inch, his nose almost against hers, "Charlie was all in favor of landing a fighter right in the front lawn of that gaudy white house and telling the entire world we were here. You were the one who wanted to keep it quiet. And what are we doing now?"

He motioned ahead of us. "We're going to go announce to the entire world that we're here, which we could have done from the beginning and saved a bunch of being drugged and trussed up!"

"If you think my judgment is that bad," she shot back, "then why the hell would you want to be with me in the first place?"

"Well, great gods, woman! If you had *good* judgment in men, would you have gotten involved with a Kamerian fighter pilot? Or *me*? I mean, I'm a Varnell! We're the scum of the galaxy, hunted and despised wherever we go!"

"Well, maybe there's a good reason for that if all of them are douchebags like you!" she blurted, then turned away from him toward the window. I couldn't see her face but her shoulders shook and I wondered if she was crying. But I knew she'd never let any of us know if she was.

A sign ahead beckoned and I sighed in relief and switched on the right turn signal.

"Look," I said, pointing. "A gas station."

Thank God.

I DIDN'T KNOW how to pump gas. It was so damned embarrassing.

"Some things," I said softly to Dani as she punched in the code the attendant had given us after she'd paid him, "shouldn't change this much. It's just a gas pump. Why does everything have to be all computerized?"

"You work on a starship built by robots," she pointed out, her voice flat, her expression neutral.

"And I came home to a world nearly as alien as anything out there." I squeezed the handle and was finally rewarded with gas flowing through the hose. "I mean, *most* people still use gas, so I suppose there's that." I'd seen what Dani had informed me were electric cars when we were back in DC but not that many. "And jeez almighty, the price of gas! It's nuts!"

"Salaries have gone up, too," Dani said, suddenly reasonable now that Gib was in the truck and she wasn't. "It's called inflation."

"Yeah, we had inflation back then, too," I told her, getting a little tired of the constant history lessons. "But most of us didn't jump through thirty-seven years' worth of it. Is that money gonna get us all the way to Chattanooga?"

She had to laugh at that despite her mood.

"We have, like, six hundred dollars left. We could get all the way to California if we wanted to. Particularly since we can't check into a hotel."

"You need to go to the little girl's room?" I asked her as the pump clicked on the last of the prepaid amount. I had no idea if the tank was full, but it should be close enough.

"Already did. You go ahead if you need to, but make sure you wear your hat and keep your head down."

"Thanks." I put the handle back into the pump, shaking my head one last time at the amount displayed digitally. "I think I will."

Not that the paranoia didn't grate at my nerves, but it had

turned into a background hum, like a cloud of mosquitoes in the forest. I had to either ignore them or let them drive me to distraction.

The convenience store was large for a back road, almost a truck stop but not for trucks. It was called a Buc-ee's and had a cartoon beaver as its logo and the inside looked more like a restaurant crossed with a grocery store. It took me a couple minutes to find the bathroom, particularly since I was trying to stare at the floor, and I nearly ran into two other people on the way out.

That was when I noticed the black duty boots, the black trousers tucked into them. They were uniform trousers and I risked a glance up and saw the badge, the gun. A cop. The gun concealed under my jacket seemed to weigh a ton, to bulge out obtrusively. I turned away from the police officer before he could get a good look at me, pretended to check out a rack of candy bars. Not that I had any money to buy one. I just had to wait for him to pass by.

"…repeat, be on the lookout for Charles Travers, approximately twenty-five years old, five foot eleven inches tall, brown hair, blue eyes, medium build. Wanted for multiple battery against federal law enforcement officers, grand theft, and fleeing across state lines. Considered armed and extremely dangerous. Known to be traveling with three other fugitives…"

He stepped away and the muted, static-filled announcement from the radio on his shoulder faded with distance. Sucking in a deep breath, I forced myself to walk slowly toward the exit.

Running or even walking fast would draw too much attention and I really didn't want attention. Not yet.

"Hey, mister!"

The call was loud but unspecific and I decided to pretend it had nothing to do with me. I didn't recognize the voice, but it could have come from anyone, not just that cop I'd seen.

"Sir!" More insistent this time. "In the leather jacket and ball cap!"

Oh, shit. I could have run. I might have made it to the truck before he caught up with me. But then, they'd know what vehicle we were driving in and Dani had told me all about how hard it was to outrun a radio and a helicopter.

Maybe if they got me, the others could still get away and get to Cordova. They'd have to keep me alive. I took a deep breath, kept my hands to my side and turned.

A teenager wearing a beaver hat held a handful of one dollar bills in front of my face.

"You had the truck on pump four, right?" he asked, his sparse facial hair not quite covering the acne. "It shut off too soon. You got change coming."

My heart thumped in my chest like the drum solo from "In-A-Gadda-Da-Vida" and I held my breath for a moment as I nodded my gratitude and took the cash, just so he wouldn't see me breathing hard from the adrenaline dump.

"Thanks," I managed, waving at him before I walked steadily and purposefully back to the truck.

The police SUV was parked right next to the front door and I looked away from it as I passed, worried it might be fitted with cameras like the one I'd been in with Dani back in Ohio. She was back in the driver's seat, the truck running, her own hat pulled low, and I couldn't even see Giblet in the back seat, which meant he'd slouched far enough down for the front seats to hide him from view. It took every bit of self-control I had not to run the last few steps to the passenger door.

"You saw the cops?" Dani asked, putting the truck into gear as I shut the door.

"Yeah, I almost ran into one of them." Almost hyperventilating, I put my seatbelt on. Dani pulled away from the pump way too slow and I gritted my teeth against the urge to tell her to hurry up. "I caught an announcement over his radio. They put out a BOLO on all of us."

"Shit." That did the trick and she gave the truck a little more gas, maybe too much as we pulled back out onto the road with a squeal of tires.

"What's a 'bolo,' other than a kind of tie?" Val wondered, not seeming as fazed by all this as we were.

"Be On the Look Out," Dani explained. "It's an acronym. It means the cops have spread the word about us out through all the state and local agencies."

"Can we get there on this tank of gas?" I asked her.

Her lips worked silently, and I figured that she was doing calculations in her head.

"Just. Maybe."

"Then we don't stop again until we get there," I decided. "We have food and water and if anyone needs to take a leak, we pull off on a side road and you use a tree. No contact with anyone if we can help it. Agreed?"

"Sounds good to me," Giblet said.

"Except for the part about peeing behind a tree," Dani added. "But yeah, agreed."

"Where I used to work," Val drawled, "even having a tree was a luxury. But I tell you what, I ain't crazy about this whole driving thing. Whatever gets me out of here quickest."

"All right," Dani said, jamming down the accelerator and whipping into a gap between two cars barely big enough for the pickup. "Chattanooga, here we come."

14

As cities went, Chattanooga was nicer than most. Of course, my basis for comparison was mostly Cleveland and Tampa, which might have been a low bar to set.

It had a certain southern charm to it and if the traffic sucked, it didn't suck nearly as bad as it had around DC or even on the Virginia back roads. Not that Dani was going to let me drive the truck again.

"Which way?" she asked, slowing down for a red light.

The city center loomed up around us, not that impressively tall and certainly not broad, yet I would still have been absolutely lost if it weren't for the cell phone mapping software. I held it up and squinted at the street names.

"Straight at this light, then take a right at the next intersection." The thing had a voice that would tell us when to turn, but

I'd switched it off. It was creepy and robotic in a way that Lenny had never been, and at least this way, I felt useful. "We're about a mile away."

My stomach rumbled and I turned back to Val and Giblet.

"Are there any of those candy bars left?" I wondered. We'd stopped for the night in the rear parking lot behind a truck stop, but none of us had gone inside, not wanting to get spotted. I'd brushed my teeth with the aid of one of the plastic water bottles but hadn't taken the time to eat anything for breakfast.

"You got the last one," Val said, handing over the white-wrapped Payday. "These things are darned tasty. We oughta' try to buy a bunch of 'em before we head back out again. Maybe Lenny can fabricate them on the *Liberator*."

The idea of an unlimited quantity of candy bars churned out by the ship's fabricators was almost as refreshing as the one I was actually eating, but I filed that idea away for later and kept my eye on the phone. At the right-hand turn, we headed away from downtown, away from the shopping district, toward a more residential area, and by the time I'd polished off the candy bar and downed a few gulps of water to complete the breakfast of champions, the navigation app told me we'd arrived.

"I think you can park on the street right there," I told Dani, pointing to an open spot by the curb. Finally able to pay attention to our surroundings more than the map, I frowned. "This seems like a weird place for a recording studio."

It was a house, so far as I could tell, or had been one at some point in the recent past. Not a very fancy one, just a normal-looking two-story house like I would have expected to find inside the limits of any good-sized city, with an alleyway for parking and not much in the way of a yard. No markings on the outside, no sign giving a hint it was anything other than someone's home.

"He likes it this way," Dani told me, shifting into park and shutting off the engine. "He used to have a studio in Los Angeles, but everyone knew where it was and he got way too many fans just dropping by."

"Then I'm sure he'll be really enthusiastic about *us* just showing up out of the blue," Gib commented, but she ignored him as she had for most of the trip.

I'd had too much time to think about what their problem was and had come to the conclusion that I had no idea and just wished they would make up their minds.

"If he was trying to keep this place secret," I asked her, "how did *you* find it?"

"Because I'm a cop," she said, rolling her eyes like it should have been obvious. I must have looked shocked because Dani sighed. "Oh, get real. It's not like I broke in and asked him for a selfie. I just wanted to see what it looked like."

"I'm not even going to ask what a 'selfie' is," I said, opening the door of the truck.

"Just wait," Dani warned me, holding up a restraining hand. "There were no cars parked in the alley or in the lot behind the place when we circled the block. I don't think he and the crew are here yet. The show doesn't start for an hour. We should catch him on the way in."

"I'm still a little leery on just hopping out and trying to talk our way in," I told her. "What if he doesn't want to listen? He could just think Gib is a guy in a costume."

"Relax, Charles," Giblet told me, popping a peanut-butter cracker in his mouth and crunching it. "Talking people into things is what I do."

"Yeah," I said, arching an eyebrow at him. "Because that worked so well with Donovan back in the White House."

"So some people are more resistant than others!" The words came out muffled around the mouthful of peanut butter. "The odds that we'd run into two of them have to be astronomical."

"Poor choice of words given that we've come here from the stars." I waved off the rest of his argument. "Don't talk with your mouth full. And finish that shit up quick in case he gets here and we need you to be able to talk without spraying cracker crumbs everywhere."

"Oh, hell, that's him," Dani blurted, pointing at the car coming down the street toward us.

It was one of those electric cars, the cool-looking ones that were named after some inventor from a long time ago. This one barely made a sound except for the scratching of the tires on the pavement as it pulled into the alleyway and parked.

"Now," Dani said. "But be cool. Don't scare him off."

I nodded, taking off the Grand Canyon souvenir cap and tossing it onto the dashboard as I climbed out of the cab. It was as cold here as it had been in Arlington, though there was no snow, and I zipped up my jacket, hands stuffed in the pockets. Eyes locked on the driver's door of the Tesla.

The man who got out was perhaps a little younger than

George, though it was hard to tell exactly because his head was shaved, hiding the gray hair that might have given his age away. He'd certainly taken better care of himself, given that he lacked the middle-aged gut I would have expected and his biceps strained against the sleeves of his jacket. A fireplug of a man, he had to be a couple inches shorter than me but probably outweighed me by twenty pounds and I got the distinct impression I didn't want to piss him off.

"Excuse me, Mr. Cordova," I said, waving casually as the man hesitated with his hand over a keypad mounted beside the front door. I figured it had to be an alarm or a lock, or something. "Could I talk to you for a second?"

The stocky man sighed but then pasted on a smile that looked genuine if a little impatient.

"Okay, man," he said, "let's take the selfie, but please, don't tell anyone where you saw me. I don't need this place getting swarmed with lookie-loos…"

"It's not that, sir," I told him, holding up empty hands. "I just have something you might want to include in your show."

Now the strained patience turned quickly to an annoyed frown.

"Then you should contact my producers. I'm not a barber, I don't do walk-ins…"

Gib came up on my right and Cordova stiffened, hands clenching into fists as if he thought this was a mugging. Then he froze when the Varnell threw back his hood and took off the sunglasses.

"Hey there," Gib said smoothly, with that resonant chord that made me take a step back like I might stumble. "My name's Giblet and I'm a Varnell. That's an alien species, in case you hadn't guessed. My friends and I…" He waved at the three of us, "…have been trying to work with your government to prepare them for a coming war but they keep trying to throw us in dark, isolated cells and want to dissect me to see how I work. We thought maybe you could help us get the word out in a way they couldn't stop."

My guts churned at the thought this Cordova guy would be resistant to Giblet's charms and my backup plan was to pull my gun and force him to let us into the studio. It wasn't a *good* backup plan. But Cordova's eyes held the same glazed expression that Mansfield's had back at the FBI office in Arlington and his smile was filled with awe.

"Holy shit, dude," he murmured, reaching out to touch the feathery down on Gib's face. "Is that *real*?"

"As real as it gets." Gib ran a finger over Cordova's bald head as if in retaliation. "And at least I still have my hair."

I stepped in, sensing that Gib's snark might get the better of him.

"Mr. Cordova, I'm Charlie Travers. I was born in 1964 in Ohio and taken from this planet by an artificial intelligence to lead a resistance against an invader from outside the galaxy. Now they're coming here and the only chance we have to stop them is for the US government to accept our help, to prepare for the Anguilar and pledge their troops to fight them, to lead the rest of the world against the invaders."

Cordova goggled at me like I'd just told him that the Moon was made of green cheese.

"What the hell are you talking about, dude?"

Dani laughed and put a hand on his shoulder, pushing him gently toward the door.

"Why don't we go inside and talk about it? This'll be the best show you ever put on."

"So, you're a black belt in Taekwondo?" Cordova asked, his eyes lighting up almost as much as they had when he'd heard Giblet speak. "That's very cool, dude. I competed in MMA, myself."

"MMA?" I repeated, then took a sip of the Diet Coke he'd given me. All of us, actually, though Val had taken one sip, made a face and tossed the can in the trash.

The five of us had gathered around an oval table with microphones at each chair and cameras pointed at the table from across the studio, though they weren't on at the moment. There was no one to man them, the crew not having arrived yet. Thankfully. We had to have this guy Bill Cordova convinced of who and what we were before anyone who might talk him out of it got there.

The studio was larger than I'd thought, taking up the entire ground floor of what had been a house, the interior walls taken down to accommodate it, and the walls behind and to the side of us were lined with huge, flat-screen TVs or maybe computer monitors. There were computers hooked up to the recording gear, video and audio, and a few laptops scattered around for unknown purposes and I thought I might have been on the bridge of a starship if I hadn't known better.

Aside from the ubiquitous tech, the rest of the studio was like a giant version of the "I love me" walls that I'd seen in the offices of Colonel Danberg and the few other high-ranking Army officers I'd known. Certificates of rank in half a dozen different martial arts, photos of Cordova with what I assumed were famous people, although I didn't recognize any of them, as well as of him inside what looked like a boxing ring and also some kind of open-top cage, dressed like a fighter. He was much younger in those photos, of course.

"Mixed Martial Arts," he explained, then laughed, rocking back in his chair. "Oh, man, that's right, you wouldn't have been around for that. It's like…kickboxing, but mixed with wrestling and jujitsu and boxing. It's so damned cool. You should take some lessons."

"I've had some training in Strada martial arts," I told him. "My wife was raised from birth basically to be a warrior, armed and unarmed."

"That sounds interesting. Maybe she could show me some of that stuff. I'm always looking to pick up new tricks."

"This is all very fascinating," Giblet said, swishing the last of his drink around in its can, "but what about this broadcast thing? We told you, Bill…I *can* call you Bill, can't I?"

"Sure, dude." Cordova shrugged, chuckling. "I mean, you're an alien. Holy shit, you're an *alien*…you can call me whatever you like."

"That's a long answer, but thanks." Gib sighed. "We told you, *Bill*, we're wanted by the federal government. Not just like criminals, but like they're going to disappear all of us and cut me to bits for study. We don't have much time. Either you help us convince people that this is real, or we leave."

"We don't *want* to do that," I interjected. "If we do that, we'll be facing the Anguilar with just the forces we can get here to Earth, and that's not going to be enough. Even if we beat them the first time, they'll come back, and we can't *stay* out here without resupply, without a base of operations, without support. Either we get help from the American government—and eventually, the entire planet—or the Anguilar are going to take this place, and there won't be anything I can do about it."

"Yeah, sure, man," Cordova assented. "I'll put you on the air. But I gotta say, *I* believe you, but just saying this stuff ain't gonna make everyone believe you." He laughed, reached into a drawer set in the table and pulled out a joint and my eyes went wide. "I believe lots of shit, and sometimes I change what I believe when I see something new." He took a lighter from the drawer and flicked it to life. I shook my head.

"Is that legal now?"

"Not here," he admitted, taking a long inhalation. When he breathed it out, I winced at the odor. "Not yet. But you know, I'm kind of flexible about the law. Hence my sitting here with you wanted fugitives. But what I'm saying is, a lot of people listen to my show because it's entertaining, or because they like to hear a lot of viewpoints, but that doesn't necessarily mean they buy into it all. How are you gonna convince them this isn't just a bit? A con?"

I rubbed at the transponder in my arm and smiled.

"Don't worry about that. This is only step number one. We have our own show to put on, but if we do it before we tell people what's going on, it'll make them more frightened. I just need to know if we can count on you."

"Oh, hell yeah!"

The back door opened with a buzz of conversation interrupting us, and my hand went to the gun holstered under my jacket, but Cordova was already standing, waving to the three younger men with long hair and tattoos and a woman with tight, purple curls and more piercings than I'd seen on a human being.

"Guys!" Cordova said, jumping up with his hands spread in greeting. "We got a change in plans. Frankie, get that archaeologist on the phone and tell him we're doing the interview tomorrow. Set things up for these four guests and we're starting the show in ten."

"Umm…" One of the three hippie-looking guys stuttered like Cordova had smacked him in the face, looking between the four of us with incomprehension before his eyes settled on Giblet and widened. "What the hell is that?"

"*He*," Cordova replied, arms crossed with a smug grin, "is a real, live alien and we're about to interview him live on the show."

The purple-haired girl stood next to the hippie, their expressions mirror images of skepticism.

"How much have you had today, Bill?" the girl asked, tilting her head in an accusatory glare, her gaze flickering to the joint still smoking in an ashtray. "It's not even noon yet, man."

"This is my first, I swear!"

"Hi there, I'm Giblet." That persuasive tone buzzed in my ears, the pheromones overwhelming even the acrid stench of pot, and I could have sworn Gib's eyes glowed in the overhead lights. "And I know we're all going to be such good friends..."

15

"YOU'RE FROM OUTER SPACE," Bill Cordova said, his expression grim and utterly serious. "So, tell me something…is Bigfoot an alien?"

Giblet looked over at me helplessly, shaking his head.

"What the hell's a Bigfoot?"

I glared at Dani, and she buried her face in her hands. Even the guy behind the camera, who looked as if he smoked more weed in a day than anyone I'd known in the eighties had in a month rolled his eyes.

"So far as we know, Bill," I said, straining to keep my temper under control, "Giblet is the only alien currently on this planet, and we brought him with us. Whether there are Bigfoots, Loch Ness Monsters, or Werewolves of London, I couldn't tell you. All I can say is that there was one planet in this galaxy where intelligent life had evolved in the last four billion years and that was here. We were it for this galaxy until the Creators came along."

"And those are the robots, right?" Cordova asked.

"They're an artificial intelligence," Dani provided, "that share a collective consciousness, but their…avatars, I guess you'd say, are humanoid-ish robots."

"They're big, tall and roll around on a wheeled base," I said. "And they have as many arms as their task requires. But they do have a head with a kind of an articulated face, though I think that's more for our benefit. The one we know, the one we call Lenny, looks just a little bit like a young Michael Keaton."

"Yeah, you keep saying that," Dani said with a grimace. "I just don't see it. If anything, maybe a young Christian Bale."

"Is he the one who played Batman in that really dark movie you like so much?" I asked her.

"It's *The Dark Knight*, not the dark movie," she corrected me. "And yes, he is."

"Eh, I guess," I allowed, then waved it away. "Like I said, that's for our benefit. I think if Lenny didn't have to work together with humanoids, he wouldn't bother with a face at all. But like I was saying, there were a lot of worlds with life, but none with sentient life except Earth. Then the Creators came along and decided that was a shame and they had to fix it. They *could* have just taken people off Earth and scattered them around the galaxy wherever we could live, but they decided that they wanted a little more variety, so they mixed our genes with the local life to create sentience. Like Gib here, whose distant ancestors were bird-like creatures who got a giant dose of human DNA."

"Wow," Cordova said, resting his chin on his fist. "That is so very much the opposite of what everyone who's into ancient astronaut theory believes! They all think that humans were the product of genetic experiments that mixed alien DNA with, like, ancient hominids."

"What can I tell you?" Dani said, shrugging. "They're wrong. We're the OG."

"In this galaxy, anyway. The Creators used to be biological, but at some point, they gave that up for robot bodies and a collective machine consciousness. And then there's the Anguilar. They're the only other intelligent species from another galaxy that we know of right now, and they're a lot younger than the Creators. And a lot more like us."

I paused. They were, I considered for the first time, a little *too* much like us. Everyone else being so human-like, I understood because of the genetic tampering. But why were the Anguilar so humanoid? I shrugged the thought off. I could ask Lenny about it later.

"And the Anguilar are the ones you say are coming to invade Earth?" Cordova asked, a touch of journalistic skepticism in the question. "I gotta ask, why would they want to do that? What the hell have we got that anyone would want? Is it like the Annunaki who want to steal our gold?"

"I don't know what an Annunaki is, Bill," Giblet confessed, "but no, no one wants your gold. There's billions of tons of gold in the various asteroid belts that are in every star system and no one has any use for it except for decoration. They want your food. They want your people to grow food for them to feed their empire. It's that simple."

"What?" Cordova barked a laugh. "You guys don't have that sci-fi shit where the ship can make you tea, Earl Gray, hot?"

"Everyone has food processing equipment that can make anything you want," Dani told him, and thank God she answered the question because I kept feeling like there were a hundred references to things I wasn't getting. "But not out of thin air. They're not gods and they can't turn stone to bread. To make food, you need food. It doesn't have to be too fancy for people to get by on it. Wheat, corn, rice, whatever. But they're trying to feed all their people and all their subject systems. And we've been choking their supplies by freeing subject worlds and attacking their logistical train."

"More important than that," Gib put in, "they want to be the only ones with the food so they can use it as a weapon to control the galaxy."

"That's the real reason they're coming here," I said. "They didn't think anything of this world because the last time they came by here, or anyone did except Lenny, we could barely grow enough to feed ourselves. Now, just this country alone grows enough to feed the world twice over. If we, the resistance, made an alliance with Earth to supply nothing but food for us, we could probably break a dozen worlds away from the Anguilar without firing a shot, worlds they don't even occupy but control with the promise of food."

"And the damn Anguilar wouldn't allow that," Gib said, a little bitterness in his voice. "They were scavengers until a few centuries ago, exiles without a home, stealing what they needed to survive, and they'd rather kill every man, woman, and child in the galaxy than go back to that life."

"Which was why I had to come back here," I told Cordova. "Believe me, I didn't really want to. I wouldn't have made the choice to get snatched up by Lenny and spend the next thirty-five years in stasis, but now that I've made a life out there, there's nothing for me here. All this place holds are disappointments and bad memories. Every good thing that's happened to me, happened out there."

Dani shot me a look of realization, as if she'd finally figured out something about me.

"Yeah, same for me," she agreed. "I was stuck in a nowhere job that I'd started to hate. I was a sheriff's deputy and it felt like I was bailing water out of a sinking boat with a thimble. Most people hated us and even the ones who said they supported us still resented us half the time. Not to mention, I'd wind up arresting the same people for the same crimes, over and over, and they'd always be right back out on the street." Dani sniffed a soft laugh. "Since then, I've helped free a *planet* and fought off two different Anguilar invasion forces."

"And killed a ruthless bounty hunter," I reminded her.

"Yeah, and that. I have no reason to come back…except to make sure that the people here never have to go through what happened to that conquered world. Earth needs to act *before* the Anguilar get here. You don't want this planet to be a battle-ground. I've seen what happens to places that are."

"Okay, I get that," Cordova said with a slow nod. He looked

over to Val. "I understand you're a Civil War veteran, Mr. McKee?"

"That was a long time ago," Val said with a shrug, then chuckled as he realized how it sounded. "I mean to say, it was a long time ago for *me*. Eight years after the end of the war before I was taken by Lenny, then another five now since. I don't think about it too much anymore."

"Well, thank you for your service, anyway, sir. Do you miss Earth? Are you happy out flying around to other planets, never seeing home again?"

"This place isn't my home anymore," Val admitted. He smiled softly. "Home is with the people I love, my friends, my family. I'm here because I want to protect them, no other reason."

Cordova waited, as if he thought the old cowboy might have more to say, but Val never failed to stop talking before the words ran out. The talk show host gave up and moved on, determined to do his job even if we'd hijacked his program.

"And what about you, Giblet? Why are you here?"

"God only knows," Gib told him, then nibbled half a Dorito before finishing. "My people don't have a home. We've been hunted and hounded off of every world we've tried to settle on and the last Varnell I came across wound up trying to kill us. The Anguilar shoot us on sight."

"Oh, my God! Why would they do that?"

I winced, wanting to warn Gib not to tell the truth, but it was too late.

"Because we all have the ability, to one degree or another, to convince people of things. To *persuade* people. That's why you accepted so readily that I was actually an alien. I am, of course, but you didn't have any real reason to believe it. Maybe I should feel bad for using my mojo on you, but I honestly don't." Gib scowled, polished off the rest of the chip. "Present company excepted, I find humans not that much more pleasant to deal with than Anguilar and I wouldn't be here at all except that Charlie is the best friend I've ever had…and I'm hopelessly in love with Dani."

Dani looked at him sharply, as if she was about to say something, but shut her mouth. Cordova did the opposite, his mouth dropping open as he glanced between the two of them.

"Wow, did *not* see that coming," he admitted.

"Yeah, you and me both, brother," I agreed. "But then, who am I to talk? I'm married to an alien."

"What do you think about that, Dani?" Cordova asked, sounding more like a couple's therapist than a talk show host. "How do you feel about Giblet here?" He shrugged. "I mean, no offense meant, and I don't want to sound like a…speciesist or whatever, but he *is* a bird-man. That's a big difference. You think you could live with that?"

Dani said nothing for a moment and I thought she might not, or that she might chew Cordova's head off for asking the question and tell him it was none of his business, which, of course, it wasn't. Instead, she surprised me by reaching across the table and grabbing Gib's hand.

"Yeah, I think I might be able to live with that."

"And that…works?" Cordova shook his head, obviously fascinated by the concept. "I mean, biologically? All the equipment lines up the right way and everything?"

Dani's face went crimson and this time, I was *sure* she was going to blow up at the fireplug of a man and punch him in the face, MMA or no, and I jumped in to try to defuse the situation.

"Look, Bill, the real reason we're here on your show is that we need people to know about this. We tried to do this quietly, tried to contact the government secretly, give them the chance to break the news to the public however they wanted because we were afraid people would panic. That didn't work out."

"They didn't believe you?" he asked.

"No, they believed all right. We handed over our landing shuttle, showed them how to fly it. And then they black-bagged us into a secret hangar at Andrews Air Force Base and were going to take us all off to some off-the-books prison and have their scientists chop Giblet up." I didn't try to disguise the anger in my tone, but I ratcheted the volume down a notch. "So, we're doing it a different way now. My way. Now, we're telling everyone who and what we are and why we're here."

I pulled the lockblade Charlie had gifted me out of my jeans pocket and flicked it open. It was something called a Zero Tolerance and looked like you could hammer nails with it.

"Hey now, let's be careful!" one of the producers said, holding up a hand.

I ignored him and shrugged out of my jacket, pulled up the sleeve of my Chicago concert T and felt for the transponder before I gritted my teeth and dug the point in.

"Damn!" I hissed, unable to be quite as stoic as I'd intended.

Blood welled out around the cut, but not as much as might have…because a flattened oval about an inch long squeezed out of the wound and I set the knife on the table, grabbing the thing between my thumb and forefinger.

"Is that some kind of…alien implant?" Cordova asked, his eyes bugging out.

"It's an emergency transponder," I ground out, wincing as red tears streamed down my arm. "My wife injected it there before I left."

One of the producers yanked open a small medical kit and grabbed a handful of gauze, pressing it against the cut. I nodded gratefully.

"And what are you gonna do with that thing?" Cordova asked.

"You said people have to see for themselves," I reminded him, standing. "I'm going to show them."

The sun was bright, almost directly overhead, which meant we'd been talking for nearly two hours. I held a hand up to shade my eyes, held the transponder in the other and pressed my thumb into a button at its center. I'd wondered how I'd know if it was working, but the slightest pulse of vibration came through the tiny device, the signal reaching all the way to orbit.

The production crew had followed me out into the street, the cameraman holding what looked like an SLR body but had to be some kind of video camera.

"This is going out live, right?" I asked Cordova as the others gathered around me.

"Oh, hell yeah," Cordova agreed with the enthusiasm of a

frat boy supervising a kegger. "After what you told me, there was no way I was taking the chance that the government would put pressure on the streaming outlets to suppress it."

"Good. Everyone should see this."

The sirens switched on only moments before the police cars whipped around the corner. I knew they'd be coming. There was no way we'd be able to get away with this without the feds finding out. My only question had been whether they'd trust it to local cops or wait until they got enough of their own people down out of Atlanta to make the arrest. I'd counted on them waiting and they had.

More SUVs. Everyone drove them now, it seemed like, especially cops. Black Ford Explorers this time, six of them, half marked FBI, half US Marshals, which must have been quite the power struggle to see who would be in charge, but they coordinated their approach well enough, surrounding us from every side.

"Don't go for your gun," I warned Dani. "Everyone keep your hands at your sides."

"I'm not letting them take me, Charlie," Gib warned, setting his feet, getting ready for fight or flight. "I already told you."

"No one's taking you, Gib," I assured him. "Just wait a minute."

"Federal agents!" one of the FBI guys yelled, leveling one of those M16-style carbines that were just as ubiquitous as SUVs in the here and now. He wore a bulletproof vest over a dress shirt and slacks, which was an indication of how quickly this whole thing had been thrown together. "Put your hands behind your heads and get on your knees!"

"Here you have it, folks," Cordova said, facing the camera. "Just like they said, it's the feds coming to grab them, trying to suppress the truth!"

"Put down the camera and get on your knees!" the FBI agent yelled, echoed by the US Marshals.

"Come on, honey," I murmured. We were *not* getting cuffed or getting put in one of those cars and if we had to go down shooting, we would. But if Laranna had gotten my signal…

The FBI and US Marshals were yelling so loud for us to get to our knees that I didn't catch the whine of the atmospheric jets until the shadow passed across the sun. Cops who were probably trained better took their eyes off of us and looked upward and so did Cordova and his cameraman. I waited until the warm wind of the exhaust teased at the back of my neck before I gave in and looked up.

The Vanguard fighter hovered above us, unbelievably huge, taking up most of the block, its weapons trained on the line of law enforcement vehicles. The lead FBI agent wasn't demanding anything anymore, just staring wide-eyed at the spacecraft, too impossibly big to be hovering if it weren't for the gravity-resist technology. His rifle lowered, not as if he'd surrendered but more like he'd forgotten he held it.

Cordova didn't seem stunned or shocked though. A huge grin split his face and I wasn't sure if he was satisfied to have proof that his conspiracy theories had proven true or if he was just imagining all the dollar signs pouring in.

"Anyone makes a move or fires a weapon," Laranna warned, her voice echoing off the buildings on either side of the street, blaring from the fighter's PA system, "I'll fry them like a turkey. No offense, Giblet."

The Varnell sneered upward and shot the fighter a bird, which was ironic, in a way.

"Now, Mr. FBI agent man," I said, stepping up to the one who'd been doing the yelling. He was mid-thirties, I judged, hair too long and gut too soft for me to really respect him, but I suppose they'd had to make do with what was available. "I think we can both see that this is above your pay grade. Get your boss on the phone, and get me someone from Washington with the power to make a deal. Because I'll tell you what, I can have a couple dozen more ships just like that come down and pick us up and you'll never see us again…but the world will know exactly what happened." I pointed at the cameraman, who was scanning back and forth between me and the fighter. "And this administration will be the ones who pissed off the first alien visitors in recorded history."

Well, not exactly. But they didn't need to know that. Yet.

16

"Mr. President," I said, shaking his hand, "you're a damned hard man to get to see."

John Louis looked exactly like what he was, a career politician. I remembered my father complaining that all politicians were lawyers, but I think even that was preferable to the way Dani had told me things were now, where most of the people controlling the direction of the country had never had a real job outside government and had no concept of the real world.

If all that could have been squeezed into one balding, wrinkled, white-haired geezer with a flaccid handshake and mouthwash breath, that man was John Louis. He'd been a senator before I left Earth, for God's sake. For all that, a haze of unreality coated the whole experience because I, Charlie Travers, who couldn't even get active duty in the Army, was talking one-on-one with the President of the United States. And I didn't even have to get the Medal of Honor to do it.

"Well, Mr. Travers," he said, chuckling like we were in front of TV cameras instead of alone in the Oval Office—alone unless you counted the four Secret Service agents, "you certainly chose an innovative method to get a White House tour."

"Oh, I *had* the tour, sir," I assured him, not attempting to conceal my anger. "It took me to the West Wing and the National Security Advisor's office…and then to an interrogation cell in a converted hangar at Andrews."

"Yes, yes, I know," Louis said, raising his hands in a gesture I'd only seen from politicians and actors. "And I can't give you any excuse, but I *can* give you the assurance that this was done without my knowledge or approval. Parker thought he was protecting me, covering the whole thing up because that was his first instinct. But if I had known, I would have never allowed such treatment."

And I could believe that as much as I wanted, but I *thought* I could believe that Louis wouldn't try to disappear us now that the whole thing was splashed all over the internet, social media and, probably, the mainstream news. Certainly, there was no way of suppressing all the videos and photos of the Vanguard.

"Please, have a seat," Louis invited, motioning to the chair across his desk. Across the *Presidential* desk. It was huge and ornate and probably cost more than I would have made in ten years as an Army officer.

The chair was, surprisingly for all that it was a work of art, not that comfortable.

"I'm kind of surprised," I told him, "that you wanted to speak to me alone, sir. I expected you'd have generals and scientific advisors and the whole nine yards. And that you'd want Giblet in here, as well."

"Oh, all that'll come, son," Louis said, waving the thought away. "But it can wait. The most important questions have already been answered, and most of them were answered while you and your merry band were on the run. We took DNA samples from all of you while you were in custody and those confirmed that you were who you said you were…the very same Charlie Travers who disappeared in 1987."

"I don't recall ever giving anyone a DNA sample before I was taken off Earth," I said, frowning.

"You didn't, but your parents did. As I understand it, when they thought there was the possibility there'd been foul play in your disappearance, they found some of your old baby teeth and gave them to the police."

My fingers tightened on the armrest of the chair as a jolt of guilt and pain rocked me. Not that my parents had cared I'd gone missing—I'd accepted that by now. No, it was at the thought they'd kept my baby teeth. I wiped at something in my eye and couldn't hold back a sniff. Louis noticed and offered me a box of Kleenex.

"I'm okay," I told him.

"I'm sorry. It's easy for us to think that this all happened long ago but for you, it must be like it just happened."

Insightful for a politician. Maybe it meant I'd misjudged him or maybe, like the best of the breed, he was an emotional vulture, ready to feed on grief when he saw it.

"Thank you, sir," was all I trusted myself to say.

"Getting back to the subject," Louis said, all that empathy melting away, "once we knew it was you and we knew Deputy Campling was who she claimed, we knew this wasn't simply a scam, that something very unusual was happening. But when we ran the DNA of your friend Giblet, well…yes, we realized we were actually dealing with alien visitation. Our engineers are still going over the lander you handed over to us but they're one hundred percent certain that no nation on Earth has the technology to construct that aircraft."

Louis sat back in his chair, the cushioned leather creaking under his weight. The man was tall, like most presidents, a good four inches above me.

"And of course, there's no other explanation for the…fighter, I guess you call it, which appeared over downtown Chattanooga." He rubbed at the side of his head as if he was fighting off a nascent headache. "I suppose you have some idea of the trouble that podcast and the public demonstration that followed has caused us."

"It wasn't our first inclination," I reminded him. "We wanted to do this quietly."

"Well, I suppose that ship has sailed." He shrugged, pursing his lips. "Oh, perhaps there's still a chance to paint this whole thing as a publicity stunt by Mr. Cordova, to say that the aircraft over Tennessee was merely a drone and that people misjudged its size via an optical illusion or something."

"You could," I acknowledged, the discomfort I felt now having nothing to do with the straight-backed chair. Had these people not learned their lesson? "You might be able to pull it off. I've seen the special effects that you guys have now. You could sell it that the whole thing was computer graphics. But that's only going to work if you tell us you don't want this deal."

"Is it?" he asked, a glint of intelligence behind those eyes, a warning that I shouldn't underestimate the man just because he was a lifelong glad-handing politician. He hadn't gotten to this position without at least being clever. "Explain to me why."

"You have a cell phone, right, sir?" I asked, gesturing at his jacket pocket where I could see the outline. He nodded and took the device out. "Well, so does everyone else. You know what that means. Hundreds of millions of people with a video camera in their hand twenty-four seven. Nothing is secret for long. If there's nothing else for them to see…" I shrugged. "Then you can convince people they saw nothing. But if you want access to this technology, if you want help with the coming war, we're going to be around constantly and someone else is going to be the one to put the spin on this, not you."

The older man grunted and fell silent. I wasn't sure if he was skeptical or thoughtful or just getting ready to fall asleep mid-conversation, but he finally focused on me again.

"You're perceptive for someone your age, son. But I suppose it's hard to say what your age is, exactly."

"I'm twenty-five, subjectively," I said. "But I've spent the last two years trying to convince slaves, smugglers, pirates, kings, and priests to help us throw off the empire that's been subjugating them for centuries. They don't have cell phones and social media, but the concepts are the same. You either take the reins and ride the situation or give up and let it ride you, as my friend Val McKee likes to say."

"Yes, you're probably right about that. You have to understand, though…this is the nightmare every president back all the way to Eisenhower has had to think about. The idea that the aliens would land on their watch and they'd have to be the one to deal with the fallout. It has the potential to change the entire balance of the world. The temptation is great to simply sweep it under the rug and pretend it never happened."

"And that would be the easier thing to do," I agreed. "Right up till the time the Anguilar come here and start wiping out your command and control structures and military capabilities with orbital strikes." My thin smile couldn't have been more plainly sarcastic if I'd drawn a sign and taped it to my chest. "Of course, that might not happen until the next administration, so it could be someone else's problem."

President Louis folded his hands on the desktop, making a face like he'd bitten into something sour.

"And you're sure of this. Sure they're coming here."

"Sir," I told him, "all I can say for sure is that the Anguilar Empire knows you're here, they know how to get here and you have what they want…and no good way to defend it. I can't say they'll be here tomorrow or in a year, but their only other option is to come at us…and we've already beat them badly every time they've tried. They have a lot of pride, but they're not stupid and they want to survive more than they want to punish the resistance. Trust me when I tell you, you don't want to be fighting them in your own backyard. It'll just take one ship getting through to kill *millions* of people. It's bad enough for worlds with defense shields and orbital weapons platforms. For Earth, it'd be a nightmare."

"And you can help us prepare for this?" Maybe I imagined the hint of desperation in the President's voice or maybe I didn't. "You can give us the weapons and technology to keep them from invading us?"

"No." At his flummoxed expression, I went on quickly. "I can give you the weapons and technology to hit them *first.* To keep them from hitting you, you'd need at least as many ships as we have and there's no way to get them quickly enough. We have five cruisers and a couple dozen interstellar-capable heavy fighter craft and that's *it.* Our ships are better than theirs, better protected, better armed, but we need all of them to protect the worlds we've already freed. If we commit them all to defending Earth, the Anguilar will just go right behind us and take back those worlds."

"You're an American citizen," Louis reminded me. "And a citizen of this world. Shouldn't your concern be with protecting Earth?"

"You were never in the military, were you, sir?" I asked.

"No, but my son was..."

"If you had been," I interrupted, "you'd have heard of the saying 'never give an order you know won't be obeyed.' I'm a human. Valentine McKee is a human. Dani Campling is a human. But we're *three* people. The only three humans in the entire resistance right now. And of the three of us, I'm the only pilot. So, if I tell a bunch of people to abandon their families, their friends and all the people they know on the worlds we've freed in order to guard *my* homeworld from destruction, how long do you think my career as commander of the resistance is going to last?"

And yeah, I was being a little bit insubordinate with the Commander in Chief, but hell, I wasn't in the Army anymore. I don't even know if I was technically a citizen since I'd probably been declared dead a couple decades ago.

"I suppose I see your point, Mr. Travers." Louis snorted a laugh. "Or should I call you *Commander* Travers?"

"Charlie's fine," I told him. "Everyone just calls me Charlie."

"Very well, Charlie. I won't lie to you. This is going to be a hard sell. You told me that your friend Ms. Campling has filled you in on how divided this country is politically. Trust me when I tell you that this whole thing *will* be politicized. There are a good percentage of the people who'll oppose it just because I support it. Another faction on both sides of the aisle are going to oppose it because it means involving us in a war. And I *will* have to get congressional approval for this. There's not a chance I can get away with involving the US military in an interstellar war without it. I'd get impeached in a day."

"I understand, sir." I shrugged. "I'll do whatever I can. Demonstrate the technology for them…hell, I could take members of the House and Senate for rides in space, if that'll help."

"It might." He rumbled a laugh. "I'd like to take you up on

that offer myself, honestly. But what I had in mind might be a little less appealing." I tilted my eyebrow in curiosity and he pointed at me. "I'm going to need you and your people to testify before Congress."

"Oh, God," I muttered, grimacing. "Really? Public speaking?"

Louis laughed heartily at that.

"Don't tell me you got to be the general of this army without ever having to speak in public?"

"Some," I admitted. "But mostly, I'm a lead-from-the-front kind of guy. We have other people who handle the diplomacy."

"Like your friend Giblet?" he asked, his smile knowing. "It didn't take too long to figure out he has some kind of hypnotic influence on people. That was one reason for the drastic measures Mr. Donovan took. He thought you meant to mind-control our people for some nefarious purpose."

"Gib can't *control* people's minds," I assured him. "He's just…persuasive. If he could control people's minds, we wouldn't have needed rescuing from Andrews. By the way, that brings up another point. And this is non-negotiable if you want anything from us. Because even if you can't help militarily, I'm still going to leave you with some technological hints that'll improve life for everyone here. But not if you don't give me this."

"Let me guess," Louis said, holding up a hand to stop me from saying it. "General Barnaby."

"Yeah. General Barnaby. If you want technological aid from us, whether or not you join in this war, you'll issue him a presidential pardon for what he did when he got me out of that hangar."

I was prepared for a fight on this, ready to dig my heels in. I wasn't going to leave George hanging out to dry. But Louis sighed and nodded.

"Granted." He raised a finger. "But he's fired. I can't change that. There's no way I could justify keeping him in his current position. It's noble that he values your friendship enough to take the risk for you, but one of the requirements of having a national security position in the White House is absolute loyalty to this country above all else."

It was a damned good thing Dani wasn't here because I had an idea how she'd respond to that, and it would involve lots of sardonic laughter and comments about post-government jobs as lobbyists for defense contractors. But for my part, I just nodded.

"I understand. George knew he was making a sacrifice, but I just don't want it to be his life."

Louis's eyes narrowed.

"And what about his son, Captain Barnaby. Your namesake if I'm not misinformed."

"What about him?" I asked, doing my dead level best to keep a poker face. There was no way they could know about his involvement.

Could they?

"Oh, come on, Charlie," Louis said with a sly grin. "You don't think we can put two and two together? General Barnaby was aided by a young man wearing Army fatigues at *just* the same time that his son was visiting home before reporting to his new assignment?"

"Mr. President," I said grimly, as serious and deadly as I could make my expression, "if you have hope of working with us, of reaping the benefits of plentiful, free energy, medical miracles, and cheap space travel, you'll agree with me that there's no evidence at all that Charles Barnaby was involved in this matter and none of us will do anything to interrupt his career."

The President looked at me for a long time, his eyes piercing through, a man used to seeing through the bluster of political opponents to the truth buried inside.

"How about a compromise," he offered, finally. "We don't… derail young Captain Barnaby's career, but we give him a temporary reassignment."

"To where?" I wondered. "The Aleutian Islands?"

"You're going to be spending a lot of time in DC," he said by way of answer. "You and those you want making your case to Congress and the American people. I'll let you decide who, but given what we know of Mr. Giblet, I think I'd recommend another alien to take his place. We'll put you up in the finest accommodations, of course, and we'll keep things as secret as we can, but you said it yourself. Everyone has a phone, anyone can take a video. You'll need a military protection detail. And I can't think of a better man to lead it than the one who already risked his life and career to help you."

"Oh, shit," I murmured.

I didn't know the other Charlie that well, but I was pretty sure he wasn't going to like this.

17

"I DON'T LIKE THIS, Mr. President."

The woman was as stern and severe as the principal of my grade school and shared her bob haircut, though I don't believe Mrs. Keough ever carried a 9mm handgun. Well, if she did, she didn't wear it under her jacket, and knowing her, I think she would have preferred a .357 Magnum.

Agent Watson had bigger worries than a few classrooms of elementary school children, and the concern furrowed her brow as much as the squint at the overhead sun.

"You should be down in the bunker," she went on, gesturing overhead. "You're a sitting duck out here in the open, sir."

"Mr. Travers," President Louis said, shading his eyes with a bladed hand as he stared up into the mid-morning sky, "could you please inform Agent Watson what one of your fighters could do to the bunker if it wanted."

Groaning under my breath, I shared a pained look with Dani before turning back to the head of the President's security detail.

"Ma'am," I said crisply, like I was reporting to a superior officer, "the particle cannons on a Vanguard starfighter are capable of penetrating the shields on an Anguilar cruiser with one shot, capable of disabling her with two or three. I'm not a physicist, but I'd estimate that each shot from that weapon is the equivalent of an atomic bomb blast. Without the radiation, thank God, because I've been around a few of those blasts and I'd rather not wind up with two-headed children."

"Now imagine what one of those things could do to Air Force One, Agent Watson," Louis told her. "And add into that the fact that our radar has *still* proven unable to track the thing despite it appearing out of nowhere in the middle of Chattanooga. It flies between the *stars*, Janice," he told her, shaking his head. "Do you think the SAM batteries or an AMRAAM from an F-35 is going to be able to bring it down?"

"We're here as friends," Dani said firmly, meeting the Secret Service agent's eyes without a hint of intimidation. "If we'd come as enemies, you'd never have seen our faces. We wouldn't have to land and make ourselves vulnerable to blow the living shit out of anything we wanted to. And the Anguilar won't either, unless someone's here to stop them from doing just that."

"Easy, Deputy Campling," President Louis said. "Agent Watson is just doing her job."

"I'm not a deputy anymore, Mr. President," Dani shot back. "I'm a…" She glared at me. "Dammit, Charlie, if we're serious about this resistance thing, we have to come up with a rank system. It was fine when we were dealing with Strada and Copperell who owe you their lives and would follow you if you just called yourself the Chief Kumquat, but if we're working with the American military, they're going to want to call you something besides Charlie."

"I'm all in favor of Chief Kumquat," Giblet put in as an aside, "if anyone cares."

"I'd just as soon you didn't speak at all, Mr. Giblet," Watson told him, and a couple of her agents surrounding us on the south lawn tightened their grips on their rifles.

"Yes, ma'am," Giblet replied with such utter meekness that it was obviously mocking.

"I was commissioned a second lieutenant in the US Army," I told Dani, "which was the highest rank I'd ever held. And I look twenty-five despite the fact that I'm sixty. I'd feel pretty damned stupid calling myself a general or something."

"George Armstrong Custer was a colonel at twenty-seven," Val reminded me. I raised an eyebrow. He hadn't spoken much since we'd arrived at the White House for the second time, which wasn't unusual for him. "Just sayin'."

"That's right," I said. "You were taken in 1873. In 1876, Custer got half the 7th Cavalry wiped out by the Lakota. It's called Custer's Last Stand. I'd rather not put myself in his company."

"Well, he was a bit of a prick when I met him during the war," Val admitted.

Watson's eyes went wide and I figured she hadn't been read into Val's origin, but before she could comment, the roar filled the sky just ahead of the appearance of the Vanguard. President Louis had mentioned SAMs—Surface to Air Missiles—and I assumed those had to be mounted on the roof of the White House, but I couldn't see any sign of them down here and I wondered if they were targeting the Vanguard. It wouldn't do anything to the fighter, but it might piss Laranna off.

"I've seen Marine One land here a hundred times," Louis told me, leaning close—probably closer than he needed to. The guy was too damned touchy-feely for me. "But I never thought I'd see an alien spaceship touch down on the South Lawn."

"I never thought I'd see it either, sir," I agreed.

"I still think you should call yourself *Commander* Travers," he confided, almost whispering it into my ear. "Non-specific, won't sound so weird to you, like you promoted yourself."

And as much as I hated to admit it, he was probably right.

"Yes, sir. I'll consider it."

Then there was no opportunity for talking because the whine of the jets drowned everything else out. Bits of grass pelted us and a couple of the Secret Service agents actually stepped in front of the President, blocking him from the bombardment of lawn particles. There was nothing they could do about the heat, though given the brisk wind blowing out of the north, the warm blast from the drives was something of a relief.

The fighter landed as smoothly as I would have expected from Laranna, just the gentlest of bounces on the landing struts before they settled into their housings and the side hatch popped open. The uniformed agents turned toward Laranna as she emerged from the cockpit, but they had their orders and didn't raise their rifles. She'd at least listened to my advice and not worn a sidearm, though I couldn't tell if she was carrying any of her concealed blades.

"President Louis," I said, stepping forward, "this is my wife, Laranna, a warrior of Strada." Laranna stepped forward and I tried to picture her as he would, seeing her for the first time.

She was beautiful. Of course, I was biased, but I had independent confirmation, and the exotic qualities of her pale, green skin and the small tribal tattoo over her left eye would accentuate that to President Louis and the others. Beyond that, though, Laranna moved like a jungle cat, lithe and deadly whether armed or not, and by the way Louis stared at her, eyes widening, mouth slightly open, I could tell the effect it had on him.

"A pleasure to meet you, sir," Laranna said, taking his hand. She sounded respectful, though I knew she wouldn't hold an Earth politician in any greater regard than she did the other planetary leaders we'd met, which wasn't much. Two years ago, I'd have expected her to be as brutally honest as Dani, but we'd both grown a bit since then.

"The pleasure is all mine," Louis said, grinning, holding onto her hand a little longer than he had to. "I have to admit, Ms. Laranna, the thought of flying in one of those things is nearly as exciting as the opportunity you folks are according us, for all that the Secret Service would probably blow their collective tops if I set foot in it."

"The Vanguard is an incredible machine, sir," she agreed. "You won't find their like anywhere else in the galaxy."

"I don't suppose you have enough of these to outfit our Space Force, huh?"

"I'm afraid there's only the one fighter wing, sir," I told him. "And they're a key part of our military organization. But rest assured, we'll be using them to defend Earth for as long as we're here. But right now, we need to use this one to get Giblet off the planet, as you suggested, before anyone in Congress or…other places get the wrong idea about him."

"I don't want to leave you guys here alone," Gib said, his eyes fixed on Dani. "You might need me."

"I do need you," Dani told him, grabbing his hand and squeezing it. "You're the best pilot we have, and I need you up there, covering my ass."

"Oh, darling," he chuckled, "you know there's no place I'd rather be than covering your ass."

"Stop," she scolded, raising a finger. "Just be sure you're listening if we need help."

"I'm always listening." Gib blew her a kiss and waved at the rest of us before he hopped up the steps into the cockpit and shut the door behind him.

"We should get clear, Mr. President," Watson said, putting a hand on Louis's arm and pulling him away from the rugged, broad-shouldered curves of the Vanguard.

"Oh, I doubt the thing'll make any more of a mess going up than it did coming down," he said, scowling at her like he was a geriatric patient and she his nurse. "But fine, we have a meeting to get to, anyway." He offered Laranna a broad smile full of gleaming, white capped teeth. "Now that the party is complete."

I took Laranna's hand as we followed Louis and his entourage of guardians back into the White House.

"Great gods, Charlie," Laranna whispered into my ear as we passed under the shade of the entrance, the fighter taking off behind us. "What the hell have we gotten ourselves into?"

"I have to say," the Secretary of Defense said after Laranna and I had finished our initial presentation, "after hearing the situation, I guess my question is, what the hell can we do against that?"

He was a retired general, from what I understood, older than George, his face a granite mask carved by some ancient tribe, his voice a distant rumble of thunder, and I had the feeling he was a terror to the troops beneath him. But I could also tell he understood. He motioned at the holographic projection at the center of the table in the Situation Room. Laranna had brought it down with her from the *Liberator*, since Lenny had felt it would make a significant impression on the "primitives," as he'd put it.

The *that* Secretary Mattheis referred to was an image of the Anguilar fleet that had come after us at Thalassia, massive daggers of metal streaking through space toward the planet. The image had been taken from the *Liberator*, so she wasn't in the picture, but the point of it had been to show the US government what we were up against. Given the horrified look on Mattheis's face, it might have worked too well.

"I mean," he went on, fingers tapping against the table, "they have directed energy weapons that can reach us from orbit, and not only do we have no defense against that, we have nothing that can touch them." I opened my mouth to try to explain, but he interrupted me. "I know, you say that you'll help us out if you're here when they come, but what if you're not here? You can't teach us to make your warships, you've already admitted that. Can you teach us how to build your shields?"

"No," I said, though I would rather have avoided the question. "The shields are a part of the hyperdrive, and you can't use the hyperdrive without power cells. We can get you some, but we'll have to steal them from the Empire. Even then, you could only produce starships, not warships. There's a difference. It'll take decades to build the facilities required to construct warships, and that's if we can even manage it."

"You've talked about us building shuttles like the one you delivered to Andrews." Madison Barrett was short and elfin, yet still she gave me the impression that people could underestimate her at their peril. She was, I recalled from our introductions before the meeting, the Secretary of State, which I figured initially would mean she'd be all about trying to figure out a diplomatic way through the situation, but she'd wound up asking more technical questions than any of the others, even the President's science advisor. "Why do those not need power cells?"

"I'm not an engineer," I reminded her, then motioned at Laranna, Dani, and Val. They'd all taken their seats, leaving me the only one standing, and I fought an urge to pace. "None of us are."

"And why don't we have your engineers here?" Barrett

demanded. "Because you didn't think we were smart enough to understand your physics?"

"No," I sighed. "It's because our engineers are all bug people, and if you guys couldn't handle a talking bird man, they'd absolutely shit themselves if they met a Peboktan. But as best as I can understand it, anything that requires…warping space, for lack of a better term, requires power cells because the cells draw energy out of hyperspace. That's the only thing powerful enough to jump to hyperspace, create shields, or fire the particle cannons. Since every one of the power cells is kind of a miniature hyperdrive, they require something that Lenny tells me is called exotic matter. It has to be created, like, inside a black hole or something. I'm not sure anyone can produce them anymore since the end of the Centennial War, but the Anguilar brought enough with them to outfit their whole fleet."

"That makes sense," the science advisor said, nodding enthusiastically. He was an odd-looking dude, skinny as a rail with an Adam's apple I could have teed a golf-ball off of and a bright red bow tie and I couldn't remember his name for the life of me. "I mean so far as *any* of this makes sense from the point of view of quantum physics. If this were something you could pull off with just a fusion reactor, it'd mean we'd have to pretty much trash everything we knew about reality, but if you apply that much power to any system, strange things can happen."

"I'm glad it's a comfort to *you*, Dr. O'Neil," Secretary Mattheis interjected, glaring at the odd scarecrow of a man, "but I'd be willing to throw physics out of the window if it meant we could defend ourselves."

"Is there any chance," Barrett asked carefully, as if worried about offending either us or the President, "that the Anguilar might be willing to work out trade? They want food and we'd like to not be enslaved and destroyed. If they were reasonable, we might be able to trade them food for these power cells?"

Laranna barked a laugh and I nodded to her.

"Madame Secretary," she said, respectful but unable to keep a hint of scorn from the words, "*all* of us attempted peaceful trade with the Anguilar first. They even agreed to it…for a while. But once they'd scouted us out and discovered we lacked the military prowess to prevent them from simply taking what they wanted, they gave up any pretense of benevolence and enslaved us."

"There's also the fact," I interjected, "that any food they got from you would be used as a weapon against the worlds they've already subjected. You'd be enabling an oppressive, murderous regime just to try to get a little temporary security."

"Wouldn't be the first time," Dani murmured.

"And anyway," Laranna went on, giving Dani a quelling glare, "you'd be taking the risk that they'd make a deal…and you wouldn't have any effective military backup in case they didn't, because if you're treating with the Anguilar, you won't have any support from the resistance."

"That sounds like a threat," Mattheis said, his expression darkening.

"It's a promise," Laranna told him, not backing down an inch. "The resistance is made up of worlds which were forced to fight their way to independence from the Anguilar at the cost of tens or hundreds of thousands of lives, or of refugees from worlds that never had the chance. They'll fight to the death for the chance to strike back, for the chance to make sure no one else has to go through what they did…but they won't be the stick to your carrot. There are no carrots in this war, Mr. Secretary."

"What we're suggesting," I took over, not wanting to let this devolve into a debate, "is that the only way Earth can be safe from the Anguilar is if we take the fight to them first." I held up my hands to stop the questions that were coming from all sides, including the President. "The choice here is this. Either you can decide to sit this out and we'll still give you the technology package." I patted the data packet Lenny had put together, a data core plugged into a holographic projector. "You'll have the technology to build fusion reactors, fabricators, asteroid mines. You'll have medical advances that'll cure cancer and let people live to over a hundred years old. And the whole time, no matter what you do with that stuff, you'll be looking over your shoulder, waiting for the Anguilar to come, *knowing* they will. Having to fight them here and knowing that even if by some miracle you win, your cities will be devastated, everything you've built torn down. Or."

I raised a finger. "Or. Or you can fight alongside us, let us train your troops and arm them with the latest weapons, things that you can dream up and we can build. You can put our technology into your fighters, your missiles, and make something better than the sum of its parts. You can take the deadly valor of the Strada and the loyalty and devotion of the Copperell and mold them into something disciplined and organized with the help of the US military. And together, we can take the Empire apart, one world at a time. They'll never threaten Earth and, what's more, if we take their cruisers, you'll get your share of them. Starships. America could have the stars, and if you help free the rest of the galaxy from the Anguilar, you'd be welcomed there. You could be part of the new government that unites the free worlds, part of the trade network that could bring Earth all the tech spread through this galaxy right here. It could turn this planet into one of the foremost in existence. But only if you have the nerve to take the risk."

"Damn," President Louis said softly, shaking his head. "You've definitely got the chops to run for office. But save the sales job for Congress. You testify in three days."

"Three *days*?" I repeated, falling back into my chair. "Does that mean you're going to back our play?"

"Sir," Barrett said, her eyes widening as she looked between the President and me, "you can't be serious. The net is already on fire about the alien ship sightings. We need to get a handle on this, put out a statement before the Speaker of the House makes our policy for us! This could wreck your entire administration and I haven't even begun to factor in how the Russians are going to react to it!"

"The situation isn't going to change just because we sit on our asses and don't make a decision," the President told her. "You're right, we do have to get ahead of this. And we do it by taking a position *before* Speaker Metz can take one for us." Louis shot me a grin. "You have three days, son. I suggest you go back to your hotel and practice your speech."

18

"GET your ass in the car...*sir*," Charles Barnaby growled, motioning at the back seat of the Suburban.

He still wouldn't meet my eyes after two days on the job, though I suppose that could have been because he was busy watching for threats. Probably not though. The rest of the team had that job, and they were all older and much rougher looking than the commander of our new protection detail.

I let Laranna scoot in ahead of me while Val and Dani took the third seat. I'd rather have all sat in the same row, and God knew the bench seat was big enough to allow it, but that would have been against the security protocols that Charlie Barnaby had put into effect. Two of us and two guards in each seat, the guards on the outside.

The driver had cranked up the heat in the SUV already and the seats were internally warmed as well, which was a Twenty-

First-Century innovation that I appreciated. The President kept the offices in the White House too warm, which I suppose was an old-person thing, but the net result was that when we'd stepped out of the private exit, it had felt even colder outside than it should have. I could have adjusted to it in a few minutes, but thanks to the comforts of the 2020s, I didn't have to. I wondered if that was somehow significant to the differences between this time and when I grew up.

"You can do this," Laranna told me, grabbing my hand. "You managed to turn the Strada and the Thalassians into allies, and these are your people."

"I was a student when I left," I reminded her, putting my head back against the rest and sighing. "That didn't give me much experience in public speaking. The Strada and the Thalassians were real people. These are politicians. There's a big difference."

"And thanks to you," Charlie said, squeezing into the car beside me, "I get to hang out with politicians all day long." He leaned up and patted the driver on the shoulder. "We're clear, Hank. Let's roll out."

Hank was a lanky, long-armed man in his early forties, with hair too long to be regulation and a five-o'clock shadow. None of the security team wore anything resembling a uniform, unless khaki pants, flannel shirts, and baseball caps counted as a uniform. Even Charlie was in civilian clothes, though his lacked the worn, well-used patina of the others. He looked like he'd walked into the department store and asked to be outfitted with the best outdoor gear they had, a city slicker on a dude ranch. I knew it wasn't all his fault. They'd probably waylaid him halfway to Georgia and sprang this detail on him.

And I knew he blamed me.

"I'm sorry about this, Charlie," I said quietly, not knowing whether he wanted the others to hear this conversation. "I wasn't given a choice. I shot my wad keeping your dad out of jail."

He stared out the window as Hank pulled away from the curb behind the lead car, then checked over his shoulder at the vehicle behind us. Not all three Suburbans and none of them black because the whole point of this exercise was to avoid being spotted. The lead vehicle was a small, gray SUV they called a Ford Bronco, though it didn't look anything like the Broncos from the eighties. The one behind us was a generic white Explorer, which Dani assured me screamed "police," but not necessarily "feds."

I thought Charlie was going to ignore my apology, but once we'd pulled out onto the main road, he murmured a command into what I thought had to be a throat mic, paused for a reply and turned back to me.

"I know," he said, finally. "I'm not upset about…" He motioned around us. "…this. I mean, it's going to be a big blank spot on my service record and I'm going to have to wait for another company command to open up in the Ranger Bats, but it could have been a lot worse. I just…it's Dad. I know he worked really hard for this job."

I glanced across Laranna to the soldier on the other side of her. He had to be listening to us, but he gave no sign of it, his dark eyes locked on his side of the street. We'd slowed to a crawl behind the snarled traffic, and if the President's motorcade might have had police escorts clearing everyone out of the way, our quest for anonymity would have made that a bad idea. Instead, we'd just suffer in silence like everyone else.

"I appreciate what George gave up to save me." I hesitated to broach the subject, but I had to know. "Is he going to be okay financially? I mean, it's not like I have a checking account here, but I think I could find some stuff he could turn into cash if he needs it."

Charlie laughed.

"Hell, you could just give him an exclusive interview on YouTube and he'd be an overnight millionaire. Do you have any idea how much money Bill Cordova made with your appearance on his show?"

"I hope he appreciates it when the Anguilar show up," Dani said, leaning forward from the seat behind us. I shot her a dirty look. She hadn't been invited into the conversation, but she'd never let that stop her. "I bet he has a bunker already, like an end-of-the-world prepper thing. I wonder if he's already heading that way."

"Charlie Barnaby," Laranna said, offering him a hand. "We haven't really had the chance to talk. I wanted to thank you. *My* Charlie might still be sitting in a cell if not for you and your father."

"It's gonna get confusing with the two of you calling me Charlie," he said, the glum set of his jaw finally cracking into a smile as he took Laranna's hand. "My friends actually call me Chuck."

"Sir," Hank spoke up, bringing my attention back to the road outside, "we got something up ahead on the drone feed."

The bearded, blond Viking in the front passenger seat hadn't spoken a word since I'd met him and he didn't now, just turned and held up a small tablet with a video feed streaming on its screen.

"This is from a small, quadcopter drone," Charlie—*Chuck* told me, taking the tablet from the Viking. "Like a tiny, remote-controlled helicopter."

I shook my head, having no trouble understanding a remote-controlled miniature helicopter but more disbelieving of the idea that it could transmit a live video feed from that distance. It had to be at least a half-mile away from us and a hundred feet up, but the video was preternaturally steady, another thing I had trouble believing.

What was happening *in* the video was even more unbelievable. The streets were blocked by thousands of demonstrators, maybe even ten thousand, and at first, I couldn't make out what they were saying over the tinny speaker of the tablet, nor could I read the signs they were waving. The drone descended and everything became clearer…and so much stranger.

"One, two, three, four!" they chanted, pumping their fists in the air in unison. "We don't want no alien war! Five, six, seven, eight! Down with this fascist state!"

The crowd marched down the street toward the White House, watched but not impeded by a handful of DC cops from the sides of the road. The signs were clear now, all of them expressing the same, general message.

KEEP US OUT OF ALIEN WARS.
NO BLOOD ON THE STARS.
KEEP THE HEAVENS PEACEFUL.

"Where the hell did these idiots even come from?" Chuck wondered aloud. "That interview was just three days ago!" He shook his head, then put a hand to his ear as if out of instinct, cupping it to block out sound from the small speaker there. "Lead, this is Two. Can we reroute?" I couldn't hear the other half of the conversation, but Chuck nodded. "Copy. Make it happen."

Chuck handed the tablet back to the Viking and leaned up into the front seat, next to the driver's shoulder.

"Hank, Lead is going to take the next right. Follow them on Alternate One. And redirect the drone to check the roads."

Now I could see it on the streets around us even as the traffic slowed. People braving the evening cold to sightsee amongst the skeletal cherry trees and snow-covered monuments slowed as well, some, the elderly mostly, turning back to avoid a possible threat. Others, particularly the young and childless, walked toward the distant sounds of chanting, or even jogged, as if the protest was like a reenactment of the Shootout at the OK Corral, done for their amusement and they didn't want to miss the show.

Though to be fair, what would I have done, if it had been a twenty-three-year-old me, fresh out of college, visiting DC and there'd been a huge protest nearby? I probably would have been running right alongside them and, given that would have been 1987, I would have been wishing I'd brought my camera.

We reached the turn, had to wait behind a line of traffic,

expensive cars by the look of them but glum and brooding with road salt and frozen slush hanging off their wheel wells. Impatient as well, given the fitful honking as a BMW and a Lexus voiced their impatience with the Volkswagen SUV taking its time to make the right on the red light.

"Oh, damn." The voice was the slow rumble of a glacier crushing boulders beneath its weight, unfamiliar. It was the Viking, and he didn't sound happy. "Problem with Alternate One, sir."

This time, I didn't even need the drone feed to see it. More protesters. Not as many as the original group, less than half the size, but making up for the lack of mass with a surplus of velocity. Younger, bigger, mostly male and jogging toward the intersection like they intended to intercept the other group before they could reach the White House. They carried signs as well, and I did have to look at the tablet to read those, since they were still a couple hundred yards away.

PROTECT US FROM THE ANGUILAR.

VIVE LE RESISTANCE!

THEIR FIGHT IS OUR FIGHT!

And a bunch of others, including, to my utter horror…

"Is that *your* face?" Laranna asked, leaning over me to look at the poster being held by one of the men in the front line of the demonstrators.

"Screen grab from the Cordova show," Chuck agreed, then touched his earbud. "Trail, can we back out of here, pull a U-turn?" He frowned and twisted in his seat.

I didn't need to hear Trail's response because I could see it.

We were blocked in, a minivan nearly touching the bumper of the Explorer behind us. Which wouldn't have been the end of the world since these guys were professionals and had left gaps between their vehicles to give themselves room to pull a quick U-turn…except the lane to our left was packed bumper-to-bumper as well, not leaving us any room to maneuver. The light had turned green and if those cars in the straight lane had proceeded, we could have made it…but the mass of protestors blocked this road just as the first group blocked the path straight.

Which left the curb to the right, except that there was actually a double right turn lane, and the rightmost of the two was under construction. The right side of our vehicles was up against a jersey barrier.

"We're blocked in," Chuck said. No panic in his voice, matter of fact, steady. He nodded to the Viking. "Cutter, recommendations?"

Huh. That had to make the Viking a high-ranking NCO or possibly a warrant officer, assuming these guys were Delta Force, which I did. I wouldn't have picked the big guy out as someone in charge.

"We stay in the vehicles, call for law enforcement backup," Cutter replied instantly, nodding toward the counter-demonstrators. "There might be a confrontation, but they'll be concentrating on each other, not us. We wait until the locals clear this shit away and…" He grinned as he looked back at us. "…I hope none of y'all have to use the bathroom anytime soon."

"Right." Chuck sighed, tapped his earbud again. "Lead, Trail, we're sitting tight. Stay in your vehicles and keep your doors locked. Lead, put in a call to the local cops for support, get this mob dispersed soonest. Priority is to clear this intersection." He reached under his jacket and pulled out a SIG, holding it low towards the floorboards, then he nodded to me. "Just sit tight. Everything'll be fine."

"We got anything nonlethal?" Hank asked, speaking to Cutter, I thought, rather than Chuck.

"Just my swinging cod," Cutter replied, chuckling. He twisted around in his seat, looking at the other three Delta operators in the vehicle. "Tink, Rooster, Monk? Any of you carrying CS or pepper spray or, hell, brass knuckles?"

The three men looked at each other, back at Cutter and shook their heads.

"I didn't see anything in the threat brief about public demonstrations," the one they'd called Monk replied, grinning.

He was, from the thin shadow of what had once been his hairline, prematurely balding and had shaved his head in protest, which might have been the source of his nickname. All these guys used first names or nicknames, another reason I figured they were Delta. Not that I was an expert on them, but I'd heard Colonel Danberg talking about the Unit with other cadets and, assuming he wasn't full of shit, these guys fit the description to a T, even thirty-five years later.

"Well, you weren't paying attention, then," Chuck told Monk, though the curl of a thin smile said he was just yanking the older man's chain, "because I clearly remember putting in my op order under Situation, Enemy Forces that everyone was a possible enemy, up to and including Congress."

"What caliber do you use for Congress?" Tink, the barrel-chested man sitting beside Dani asked.

"The hard part isn't what caliber to choose," Hank put in, "it's the optics. I mean, there's so much thermal distortion from the hot air they put out, how you gonna get a long-range shot?"

A low chuckle ran through the vehicle, including, to my surprise, Dani. Not Laranna or Val, though, probably because they didn't get the context of the joke. Well, Laranna didn't for sure and I didn't know if Val was used to that sort of humor about the government back in his day.

"Oh, boy," Hank murmured, tapping his window. "It's kicking off."

Through the windshield and a haze that the defrosters couldn't quite keep ahead of, the two groups of demonstrators met. Their chanting and yelling had turned into a solid wall of noise, no longer separable into coherent syllables, canceling each other out like white noise as the two groups had closed in on the intersection. The counter-demonstrators reached the crossroads first, and there weren't nearly enough DC cops there to stop them, or at least that must have been what the police in attendance thought because they didn't even try to get in the way, and Hank noticed that, too.

"DC's finest earning their pay again," he murmured.

The counter-protestors, the ones carrying *my* picture around, planted themselves in the street, one line filling in after another, cutting off the road to the White House. The oncoming anti-alien demonstrators slowed to a gradual halt, an accordion effect running up and down the throng of ten thousand people like this was the interstate and someone had to stop for a traffic accident.

The two sides stopped maybe twenty yards apart like there was an invisible barrier between them, at first just chanting their slogans at each other, priests of different religions hurling prayers and spells at the other side and hoping their own gods would come out on top. If it had stayed like that, maybe things would have worked out. There's a certain inertia to crowds that big, and objects at rest tend to remain at rest unless acted upon by an external force.

But people aren't inanimate objects. Often, they're much dumber than inanimate objects, and this was no exception. All it took was one guy. I don't know which side he was from, couldn't see the spark that ignited the confrontation, I only saw the surge forward from both sides, covering that twenty yards in seconds. Chants and taunts became bellows, screams of pain and fear, and even through the closed windows and the rumble of idling engines, the sound of flesh striking flesh penetrated.

The two crowds mingled at the front, merging with each other like different-colored paints spilled on the floor of an art studio, merging from yellow and red to a messy orange. In seconds, the whole scene descended into chaos, the blood-red rays of the setting sun throwing it into relief, an abstract painting brought to life, Picasso's "Guernica" playing out in front of us.

"Shit," Chuck said softly. He touched his earbud again. "Home base, this is Two. We have a situation here. Any timeline on that law enforcement support?" He rolled his eyes, but didn't let it leak through into his voice. "Copy. Keep us updated." A tap to turn off the mic and he shook his head. "Traffic is snarled up with a couple accidents. Gonna be at least ten to fifteen minutes. They have a helo warming up at the pad to keep an eye on things, but unless the demonstration proves an immediate threat, we're on our own."

"And what else is new?" Tink muttered. "Why should this be any different than Syria or Yemen?"

"It's heading this way," Hank warned.

If this had been some ancient battlefield, the line with more power, more esprit de corps, more initiative, would have penetrated the other, driven the enemy before them and turned them running back the way they came. But neither of these forces had the discipline of an army, so instead the fight spread outward laterally…mostly our way. Humanity broke over the line of cars like a wave, each of the stream of combatants cohering into real people as they drifted closer to us.

Here a bearded, beer-bellied twenty-something wrestling a man in his forties, the older man's face half-covered by tattoos. Their signs were gone, discarded in the chaos, so I wasn't sure which of them approved of my presence and which one thought I was evil incarnate, and by the looks of the two, I would rather neither of them was a supporter. Neither knew how to fight, that much was clear, and they tumbled away without either of them landing a solid punch.

I let out a relieved sigh. These people were out of control, sure, but they were focused on each other, not some random SUV. If they broke a few heads, well, that was a shame, but I hadn't asked anyone to protest for or against me.

"Charlie," Laranna said, her eyes fixed on a spot to the right, away from the bulk of the combatants, on the other side of the jersey barrier. "What is that man carrying?"

Every eye turned in the direction she indicated, and I think we all saw him at once. He was average looking, nothing standing out except the black balaclava he wore over his face. Some of the protestors on both sides concealed their faces beneath scarves or what looked like surgical masks, but this guy's reminded me of an SAS agent…or a ninja. It matched the black duster draped over him, so long it nearly scraped the ground. Long enough to have concealed the four-foot black cylinder he swung to his shoulder, pointed directly at the Suburban.

Cutter, the one I'd thought of as the Viking, yelled the warning before my mind could process it, though given another two seconds, I would have recognized the black tube for what it was.

"RPG!"

Before anyone could move, a flare of igniting rockets and a cloud of smoke obscured the man in black and a Rocket Propelled Grenade streaked into the front of the SUV. Light and smoke and a blast so loud that all sound faded, and I descended into the blackness.

19

"Travers! Wake up, dammit!"

"Charlie, can you hear me? You have to get up…we have to get out of this vehicle."

The voices were distant, muffled by a wall of haze and nearly drowned out by a high-pitched whine, like a swarm of pissed-off mosquitos. I wished they would all shut up. My head hurt…hell, my whole body hurt and I didn't *want* to get up, even if the car was on fire…

Wait a second. I pried my eyes open. The car was on fire.

"What the hell happened?" I blurted, sitting bolt upright, then coughing my lungs out as burning rubber and gasoline choked out the air. The cab of the Suburban had filled with acrid smoke, although the fire, so far, was confined outside the windshield, roaring up from the wreckage of the engine compartment. Some of the heat still reached us even through the dash, prickling my skin as the moisture evaporated like I'd walked into a pizza oven.

"RPG," Chuck Barnaby said, spitting blood out onto the floorboards. I thought for a second he might have internal injuries until I saw the blood running from his nose and a cut on the side of his head that matched the crack on the side window. He'd bounced off of it. "They'll be coming to finish us off. Everyone out my side."

The door resisted him, and it took two blows with his shoulder before it opened and a blast of cold air washed away the stifling smoke, bringing me back from the haze of semi-consciousness to full awareness. Laranna was fine, didn't have any bleeds, burns, or bruises that I could see in the bare instant I had to look at her before Chuck was out the door. Dani and Val and the two Delta ops in the third row were pushing the right half of the second-row seat up already before Monk could even get out of it, so I assumed they were at least mobile.

Hank and Cutter were a different story. The Suburban had to be some kind of armored security model, or we'd all have been dead, but even whatever shielding the thing came equipped with hadn't been enough to deflect the full concussion of the rocket launcher. Spiderwebs of cracks splintered the windshield into a mosaic done by the most boring artist the Renaissance had to offer, colored only by the black smoke pouring from the hole where the hood had been. No fragments had made it through, but the airbags had gone off on both the driver and passenger's side and either their eruption or the blast that had caused it had left both men hanging out of their seat belts, eyes unfocused.

Hank had pulled out his SIG handgun, but the blast had knocked it out of his hand, leaving it half in one of the cupholders in the center console and I grabbed it on my way out. This wasn't the first time I'd been blown up and if there was one thing I'd learned from the experience, it was that the next step was usually getting shot at.

"Taking fire!"

Damn, I hated being right all the time.

The warning didn't come from Chuck, who was busy trying to pull Hank's door open, but from one of the men in the lead Bronco. My ears had begun to recover, slower than my brain but enough that the chatter of small arms penetrated the ringing, followed by the *tonk-tonk-tonk* of bullets impacting against the metal on the passenger's side of the Ford.

Luckily, the RPG had been reserved for us, giving the four operators in the lead vehicle time to get out…and luckily, they had more than handguns. Two of the men were ducked behind the jersey barrier, their hands filled with the same sort of carbine or submachine gun I'd seen in the hands of the Secret Service, something that hadn't been around when I'd read my last issue of Guns and Ammo. I couldn't see who they were firing at—besides the impromptu smoke screen, the sun had dipped below the horizon while we'd been waiting in traffic and the bright beams of headlights combined with the deep shadows in the construction area to turn that entire side of the street into a gray haze.

I didn't know if anyone could see them or not, the demonstrators had definitely *heard* the explosions and gunfire and whether they'd been my supporters or detractors, they all shared one thing now—a deep, instinctive need to run like hell. Their shouts and screams were a vocal backing to the staccato drumbeat of the guns and the glow of headlights showed a kinetoscope view of sprinting former rioters.

In the split second left to me to make a decision about my next move, information washed over me and I grabbed furtively at the pertinent bits, building my own mosaic. This was, I'd come to understand, the thing that made me different than most people, maybe the thing that had drawn Lenny's attention in the first place when he'd taken me. Most people, when faced with the prospect of violent death, panicked and ran. Others froze up, if even for a few seconds, long enough to die. And even those who didn't run or freeze up often acted according to instinct or training, whether or not those instincts were giving them the best plan of action for their circumstances.

At some point in the last two years, I'd learned to slug my brain into motion when the bullets or pulse rounds started flying, to fit all the facts into a series of bullet points on the whiteboard inside my head and come up with the best plan. The bullet points were as clear as the actual bullets. These weren't rioters. This wasn't some spontaneous outbreak of violence by bad apples at a protest. This was a targeted hit—and we were the targets. Maybe even just *me*. I didn't know who, could only guess why, but these guys weren't going to run. They were professionals. The return fire was keeping them back, behind cover probably, but that wouldn't last long.

"Laranna," I said, turning back to her as she helped Dani out of the back seat. "You have your comms?"

She nodded, holding the small device up. She'd run through a metal detector on the way into the White House, but they hadn't tried to take the comm, apparently having learned their lesson the first time back in Tennessee.

"Whatever's on patrol, get it down here…now!"

I didn't wait for her to answer, just took a deep breath and ran around the front of the SUV to the passenger's side. The wind blew the smoke in that direction, which made for good concealment but no cover at all, and I ducked low, nearly crawling the last few feet to stay behind the concrete jersey barrier as incoming rounds punched into the windshield, plucking bits of glass out of its bullet-resistant layers.

Monk had stayed in the car and was trying to get Cutter free of his seat belt and get his door open, since there was no way anyone was going to be able to haul the big man over the center console and out the driver's side. The door popped open about an inch and through the cracked window, Monk's scowl of frustration told me he wasn't able to get it open any farther. I shoved the SIG into my jacket pocket and grabbed the door handle, planting my foot against the central column and yanking backward with every ounce of energy the adrenaline had gifted me.

I wasn't sure which would give first, my back or the bent and twisted hinges, but I assumed from the tortured squeal of metal that it had been the door. It gave way, opening a good three feet and I tumbled backward, barely catching myself with the handle. A spray of bullets tore into the metal beside my hand and movement teased the corner of my eye, lit up by the fire.

One of the masked men in black lurked there, balaclava

hiding his face but not his eyes. They were cold and determined, but the M16 carbine wasn't cooperating, the bolt locked open on the last round he'd fired into the Suburban. Which gave me just enough time to grab the SIG out of my jacket pocket. I had, I realized abruptly even as I lined the sights up and took the slack off the trigger, never killed another human being. It was a fine distinction, but one I think my subconscious had been making these last two years without my knowledge, because when the gun kicked in my hand, the bullets might have been ripping through *my* chest instead of his.

Two to the chest, one to the head, what had been called the Mozambique Drill here, but the Strada taught it as well, and his head snapped back at the last shot before he toppled backward, the carbine and its empty magazine clattering to the pavement separately. I kept the gun extended in both hands, scanning back and forth for a moment to make sure no one else was charging the truck. Muzzle flashes still flared from behind other jersey barriers and from the cover of abandoned vehicles, their passengers having deserted them to flee the explosion and gunfire, but they were all directed at the Bronco.

I kept the SIG in one hand, reaching in to grab Cutter under the arm with the other. The man was semi-conscious now, but blood trickled from his ears and nose and he nearly collapsed to his knees when I got him out of the vehicle. Which might have been a good idea, as far as keeping beneath cover went, but Cutter had to weigh in at somewhere over 220 pounds and I didn't want to think about trying to lift this guy back to his feet. I grabbed at his belt and leaned him into me, staggering beneath the weight but managing to stay upright as I guided him back around the other side of the Suburban.

Chuck and Tink had managed to extract Hank and had him leaning up against the rear driver's side tire, while Laranna, Dani and Val were with Monk, taking cover behind the Explorer. I let Cutter lean back against the rear quarter panel of the Suburban and slide to the ground, his eyelids fluttering as he began to come back to himself.

"Where the hell is that helicopter, Chuck?" I yelled, both so that he could hear it over the harsh chatter of gunfire and so that I could hear myself through the ringing.

"On its way," he said, frustration warring with fear in his expression and, I thought, winning. "I think we'll be okay as long as..."

Whatever he'd been about to say, it was lost in an unmistakable whoosh, the same one that was the last thing I'd heard without the benefit of the incessant ringing. Clenching my teeth in anticipation, I crouched down beside Cutter, expecting this second RPG rocket to slam into the other side of the Suburban and kill us all.

But the attackers went for the source of the most return fire and when the blast hit, it rocked the Bronco onto its driver's side wheels with a wash of heat and a hail of shrapnel against the front of the Suburban.

"Dammit, no!" Chuck yelled, breaking cover and making a run for the lead vehicle even before its ruined right side touched pavement again, bouncing as it settled into its suspension.

The four men who'd been using it for firing positions were

laid out flat on the ground at either end of the burning vehicle, lit up with unnatural clarity by the flames. I didn't know their names, hadn't met them, and Chuck had only met them a couple days ago, but we both rushed into the storm of incoming fire, intensifying now that the enemy could advance without fear of being shot.

Chuck grabbed one of the two men sprawled out at this end of the Bronco and dragged him back behind the body of the vehicle and I took the other. A handful of his jacket was as much of a hold as I could manage and, by all rights, I shouldn't have been able to pull someone who weighed close to two hundred pounds one-handed across twenty yards of pavement, but my old friend adrenaline lent a helping hand again. He'd take his payment later, when I was cramping up in bed with my back and shoulders on fire, but for now, boundless energy burned through my veins and I felt nothing but urgency.

I didn't look at the man until I'd dragged him behind cover, and when I did, all that energy went out of me like the air leaking from a balloon once it had been pierced by a pinhead. He was clearly dead, his eyes open yet unseeing, and I was about to leave him and head for the other two victims, but Laranna bounded past me. A warning came to my lips, but I bit down on it, knowing in my head that she'd trained for this sort of thing since she was a little girl and was better at it than I was, even if my heart had other ideas.

Instead of worrying about her, I leaned over the dead soldier and grabbed the carbine, yanking the sling over his head, trying not to think about how ghoulish it felt. Whoever was attacking us, they weren't going to give us a time-out so we could be respectful of the man's death. That much was clear from the dark, shadowy figures bounding forward, taking advantage of the lull in firing to advance on our position.

I'd never used the weird carbine and had no idea where the safety might be or even how to reload it, given that the magazine seemed to be laying on top of the barrel, but the sights were simple and a trigger is a trigger. The optics were the same kind that Dani had on her service weapon, the same kind I'd seen on so many guns since I got here, with a red dot hovering across my vision to show where the bullets would impact. It was simple to use, just keep both eyes open and put that red dot where I wanted to shoot.

Bullets spanged off the side of the wrecked Bronco but I shut them out, shut off the part of my brain that wanted to run and hide and concentrated on gently stroking the trigger. The gun was full auto, I knew that from watching the others, so I made sure to let off the trigger almost immediately and I still fired off at least three rounds. A dark figure tumbled forward, losing his balance and collapsing to the gravel surface where the road had been ripped up for repair. Still moving, not dead yet, but out of the fight and that was all I cared about right now.

The next slowed his rush, seeing the fate of the lead man, heels digging in and sending up a spray of debris. Not fast enough. The carbine had little recoil and was childishly simple to aim, and transitioning to the next target took less than a second. Slightly longer pull, maybe four or five rounds, and this time when they hit, the man in black pitched forward, his rifle falling from nerveless hands.

That left at least a dozen of them still out there, rushing for cover, having gained enough ground that it would only take minutes for them to overwhelm my position, less if I couldn't figure out how to reload this weapon. And that wasn't figuring on the RPG shooter. I couldn't find him in the darkness, didn't know if he was out there among the others still advancing or if he'd huddled behind a vehicle, waiting for a chance at his next shot.

Movement out of the corner of my vision nearly brought the muzzle of my weapon tracking to the left until I realized it was Chuck, taking up a position beside me. He'd salvaged one of the compact carbines himself and fired off a burst before turning to nod at me. The rifle wasn't as loud as I'd thought it would be. I knew mine hadn't seemed painfully loud, but I'd figured that was the auditory exclusion I'd read about, where the adrenaline shut out the noises of the firefight. Looking at Chuck's weapon, though, I realized the things were fitted with suppressors. Shorter than I might have imagined, probably another thing that had improved while I'd been gone and, for once, I was grateful for the difference since it saved my eardrums from further insult.

"We have to find that RPG," Chuck yelled in my ear. "One more shot from that thing, and we're done."

I hadn't noticed Laranna coming up behind us until she put a hand on my shoulder, and it took all my self-control not to jump out of my skin. She'd picked up a combat knife from somewhere, probably from the men she'd gone to pull to safety, and she held it out to the side like she'd trained with it her whole life.

"The other two soldiers are injured but alive," she told me. She nodded forward into the shadowy haze ahead of us, where the enemy still lurked. "Keep them pinned down. I'm going out there to find the man with the missile launcher."

"Are you crazy?" Chuck asked, the whites of his eyes showing as they went wide. "You'll get killed!"

"Make sure I don't, Charles Barnaby," she told him.

Then she was gone, disappearing into the night. I didn't bother arguing with Chuck, just leaned around the end of the Bronco and put another short burst into the edge of a jersey barrier, forcing the man behind it to duck further down.

Where, I wondered, were the cops? Not the ones who Chuck had called, nor even the rescue helicopter. They were all ten to fifteen minutes away and while it certainly felt like this fight had gone on forever, it must actually have been less than five minutes from when that first RPG had flown. All this would be over long before any of them arrived. No, I was wondering about the DC cops who'd been lined up along the route of the demonstration. They had to have heard what was happening, but not a one had come to investigate. Maybe RPGs and automatic weapons were above their pay grade.

They weren't the help I was counting on.

A muzzle flash from behind a fishtailed sportscar drew my attention as the fusillade of rifle bullets passed through the side windows of the Bronco, and I answered with a long burst of my own even though I couldn't actually see the shooter. I had no idea if I'd hit him but the idea was to provide covering fire and I had, at least, forced him to take cover.

Movement to my left, just the barest hint of dark against dark, heading from our lines toward theirs before it disappeared into the shadows again. Laranna. It was a pleasure to watch her work.

"Hold your fire," I told Chuck. "By the way, what *are* these guns, anyway?"

"FN P90," he informed me as if that explained everything. "5.7 by 28mm Personal Defense Weapon. Holds fifty rounds in the mag."

Well, that *did*, at least, explain why I hadn't run out of ammo yet.

Motion again and Chuck and I both swung our weapons to cover it, but the glint of a distant headlight off a silver blade told the story. It was Laranna and she'd made her way behind enemy lines. A black-clad body fell out of the shadows, sprawled over the top of one of the concrete barriers but Laranna didn't bother to take his weapon, perhaps because she had no training with human rifles, or perhaps because she had more throats to cut and didn't want to make noise.

"Damn," Chuck murmured, and remembering the Krill she'd dispatched to save my life when we'd first met, I couldn't help but agree. I'd gotten so used to the two of us doing all our fighting from the cockpit of a Vanguard that I'd nearly forgotten what a nightmare she could be with a blade in her hand.

A dark blur moving left to right, briefly lit up by the muzzle flash from an M16, then a thrashing and kicking in the shadows of a white government work truck left here by the road construction crew and a pair of black-clad legs fluttered and went still.

And someone noticed. They were as panicked by it as I might have been, standing from cover to get a better shot at her, a perfect silhouette with the crimson reticle floating over their torso.

Chuck and I fired at the same time and the gunman spasmed with the impacts, not falling over but simply sitting down like he'd suddenly succumbed to fatigue. As if we'd lit up a neon sign when we'd opened fire, more of the enemy rose from cover, laying down a torrent of lead that hit the sides of the Bronco and the Suburban and made me very thankful that the suppressors on the FN carbines concealed the flash from our muzzles and the headlights behind us conspired with the smoke from the burning cars to hide our silhouettes from the shooters.

At least that was what I told myself as a logical excuse for why I didn't dive for cover, though the real reason was that Laranna needed me to keep their attention directed our way. If I hadn't stayed upright, I wouldn't have seen the shape of the RPG launcher pop up from behind an earthen berm, the tube swinging around toward us faster than I could aim the FN...until it jerked upward, firing straight into the air.

I followed the white streak of the rocket as it arced over our heads and spent itself in the middle of the street, a chest-deep thunder and a snare drum rattle. Something white hot buried itself in my left calf and I cursed reflexively, but I had it better than the RPG man. The tube slipped from senseless hands and he slumped backward to the ground, Laranna standing over him like the angel of death.

She might have made it back to concealment but while fortune might favor the bold, it sure as hell screwed us over when those gunmen followed the arc of the missile back to where Laranna crouched with nothing more powerful than a knife in her hand. Muzzles flared and she threw herself behind the berm just ahead of the incoming rounds.

I took one of them down, but the others got the hint and fired from behind their shelters and before I could find another target, the endless fifty-round reservoir of the P90 finally ran dry. Chuck kept shooting, careful, short bursts, while I tossed the gun aside and pulled the SIG from my pocket. I wasn't sure how many shots I had left in the pistol, but I did know it was faster than finding a spare mag and trying to reload a gun I'd never seen before today.

It wasn't going to be enough. The gunmen, sensing the reduction in covering fire and probably thinking it was now or never since they'd lost their most powerful weapon, rose from their cover and surged forward, bent on taking us out no matter what the cost.

Crimson fire rained from the sky, exploding against the pavement in front of us with a crash of rolling thunder, turning the construction work truck into a twisted, burning hulk in bare seconds. And chopping across the line of black-clad gunmen like the wrath of a fire god sent from on high.

Or just like the pulse cannon on a Vanguard fighter. The craft hovered a few hundred feet above the intersection, in front of God and everyone, and in the distance, half a mile away, the crowds that had run away from the violence or come to seek it out stood in awe, watching it come in for a landing.

The hatch to the cockpit opened and Giblet stuck his head out, a pulse rifle in hand.

"You called?" he said, then took a look around at the carnage and shrugged. "You sure these people can help us, Charlie? Because frankly, this whole place looks like a damned nightmare."

And I couldn't argue with him at all.

20

"I CAN'T BEGIN to tell you how sorry I am about this," President Louis said, hands smoothing down his hair as if he'd just woken up even though it was only eleven at night. Then again, thinking about Poppa Chuck, maybe he *had* already been asleep.

I wasn't sure where we were now. The chopper had arrived shortly after Gib had pulled our asses out of the fire, a day late and a dollar short but at least the Marines had been able to get our wounded to the hospital. Including me, though all I'd needed were some tweezers to get the tiny piece of shrapnel out of my calf muscle and a grand total of four stitches. Barely worth showing up for.

Chuck's team hadn't been so lucky. At least one had been KIA on the scene and four of the others had barely been conscious when they'd been carted away on gurneys. I hadn't seen Chuck again that night and I had to assume that was because he and his people were being treated by the normal medical staff at Johns Hopkins while the rest of us were entrusted to doctors and nurses who could keep their mouths shut. Particularly about Laranna.

She had a slight concussion, at least as far as the doctors could tell given her slightly different physiology, while Val and Dani were fine other than a few cuts and bruises. It had been tough to convince Gib of that and get him back into the air. He'd demanded to come with us, to take Dani to the hospital himself, but she'd finally got him to understand that if he didn't get back up on patrol, we'd be vulnerable to another attack.

Uniformed Secret Service had escorted us to the hospital, and we'd taken the same chopper from there back to the White House. From the South Lawn we'd been taken down an elevator to…somewhere. Maybe it was the presidential bunker I'd heard them talking about, but there were no helpful signs indicating that, just gray walls and locked rooms. And Secret Service agents and not a few Marines. They glared at us as we were brought through the corridors, as if this was all our fault, somehow. And I suppose, in a way, it was.

We'd been deposited in a room that wasn't quite an office, nor exactly a meeting room for all that it had multiple monitors and tables. It had more the look of a break room though, with a refrigerator, a microwave, and cabinets filled with snack food. And then left alone for two hours.

The adrenaline had abandoned me long ago, but the shakes hadn't come until I'd settled into the plush leather couch arranged at the center of the monitors. Without warning, my breath had come short, my hands shaking, and I'd squeezed my eyes shut against tears that tried to come against my will. Laranna had been there, too, though, and she'd known. She'd squeezed my hands tight in hers and leaned against my shoulder, and I knew she had the same feelings, though she'd been taught how to deal with them since she was a child.

We'd sat there for a long time in silence, her hands on mine, not looking up at the others until Dani had deposited mugs of coffee and paper plates loaded down with ham sandwiches in front of us on the coffee table.

"Eat something," Dani had urged. "God alone knows how long we're going to be sitting here."

Val hadn't needed her to twist his arm, grabbing one of the sandwiches and digging in immediately, but my stomach had tightened at the very thought of food until Laranna had grabbed the two plates and put one in front of me. I'd given in. If this was the presidential bunker, they kept a nice kitchen. The ham had been fresh and so had the bread, and though I was no coffee connoisseur, it wasn't bad for instant.

The heavy, solid metal door to the room hadn't opened for another hour, dour-faced Secret Service agents slipping through and taking up positions on either side before the President had entered, along with four others, three men and a woman. One of the men I recognized all too well, George's boss, Parker Donovan, though his expression seemed chastened when he entered. The others I didn't know, though one wore the uniform of an Army four-star general, so I assumed he had to be important. He was certainly tall enough, taller even than Donovan, though not as stern looking. Softer around the edges, with a fringe of graying brown hair cut close.

The other two were political animals, I could tell by their tailored suits, the man short and slight, reminding me of an accountant behind his thick glasses. The woman was nearly my height, though some of that might have been the heels. She looked as if she strived to combine the fashionable look of a politician with the professional demeanor and muted colors of a police officer, and her eyes widened just slightly when she caught her first glimpse of Laranna.

"Mr. Travers," the President had said as the door closed behind him, "Ms. Campling, Mr. McKee…Ms. Laranna. Allow me to introduce General Ben Gavin, Chairman of the Joint Chiefs, CIA director Lawrence McKinnes, and FBI director Gladys Perez." His lip had curled in a wry smile. "And National Security Advisor Donovan, you already know." He'd motioned at one of the tables. "If you would sit with us, I think we have a handle on what happened."

"Let me guess," Dani said, turning her chair around and sitting in it backwards. "It was the Russians."

"It was the Russians," McKinnes and Perez said together as if they'd practiced it. McKinnes reddened at the unintentional chorus and Perez went on.

"Most of your attackers were…well, burned to a crisp by whatever weapon your aircraft used on them."

"Scalar pulse cannon," Laranna told her. "It fires from self-consuming thermal cartridges."

"Kind of like a Vulcan," I put in. "The gun, I mean, not like the alien."

"Yes, well," Perez continued, the muscles tensing beside her eyes as if she were fighting to keep from rolling them. "As such, they were unidentifiable. Except for the one with the RPG, who you killed with a knife, I believe, Ms. Laranna."

"Just *Laranna* is fine," she insisted. "And yes. The blade was poorly balanced, but then, I suppose most of your soldiers aren't truly versed in fighting with edged weapons."

Donovan gave President Louis a goggling stare.

"Are you *sure* you want to put her in front of Congress, Mr. President?"

All the shakes, the nerves, the pent-up anger fueled the red haze that fell over my vision at the National Security Advisor's words.

"Mr. Donovan," I growled, not caring even a little that I sounded threatening, "given what you tried to do to my friend Giblet, I think if I were you, I'd keep my damned mouth shut unless I had something constructive to contribute."

Donovan's chair scraped across the tile floor and he came halfway out of his seat, his expression that of a man not used to being talked to that way, but the President stopped him with a hand on his arm.

"Sit the hell down, Parker. You deserve that. In fact, I think if Mr. Travers here weren't concerned with alienating us, he'd likely have punched you in the face the second you showed up here."

Yeah, the thought had crossed my mind, and despite what Louis had said, what had stayed my hand wasn't worrying about screwing up the deal, it was the odds of getting out of this bunker alive. They hadn't let me keep either the P90 or the SIG.

"As I was saying," the FBI director went on, casting a baleful glare at Donovan, though I got the sense it was more because he'd interrupted her than it was for what he'd done to us, "we were able to get a positive ID on the dead man with the RPG. His name was Stefan Vučić, until five years ago, a senior NCO in the Serbian Army." Perez pulled out her phone and tapped the screen a few times until one of the monitors across from the couch displayed a file photograph of a horse-faced man in his early forties, strands of gray lightening his otherwise jet-black hair, his eyes dull and dead even in life. "There's no official record of him after he left military service, but our sources tell us he was recruited by the Wagner Group."

I blinked, shook my head.

"The which?"

McKinnes took over, looking grateful to have something to explain.

"The Wagner Group is a state-sponsored private military company…mercenaries, basically, but almost exclusively hired to do the unofficial, off-the-books dirty work for the Kremlin. They've been active in eastern Europe, Ukraine, and Africa and they've been accused of innumerable atrocities against civilians. They're what the Kremlin uses when it wants plausible deniability." He smiled about as condescendingly as he could. "That means when a government…"

"I *know* what plausible deniability is," I assured him. "I'm from the 1980s, remember? Iran-Contra ring a bell?"

McKinnes frowned and I wondered if it *did* ring any bells for him. Not that I would have expected the average Joe back in 1987 to know much about some covert operation the CIA did in the 1950s, but this *was* the director of the agency.

"And we don't think the timing was coincidental, either," Perez interjected. "Two opposing demonstrations *that* large organized only a couple days after you going public?" She shook her head. "We're still tracking down the organizers, but the people we've interviewed so far say the whole thing was put together via social media and that transportation was provided. For *both* groups. I have a feeling once we trace that money, they'll both wind up having been funded from the same source." She sighed, resting her chin on her hands. "Of course, that'll be some bank in the Caymans and the trail will go dead there because we're not dealing with idiots. The RPG is a dead end, probably smuggled in from Mexico and to there from Central America. The other weapons were reported stolen from a National Guard armory in upstate New York fifteen years ago."

"Does anyone else want coffee?" President Louis asked out of the blue. "I need some coffee. I'm not used to staying up this late anymore." He smiled genially at McKinnes. "Larry, why don't you get us a few cups of coffee?"

I thought McKinnes's eyes were going to bug right out of his head, and I suppressed a laugh.

"Yes, sir." The CIA director pushed his chair back and went to the coffee maker, clattering mugs and smacking bags of instant coffee against the counter in what could have been a movie-clip case study on passive-aggressiveness.

"None for me, Mr. McKinnes," I told him, trying to be helpful. "I just had a cup."

"I could do with another," Val said, offering the CIA director his empty mug. The balding little man snatched it out of his hand without a word.

"So, it was the Russians," Dani prompted. "What are you gonna do about it?"

"There's not much we *can* do, officially," General Gavin spoke for the first time since they'd sat down. His voice was surprisingly pleasant, deep and sonorous like a radio announcer. "As Mr. McKinnes said, the Wagner Group is designed for plausible deniability. We can't even prove that this Vučić fellow was actually employed by them. Maybe if the others hadn't been so badly burned and…" He snorted. "…*exploded*, we could trace them back directly."

"Gib likes to be thorough," Dani admitted, smiling broadly. "After all, he didn't have too long to assess the situation and he knew we were in immediate danger. He blew up the right people and didn't cause any collateral damage, which is pretty impressive given the circumstances."

"I agree, ma'am," Gavin told her, "particularly given the casualties that your protection detail took."

"I know the one guy died," I cut in, finally getting the chance to ask. "How are the rest of them?"

"Several shrapnel wounds, but those are mostly minor," he told me in a tone that spoke volumes about how much he cared for those men. "Four of them have serious concussions that might turn into TBI." I must have looked as blank as I felt at the term, because he clarified. "Sorry, Traumatic Brain Injury. Long-term cognitive effects, possibly."

"Yeah," Val agreed, sighing heavily. "We didn't have a fancy word for it back in my day, but I knew boys like that after the war. Touched, we called 'em." A shudder went through me without my volition at the understanding that he meant the *Civil* War. I knew it on an intellectual level, but every now and then I really *knew* it.

"Damn," I murmured. "Is Chuck…I mean, Captain Barnaby okay?"

"He's fine. He wasn't harmed, though God knows how both of you didn't get yourselves killed." Gavin's eyebrow shot up. "I reviewed the footage from the dash camera of the Explorer. You both deserve medals for putting yourselves in harm's way like that."

"I think my term of service probably ended almost thirty years ago," I said, "but Chuck certainly deserves one."

"We'll let the Russians know that *we* know," the President cut in, his furrowed brow hinting at annoyance from being left out of the conversation. "And we'll also let them know that any further action will be considered an act of war."

"Were they trying to snatch us or just kill us?" Dani wondered.

"They were trying to kill us," I assured her. "They didn't have any extraction plan that I could see. They had to know everything would get shut down. I'm just guessing, since I don't know a damn thing about Russia in the 2020s, but if they're anything like the old Soviet Union, they'd probably be very happy if the

United States didn't get access to fusion energy and alien weapons."

"Exactly," McKinnes agreed, setting mugs of coffee in front of Louis, Gavin, Donovan, and Perez. He hadn't asked them how they wanted it, which either meant he had an eidetic memory or President Louis had used him as a dogsbody before. I also noticed he hadn't gotten a cup for himself. "And that's not going to change just because this attempt failed. Think about it from their point of view. If we do make this deal, they probably assume we're cutting them out of it."

"Because we *are*!" Gavin insisted, staring at the CIA director like it was obvious. "There's no way we're handing energy weapons that can destroy cities over to the Russians!"

"But what about the non-weapons technology?" Perez wondered. She raised a hand in acknowledgement at the stares from the other advisors. "Granted, this is beyond my purview, but couldn't we buy them off by promising them fusion reactors and medical technology?"

"This is all a conversation for another time," President Louis told them. "I wouldn't feel comfortable making decisions like this without the Secretaries of Energy, State, Health, and Welfare and half a dozen others here to add their comments." He nodded to Gavin. "But you're correct, we're not giving the Russians access to weapons technology, particularly not when they're already under sanction for their aggression with their neighbors."

"I know you said it's not a debate for right now," I cut in, an idea gnawing at the back of my thoughts, "but consider this for future reference, Mr. President. This technology isn't…" I struggled for a word. "It isn't something you can put in a box as harmful or not harmful. If you give the Russian government fusion reactors and fabricators, they can use them to crank out a million tanks in a few months. If you give them cheap space drives, they can go nudge small asteroids that'll come in and hit your cities. If you give them the medical technology we're talking about, they can use it to put any soldier back on the front lines a couple days after anything but the most serious wounds. It's going to change everything even if you don't send troops to fight with us."

"Well, that's certainly depressing," President Louis admitted, slumping in his chair, coffee cup still held in his hand as if forgotten.

"No, sir," McKinney said, his expression equally morose. "What's depressing is that the Russians might be able to figure out that the opposite is also true." At the President's curious glance, the CIA director went on. "Right now, they're butthurt about not being the ones to get city-destroying energy weapons. But eventually, they're going to figure out that we can give those fusion reactors and fabricators to their rivals…and those nations will be able to turn out not only a million tanks but a million *drones.* And poof, there goes their numerical superiority."

"Well, that's bad news for *them,*" the President said with a shrug. "Why's it bad news for us?"

It wasn't McKinney who answered the question, though. It was Dani, and she'd gone pale.

"Because the second they figure that out, they might decide

they have nothing to lose by nuking the hell out of the US before you get the chance to cut a deal with us."

Now the President's visage matched hers, the air going out of him.

"Surely, they wouldn't be that crazy…"

"The Anguilar," I told him, shaking my head slowly, "not too long ago decided that rather than lose control of a system, they'd rather destroy an entire planet and everyone on it. They killed billions. And if we hadn't stopped them, they would have done it again."

Everyone went silent, chewing on that thought, I supposed, but our contemplation was interrupted by a knock on the door. A Secret Service agent opened the door from the outside and a younger woman with hair dyed an unnatural shade of red and fashion choices that would have looked more at home in a vintage science-fiction movie barged into the room, shoving the agent aside.

"Mr. President, we have problems. *Big* problems."

"Thanks very much for stating the obvious, Mary," Louis said. "Do you have something specific in mind or did you just come down here to make me feel bad?" He scowled as if realizing he'd forgotten to introduce her. "Ladies and gentlemen, this is Mary Stanhope, my press secretary. Mary, you probably know who they are."

"*They*," she said, making air quotes, "are a huge pain in my ass is what they are."

She looked at the active screen with the mercenary's picture still hanging on it and tapped at her own phone. A video replaced the file photo, and I recognized it immediately. It was the intersection in DC from a few hours ago, not a mile from here.

"This has been all over social media for the last three hours," she informed us, glaring at me like it was all my fault.

"From the angle," Perez said, squinting at the two crowds of demonstrators meeting at the intersection, "it had to be taken by a camera drone."

"Probably an indie journalist covering the protests," Stanhope agreed. "Keep watching."

Everything unfolded as I remembered it…until it didn't. The entire firefight, including the RPG launches, had been cut out of the video. One second, the fight in the street raged, getting closer to our vehicles…and the next, the Vanguard appeared as if out of midair, firing its pulse gun at the ground. The explosion of the RPG against the Suburban's front end had been spliced in just after, then the next missile hitting the Bronco, as if the pulse fire from the fighter had done the damage. I swallowed hard as the video cut to the crimson pulses smashing into the Wagner Group mercenaries…except from this angle, with the haze of smoke and shadows, there was no way to tell them from the demonstrators.

The firing seemed to go on a lot longer than I'd remembered during the event, which might have been manipulation as well, and once it ended, the view cut to the protestors running in terror. Then back to the Vanguard landing, zooming in on Giblet coming out with a weapon in his hand.

"It didn't happen that way," Val said, looking as if someone had slapped him in the face.

"Of course it didn't," Stanhope snapped. "And we have

footage to prove it. The problem is, *they* got theirs out *first.* No matter what, from here on out, we're going to be fighting against their narrative instead of running with our own."

She jabbed a finger at the screen, where a chubby, balding man was speaking, his words muted. But under his image were the words: LOUIS ADMINISTRATION WORKING WITH ALIEN INVADERS WHO MURDERED PEACEFUL PROTESTORS.

"By tomorrow morning," Stanhope said, "this is going to be on the news shows. I'm hoping you'll order the release of the video from the dashcams so we have something to counter it, but it's going to be an uphill battle. And half of the American people—and of Congress—wouldn't believe you if you said the sky was blue."

A lead weight took up the space where my stomach had been, and I fervently wished I hadn't eaten that sandwich.

Stanhope shook her head and, in two words, put the entire matter into perspective.

"We're screwed."

21

"I think I made a mistake," I admitted into the darkness.

"What?" Laranna whispered in my ear, teasing at my chest hair. "We've been married a year now. If I found fault with your technique, I would have told you by now."

Chuckling, I kissed her hair, running a hand down the soft skin of her back, feeling a slight film of sweat. The hotel room was warm enough that we'd kicked the comforter off the king-sized bed and I certainly didn't miss it now, after the exertion of the last half hour. We both should have been too exhausted to do anything except sleep, but that was another effect of those adrenaline dumps, and not one I minded so much as the shakes and sweats.

I wasn't even sure what time it was, since one of the first things I'd done when we'd been dropped off was to unplug the digital clock with its obnoxious red glow. We'd been given cell phones to allow the White House to contact us, but I'd turned those face-down. All I knew was that it was still dark, though I intended to be sleeping far past sunrise, thanks to the thick curtains.

"I mean," I clarified, "I think I made a mistake coming back here. This has all turned into a nightmare. They're talking about nuclear war."

"I don't know if I should feel insulted," Laranna said, turning over and leaning on her arm, her smile barely visible from the thin slice of hallway light coming under the front door, "that I wasn't enough to distract you from all that."

"I'm sorry," I told her, letting my head fall back against the pillow. "I just didn't mean for any of this to happen. I thought..." I sighed. "I don't know what I thought. Maybe that us showing up and giving everyone a common enemy would make things better, would bring everyone together."

Laranna giggled.

"And then, as Dani so eloquently puts it," she surmised, "they'd all join hands and sing Kumbaya?"

"Yeah, something like that," I admitted.

"You've been spoiled by how easy things have been so far."

"*Easy*?" I repeated. "You think the last two years have been easy?"

"Not the fighting part," she told me. "I mean the diplomacy."

"What diplomacy?"

"Exactly," Laranna agreed. "Everyone's been desperate, ready to follow anyone who gave them hope. We all knew things would be more complicated than that here. Though I hadn't expected anyone to try to kill us this soon into our visit."

"Really?" I asked, raising an eyebrow, though she probably couldn't see it. "Because it sure seemed like you were ready. The only thing you were missing was your own knife."

"The knife was all right," she allowed, clucking diffidently. "I could have gotten used to it. I wish they'd let me keep it. I feel naked without a single weapon at hand."

"You *are* naked," I reminded her. "Anyway, the government doesn't like anyone not under their control to be armed. I mean, they can't stop it, but they don't like it."

"Sounds paranoid."

"A little," I agreed. "What are we gonna do? If we can't convince them?"

"I know it's painful to think about," she said, stroking a finger down the side of my face, "but you're going to have to think about the possibility that we can't help them. That they won't allow us to. I know it's difficult to accept about your home, but you were right when you said we can't just stay here and protect them forever. The Anguilar would just attack Strada again, or Thalassia. And without the help of your world, we'd gain nothing."

"We just have to convince them." I tried to make the words hopeful, but they sounded morose even to my own ears. "We still have a chance. They have to listen. We have to make them."

"Get some sleep, my love. They won't wake us early tomorrow, but they *will* wake us. And I think the next few days are going to require all our energy."

"Not all of it, I hope," I told her, pulling her close again. "After all, this *is* the best hotel in DC. And God knows, it's the most comfortable bed we've had in the last two years. Be a shame to waste it…"

I OPENED the door at the first knock, knowing who it was.

Dani and Val stood in the hallway, which I expected. What I *didn't* expect was how they were dressed.

"Wow," I said. "You guys clean up good."

"Thanks," she said. "You two look pretty good yourselves."

Val's suit was similar to the one that had been dropped off for me yesterday afternoon, but somehow seeing the old cowboy wearing something that cost more than I'd earned in my entire life was more jarring than the feel of the fabric against my own skin. Except the tie. I hated the damned tie.

Dani, though…I realized I'd never seen her in a dress before, and the pale blue of the off-the-shoulder gown went well with her hair. I felt bad for Giblet that he wouldn't get to see her in it. And I felt good for me that I'd had the chance to see Laranna in hers. It was black and set off the pale green of her skin so perfectly that I had to think it had been designed for her. High-necked, it left her arms bare as if to let all of Congress and the TV cameras get a better look at the alien.

"Did you get a haircut, Val?" Laranna asked, stepping forward to flick a dark strand out of the man's eyes.

"They sent somebody by," Val admitted, shrugging. He

rubbed at his chin, the beard there shorter than it had been, the gray in the edges of it cut away. "Trimmed the old chin-whiskers, too." He tilted his head toward me. "What about you? You ready for this?"

"Oh, not at all," I assured him. "I don't suppose you have any experience addressing the Congress of the United States from back during the war, huh? Any advice to give?"

"The opportunity never presented itself," he said. "But if I have any advice to give, it's don't let me talk to any of these high-falutin bastards or I'd be tempted to tell them exactly what I think of them." He shook his head. "I been watchin' the TV in my room and some of the shit these people think is entertaining makes me want to puke."

I grunted agreement, though I hadn't bothered to watch TV in the spare time we'd had yesterday between fittings for clothes, haircuts, dinners served in our room and finally, coaching in how to speak to the gasbags of the House of Representatives and the Senate. I'd watched enough TV in high school and college to let me figure out where it might have gone in the last few decades.

"Hell, if you think TV's bad," Dani told him, "you should try surfing the internet."

"Aren't we supposed to be going soon?" I asked, glancing back at the time on the kitchenette's microwave. "I assume they don't want us wandering around alone."

They'd rented out the entire floor just so no one would catch a glimpse of us, and the only people we'd seen had worked for the White House. They were all gone now, though, and we were supposed to be at the Capitol in less than an hour. It galled at the part of me that still lived by the old Army rule that five minutes early was ten minutes late.

'Well," Dani said, making a face, "if we're not leaving, I'm going to go sit down. These heels are already killing me. It's freaking ridiculous that I have to wear the things."

"They're totally impractical," Laranna agreed, picking up a foot and running a finger down the long, thin heel. "Impossible to run in and a detriment to unarmed combat. Though I suppose they could be useful as improvised weapons."

"Hey, how do you think I feel about this damned tie?" I pointed out, tugging at the knot. "It feels like I'm being hanged very slowly. One of the main reasons I wanted a career in the military and not business was so I wouldn't have to wear this torture device."

"You could use it as a garrote."

I hadn't noticed Chuck walking up behind us, which bothered me. Someone had just tried to kill us a couple days ago—I should have been more alert, but I'd grown a bit too complacent huddled inside the tenth floor of the luxury hotel.

"That's what I keep telling myself, anyway," the younger Barnaby added, jerking at his own tie as if he wanted to rip it off.

No more khakis and flannel shirts for our bodyguard now. He'd dressed to blend in, his suit not as expensive as the ones they'd provided for Val and me but still well-fitted enough not to draw attention.

"You back on board the protection detail thing already?" I asked him, offering a hand. "I thought you might get a little time off after what happened."

"They offered it," he acknowledged, shaking my hand first, then the others. "I said no. Somebody wanted to kill you bad enough to go through me and my people, that means I can't let them get another shot."

"What about your team?" Dani asked him. Chuck might have been a professional but when she spoke, he seemed to notice her dress for the first time and caught himself in the middle of a double take.

"They're..." Chuck grimaced. "Well, you guys know that Master Sergeant Melendez didn't make it. Of the rest, it's looking like they'll all be okay eventually, but Hank, Cutter, Pablo, and Jake are going to be in rehab for a few months. So the whole squadron is out of action until then. But seeing as how I only had two days to get to know the last group, someone upstairs felt that the fact I have no time at all to get to know this one won't be a detriment." He nodded back down the hallway.

An average guy in an average suit strode purposefully down the hallway from the elevators, as nondescript as anyone I'd ever met. Average-length brown hair, nothing prepossessing about his brown eyes other than their watchfulness.

"Everything's clear downstairs, sir," he said, jerking a thumb back at the elevators. "Though I still say we should take the stairs."

"Sure, no problem," Dani told the new guy, pointing at her heels. "It's just ten floors. One thing first, though—we switch shoes."

The bland man smiled thinly, nodding to Dani.

"Point taken, ma'am."

"Everyone," Chuck said, "this is Gray. Gray, this is everyone. Introductions out of the way, let's get to the elevator before the other guests get pissed that we've shut them out of the system."

"Gray, huh?" Dani asked, smirking at the man as we boarded the open car. "I assume that's not your real name."

"He's a gray man," Chuck supplied, hitting the button for the parking garage. "No one notices him. Or at least that's what they told *me*." He grinned at Gray. "For all I know, they could be lying to me about their nicknames. I'm just a Ranger officer, after all."

"Well, *nearly* a Ranger officer," Gray teased as the doors slid shut. "I mean, you didn't actually get to report to your company yet. But since you did save Cutter's life and he's been my friend since the 82nd, I'll let it slide."

"*He* saved Cutter's life," Chuck corrected the older man, pointing at me. "I pulled Hank out of the line of fire."

Gray nodded to me.

"I saw the video of what you did, Mr. Travers. You and Chuck kicked ass…though not as much ass as Ms. Laranna here." The broad smile was full of white teeth, the only thing not gray about Gray. "If you weren't married, ma'am, I'd invite you out for a drink and a lesson on knife-fighting."

"Is the skill really so rare on this world?" Laranna asked. "One would think there'd be more emphasis on bladed weapons when your planet is only a few hundred years removed from using them exclusively for battle."

"Oof, Gray," Chuck said, laughing. "I think she just called us all primitives."

"Aren't we?" the older man mused. "It's hard to look at what happened a couple days ago and argue against it."

"Violence doesn't make you primitive," Laranna corrected him. "The rest of the galaxy has been at war for centuries. What might make you primitive is being stupid enough to ignore that reality."

"Save it for Congress," I told her.

"Just warming up," she promised sweetly.

The elevator was fast compared to the ones I remembered from Earth but still painfully slow compared to the ones on the *Liberator*, and absurdly, claustrophobia closed in on me in the long seconds it took for us to reach the basement garage.

"Hold up," Gray said as we stopped.

He drew a handgun—not a SIG and not plastic, for a wonder. It was a 1911 of some kind, like the old Colt .45s the Army used to issue, but smaller and fatter in the grip. It did have one of those electronic sights, though, and annoyance tugged my lips into a frown as Gray slipped out through the opening doors.

"Does *everyone* use those red dot things?" I complained to Chuck. He had his own weapon out and I motioned to it. "No one uses regular sights anymore?"

"You're too young to be a crotchety old Fudd," Chuck told me, keeping his eyes on Gray as the older man checked both ways in the concrete-walled hallway beyond the doors. "And being a Luddite isn't a good look for a guy who flew down here on a spaceship."

"We're clear," Gray reported, waving us forward.

The vehicle waiting for us was, surprise, surprise…a Suburban. Green this time.

"Do y'all have an advertising contract with Chevy or something?" I wondered, waiting for Val to join the silently brooding operator in the third row before I clambered inside, which was harder wearing the monkey suit.

"The federal government did bail out GM when they were about to go bankrupt a few years back," Dani told me. She and Laranna both joined me in the second row, neither woman willing to try to squeeze past into the rearmost seats while so formally dressed. "But I think it became the official federal government vehicle of choice a couple decades ago."

"They're nicer than a deuce and a half," Chuck told me from the front seat. Gray drove, which was a change from the last time, but what did I know about Delta Force standard operating procedures?

The engine roared as we pulled out of the parking structure, this time on our own. We passed out of the garage, the midmorning sun straining the limits of the tint on the windows, but no other cars fell into formation with us.

"No escort?" I asked him, looking around ahead and behind us.

"Not on the ground," Chuck agreed. "We got two armed Blackhawks overhead, though. And a V-22 on patrol."

I didn't ask what that was, since I figured if we needed it, we were already screwed.

"Did they ever figure out," Dani wondered, "how the Russians knew we were in those particular vehicles?"

Which was a good question and one I hadn't thought to ask. I kicked myself mentally at another indication that Laranna had been right and I had little experience in the whole diplomacy thing, much less counter-espionage.

"The working theory," Chuck replied, scowling probably not at the question but more at the implications, "is that there was a leak somewhere in the White House. Too many people knew which vehicles we were taking and where they were going. This time, the whole thing is need-to-know and, if I can believe General Gavin, they're keeping a tight lid on things this time. Knock on wood." He rapped a knuckle against the side of his head.

"Have you had the chance to talk to your dad?" I asked him, not knowing when I'd get another opportunity.

"He's doing okay." Chuck smiled. "He told me that he's going to take advantage of the time off to do some traveling to places that aren't, to quote him, full of assholes."

"That sounds exactly like the George I know," I said, laughing.

The laughter died as we turned onto Pennsylvania Avenue. Stuck in our hotel room, avoiding watching the news, I hadn't seen the images before, but what had been a pleasant winter scene on our initial drive into the city had turned into something from a dystopian future. The sidewalks were cordoned off by barriers and cones, with armored vehicles at every intersection manned by police tactical units carrying automatic weapons.

"Holy shit," Dani murmured.

"Yeah," Chuck agreed. The rest of his team hadn't said a

word since we'd begun the drive, a lot less talkative than the crew we'd ridden with before the attack. And maybe they had reason to be. "Officially, it's because of the risk that there might be more terrorists in the area, but I think the real reason is them."

He tapped a finger against the right-side window and I followed it up the hill to the demonstrators. There'd been thousands before. Now, there were *hundreds* of thousands. On both sides of the road. And as we drew closer to the capitol dome, the iconic symbol of the American government that I'd known since my childhood, a shining city on a hill, I heard them chanting. So loud that it made the crowds of two days ago seem like a quiet conversation between friends.

The same slogans, though this time throngs of police and what I thought might be national guardsmen kept the two groups a couple hundred yards apart. Passing by, I saw a half a dozen people try to get past the police lines and wind up on the ground, handcuffed and taken away to a waiting van.

"Where the hell are all these people *coming* from?" I whispered.

"Three or four states away," Chuck told me. "In chartered buses. We're containing them as best we can, but there's no way to arrest a hundred thousand people. I hope you've got some good arguments for Congress, Charlie. You're going to need them."

22

"EVERYONE," Laranna said softly in my ear, "is staring at me."

"Well, you're green," I told her, shrugging, then stifling a yelp at the poke she gave me in the ribs.

She was right, of course. They tried not to be obvious about it in most cases, but the glances kept coming, and the older the attendee, the more likely they'd be gawking like a customer in an old-time freak show. Not a one of them had talked to us as we were seated, though maybe that was because of Chuck and his security detail. I hadn't asked him if Congress-critters were allowed to approach us, but they apparently assumed they weren't.

What was worse, we were up in the front near the dais and not only did that mean everyone had a great view of us, it also gave me a taste of what was coming when I had to get up and speak in front of what had to be over six hundred people. Four hundred thirty-five representatives, a hundred senators and however many guards, police, Secret Service, etc…not counting the President's staff.

The crowd stirred and mumbled as a man ascended the speaker's platform and the sergeant at arms called the House to order, but I barely heard the words, still thinking about the speech I'd rehearsed. I knew how it would go, the Speaker introducing the President and the President delivering his load of crap about how this was America's finest hour, and everything was a *wah-wah-wah* like Charlie Brown's teacher in my head because my thoughts drowned out even his voice.

I knew what he was going to say, anyway, because our handlers had given us a copy yesterday. It was well-written, and I suppose well-delivered, though Louis didn't impress me much as an orator, not after Reagan and the movie clips I'd seen of Kennedy. Maybe the art had passed this generation by or maybe it was just this particular stiff but if I was any judge, he'd have trouble inspiring a starving man to eat a cheeseburger. Luckily, he had visual aids, video and photos we'd provided for him of the Anguilar, their cruisers, their fighters, as well as the *Liberator* and Vanguard fighters. Images of the Strada, the Copperell, the Peboktan, the Krill. And Lenny. That one got the biggest reaction and more than one Congress-critter mentioned *The Terminator*.

"…and rather than hear all the details from me," President Louis finished before I'd even gotten to the end of going over my own prepared speech, "I should allow you to hear it from those who brought us these tidings, these wonders…and this warning. First, and this *is* a first in all the history of this nation, in all the history of humanity, allow me to present to this august body of America's leaders a powerful leader, a great warrior who demonstrated her valor in battle when her people were ruthlessly attacked by terrorists sent in what I believe was an assassination attempt by the Russian government. She saved them by taking out a Wagner Group mercenary who was about to kill American soldiers of her bodyguard with a rocket launcher…while she was armed only with a knife." Louis beamed as if he'd watched the scene in an action movie, which bugged me. For us, it hadn't been a movie, it had been too damned close to death. "She is the first representative of an alien race to visit this world. Ms. Laranna would you please come forward and address the combined House and Senate of the United States of America?"

This had been, so I'd had it explained to me, a great departure from the usual way of doing things, allowing a foreign leader to address Congress. It had taken all the political capital the President could afford to expend to get the Speaker and the President of the Senate to agree to it, though the footage the White House had released of Laranna knifing the RPG gunner had undoubtedly helped the cause. Still there was a murmur through the assembled collection of self-important windbags that called itself the best the country had to offer.

Laranna gave my hand a squeeze and winked as she stood, and I pushed my anxiety aside to appreciate the view as she took that dress up the stairs to the dais.

"Put your tongue back in your head, Charlie," Val advised, leaning over to whisper in my ear. "You get to go home to her every day."

"And don't think I'm not grateful," I murmured back to him.

Laranna took a moment to compose herself, her eyes flickering downward to the notes left for her, then back up to the teleprompter where they were projected. She looked away from the cheats, needing neither.

"I am," she said, "Laranna, a warrior of the Strada. I've walked dozens of worlds, fought as many battles, and braved the worst that pirates, raiders, bounty hunters, and the Anguilar Empire could throw at us to stand before you today. My world, Strada, spent decades under the heel of the Anguilar while I slumbered in stasis, unknowing, forgotten. They'd given up hope, and when I discovered how long I'd slept, I did as well. I thought my home lost, and it very nearly was. Our people had been slaughtered, enslaved, the ones allowed to remain in their homes forced to turn over half of what food they could grow, forced to inform on their own people, to turn anyone who dared speak of resisting over to the Anguilar. The alternative was to court destruction, to invite orbital and aerial bombardment by Anguilar cruisers and fighters that would destroy those few cities the conquerors had allowed to stand."

The murmurs and whispers had fallen silent at her voice, and she leaned forward over the platform as if looking every one of them in the eye.

"And each day, we grew weaker, our men and young women dying in the mines or wasting away with endless labor in the fields, our hope dying with them. Only one tribe resisted, *my* tribe, the remnants of my home city, and they were driven into the deep forests, terrified to take any action which might lead the Anguilar back to them."

She smiled.

"I was determined to help them. Perhaps so determined that it drove me to recklessness, and I was captured in an attempt to steal weapons from the Anguilar to fight for my world. That might have been the end of this tale…*should* have been, for I had no right to expect help. But Charlie Travers, a man from Earth, from this nation you call the United States, came to my aid anyway, knowing the danger, knowing how little chance of success there was. He and the others, my friends, my *family* now, risked everything to free my world both out of love for me and out of love for the notion of liberty, out of the hope that all intelligent beings in this galaxy should be free to rule themselves, to keep the fruits of their labor. To raise their children and tend their land and live free from the threat of destruction."

Laranna shrugged.

"And we won. Thanks to Charlie and the others, we freed my world, forced the Anguilar to retreat from it. Again, all this might have ended there. We'd accomplished more than we had any right to imagine we could and the smart thing to do would have been to, as you say, quit while we were ahead. But that isn't how Charlie Travers thinks. Instead, Charlie and I and Gib and the rest of our friends committed to freeing other worlds, to spreading Strada's newfound liberty across the stars, to the other worlds oppressed and enslaved by these invaders from outside our galaxy." She'd been sweeping the crowd with her gaze, but now her eyes met mine. "It's why I came to respect, to admire, and then to love him, because we shared a passion for justice, an inability to look away from the work that needed to be done."

The words combined with that dress just melted me and if it weren't for the expensive suit holding me together, I would have slumped in the chair, nothing left of me but a big smile.

"If I leave you with nothing else, if you learn nothing else from my words today, I'd like to impress on you something that will run counter to your beliefs, your instincts, the way you were raised. You've thought your entire lives when you looked up at the night sky that the stars were impossibly distant. That this galaxy was monstrously huge, an academic concern good only for the beauty they provided. I was not born with this misapprehension. My people never had the luxury of the conceit that what happened around those distant stars didn't affect them. Now, neither will yours. You may think this is a bad thing, a loss of innocence, but in other ways, it's a source of hope. You can look at those stars and know they're not stark and lifeless, not so distant. You can know that the people there once had the same problems you do now, and you can trust in the fact that there are solutions to them…more than one world can produce on their own. You can rest, comfortable in the fact that you will walk among those other worlds someday, that it *is* possible. But these truths hold less comfortable ones, the fact that you can no longer afford to ignore those distant specks of light. That their beauty holds danger, and that danger is coming here."

So far, she'd kept to the script, to the speech as we'd agreed to it yesterday, but I knew the look in her eyes as she turned her attention back to the audience, guessed what was coming.

"It would have been easy for us to ignore those dangers. We have our own war to fight and the possibility that Earth will be a front in it might have been a purely academic notion, regrettable yet unavoidable."

President Louis frowned, probably reading the speech written for her and noticing she'd strayed, but before he or any of his handlers could try to signal Laranna, she finished up quickly.

"But we all love Charlie. For me, he is my life-mate, for the others, family. And Charlie loves this world. We are only here because we don't wish for him the pain of losing his home as some of us lost ours. Keep that in mind as you listen to him. None of us need to be here and the resistance doesn't need Earth. We can win our war without you. You can't win yours without us."

Laranna bowed her head slightly.

"Thank you for allowing me to address you today. May the gods grant you wisdom in your decision."

The President and most of his party stood immediately as Laranna stepped down from the podium, their applause drowning out any of the murmurings of doubt that might have arisen at her final words. She sat back down beside me and I kissed her, ignoring the cameras and the staring politicians.

"You did great."

"Are you nuts?" Mary Stanhope hissed, leaning down from the seat behind us. "You're basically telling them you'll abandon them if they vote the wrong way!"

"Because that's exactly what's going to happen," Dani snapped back at her, teeth bared in a snarl. "And maybe someone needs to show these people a stick before we offer all the carrots."

"Thank you, Ms. Laranna," President Louis said, retaking the podium, still applauding. "Those are hard truths but ones we have to hear, ones that won't change just because we don't want to accept them."

Well, at least Louis had the ability to think a little on his feet. Either that or he had speechwriters giving him tips via an earbud like a modern version of Cyrano de Bergerac.

"But now, I would like to present to you the young man who we have to thank for the chance to become part of the galactic community, the man who's come to us with gifts of incredible technologies which have the potential to change the world, to improve the lives of billions of people. Please join me in welcoming a fine young American, Charles Travers."

I buttoned my jacket as I rose, grateful that it at least gave my hands something to do besides shaking uncontrollably. I'd had dozens if not hundreds of people try to kill me these last two years and I'd never been more nervous than I was when I shook President Louis' hand and stepped behind that podium.

The applause didn't help, both because it set up an expectation I didn't know if I could meet and because it was very clearly split along party lines. These people had no idea who I was, they just knew that I was the one responsible for all the crazy demonstrators outside and the influx of calls and emails they were getting from their constituents.

"Mr. President," I said, "Mr. Speaker, esteemed members of

the House and Senate, it's my honor and privilege to be invited to speak to you today."

Not to mention my recurring nightmare. But I didn't say that. Not that I had to with the dirty look the Speaker gave me. He was a middle-aged man, probably thirty years younger than the President, and from the briefing I'd been given, wasn't at all crazy about the idea of the United States getting involved in any war, much less an interstellar one. I couldn't blame him for that, but I still had a job to do.

At least I didn't have to waste time explaining the entire situation, from Lenny to the Kamerians to the Anguilar, because the President had summarized it all in his speech. That just left me with the hard part—convincing all these skeptical politicians that any of it was true.

"Some of you may have heard my story, but I don't know if you believe it. That's forgivable because sometimes, I don't believe it myself."

I was talking too loud and Stanhope signaled me from the third row to bring it down a notch. Sucking in a deep breath, I tried to bring my volume and my heart rate under control and not look at individual faces in the audience, instead softening my focus and letting them all merge into an indistinguishable blur. Except for Laranna. I focused on her and talked to her specifically.

"I'm just a kid from Columbus, Ohio. I was born to a normal family, and if at the time I thought I had special problems that no one else had to deal with, now I understand that my life wasn't any harder than most kids my age. I played sports, ran track and cross-country, listened to music, hung out with my friends. I went to college in Florida because I wanted to get away from home, got an Army ROTC scholarship to pay for it. I wanted a career in the military both because I felt I'd be good at it and because I wanted to be part of something bigger, a greater purpose." I laughed softly. "I think I've found that."

Laranna nodded encouragement and I went on.

"I don't look it, thanks to the suspended animation technology on the ship that took me away from here, but I was born in the mid-1960s, early enough that I remember watching the moon landings on TV. Early enough that I was in high school when the first space shuttle launched. Early enough that once upon a time, we all believed that by the 2020s, there'd be humans on Mars, that nothing would stop us from reaching for the stars. I returned to see a lot of technological improvements since the 1980s, but I also found a world where the American government had gotten out of the business of space exploration. It's considered too expensive, not worth the investment. There are more important things happening here on Earth that demand your money and attention. I get that. But I think it was shortsighted before, and now, with what you know, it's irrational."

A screen set up on the wall showed files from the packet Lenny had sent down with me, showing schematics for a space drive using fusion power.

"With the technology we've given to you, even if you reject our offer and we leave this place, you're going to be a spacefaring civilization in years, not decades. You'll have the capability to bring in resources from the rest of the Solar System, build colonies on other planets…even do things that sound crazy, impossible, like terraforming Mars and mining the atmosphere of Jupiter. America can lead the way, can turn this world into a utopia where no one has to do without, where no one has to go hungry, where no one in any country has to lack for clothing or shelter or power. That can be your future, the one I imagined when I was a kid in kindergarten watching the first men walk on the moon. And I'd love to see that happen."

My grim frown didn't need to be rehearsed or faked. It came from the heart.

"But it won't last. Because the Anguilar know where you are. They've always known. You wonder why this world hasn't been openly visited by aliens before, if they're so prolific, if intelligent life exists throughout this galaxy. It's because we didn't matter. Because the last time anyone except the Creators bothered to check on us, we were hopelessly primitive, a few hundred million of us waving around swords and thinking we'd done something monumental if we sailed a ship out of the sight of land. The Creators knew better—they came and got me, after all." And thank God I didn't have to explain the Creators to them. The President hadn't told them everything in his speech, but the White House had released a press briefing explaining the reason why alien life was so similar to our own and if the politicians I addressed hadn't bothered to read it, then to hell with them.

"But they weren't about to tell anyone else, and the Anguilar were too busy conquering the civilized parts of the galaxy to go look for themselves. That's changed now and it's partly my fault."

There was no hiding the mumbling and chatter at that admission and a couple of the more boisterous demagogues yelled something about how we were forcing them into war. I ignored them.

"When the Anguilar could expand their resource base just by invading another world and taking their produce or by demanding a greater percentage of the food production from a planet they already controlled, they were happy with what they had. But when we started taking back the worlds they'd enslaved, they started getting desperate. They not only have to feed their people, they need a monopoly on the food supply to keep a stranglehold on the populations they already control. And they're not about to put their own people out into the fields growing food. They need them to lead their military, to build their warships. And if they stop building those warships and growing their military, they know we'll roll them up even faster." I shrugged, adlibbing even though I'd been instructed not to. "I suppose if they were inclined to peace overtures, this would be the perfect time for them to offer to give back some of the worlds and let the populations resettle from others in exchange for a cease-fire, but that would require them to consider anyone else as real people. Which they don't. We're nothing but assets and liabilities to them, either potential subjects or potential obstacles."

Stanhope glowered at me and I got back on script.

"They know you're here now, and thanks to the mercenaries they hired to hunt us down, they also know how far the Earth has come since the last time they surveyed it. Eight billion people."

I looked around and made the mistake of meeting the stares of some of the people in the audience. A younger woman, mid-thirties at the most, with a long, sullen face and dull eyes. A man who had to be in his eighties and who I thought had fallen asleep. A bald, stern man who was either angry at me or possibly life, his arms crossed over his chest. Skepticism on some faces, wrath on others, and yet…some faces held utter awe and wonder, their thoughts written across them. *That I could live to see this…* It was in those who I put my hopes.

"Eight billion people," I repeated, "and yet you feed them all. Anyone who goes hungry does so because the food can't get to them, not because there's food lacking. Enough food for the Anguilar to use it to control a dozen subject worlds, that's how they see you. A world that can't defend itself. That's how they see you. That's what you are…now. But if you join with us, if you help us strike them first, keep them dancing back and forth to defend what they hold, they won't have the opportunity to marshal their forces against Earth. America will stay as it's always been, defended by distance, by oceans, but this time oceans of stars. You'll send your sons and daughters into harm's way as you always have, to guard what they leave behind,"

I hesitated. This wasn't in the speech they'd written, but it came from my heart and to hell with them if they didn't like it.

"Like the words of the last verse of the 'Star-Spangled Banner,' the verse everyone forgets exists. *O thus be it ever when free men shall stand…between their loved home and the war's desolation.* That's where I've been. It's where I'll return once I leave here. If you won't fight with us, we'll keep up the fight without you. I'll do the best I can to make sure the Anguilar are too busy with me to come to you. But I can't guarantee that it'll be enough. I can't guarantee that I can keep you safe. Only you can do that. We'll provide the transport, we'll help you build the weapons. But only you can defend this land. Only you can make the decision." I offered them a smile, for all it was worth. "And the star-spangled banner in triumph shall wave o'er the land of the free and the home of the brave."

23

"I THOUGHT it was a damned good speech," Val offered, saluting me with his shot glass before he gulped it down.

Our floor of the hotel had a bar, though we hadn't frequented it the last two days, having too much to do. But we'd done it. There was nothing else to be said, no other hand to be played. Now we could only wait. So, we might as well drink while we were doing it, particularly when the bill went to the federal government.

No bartender…I suppose the security detail hadn't trusted any to be on the floor with us. But it had come fully stocked and beautifully decorated, with wood paneling and leather seats, large enough to accommodate the entire floor and a couple others besides, yet empty except for the four of us.

"It was a little old-fashioned," Dani allowed, tilting the bottle of vodka to refill her own glass, squinting as she did, as if she saw two of the glasses and was trying to split the difference. "I liked it, but you gotta remember the crowd you're dealing with. Half these people don't believe in the country or the government they're supposed to be running. They not only didn't recognize the 'Star-Spangled Banner,' they probably consider it fascist or imperialist or something." She took the shot without hesitating, then frowned at the glass. "There must be something wrong with this vodka. My lips are going numb."

"You Earth people," Laranna declared, sipping from her glass like it was bourbon, "can't handle your liquor."

"That's disgusting," I told her. "I think Strada must be related to the Russians somehow. This is how you drink vodka." I took the shot in one gulp and made a face. "If you have to drink it at all."

"It's not that bad," Val opined, shrugging, peering into the clear liquid, sloshing it around his glass. "Better than what we used to drink in the bars in cow towns. That stuff'd rot the lining of your stomach right out. When's this vote, anyway?"

"Tonight," I sighed, leaning back against the bar, the stool creaking beneath me. "Emergency session of both houses. They'll stay until they vote."

"And what exactly are they voting on?" He shook his head. "I mean, I've never been clear on that part."

"To authorize the military to send troops back with us for familiarization and training. It's a baby step, so hopefully it won't get too much pushback."

"Have any of you been watching the news?" Dani asked, eyes

narrowing as she stared at me like I'd just declared the sky was green.

"I've done my best to avoid it," I admitted.

"Yeah, well, things are getting ugly." She got up from her stool and fumbled around behind the bar, finding a remote control and pointing it at the small, flat-screen TV located above the fountain.

It popped to life on some kind of show about real estate and she cursed softly.

"I'm a freelance hamster trainer," Dani mocked, "and my wife is a part-time harmonic tuner. Our house budget is three point two million dollars."

She switched through the channels until she came across a news channel…one of, like, half a dozen I'd seen the last time I'd flipped through the menu on a modern TV.

"I still can't believe," I murmured, "that there are channels that have nothing but the news all day, every day. How the hell can they find enough news to fill all those hours?"

"They make it up, mostly," Dani admitted. "Now shut up and listen."

It was a commercial for an erectile dysfunction drug, and there sure seemed to be a lot of those commercials. I wondered if the problem had increased over the last three decades or if people just didn't talk about it back in my day. I kind of wished they *still* didn't talk about it. Thankfully, it didn't last long, but when the news programming returned, there was five minutes of celebrity gossip about some singer who looked like he was twelve years old dating an actress a foot taller than him before they finally switched to the actual news anchor.

The announcer was a slender, handsome man with salt-and-pepper hair and a too-smooth voice, though the images being shown behind him were not smooth at all. I couldn't tell the city, but it looked European. The violence was universal, could have come from news reports I remembered of the revolution in Tehran or the riots in Los Angeles and Detroit. No demonstrations, no picketing, just naked panic and destruction. Fires raged out of control, consuming businesses whose signs I couldn't quite make out, not even what language they were in, and past them surged crowds of tens of thousands.

"The scenes you're seeing," the anchor told us in his dulcet tones, "are happening live in Paris as crowds of protestors have begun setting fires and destroying homes and businesses. The protests began a few hours ago after the testimony in a special joint session of the American Congress by Charles Travers and the extraterrestrial Laranna, representatives of the so-called resistance against the alleged threat of the Anguilar."

The image shifted from the violence to images of Laranna and I and, on the other half of the screen, one of the pictures we'd provided of an Anguilar officer, his face lean and cruel, his eyes black and dead.

"The existence of extraterrestrials has been confirmed by independent labs who've analyzed genetic material from both Laranna and the Varnell pilot called Giblet and reported that although their DNA is similar to humans, it's not identical and couldn't have been produced by our current technology. There have also been independent confirmations of the capabilities of their spacecraft via analysis of the videos taken in Chattanooga and Washington DC. However, we have nothing but the word of Travers and his friends that this oppressive alien empire exists or that their intentions toward Earth are hostile."

"This entire situation is unacceptable to me." It was the horse-faced woman I'd noticed during my speech, standing at a podium beside three others I didn't recognize, clustered around her while she did the talking to the gathered reporters. "We're being asked to declare war against another sentient species with no proof that they mean us harm, no proof that they aren't amenable to diplomatic negotiations."

"The concerns of members of both parties are noted," Mary Stanhope said, speaking from a different setting, cut in with the rest of the recordings as if she were responding to horse-face. "However, we're not asking for a declaration of war against anyone and the assertion that we are is misleading to the American public. This is merely a vote to move forward with an agreement in principle for a mutual defense treaty with the resistance. As part of this process, we would, of course, send representatives to assess the situation with the Anguilar in person, to be transported to the front lines by the resistance. No hostilities would be declared, and no American troops would be committed until and unless our analysis of the conflict matches what they've told us. But it would be irresponsible to allow this opportunity to pass without at least investigating it."

"How would you respond to the concerns of other nations, including our allies," an unseen reporter asked, "that the United

States is risking involving the entire Earth in an extraterrestrial conflict without consulting the United Nations or even NATO?"

"Again, we're only talking about preliminary investigations into the situation..." Stanhope began, but the news anchor cut the clip off.

"Sources within the French and British government have told us that they've been briefed on the situation by the Louis administration but haven't been asked to advise on the negotiations with the resistance..."

Dani shut the television off and tossed the remote down with a snort.

"Declaration of war. Like anyone would ask for that yet. They haven't even met a real Anguilar! But what do they think is gonna happen if they vote this down? Do they think this all just goes away? That everyone's going to forget we exist?"

"They're scared," Laranna said. "Who can blame them?"

"This hasn't gone the way I thought it would," I lamented, wondering if I should get another drink. I *needed* one, but that didn't mean I should get one. "But I don't know what else we could have done. Maybe we should have kidnapped the President and taken him out to Copperell and rubbed his damned nose in it."

"Maybe there *was* no good way to do this," Laranna said. She slid out of her seat and slipped an arm around my shoulder, leaning her head against mine. "Maybe this is the best we could do. We've told them the truth, given them as much help as they'll let us. We may just have to hope it's enough."

"It won't be," I insisted sullenly. Maybe it was the vodka, but darkness had settled over my mood like a thunder cloud on a midsummer afternoon in Florida. "It'd take decades for them to construct useful defenses even if they started working on them tomorrow. Just building a fusion reactor would take years without us bringing in Peboktan to help them."

"Let's not get all down already," Val insisted. "The vote hasn't happened yet."

"Yeah," Dani agreed. "I mean, there's always backroom deals going on in politics. The President could be busy making phone calls to everyone, having secret meetings."

I nodded. She was right.

"How late are we gonna wait up for them?" Val asked, yawning, only remembering to cover his mouth at the last second.

"It's almost midnight," Dani announced, checking her cell phone. We'd each been given one by the security detail, though I think it was more for them to be able to keep track of us than for our benefit. "I feel like an old lady going to bed this early." She nodded at the TV. "Usually, the debate would be televised, but I checked earlier. It's blacked out for security reasons. Guess they haven't shared everything with the public yet." She frowned as if thinking of something, then pointed to her phone and put it down on the bar, motioned in a "gimme" gesture to all of us.

I squinted at her doubtfully, but pulled my own cell out and handed it to her. She set it beside her own and then Laranna and Val got the idea and did the same. Dani switched the TV back on with the remote and turned the volume up near maximum, blaring yet another drug commercial out at full blast, and I winced, covering my ears.

Dani moved to the doorway of the bar, motioned for us to follow.

"What's the deal?" Val started to ask, but she shushed him and waved at the hallway.

Once we'd joined her a few steps down from the entrance, away from any doors or windows, Dani pulled us into a huddle and whispered so softly I could barely hear her.

"Cell phones can be bugged," she informed us, "and we need to have a private conversation. Laranna, do you still have your comm?"

Laranna didn't speak, taking Dani's words to heart, just held up the device, even smaller than the cell phones.

"We need to decide," Dani went on, "whether we trust the government to not do something stupid if the vote goes bad. They've already kidnapped us twice."

"I think the first time was technically a legal arrest," I pointed out. "Since you disappeared from a police station after what was officially reported as a terrorist attack."

Dani gave me a dirty look and I shrugged, fell silent.

"Why would they make a move against us?" Val cut in, shaking his head. And talking too loud. He'd spent the last few years around high technology, but he had yet to develop the paranoia of anyone who grew up with the idea of surveillance equipment. "After all, everyone knows about us, they can't think they can make it all go away just by making us disappear."

"They also know we have air support available that they can't counter," Laranna pointed out. "They've seen what a Vanguard fighter can do, and we told them that the *Liberator* is only a few minutes from orbit if we need her."

"Because of what they're afraid we might do if they say no," Dani told them. "I don't think you guys are looking at it from their point of view."

"And what might we do?" Val asked, throwing up his hands. But the answer came to me as if Dani's paranoia was catching.

"We might go to the Russians. Or the Chinese."

"Or the French," Dani agreed, nodding her approval. "Or the Iranians. You and I know we aren't going to do that, but would that asshole Donovan believe it? Would that little, bald CIA ferret?"

"There's not much we can do unless you want to leave now," I said after a moment's consideration, then glanced around. "And I sure as hell hope they don't have cameras looking at us right now because this looks more like a group hug than a conspiracy cabal."

A loud ping sounded from down the hallway and we spread out automatically, my hand reaching for a gun I wasn't carrying. It was the elevator. I looked to the others, found them staring at me, waiting. Sucking down a deep breath, I settled myself and walked toward the opening doors.

Chuck was there, which I expected…and behind him was Parker Donovan, which I had *not*. The National Security Advisor looked like he hadn't slept in three days, or if he had, it had been in his rumpled, wrinkled suit, the haggard exhaustion dragging his features down into a hound-dog sadness.

"Kinda late for a visit, Mr. Donovan," I said, nodding to the man.

"Mr. Travers, Laranna, Mr. McKee, Ms. Campling," he said, looking each of us in the eye as if this were a formal occasion… or we were being arrested. "Before I get to the reason I'm here, I just wanted to tell you all that I apologize for what happened when you first came to me. I didn't know your true intentions and I could tell that I was under some sort of influence from your friend Giblet. I acted hastily and possibly illegally. Given what I know now, I regret it."

Dani didn't look like she wanted to accept the apology, so I did it for her since I was supposed to be the leader, and thus, obligated to act more maturely than I would have been inclined.

"Thank you, Mr. Donovan," I told him, doing my best impression of sincerity. "I appreciate you telling us that and I understand how things were a bit…confused."

"You didn't come all the way here for that," Dani accused, not at all following the tone I'd tried to set. "What's wrong?"

"Perhaps we should sit down," Donovan suggested, but Dani was already shaking her head.

"That always means bad news and I'd rather take bad news on my feet."

"Very well." The National Security Advisor sighed. "The measure failed in both houses."

"Shit," I hissed, fists clenched. I wanted to punch something, but the walls looked expensive. "By how much?"

"Along party lines except for a couple defectors each way," Donovan replied, spreading his hands helplessly. "We're not giving up. We're trying to call for formal hearings…but that'd mean you'd all have to testify in front of House and Senate subcommittees and it could take weeks, if not months."

"There's no way we can stay here that long," I told him immediately. "We're a significant chunk of the resistance leadership, not to mention we brought half the Vanguard fighters and one of our only five Liberator ships with us. We can make cargo and personnel runs here on the regular, but weeks or months isn't going to happen."

"Is there nothing that can be done sooner?" Laranna asked.

"We can send certain…observers with you, perhaps," Donovan acknowledged. "For a limited time. They wouldn't be authorized to carry out any military operations, they could only advise, teach, report back, that sort of thing. Men like Captain Barnaby and his team, for example." He nodded to Chuck, who grinned broadly.

"If you're talking about sending me up in a spaceship, sir," Chuck enthused, "let me tell you right now, I volunteer. Who in their right mind wouldn't wanna be the first American to go to the stars?"

"Hey now, fella," Val said with a scowl, "I think I got you beat by about a hundred and fifty years."

"You know what I mean," Chuck insisted, waving it away.

"I'll have to run it by the President," Donovan warned him. "But I think it goes without saying that we'd probably be better off if we had some official eyes on the situation out there."

"So you wouldn't have to just go by our say-so," Val assumed.

"Exactly. I also wanted to make sure you hadn't…decided on a backup plan." Donovan arched an eyebrow. "Have you?"

I shared an "I told you so" look with Dani before I responded.

"We're not planning on making the same offer to the Russians or anyone else," I assured him. "It wouldn't work even if we wanted to do it. No other nation has a military large and technologically advanced enough to do any good against the Anguilar."

That had been Dani's assertion and Lenny had confirmed it once he'd read the entire internet and sifted through the obviously false parts. China and Russia had more raw manpower but neither nation's military was well-organized or well-trained enough to be anything except cannon fodder against the ground forces of the enemy. Which might have served its own purpose, but I wasn't about to reward either of those governments for wasting the lives of their soldiers.

"Well, that's something, at least." Donovan sighed. "I was hoping I could bring better news. But looking on the bright side, we'd have had to independently confirm this whole thing anyway, and it's possible to make certain preparations in case the vote goes our way, but…" His eyes took on the pained expression again. "I don't know how we're going to be able to get this passed without you here to be the face of it. The longer you're gone, the longer this is out of the public eye, the less people are going to believe it. If there are people out there who won't believe that the Earth is round, imagine how easy it'll be for them to convince themselves that this is all some government conspiracy."

"I get that," I admitted, "but maybe…"

The beeping startled me, not because I hadn't heard it before but because it seemed out of place here. It was Laranna's comm. I stared at it right along with everyone else, their wide-eyed expressions likely matching my own. We'd left strict instructions for Lenny and the others to wait for us to contact them, to not call us because it might be an unwelcome reminder to the people we were trying to convince we were allies that there were armed ships floating above them.

Laranna pushed the button on the side of the device to accept the call, taking it over the speaker so we could all hear it.

"Laranna here."

"It's Gib." His voice was small and distant over the speaker. "Sorry to interrupt, but playing footsie with the natives is going to have to wait. I just got a transmission from Lenny to relay to you...he couldn't reach you from his current position."

"What is it, Gib?" Dani asked, leaning over the comm.

"Sensors just detected hyperdrive transitions out past the orbit of your fourth planet."

"Mars," I supplied automatically, trying to push down the panic from what I knew this meant, waiting until I got the facts. "How many and what's the drive signature?"

"They're Anguilar cruisers, Charlie. A dozen of them. And they're heading straight for Earth."

24

"Yes, sir!" Donovan snapped, sounding from this side of the conversation as if he was losing his patience with the Commander in Chief. Beads of sweat trickled down the older man's forehead and a muscle twitched in his cheek as if he'd woken from a nightmare only to find himself engulfed in yet another. "Twelve. One-two. Capital ships all inbound from Mars orbit."

He put a hand over the phone's speaker and glanced at me as we headed down in the elevator, the four of us, the National Security Advisor, and Chuck.

"What's their ETA?"

I passed the question over the comm to Gib, who passed it to Lenny and by the time we got a response, the elevator was already opening at the lobby. Not the parking garage this time, though that had caused a lot of heartburn with the security team, but there was no time for White House meetings or motorcades.

"They *could* get here in hours," I told him, "but they're holding position right now, probably running scans. Once they figure out you don't have any orbital defenses, they can jump in closer and then it's minutes, not hours."

Gray and the rest of the security team waited for us in the lobby…and no one else. Not that I expected a crowd of people here after midnight, but even the front desk clerks had been chased away and I wondered how they felt about that. I understood why they'd left though. Gray and the others were in full battle rattle, body armor, helmets, night vision, and those M16 style carbines with all the high-tech crap hanging off of them. Six of them, not counting Chuck, which I'd come to understand was the standard Delta Force team. There'd been two teams on the detail before when we'd been attacked, but since we'd gone lower profile since then, we were down to one.

"Out in the parking lot, boys," Chuck said, motioning at the revolving doors. "Clear an LZ and don't let any vehicles pull in."

Gray and the Delta team rushed out into the deep of the night and Chuck held us in the lobby for a few seconds with a clenched fist held in the air until he got a report over his ear bud and waved us forward. He lacked the body armor and carbine, but he did have his sidearm drawn and I envied him the luxury. The Anguilar wouldn't be here yet but there was still the possibility of the Russians.

A cold wind slapped me in the face the second I stepped

through the door, as big of a wakeup call as the one Giblet had delivered to us, none of the buzz remaining from the vodka, though I doubted any of us would pass a breathalyzer test. Luckily, we didn't have to drive.

"Gib's flying cover," Laranna reported, looking up into the night sky, the stars drowned out by the city lights and the haze of clouds.

I followed her gaze and a few snowflakes teased at my cheek with a last kiss of the Washington winter before a familiar green glow shone down through the haze. I'd seen its like for the first time two years ago as my subjective timeline ran, thirty-seven by the clocks here on Earth. It had changed everything for me, taken my life on a different path and I wondered if the same symbol in the sky tonight meant a different life for everyone on the planet.

For better or for worse.

The shuttle descended almost soundlessly. Not quite, not like I'd imagined so long ago, on that night walk in central Florida back in 1987. There was a whoosh I hadn't noticed back then, the landing jets taking her down with the help of the gravity-resist field as the almost-a-flying-saucer landed between the luxury cars and rentals without so much as scratching their paint.

Donovan gasped at the sight of her, as if he hadn't really believed until now, not even after watching the videos from Chattanooga and the battle at the intersection. Doubting Thomas, not truly accepting the miracle until he could put his finger through the nail holes in Jesus's hands.

"Mr. President," he said, clearing his throat as if he couldn't speak at first, "their spacecraft has landed. They're heading back to their ship."

The hatch opened, the steps folding out and Donovan met my eyes, his face thrown into sharp relief by the glare and shadows of the parking lot.

"The President wants to know what your intentions are, Mr. Travers."

I looked to Dani, Val, Chuck. Humans like me with ties not just to this world but to this country, all with a sense of duty that had led them to be cops or soldiers…or both. And then Laranna, whose only link to this world was me, yet I knew she'd gladly fight to the death to protect this place if I ordered it. They all would, all the hundreds on the *Liberator*, but did I have the right to ask?

As if reading my thoughts, Laranna leaned close and whispered the answer in my ear.

"It's why we came, Charlie."

I nodded.

"We're going to defend this planet, Mr. Donovan. No matter what the cost."

"Then I'm going with you," Chuck declared, his stance, his expression daring me to tell him he couldn't. "My job's to keep you safe and no one's countermanded that order yet."

"The hell with that," Clay said, stepping up beside the officer. "We're all going. If there's fighting to be done, I figure you guys are going to be doing it before anyone down here."

I shrugged at Donovan.

"You wanted observers. This is about as close to the Anguilar as anyone's going to get." Turning back to Chuck, I sighed. "You'd better not make me regret this. If anything happens to you, your dad's never going to speak to me again."

"My dad," Chuck shot back, stepping through the hatch into the lander, "knows what it means to be a soldier." He paused and looked back at me, up at the cockpit. "There's an orange guy flying this bird."

"Don't be speciesist, sir," Gray told him, squeezing by. "The lady out there's green but I ain't holding it against her."

"Talk to me, Lenny," I said, striding onto the bridge with Laranna at my side, Dani and Chuck close behind. "What're those assholes doing?"

The ride up had taken over an hour and by the end, I'd been antsy enough to crawl right out of my skin, but Gib had insisted that the situation was stable all the way up to Lunar orbit and the docking with the *Liberator*.

I hadn't been so keyed up that I'd missed the reaction of Chuck and the Delta Force team, though. Chuck had tried to keep from gawking like a tourist in New York City but hadn't been able to manage it. His eyes had been wide, jaw slack as we'd ascended through the atmosphere, and once we'd reached the Moon, circling around to its dark side to find the floating, metal mountain that was the former Kamerian Zoo Ship, the former Creator warship, he'd gone speechless.

The Delta operators were hardened men who'd seen the elephant, as Poppa Chuck used to say, who'd made careers of being prepared for anything, but even Gray hadn't proven capable of suppressing an expression of awe and wonder. By the time the hangar bay had swallowed us up in its gaping maw and the lander touched down between a double row of fighters, only Chuck had managed a question.

"Why is there gravity?" he'd asked, shaking his head, then glanced over with a start as the hatch had popped open.

"Are you a physicist?" Dani had replied with a question. Chuck had shaken his head helplessly and Dani had laughed in return. "Well, if you were, you still wouldn't understand, so it's better not to think about it too much."

I'd put Val in charge of getting Gray and the others outfitted with useful weapons and armor and told Giblet to get the fighter crews ready for launch before I'd headed to the bridge. Chuck had come along rather than staying with the Delta team and I hadn't questioned it. He was the commanding officer, which meant he had an obligation to stay up on the big picture. Plus, it was pretty obvious he was bursting with curiosity.

"They haven't moved yet," the robot said, turning from the control display to greet us. "I believe they haven't yet detected the *Liberator*. Our drive field is at minimal output and this moon has disguised our gravitational signature."

If Chuck had seemed awed before, when he saw Lenny, he might have gone catatonic. I put myself in his shoes, remembering the first time I'd seen the robot, how flabbergasted I'd been by the silver giant with the metallic yet human-like face.

"That won't last long," Laranna opined, peering at the tactical display, where the dozen cruisers still waited in a globular cluster. "Once they're satisfied that there are no warships, no defense platforms, they'll move in." She cocked an eyebrow at me. "The question is, should we let them?"

I frowned, knowing better than to object before considering what she'd said, but Dani hadn't known Laranna long enough for that forbearance.

"Why the hell would we do that?" she blurted, waving at the screen. "The farther away they are, the less damage they can do to Earth."

"If we allow them to think their invasion is unopposed, they may not jump in to minimum distance," she explained. "The longer they take to approach, the more time we have to prepare for them." Laranna shrugged. "The downside is, that also means we have less opportunity to engage them before they reach firing range of the planet."

Nodding thoughtfully, I turned the pros and cons over and around inside my head.

"The Vanguards have more of an advantage when they can micro-jump," I decided. "We'll launch the fighters and keep the *Liberator* in Lunar orbit, drive field low enough that they won't see her. If anything gets through, Lenny, you'll be our last line of defense."

"You're in command, Charlie," Lenny said, tilting his head to the side in what might have been an expression of doubt, "but you must know we lack the firepower to take on this many ships. They will get past me and they *will* launch fighters…and troop landers."

"Yeah, I had an idea about that," I said, turning to point a finger at Chuck. "We have a company of Strada warriors on this boat, but their officers don't have much combat experience. How'd you like to take command of them?"

"A company like her?" Chuck asked, nodding to Laranna.

"Well, not as good looking," I allowed, "or as smart or deadly, but close."

"Sure. But to do what?"

"The Anguilar don't have enough troops even in twelve cruisers to occupy even a single city," I explained. "That means they're going to strike somewhere they consider central, a target that, once they control it, along with the threat of orbital and aerial bombardment, will give them an unassailable political and strategic position."

"You're thinking…" Chuck glowered, shook his head. "Naw, they wouldn't."

"They might. But if I'm wrong, we can't be sitting in one spot, we need a mobile force to take them on. We have enough cargo ships to carry the Strada and their armored vehicles anywhere on Earth. I want you with them."

"What about Gray and the Delta team?" Chuck asked. "Are they coming with us?"

"No," I said, smiling thinly. "I have another job in mind for them. Laranna, can you introduce Captain Barnaby to the Strada infantry and have them get him armored up?"

"Of course," she said, though I did notice a twitch in her

eyebrow, not exactly doubt in my judgment but more curiosity as to what I was up to.

"Then get suited up and meet us in the hangar bay. Dani, you still wanna be my gunner?"

"Not really," she sighed, "but you're always at the front of the fight, so I might as well."

"Then let's get to the Vanguards." I paused halfway to the bridge entrance and turned back to Lenny. "You've always said I was in command. Do you mean it?"

"I think you know that I do," Lenny said, that great metal head cocked to the side, a dry smile clicking into place with the movements of silver plates. "But whenever you ask me that, I know you're about to give an order you know I'll disagree with."

"But you'll do it anyway, right?"

"Have I ever gone against your orders, *sir*?" Maybe there was sarcasm in that question and maybe there wasn't. I had a hard enough time reading flesh-and-blood people, much less alien robots.

"Then you won't do it this time," I said, "when I tell you that there's no retreat from this fight. We're not letting the Anguilar have Earth."

The AI robot rolled across the bridge to loom over me only a few feet away, though it felt more like he was getting closer for privacy rather than intimidation.

"I know this world is your home, Charlie, but we have to be realistic. The forces we have here represent a significant portion of our military capabilities. If we lose half our Vanguards and one of our five Liberators, the resistance is effectively dead. We'd have to withdraw back to Sanctuary and abandon Strada, Thalassia and the other worlds allied with us."

"And if they take this world," I countered, "then they'll have access to more resources than any of the others because the mines are pre-dug, the equipment already built and running, the farms already working." I jabbed a finger up at his face, even though I knew that wasn't actually where his optical sensors were. "And if you're thinking that there's so many people on this planet, the conquest would tie up their forces for years, think again. You don't know humans. They'll take out the government centers that might oppose them, intimidate the rest from orbit where they can't be touched and blackmail half the world's food production without needing to occupy more than a handful of territories. They'll turn one nation against another, use us to enslave each other and I'd be willing to lay you odds that we'd be fighting human conscripts in Anguilar armor in a year. Losing this world will kill the resistance a lot faster than losing this ship. So, we're doing it my way. Am I clear?"

"As always," Lenny said, nodding and backing away.

"Good to know."

I turned and left him there, but I couldn't leave the doubt behind. Lenny had come clean about how he'd used and manipulated us and our entire populations for centuries, how he and the other Creators had engineered the entire galaxy, and he'd sworn there were no more secrets. The problem was, even if I could accept that an AI robot was a person, which I thought I had… could I accept that they would suddenly grow a set of morals?

"There're wheels turning inside that little brain of yours,

Travers," Dani accused as she fell into step with me, heading down to the hangar bay. "I can see 'em. What's the plan?"

"I got lots of plans," I told her, glancing around uncomfortably. Lenny could hear me anywhere on this ship. Normally, I didn't think about that. "Let's see if I get the chance to use any of them."

25

I HADN'T DONE a combat launch out of the *Liberator* in months. Maybe that was why the emergence from the harsh white and yellow glare of the hangar bay into the star-dusted blackness still felt novel, like being born again and not in the religious sense. My breath came short, the thrusters pushing against my back like a schoolyard bully, letting me know I should expect a fight.

The Moon, though...that was new. This close, it wasn't just the silent partner of Earth but a world in its own right, massive and pockmarked with eons of abuse, our bodyguard taking the punches from billions of years' worth of meteors. This was the Moon that Armstrong had stepped onto when I was four, a little, black-and-white figure on our black-and-white TV, yet it had captured the imagination of this little boy and tens of millions of others.

Maybe that little version of Charlie Travers had dreamed of

someday flying past the Moon in a spaceship, but I doubt it had been anything close to this scenario and there'd been no alien invaders involved.

"Gib, Laranna, your squadrons good to go?"

I hadn't given up on the call signs, not entirely, and everyone still had a number attached to their fighter's avatar in the IFF display, but those were more useful for when I had to address individual crews. I knew everyone by name, but even a second's hesitation trying to put that name together with a fighter could mean disaster. Giblet and Laranna, not so much.

"First squadron formed up," Laranna reported, and the sensor image of the space behind me confirmed it, six fighters lined up in an uneven wedge to my portside.

"Second squadron ready," Gib told me. He always sounded so businesslike when he was flying…well, not *always*, but often enough that it struck me how different it was from his usual demeanor.

Thirteen fighters including mine. I didn't have a wingman, which wasn't ideal, but we were hamstrung by having to keep as close as we could to two full squadrons back on Thalassia to make sure the Anguilar didn't launch an effort to retake it while we were busy here. Two squadrons there, Liberator ships at Sanctuary and Strada, and we were stretched about as thinly as we could be without breaking. *Maybe* without breaking, we hoped.

"Keep the Moon between us and the cruisers as long as we can," I cautioned, which was probably repeating myself but it made me feel better to reiterate the plan, as if it was a prayer and repeating it made it more likely to be answered. "The goal is to keep them occupied out there, in the outer system as long as possible, which means we need to make sure they don't see the *Liberator* until the last minute. Don't get decisively engaged. Hit and run, make them launch their fighters out there instead of within range of the planet."

"And don't get killed," Gib added. "We don't have the fighters to spare. No suicide charges, and if you feel like you could take down the whole cruiser if you just exposed yourself to enemy fire for another ten seconds…don't. The only thing between that planet and those Anguilar is *us*."

"Well put," Dani said, and I glanced back at her, caught the grin through the open faceplate of her helmet. "You remember that, too, Gib."

"Your wish is my command, my love."

"All right, that's enough, you two," I interrupted, grinning despite everything. So much for being professional. "First and Second, follow me out, keep it slow. They might think we're just a flight of missiles launched from the surface, and I'd like to *let* them think that until we reach safe jump distance."

The throttle jiggled unsteadily under my hand, as if it fought me, wanted to open up and leap away from the shining white of the Lunar seas and rush at the enemy headlong. There was a boat-chop rumbling to the drive at low thrust, an uncomfortable vibration that not even the inertial dampeners could negate and, as counterintuitive as it was, a cold twist in my gut was sure that the enemy would spot the chop like a wake through a pond.

I couldn't see them, of course. The Anguilar were nothing but distant blips on the sensor screen, millions of miles away.

Stay there, I chanted inside my head. *Stay there just a few more minutes.*

The green line across the navigation screen taunted me, the minimum safe jump distance. Dani had already programmed the maneuver into the nav computer—all that remained was to get to that line and hit the controls. Before they saw us and jumped in. Simple. No problem at all. They wouldn't notice us. We were slow, running warm but not hot. Cold enough to be rockets fired from a base on the Moon. That might surprise them a little, the idea that the primitives had a base on their satellite and had enough forethought to arm it with missiles, might give them pause, and that was okay. As long as it made them stay out there just a little longer…

It did not.

"Oh, dammit!" Dani snapped and I knew what had happened before my gaze flickered from the nav screen to tactical.

Three of the cruisers snapped out of existence from the globular formation out past the orbit of Mars, and, before I had time to consider what that meant, they demonstrated exactly what it meant by reappearing right at that stupid green line, taunting us.

"Split!" I ordered and didn't have to specify who went where because that was one of the things we practiced constantly.

Laranna was on my portside and broke to that side and down relative to my position, with her fighters in tow, maneuvering jets flaring as the six Vanguards banked in a motion that shouldn't have been possible in a vacuum but was thanks to a surplus of power, the inertial dampeners, and the gimbaled main engines.

Gib and his squadron headed starboard and up and that just left me to decide which ones I would follow.

I did neither and Dani yelped as I spun our Vanguard down relative to the ecliptic, the plane the planets were arranged on relative to the Sun, and opened the throttles. The explosive thrust slipped past the dampeners and slammed us into our acceleration couches with bruising force, taking us down and out of the line of the direction of travel for the three Anguilar ships…just as they opened fire.

There was no good reason why particle cannons should be visible in a vacuum. I was no physicist, but even I knew that the whole Sci-Fi movie thing with streaks of light going through space when they fired their lasers was heavy on the fiction, light on the science. Lasers were invisible in a vacuum and so should particle beams have been. But these weren't. They were crackling, white bolts of lightning from an evening thunderstorm, searching for anything that stood out from the ground, whether it be a tree or a space fighter.

We weren't there when the beams of destruction passed through, thanks to the superior maneuverability of the fighters. They were smaller and had a hell of a lot less power to play with than the cruisers, but a Vanguard massed thousands of times less and even with the inertial dampeners, mass needed energy to move it.

I opened my mouth to give the order not to jump, thinking that the Anguilar might not realize the fighters were Vanguards, but that was a fool's wager. If they were here, they'd read Seraph Nix's report and they'd know about the starfighters. No point in hamstringing our tactics on a hope. Better to just see how they reacted to the split.

The outer two did just what I expected them to, following the fighters around, angling for another shot, and ideally, I'd wanted the third cruiser to come after me, to distract all three of them from their actual target. Unfortunately for me, while the Anguilar were as cruel as cats to anyone they thought of as an *other* and not overly loyal to anyone but themselves, they weren't necessarily stupid. Starblade fighters streamed out of the third cruiser's hangar bay, swarming downward from its position, hunting for me.

"They didn't buy it," Dani advised, reading the situation with admirable clarity, particularly since she hadn't shown much acumen at the whole pilot thing and didn't even really care for being a gunner.

"No, they didn't. Watch for fighters. And hold on…I'm coming back around."

Watching for fighters wouldn't be the hard part. They were everywhere, two dozen of them, burning hard to try to reach me before I could make it to minimum jump distance. Too bad for them that wasn't what I had in mind. Holding on, now…that wouldn't be so easy.

I'd taken out a jet-ski a couple times in the bay and there was one move I loved doing with the machines. Full speed in one direction, let off the throttle completely, twist the wheel around a hundred and eighty degrees and open the throttle full power. Do it right, and I could be heading back in the exact opposite direction without pulling off a broad, curving turn. The downside was, my grip on those handles had to be *really* solid or I'd go flying off the back of the machine the way Jill had that one time.

Dani wouldn't go flying out of the fighter, but she might feel like she was. Cut the throttle, twist the gimbals in the opposite direction and open up again, full thrust. Our acceleration couches were on gimbals of their own, slaved to the controls, and they'd started to spin before I began the braking thrust, but hadn't quite reached full opposition. The lateral thrust shoved me against the side partitions of the seat like a bully pushing me into a school locker and if not for the interior helmet padding, I would have banged my head against the chair hard enough to leave me stunned.

As it was, stars filled my vision for a few seconds and I blinked, trying to clear my eyes as we headed straight back into the oncoming wing of Starblades. They weren't ready for it, mostly because none of them could have pulled the maneuver off, even if their drive pods were on rotating mounts the way the Vanguards' were, because it would have ripped them in half. The first shots at us were wide and wild, slashes of crimson, scalar energy fed by thermal cartridges not too different from the Vulcan on an Air Force fighter plane.

I didn't try to maneuver to avoid them, concentrating on spinning the drive pods again, taking us back the way we'd come. I pitied any society that got the engine technology before they got the inertial dampeners, because any one of the moves I'd made over the last thirty seconds would have smashed Dani and me into a thin, fine paste on the floor of the fighter without the things. And God alone knew how they worked, because I sure didn't.

The Starblades flashed past us on either side, unable to change their direction as quickly, but the last pair of wingmen in the formation managed to aim their pulse guns before they did and the Vanguard shook with the transformation of thermal energy into kinetic by the Kamerian fighter's shielding. Not too violent after the pain the thrusters had inflicted, but a kick in the ass, a reminder that even with the shields, we weren't untouchable.

The cruiser hadn't turned toward me before, instead maneuvering into what I thought was a course for Earth orbit, but she must have seen me coming now because the steering jets flared on opposite ends of the massive starship, halting its spin. Not fast enough.

The silvery wedge shape filled the main screens, blotting out the stars, close enough for the tactical computer to blink a warning at me that we were in range of her particle cannons. But that meant she was in range of ours. A nudge to the steering yoke and the targeting reticle floated over the bow maneuvering thruster bank. I touched the trigger.

That was the beauty of the Vanguard. So much power crammed into such a small ship, and not least of that was the particle cannon. We could cram one of the weapons into a lander, and had, but the problem was, each of the weapons needed its own dedicated power cell and given how hard they were to acquire, no one wanted to put them in a ship small enough that it might get itself blown up. The Kamerians hadn't shared that philosophy and, for all their failings—which had included megalomania and a desire to rule the entire galaxy—I had to admire their engineering prowess.

The lance of coruscating white energy lit up the cruiser's defense shield like a Christmas tree ornament, a half-sphere of crackling static, enough to stop most of the shot. But not all of it. It wouldn't have been enough to do more than blast apart hull plating anywhere else on the ship, but the maneuvering thruster drive bells were broad, a weakness in an otherwise seamless hull. The influx of charged particles ripped apart the drive bell in a flare of yellow and orange flame, the expulsion of gas sending the cruiser into an involuntary spin.

Again, not stupid. The captain of that ship knew what had happened, knew what he had to do. The main drive roared defiance and the cruiser leapt forward under full thrust, fighting the lateral propulsion of the destroyed steering module with a gush of white flame. But that meant his guns were pointed away from me and my particle cannon had recharged. Targeting the exact same spot, I fired again.

That was the thing about the defense shield…it was arranged in quadrants. I wasn't sure of the technical details about the why of it, but the how was simple enough. Put enough energy into one quadrant and it would overload. Just like this one did. There was already a ragged gap in the hull where the steering pod had exploded, and when the stream of artificial lightning pierced the shield and the gaping wound, it was just a clean run right through to the drives.

It might not have exploded. I'd seen it happen both ways.

Sometimes, the main engine went dark and the ship just drifted off aimlessly into the blackness, leaving behind a detritus of escape pods and landers trying desperately to make it back to the last habitable planet. That wasn't particularly satisfying…but this wasn't one of those times.

The drive blew spectacularly, a miniature supernova that consumed the cruiser in a sphere of white fire, expanding so far outward that our own shields glowed with the strain before I was able to pull away from the blast.

"You had to kill one all by yourself, didn't you?" Dani asked. "Don't get too cocky…those fighters are on their way back."

One look at the sensor screen told me she was right about that. They'd managed to get turned around and all two dozen of them were coming straight for us like we'd just blown up their ride home or something.

"All right," I told her, hand hovering over the throttle control. "Hold…"

"*Don't* say hold on," she snapped.

"Okay, I won't."

Starblades disintegrated in showers of charged particles and I pulled away at the death of the last of them, messier than the others, coming apart at the midsection under a burst from Dani's pulse turret. The view out of the main screen blurred with the turn, stars, Earth, Moon, a kaleidoscope of colors and shapes and I shut it out, focusing on the sensor screen, but it whirled as well.

"Oh, Charlie," Dani said, her voice in a nervous singsong, "we got a problem."

The screen cohered in my vision and so did the problem. Not

the other two cruisers. One of them was already listing, broken at the spine, her drive dead, Giblet's squadron peeling away from her corpse, while the other had vanished inside a roiling cloud of fire. But the bare minutes it had taken had been enough for the other cruisers to decide they couldn't wait around any longer. All nine had jumped in and were burning straight for the planet.

"Not stupid," I murmured.

The three cruisers had been a probe, a test of the defenses…a bad one. The commander had underestimated us, and the bastard was smart enough to know it. More than that, he was smart enough to know why we were here and how to distract us. Fighters streamed out of the cruisers, and behind them, troop transports. Heading for Earth.

26

MAKING decisions in a fraction of a second was one of the three vital characteristics of a great leader according to the Strada, or so Laranna had told me. She was of the opinion that was the reason Lenny had picked me to command the resistance, though how he could have known that about me back in 1987 was an open question. Dani had told me about social media and I'd seen the personal information on the internet, so it would have made sense in the 2020s, but not back then.

Somehow, he'd guessed right. And I hoped I did.

"Laranna," I snapped, "follow them down, take out the fighters. Gib, stay with the cruisers!"

And just like that, I'd had to send the woman I loved chasing after hundreds of fighters and my best friend into the teeth of more cruisers than he could survive, and I'd made the choice in less than a heartbeat, like it was the easiest thing in the world. Like I wasn't scared shitless.

"Lenny, get your ass in the game." And that one hadn't been a hard decision at all. "Get on those damned cruisers! And launch the Strada ground forces in the landers. Get them following the Anguilar transports."

"As you command, Charlie," was the robot's oddly worded reply, and once again, I fought a suspicion that he didn't agree with my decision.

I had other things to worry about now, though. Like trying to figure out how to contact Washington on the comms. They'd given me a frequency for a direct connection, but I'd never attempted to use the comms on a Vanguard to send a regular microwave signal, much less while I was flying the plane.

There.

"This is Charlie Travers, please come in. White House, do you read?"

It took several seconds, and I was about to give up on it, lacking the time to wait on hold, when static burst over my helmet speakers, followed by the familiar voice of Parker Donovan.

"Tell us what's going on up there, Travers." He sounded tense, like he'd seen enough to guess.

"We've taken out three cruisers, but the remaining nine have launched fighters and troop transports. I don't know for sure where they're heading but we have fighters and landers on their tail. You need to get your fighters, air defense, and ground forces mobilized around the capital, in case that's where they're targeting."

"Do you believe that's the target, Travers?" Donovan asked tightly, voices raised behind him as others called out commands and urgent questions. "We need to know."

"It makes sense. The Anguilar always go for the most centralized command of the local government. I could be wrong, but if you have to make a choice, that's the one I'd go for."

"Copy that. Keep us in the loop."

The voice was replaced by static and I cut the connection, filled with an irrational guilt at the thought that they'd follow my advice and I'd wind up making the wrong call. I'd been making calls that affected whole worlds without the slightest bit of self-doubt, but here, with my world, my government, I suddenly felt like the twenty-five-year-old ROTC second lieutenant that I was.

"And where are we going?" Dani wondered, pulling me out of my thoughts.

Good question. A harder call to make. They could use me down there. There were a hell of a lot more fighters than they could take out and more troops than anyone on Earth could handle. But the real reason I wanted to go that way was because that was where Laranna was, and that was another of the Stradan three vital characteristics of a great leader…they knew why they did things.

"The cruisers," I told her. "We're going after the cruisers."

The whole thing was a tableau laid out in some Renaissance painting, Michelangelo decorating the ceiling of the Sistine Chapel with a war in heaven. The cruisers were huge individually, but nine of them so close I could see them with an unmagnified optical camera was like the New York City skyline ripped out of the Earth and transported into orbit. The Moon hung behind them, the frame of that macabre painting, the night sky of the western hemisphere ahead, Starblade fighters and troop transports disappearing in the distance into glittering dust falling from the heavens.

And after them we came, thirteen Vanguards, not nearly enough. The *Liberator* was on her way, though I couldn't see her behind the Moon, but even for the magic tech in the ancient Creator ship, physics still placed shackles on how fast she could accelerate, on how long it would take her to reach orbit. Minutes that we didn't have.

Minutes we'd have to buy. Gib and his squadron roared ahead of us, their drives torches burning against the night, and I chased after them, heedless of the firepower waiting at the end of the pursuit.

Again, the Anguilar commander was too damned smart. He knew what we were, knew what we could do and, unlike the three ships he'd sent to scout, he knew how to beat us. The cruisers moved as one, a practiced maneuver, their bows coming around, bringing their particle cannon batteries to bear. All nine ships fired as one and reality itself ripped to shreds with enough energy to obliterate a city, aimed at us.

Too far yet, even for those huge guns, and he had to know that, too. The shields on Gib's fighters glowed white, surrounding the Vanguards with a bubble of protection, but each of those bubbles shook like a mighty wind had taken them.

"Break off, damn you!" Dani said under her breath, watching the same show play out that I was.

Gib couldn't have heard her, but he listened anyway, leading his birds in a sharp bank up and starboard. I was farther back, far enough that the particle blasts hadn't even lit up my defense shield, but that wouldn't last long. The cruisers and I were both headed the same direction, into high Earth orbit, and if I kept that trajectory, they'd be in firing range in seconds. Gib had gone up, so I went down.

Yeah, I know, up, down, right, left…none of that meant anything in space, but we had to think and talk about it somehow, and relative positions were the only way. What's more, ships working together needed common frames of reference, which meant as a practice, all of us maintained the same basic orientation relative to each other and the ecliptic of the system we were flying in. So the Earth's North Pole was up, its south pole was down, and we figured out left and right from there. Maybe it would have been more scientific to use 360-degree numerical references, but it would have been just as arbitrary and harder to figure out.

I went in the direction of the South Pole and outward, and cleared the firing arc of the cruisers just as three of them opened up on me. Still at maximum range, but close enough that yellow warning lights flashed and a gentle tremor ran through the fighter as the shields crackled, the mast of a sailing ship in a lightning storm green with St. Elmo's fire.

I didn't think about how to fly the plane anymore. That had been a tension in my neck and shoulders every time I was at the controls when I'd first been learning the Vanguard, unnoticed until it was gone. Now, it was almost like driving a car or riding a bike, something my reflexes did without input from my conscious mind. I decided where to go and I went there.

Thinking would probably have gotten me killed since the only thing keeping us alive was speed and agility. The cruisers moved like they shared a central hub, the nine of them rotating to keep a firing arc at every angle of attack because they knew we'd *have* to attack. We had to finish them and get down to engage their fighters, while they could take their time and keep us pinned down… and if we gave up and dropped into the atmosphere, they could pour fire on ground targets and there'd be nothing we could do about it.

They hadn't counted on two things, of course.

One, we were damned good at our jobs and neither Gib nor I was going to sit back and let them play porcupine. And two, there was also the *Liberator*.

She cleared the Moon just as a ravening particle blast missed our cockpit by less than half a mile, her massive bulk appearing out from behind the fading white energy like a ghost ship from a bygone era. And for the Anguilar, she might well have been. I kept the Vanguard in a curving arc, steering jets flaring, drive pods at different angles, the lateral acceleration a sucker punch to my ribs that just kept on coming, squeezing us into the gap between the firing arcs of two of the cruisers, waiting…waiting for them to notice.

When they did, it was obvious. The commander of the Anguilar flotilla had run them tight, like they were a fighter squadron or a tank company rather than capital ships, but with the appearance of the *Liberator*, they split out of their careful formation. Not panicking…whoever this guy was, he was better than that. But turning one defensive picket into two, three of the cruisers facing the oncoming Creator ship, the rest still maneuvering to keep Gib's squadron at bay.

"Umm…" Dani said, and when I looked back at her, a perplexed look had settled over her features. "We have an incoming transmission."

"Earth?" I wondered, thinking Donovan had already gotten impatient for a status report.

"No. The Anguilar."

I'd been watching the nav and sensor screens, ignoring comms, but at her words, my head snapped up and I saw the image accompanying the transmission. It was an Anguilar officer, and the code was theirs. It could be an attempt at a distraction, something to slow us down or deceive us. Maybe an attempt to gain intelligence. But intelligence-gathering went both ways.

"This should be interesting," I murmured. "Put him through."

If he was trying to distract me, I'd have to make sure it didn't work. I'd guided the Vanguard into a gap between the two defensive formations, the two groups of Anguilar cruisers just out of particle cannon range of each other, like the commander had been an American soldier and wanted to make sure one grenade wouldn't take out both. That put me well out of range of their pulse turrets as well, not that they still didn't try to shoot at me. If they'd kept any fighters back for protection, it might have been more difficult, but the gap gave me a few seconds for this diversion.

"Are you the human called Charlie Travers?"

It was audio only, but the haughty, high-pitched tone of an Anguilar was obvious.

"Yeah, that's me. You call to offer an unconditional surrender? Because that's the only thing I want to hear from you."

I expected outrage. That seemed to be the usual Anguilar response to any haughty response from their lessers—and to them, everyone was lesser. Instead, I got a laugh.

"I've been told of your exploits, Commander Travers. Though I suppose I didn't truly believe until your planes destroyed three of my ships in minutes. That was my fault, a poor decision, but one I hope to make up for now."

Great. *Commander* Travers. Now the President *and* this Anguilar bastard were calling me that. I was about to tell him to address me as Grand Admiral Travers, but he wasn't done yet.

"Allow me to introduce myself." Now the video feed *did* pop up, a projection over the comms board, a typical Anguilar male from the shoulders up. Maybe a little older than the ones I'd run into so far, if the lines in his face and the gray in his feathery hair were any indication, a little more battle-hardened if the scar crossing his right cheek hadn't come from opening a can of tuna. "I am General Zan-Tar of the Emperor's Own."

"A general, huh?" I repeated. "The last Anguilar officer I killed was a colonel. I guess I'm climbing the ladder."

"Yes, Colonel Mok-La," Zan-Tar acknowledged, smiling thinly. "He was a driven man, single-minded in his pursuits, often to the detriment of the Empire as a whole. If you hadn't provided him with a respectable death in battle, I fear we would have been forced to subject his bloodline to the humiliation of a public cleansing."

"I'm happy to have saved them the embarrassment," I allowed, adjusting my course as a burst of pulse fire got close enough to give the edge of our shield a fringe of red, imparted the slightest of plumb-bob sway to the course of the Vanguard. Zan-Tar…I'd heard that name before. I couldn't quite place where, but it had to have been either on Copperell or during the *Nova Eclipse* operation. It probably wasn't important.

"I'm sure they're grateful," Zan-Tar agreed. "But back to why I'm bothering you. This entire attack is a waste of time, money, and resources, Commander Travers. May I tell you what's going to happen here?"

"Please, do," I urged him. "Pardon me for just a moment, have some business to take care of."

Cutting thrust, I spun the Vanguard toward the cruiser on my left-hand side and fired off a particle cannon blast. Too far away to do much and not aimed at anything particularly vulnerable, but it battered her shield and reminded them that I wasn't sitting here twiddling my thumbs while Zan-Tar buttered me up.

The cruisers reacted the way I'd hoped they would, shifting positions, trying to swing their main guns around to cover me, but I nudged the fighter away, slightly out of range. The *Liberator* was only minutes out of firing range, and Gib, I saw on the tactical display, had taken his squadron on a broad arc around the other group of cruisers, trying to outmaneuver them.

"How this will unfold, Commander," Zan-Tar went on as if nothing had happened, "is that either we will win this battle but take further casualties and be unable to take the planet, or you will win, and take losses you can't afford…and then, we'll return, with more ships, more fighters, more ground troops. Because we *have* more and can lose every single ship and every single soldier in this system without it crippling our military. You'll be forced to keep every ship you have in the Sol System to protect it and then, while you're busy defending your homeworld…we'll be equally busy undoing all that heroic work you've done in places like Strada." He shrugged. "Of course, it *will* cost us. We have more ships than you, but they're not cheap to replace. We have food sources and can acquire more, but every world we take to produce resources for us requires a concomitant investment of troops and ships. I'd like to propose a mutually beneficial agreement."

Oh, shit. If he was going to offer the deal I'd already assured everyone that the Anguilar were too self-involved to consider…

"We can't trust this world to its current rulers, of course," he said, and I kept my sigh of relief internal. "They're far too divided and inefficient. Instead, consider this. This system is far enough away from the Imperial Headquarters for me to sell them this, particularly given the heartburn you've caused all the way up to the top. You stand out of the way and allow us to take control of this world, then we put you and your…" His lip curled in derision. "…*resistance* in charge of it. You provide the security, give us a quarter of the annual crop yield and half the current production of mineral resources. We don't care how you do that," Zan-Tar added. "It's your system. Bring the minerals in and mine them from asteroids if you like, as long as you're paying for it. In return for your pledge to cease hostilities with us and not to provide aid or comfort to those who do, we'll agree to forego any further attempts to retake Strada."

I blinked in disbelief. Not because the offer was worth considering but because just the Anguilar being willing to make it was hard to fathom. This was another one of those damned leadership moments. I wanted to tell this guy to take his proposal and stuff it, but two things stopped me. One, I needed to know how far the Anguilar were willing to bend on this. If this was just the product of a sensible general or that of panic, desperation.

And the other, the one that really galled me, was that, despite how I felt about it, despite how the other worlds of the resistance might feel, despite how badly it would piss off Val and Brandy if I gave up hope of freeing Copperell…the people of Earth deserved the chance to make the choice for themselves. If I made it for them, how was I any better than the Anguilar?

"What if I said to you," I replied cautiously, hands guiding the Vanguard automatically through a rolling arc as I kept the bulk of one of the cruisers between me and the second, "that I'd consider your offer if I could leave the current government in charge on Earth? We'd provide the food and the minerals, just like you asked, but they'd stay in charge…at least of the Earth-Moon area."

Dani stared at me in obvious horror but I avoided meeting her wide-eyed gaze, holding my breath, waiting for the reply. Hoping it would be no and feeling like a complete shit for it. Yes would mean the end of the war for now, would allow Strada and

Earth, at least, to live in peace. We could bring the refugees from Sanctuary here, resettle them on Earth and consolidate our defenses in the two systems in case the Empire went back on the deal. People could go back to living real lives. Laranna and I could have children and not have to worry about one or both of their parents going off to die in battle.

"I'm afraid I haven't been given the latitude to offer that," Zan-Tar replied sadly. And I actually believed he *was* sad about it, not putting me on. "In fact, it took a considerable amount of my political capital with Emperor Kan-Tal-Vin the Fifth to allow me to make this offer. You must understand how this looks to the Senior Bloodlines. The Anguilar take what they want. It has always been thus."

"Then I'm sorry, but I have to say no. We do what we do so people can have the freedom to rule themselves. If I take that from them, what am I fighting for?"

Zan-Tar's brow furled as if he was trying to understand the thinking behind that, but finally, he shook it off like a dog coming in out of the rain.

"I regret that this must happen, Commander. It isn't often that I admire an opponent who is not one of our people, but you've shown the sort of daring I appreciate in my own officer corps. I hate to kill you, but I will. My duty to my bloodline demands it."

And that was as close to sentiment as I was ever going to get from an Anguilar, closer than I'd ever thought I'd come.

"And I'd hate to die," I replied. "But I will if I have to. My duty to my family and my country demands it." And the planet, too, I guess.

Zan-Tar offered what I recognized as an Anguilar salute.

"Then to arms, Charlie Travers. And may the gods smile on your death."

27

The bastards didn't waste any time.

I'd thought Zan-Tar was smart before I'd put a name to him, but he'd been toying with me, lulling us into a false sense of security with the slow movements and defensive posture of the cruisers. The moment the transmission ended, all nine of the vessels leapt into the fray like a pack of dogs set loose from the leash by a hog hunter. Springing into action, they took full advantage of the power at their disposal and six of them spread out to flank the *Liberator* while the other three spun with surprising agility and launched headlong into Gib's squadron.

Another split-second decision, another where I had to know why I was doing it. I wanted to help Gib and I could have told myself it was because we needed to preserve the Vanguards, but the real reason was that he was my friend. The *Liberator* was vital not just to the resistance but to all those Strada warriors if they ever wanted to get home, and there was no way she could take on six cruisers by herself. I jerked the controls to the left and upward and pushed the throttle open.

The Earth rushed by beneath us, a blur of continents, light and dark as we crossed the terminator and Dani made a weird, choking noise, wordless but I knew what it was. She'd been about to object to us leaving Gib and his squadron to their own devices but had bitten down on the complaint, knowing how it would sound. I appreciated that, and the trust she was putting in my judgment.

"Lenny," I snapped into the comms, "break low, use the planet to slingshot you around, rake them with a broadside as you pass and I'll hit them from behind."

"Rake them with a broadside?" Dani asked me, laughing at the absurdity of it despite the situation.

"What's the use of being a space captain if I can't say shit like that?" I said, shrugging.

If someone had asked me five minutes ago what the hardest part about being a commander was, I would have said having to send my friends and loved ones off to battle without me. Two minutes ago, I would have changed that to being forced to make decisions that affected hundreds of millions of people without the time to consult any of them. But right now, my answer would be the fact that I was engaged in one battle and unable to keep track of the others.

Lenny had followed my orders and turned back toward Earth orbit, increasing boost to the point where I worried he'd shoot right past the planet. I should have known better, of course. The

Copperell and Peboktan crew who manned the bridge were the best and wouldn't make a mistake like that…or maybe Lenny wouldn't let them. His programming prevented him from being involved directly in the battle, but I knew firsthand that it would allow him to preserve the ship against navigational dangers, even in combat.

Whichever it was, whatever trick of physics and engineering they used to pull it off, the *Liberator* speared down into the atmosphere, the Anguilar ships arcing toward her, unable to get a weapons fix before she was out of their firing arc. The *Liberator* didn't have that problem. She cut her engines and spun on her axis, her twin particle cannons slicing across her closest pursuer like a pirate cutlass. The Anguilar cruiser's shields expanded in a halo of angelic white for a full second before the protective barrier collapsed under the influx of raw energy, taking the ship with it.

"Yes!" Dani yelled, pumping her fist like her team had just scored a touchdown.

Unfortunately, this *was* just like a touchdown in that the ball got kicked back to the other team after. The spin back around to face her direction of travel cost the *Liberator* time and one of the cruisers took advantage of it, imitating her maneuver, cutting thrust long enough to aim her nose emitters at the Creator ship.

I saw it coming, my lips skinned back from my teeth to call a warning that wouldn't come in time and wouldn't make any difference if it had. The twin blasts took the *Liberator* amidships, the first direct hit I'd seen her take the whole time I'd been sailing on her, during all the space battles we'd been through. Her shields bloomed in layers of blue and white, a supernova spreading like ripples in a pond as the fields shed energy outward for dozens, maybe hundreds, of miles before the glow disappeared.

She didn't blow up. That was the good news. I'd expected her to, but I'd underestimated how well the Creators built their ships. A blackened, bubbling scar the size of a semi-truck marked her portside hull, though I couldn't be sure from thousands of miles away even with the telescopic cameras if the blast had penetrated. Her drives still worked, the desperate plume of white still pushing to outrun the enemy ships.

"She won't take another hit," I judged, my voice so much calmer than it had any right to be given the roiling in my guts. I touched the comms. "Lenny, slingshot out past the Moon, use your hyperdrive to get clear."

"And then what?" Dani asked, not waiting for Lenny to answer. "We can't take on these ships with just half a dozen fighters."

"Hopefully, they'll follow her," I said, as much of an explanation as I had time for…and honestly, as much of a plan as I had.

Except for this. I pushed the throttle forward to the stops, which was about as much technical detail as I knew of the actual thrust of the fighter except that it was fast. Faster than the cruisers at least in the short run, and I caught up with them before they could catch up with the *Liberator*. The price for the acceleration was pain. That was the real limit of how hard the fighter could boost, I thought sometimes with the non-scientific bent of my non-physicist brain. The harder I boosted, the more inertia slipped through the dampeners and the more my face pushed back into my skull, the more my ribs creaked.

I bought space with pain, and it was worth it. The targeting reticle floated over the drive pods of a cruiser and I touched the trigger. Close enough this time that the lance of white fire speared through their shields almost without stopping and the Anguilar ship twisted away on a jet of superheated gas. The drives went offline, deprived of the power feed from the cells, but the ship still tumbled under the momentum of the wound in her side…into the atmosphere.

I couldn't wait around to see, but the tactical computer told the story. That ship was heading down, would burn up before it reached the surface.

Another one bites the dust.

Which reminded me, I'd forgotten to put on music. No time now, but I missed it. It helped me to forget the why of what we were doing, the real consequences, and just be in the moment. I could have used it now, because the rest of those damned cruisers had realized I was here. Four of them, one of me. I rolled planetward, toward the atmosphere myself, trusting that they couldn't follow me there.

They tried. Lightning crackled into auroras from the particle blasts seeking us out, and the upper atmosphere tugged at our wings, offering safety, illusory or not. I feathered the engines, dipping lower, trying to put distance between my Vanguard and the remaining cruisers. Trying to keep them focused on me.

"Charlie." It was Laranna, her voice distant and staticky over my headphones. "Charlie, can you hear me?"

And I could, just barely, probably because my dip into the atmosphere had taken me halfway around the planet, with the Pacific coast passing by below.

"I copy, Laranna," I replied, happy just to hear she was still alive. "What's the situation?"

More thunder interrupted her reply, turbulence battering the Vanguard from the fusillade of particle cannon fire raining down. Three of the cruisers had broken off pursuit, but one braved the thicker atmosphere, counting on gravity-resist and the raw thrust of her engines to overcome the increasing friction. She was getting closer…

"We're tangled with the Starblades," Laranna said, strain in her voice, probably from the g-load her fighter was pulling. "Can't shake loose for air support. The transports are landing in DC and your friend Chuck is down there coordinating the Strada with the local forces." A burst of static drowned out her words and panic surged in my gut at the thought I'd lost her, but her IFF transponder still shone bright blue and when she spoke again, it was with a grunt as if she'd just burned through a high-g maneuver. "We need help down here."

Dammit.

"I'll get it to you as soon as I can," I promised. "The *Liberator* took a bad hit and she's out of the fight. We're dealing with multiple cruisers…"

I'd screwed up. The dangers of trying to command and fly a fighter at the same time, I'd let the cruiser get too close. In my defense, what the Anguilar captain did was pretty clearly suicide, but either they knew I was the one flying the Vanguard and wanted very badly to take me out or he had some horrible target fixation. I'd brought the Vanguard down to twenty thousand feet, thick enough that the air shook the fuselage and forced me to ride the steering yoke like an old pickup on a dirt road. The starfighter wasn't built to excel at atmospheric combat, but the Anguilar cruiser wasn't built to fly in the soup at all.

Friction heated the forward edges of the warship to red hot as she pitched and yawed like an eighteenth-century sailing ship on a storm, but Captain Ahab just wasn't giving up on this great white whale of the resistance. From hell's heart, he stabbed at me...or at least he fired his particle cannon. Thermal blooming rushed back over the nose of the cruiser, lighting up her shields, the kinetic energy adding to her instability.

Not that the particle blast did *our* stability any good. The fist of God crashed into the fighter, snapping my helmet back against the padding and the notion of up and down became just as relative as they were in interplanetary space.

I might have cursed. I know Dani did, but with the flood of searing heat and the Vanguard being shaken like a dead squirrel in a hound dog's mouth, the cursing might have been inside my head. Blood trickled down my lip where I'd bitten it and stars filled my eyes, fighting my attempts to differentiate them from the flashing warning lights, but my hands were still wrapped around the steering yokes, and I knew a sure way to get out of the spin.

Tilting the yokes in different directions spun the drive pods on their gimbals, both of them aimed downward. Thrust shoved me straight down into the seat, the brutal acceleration feeling as if it had taken inches off my height, and whatever abuse my body went through was nothing compared to the shrieking and groaning of the fuselage under the structural stress, but the fighter broke out of its flat spin.

Just in time to watch that Anguilar cruiser nose in, tumbling out of control, her drives cutting off. She'd flown too close to the Sun and the wax on her wings had melted.

"They're going down," Dani whispered in awe, staring at the view from the belly cameras on the main screen. "I wonder where they'll crash."

We were somewhere above the desert southwest, though the barren, red rock below didn't come with map lines, so I had no idea what state we were over. No cities stood out from the wilderness, but that didn't mean the cruiser wouldn't find one.

"There's nothing we can do about it," was the only answer I had for her. "We have to get back upstairs."

And hope the fight there wasn't already over.

THERE WAS no danger of that, as it turned out.

The situation had changed by the time I pulled our Vanguard out of the atmosphere and back up into high orbit, though I couldn't say if it was better, worse, or just different. It was definitely better, numbers-wise. Between the *Liberator* and our Vanguards and the one ship captain's sheer bloody-mindedness, we'd taken down three of the Anguilar cruisers sent after Lenny, while out in cis-lunar space, Gib and his squadron had managed to dispose of one of the three sent to deal with them. The remaining pair of cruisers stood them off just out of firing range, and Gib had, to his credit, followed Dani's orders and mine. No friendly casualties according to the IFF…or at least none of the Vanguards damaged badly enough to take their transponder offline.

The *Liberator* was another story. She was still running ahead of the three cruisers, but only because she had a head start. The Creator ship limped at what looked like half her usual speed, not yet to minimum safe jump distance. If she could even make the jump in the first place.

"Lenny, how bad is it?" I asked, hoping the message would even get through to him. The cruisers could be jamming, or the ship might be damaged too badly to receive the transmission…

"I may be indulging in what you humans consider understatement," he replied after a moment, "but I would judge that there is good news and bad news."

"Oh my God," Dani moaned. "He sounds like a virtual assistant telling dad jokes."

"What's the good news?" I asked, playing along.

"The damage we've taken is reparable without requiring a spacedock or external construction gantry."

That *was* damned good news, since we lacked either of those, not just here but *anywhere.* Only the Anguilar had those sorts of facilities, which was one reason we didn't build our own warships.

"And the bad news?"

"The bad news," he said, the words pitching downwards like they slipped off the edge of a cliff, scrabbling for purchase with their fingernails, "is that the repairs will take hours, if not days, and until they're completed, the sublight engines are at half power and the hyperdrive is completely offline."

Oh, yeah, that *was* bad news, all right. But he wasn't finished yet.

"And of course," he continued, sounding as if the entire matter was a casual aside, "without the hyperdrive, the shields are inoperative."

"Of course," I murmured. If there'd been mechanical gears in my brain, they would have been grinding, smoke pouring out my ears. "Val, do you copy?"

He probably wouldn't be on the bridge, but he'd have his personal comm handy and it would be linked to the ship's receiver.

"I got ya, Charlie," he replied immediately. "What ya need?"

"Is the Delta team geared up?"

"Been that way for a couple hours now," he confirmed.

"Get them and an emergency flight crew into an armed lander…and you. Launch immediately and head this way."

"What do you have in mind, son?" Val asked, a little doubt in his tone.

"Nothing you're going to like," I admitted. "But if it's any consolation, I'm going to like it even less."

28

"You sure this is a good plan?" Giblet asked, the message slightly garbled, transmitted backward past the flaring exhaust of his fighter's drives as it and the rest of his squadron boosted away from us.

"Lenny needs you and your birds more than I do," I assured him. "Keep those cruisers off him."

The squadron had turned so abruptly that the cruisers hadn't yet had time to pursue and the two Anguilar vessels seemed forlorn and abandoned for a moment. That lasted all of the time it took to form the thought, before the cruisers turned ponderously on gouts of steering thrusters, ready to either chase down the starfighters or add their number to the force hunting the *Liberator*.

Only one way to change that. I activated the comms board and called up the frequency General Zan-Tar had transmitted from, sending a hailing signal. He might ignore it. He'd seemed like a professional soldier, and an experienced one at that, which might mean he'd see through this as the distraction it was. But then again, he'd been the one who wanted to negotiate.

A flickering hologram above the comm board rewarded my gambit.

"Your people are skilled pilots," Zan-Tar acknowledged, not seeming to be overly affected by his losses. "Though given the damage to your mothership, that may be due to our inexperience fighting craft so small yet with such powerful drives and weapons. The Kamerians built well." The general smiled without warmth. "Yet try as you might, you won't stop us from getting to that ship. If we achieve nothing else with this battle, we'll strip you of yet another of your limited warships. And as formidable as those fighters are, you can't travel for weeks in them. You should have taken my offer."

"Tell me something, General," I said. "The reason I called was, one of your captains sacrificed his entire ship following me into the atmosphere to try to take me out. Didn't even think twice about it. Do you want me dead that badly?"

"We all serve the Empire, Commander Travers," he replied grimly. "Whether in life or in death."

"Just one more thing then," I told him. "You *do* know I'm in this fighter off by itself, don't you? Which ship are you in? I'm betting it's one of the two that are running away from me right now. If you want the both of us to serve the Empire so damned much…why don't you turn around and fight me?"

I switched the transmission off and watched the sensors as

well as the main viewscreens, waiting to see whether it would work. Both the cruisers were burning toward Gib and the *Liberator*, but one of them cut its drives, maneuvering jets burning hot as it spun around to meet my charge.

"You know," Dani said, "you might want to let me know your plan before you go putting us up against an enemy cruiser head on. Not that I'd chicken out or anything, but I'd like some time to mentally prepare myself."

I nodded, though I didn't take my eyes off the sensor screen, didn't speak because I had a hard enough time doing math in my head without trying to talk at the same time. The cruiser had to decelerate to bleed off its inward momentum before heading toward us, while I'd set our course in a swooping arc that crossed her forward trajectory.

And off to the right of the image on the sensor screen, burning in from just shy of lunar orbit, was the lander from the *Liberator* with Val and the Delta Force team aboard her. Even our landers could reach speeds that would make the space shuttle blush with embarrassment, but it would still take a couple minutes for the small vehicle to reach us. The tricky part would be staying alive that long.

Another screen flashed for attention, a warning that the fighter would be in range of the Anguilar warship's particle cannon in seconds. It was all about angles, where they intersected and how long we'd be in the path of their weapon.

"Don't have time for a full mission brief," I murmured distractedly to Dani, "but I will tell you this. I'm not planning to meet them head-on."

We were ten seconds from their firing arc when I angled the drive pods downward and gave the Vanguard a kick in the ass. Physics were still physics, which meant switching off the thrust in one direction didn't negate our motion along that trajectory, but the upward acceleration added yet another angle to all the ones before, a hypotenuse to the triangle that lifted us out of the cruiser's target zone less than a second before she fired. Even then, the shot grazed the edge of the defense shield, lighting it up with static discharge, the biggest bug zapper on the biggest back porch in the universe.

Dani cursed again reflexively as the fighter shuddered from the near-miss and I tsked, continuing the upward and forward arc.

"You should really try to clean up your language," I told her, tightening my stomach muscles to work against the g-forces trying to squeeze the blood out of my extremities, a trick I'd read about in a book on naval aviators that I'd picked up after watching Top Gun. "After all, we're like…ambassadors here, sort of. Gotta make a good impression."

"Yeah, you're a real boy scout," she snapped back.

I would have told her that yes, I *had* been a Boy Scout, but I needed to save that breath for the strain of the next maneuver. Flip the drive pods and the seats with them, decelerate hard enough it felt like a full-grown Brahma bull was sitting on my chest for a good ten seconds, flip again and boost the other direction. My eyes didn't want to focus and I had only the vaguest idea of where I was or if the move had worked the way I wanted it to until a shake of my head cleared my vision and I found myself staring straight into the point defense turrets over the cruiser's hangar bay from only a few dozen miles away, practically spitting distance in space.

If I'd taken a second longer than I should have to recover from the braking boost, Dani hadn't. She opened up before I had the chance, raking the turrets with our own pulse guns for two full seconds before I could nudge the nose of the Vanguard into position and line up the targeting reticle.

Lightning streaked across the space between us and ripped a jagged hole through the hangar bay doors, atmosphere spewing out on fire until interior seals cut it off, and when they did, I fired again. More burning atmosphere and this time, it cut off more slowly, draining a greater area before the emergency barriers slid into place at some deeper point in the ship.

This time, bodies tumbled out along with metal debris and the cruiser did what I knew she'd do, trying to blast clear with her main drive while she spun around, searching for a shot at me. She might have gotten it, and even if the only weapons at the rear of the ship were pulse turrets, enough of those focused together on the Vanguard would have penetrated our shields before we could get clear.

But getting clear wasn't what I had in mind. Out of the corner of my eye, I saw the blue dot on the sensor screen that was the troop transport. They knew what to do next and so did I.

Instead of evading, I blasted us forward through the white-hot edges of the hangar bay doors, flipping the drive pods just before we crossed inside, from the brightness of the sunlight reflected off the Earth and the Moon into the darkness of the metal cavern. Another braking burn, painful for us, more painful for anyone still inside the hangar bay, and the exhaust from our drives baked an Anguilar shuttle into twisted, charred metal before it stopped us.

The Vanguard touched down with a jarring thump and we were inside an Anguilar cruiser. I sucked in a breath, the reality of the situation hitting me as hard as any of our high-gravity boosts, then cut loose from my restraints with a tug on the quick-release. I wanted to look over my shoulder, but good sense over-rode instinct and I watched the feed from the rear cameras instead. I wasn't sure who was piloting the troop lander, but they had the makings of a fighter jock. The bulbous craft, fatter and longer than a regular shuttle, barely fit through the hole I'd blown in the hangar bay, sparks scattering as the portside wing scraped metal.

The lander pilot even had the good sense to skew his course to the right of the Vanguard, making sure we could get out of the bay if we had to, before he cut thrust and let the internal gravity do its job.

They were down. Show was about to start.

"Stay on the pulse guns," I told Dani, vaulting out of my seat, the soles of my flight suit thumping hollow against the deck next to the hatch.

The locker beside it swung open at a touch on the security plate to reveal a pulse carbine and a tactical harness with spare drums for it. The setup was awkward, and I made up my mind if we actually managed to make this thing work with the government, the first thing I was going to do was fabricate pulse rifles set up more like a good, practical M16 with regular magazines. For now, though, I cinched it tight and threw the sling over my neck. I'd thought when I picked up my first pulse rifle, one I'd taken off the corpse of a pirate, that no one out here used slings, but it turned out that was just the way that particular pirate crew preferred it. Damned good thing. Slings were useful.

"Faceplate down," I cautioned Dani. "I'm opening the hatch."

"Of course you are," she muttered, but we both snapped our visors into place and the internal air systems clicked on, followed by the hiss of the blowers.

The standard procedure would have been to evacuate the interior of the Vanguard through the fans before I opened the lock, but time was a little short, so I just let loose the latch and the door sprang open, slamming downward with all the force of the fighter's internal air gushing out into the vacuum. Gravity still worked even without air or power and when I hopped down off the edge of the doorway, the weight of the armor, ammo, and rifle forced me into a crouch. Probably a safer position to scan my surroundings anyway.

The hangar bay was nearly empty, the Starblade fighters and troop transports it had once held gone now, invading the capital. Two small landers were all that remained and one of them had been destroyed by our landing, leaving a single shuttle at the far end of the bay, a good hundred yards away. The bay stretched the entire length of the widest section of the cruiser's hull, big enough and empty enough that we could have played football in the compartment. The other side didn't have any players around at the moment, though, probably because of the aforementioned lack of any fighters or troop transports.

And, of course, there was a big damned hole in the wall. The particle cannon packed a huge wallop, and the blast had passed upward at a slight angle, smashing through three bulkheads just that I could see before exiting through the dorsal hull. A patch of distant Earth shone blue through the gap…and didn't seem to be moving. That was either a good thing or a bad one depending on the why. If the captain of the ship was paralyzed with indecision, it was good. If he was intent on not going anywhere till he sorted us out, it was bad.

Rising, I turned back to the troop transport.

"Val, report," I said, waving at the armored, helmeted figures trundling down the ramp of the ship.

Operating in a vacuum was surreal, the only sounds the vibrations of my feet on the deck traveling up through my suit, the harsh intake of my own breath. When Val answered over my helmet's headphones, he could have been miles away rather than standing in front of me, the rugged lines of his face barely visible through his visor.

"Got Gray and them other boys, along with two Peboktan engineers and four Copperell bridge crew. Everyone's strapped but I wouldn't count on the tech types hitting anything farther away than the end of their arm."

"Gray, you got the hang of the vacuum suit thing?" I asked, hoping the man was one of the half-dozen armored shapes behind Val, though there was no way to tell him or any of the

Delta operators from the tech crew other than, perhaps, the more comfortable way they held their weapons.

"Believe it or not, Mr. Travers," he said, his tone as calm and casual as if we were back in that hotel, "this isn't the first time I've been in a space suit." He stepped out of the pack and I knew it was him from his thin smile under the plastic of the faceplate. "And no, I'm afraid I can't tell you any more of that story. Need to know and all that."

I laughed at the absurdity of need to know under the circumstances, but the laugh was interrupted by a flash of light from across the compartment. Not from the big-ass hole in the wall but the other end, where there was still an intact doorway…and through it charged a dozen Anguilar soldiers in full armor, firing scalar pulses at us on the run from a hundred yards away. Which was the only reason I wasn't dead.

The flash of light had been a stream of pulses passing less than a foot over my head, smacking into the nose of the troop transport in a shower of sparks.

"Take cover!" I yelled, pushing Val and Gray backwards with one hand, bringing up my rifle with the other.

I never got the chance to use it. The limiting thing about particle cannons was that they needed a straight-line shot from the cylindrical accelerator and the beam was too powerful to be bent or diverted. Your ship had to be pointed at whatever you wanted to shoot. The pulse guns didn't have that problem and the turrets on the wings of the Vanguard rotated freely in ninety-degree arcs. Just enough mobility for Dani to traverse the right-hand turret all the way to its stops and fire a couple hundred rounds into the oncoming enemy.

A solid line of red hosed across the ranks of Anguilar troopers, blasting them into a loose collection of crystalized flesh and blood in the space of two seconds. One minute a mortal threat, the next nothing but charred and quick-frozen hamburger splattered against the wall.

"Holy shit," Gray muttered, slowly lowering his rifle. "That's better than a Ma Deuce."

"Unfortunately," I told him, "like money, you can't take it with you." I waved like the statue of the infantryman at Ft. Benning. "Follow me. We have a ship to take."

29

"Doesn't make any sense," Val said, his voice obscenely loud in my ears when we should have been silent and tactical. I never would get used to the soundproof helmets and headphones. "Where the hell is everybody?"

"Makes perfect sense," I countered, tapping my helmet, then motioning around us at the empty corridors of the cruiser. "Half this ship is in a vacuum. The troops and pilots mostly launched for the assault on DC and the crew is probably in space suits, sealed into their compartments. The big question is, are most of them on the bridge or in engineering?"

"That's why you get paid the big bucks, right?" Gray asked, for all his training in a space suit, not grasping why it was rude to step into someone's radio conversation. "To make that decision."

He was right though, and as we approached the intersection, the decision loomed. Anguilar ships were arranged horizontally, just like every other vessel with on-board gravity control and inertial dampeners, which was better for us, since it meant we wouldn't be dealing with elevators that could get locked out remotely or stairwells that could become deadly chokepoints. Instead, the Anguilar opted for ramps between one level and another. We'd come to the intersection between three levels. The ramp upward headed to the bridge, the corridor forward to the crew quarters and storage bays, and the ramp descending would be for access to engineering.

There was no way to know how many soldiers or security troops the ship's captain had kept back, but it couldn't be too many.

"Val," I said, making the decision a half-second before the words rolled out, "take the Peboktan and three of the Delta team and go secure Engineering. Don't give them the chance to sabotage the ship. You have the cracking pod, right?"

Val held up the device by way of confirmation. It had been something Lenny and Brandy had devised with Mallarna's help after we'd come back from Copperell with the fabricator for their ship's ID transponder. The device had also included the code algorithm for the internal security locks on Anguilar ships and bases, and it had just taken a little Creator computer technology combined with one of our comms to turn that data into what was basically a skeleton key for Anguilar ships.

"Hope it works," Val added. "You know we haven't really tried these things out yet."

"Consider this their first field test," I told him, patting the one affixed to my gunbelt to make sure it was still secure. "Dani, do you read me?"

"Yeah, I'm here," she replied from back at the Vanguard. "And you damned well know it, since you left me here."

Yeah, she hadn't been too happy about that but there was no way I was leaving the Vanguard and the transport unguarded. The last thing we needed was to come back and find that the Anguilar had sabotaged them or worse, stolen them. If the Anguilar felt like abandoning ship, I was all for it, but not on *my* birds.

"I left you there," I reminded her, "because no one else besides me knows how to fly the Vanguard. We're splitting up to take Engineering and the bridge. If you don't hear from us in five minutes, launch and disable this ship. Try not to blow the bastard up if you can help it, but do *not* allow it to boost to jump distance. Copy?"

"Yeah, I copy. I won't let the big, bad Anguilar take you away for public execution, Charlie."

I sighed, switched frequencies to the dismounts gathered in a semicircle around me. They'd separated already into two groups, and at least the Delta operators hadn't argued with me about splitting up.

"Gray, you coming with me or Val?" I asked. Not that it mattered much…I hadn't been in combat with these guys the way I had our original team. I just wanted to make sure I knew at least one of the names of the people who'd be backing me up.

"I'll stick with you. Temu and Gus will be coming with me.

Boz, Fish, and Parker will be going with Mr. McKee. Boz is the senior NCO for the group," he added.

I shook my head at the stream of nicknames. I understood they probably used them rather than their real name and rank for purposes of operational security, but who did they think *we* were going to tell?

"Boz," I said, looking in the general direction of the Engineering team, "your priorities are to take the Engineering section as intact as possible and to keep the Peboktan techs safe so they can get control of the drives, life-support, and power. Listen to Val and don't shoot anything if you don't know what it does."

"Hell," one of them, I didn't know which, commented dryly, "I don't know what *any* of this shit does."

"Then don't shoot any of it unless it's shooting at you," another told him, leaning over as he did. He was a broad-shouldered man, straining against the biggest suit we'd had available on the *Liberator*, and I assumed that was Boz. I got a hint through the glare reflected on his visor of a wide, open face and a leering grin. "Don't worry, sir, I'll make sure they don't break anything important."

"Val, we don't have much time," I reminded the old cowboy. "If you can't take the section, we're going to have to disable the drives and abandon ship. Use your best judgment."

"I always do." He offered me a casual salute before heading down into the bowels of the ship soundlessly, like I was watching this on TV with the volume muted. "Good luck."

"You want me up front, sir?" Gray asked, hefting his rifle. We'd barely had time to let him and his team test-fire the pulse weapons before we'd left the *Liberator*, but the rifles weren't that complicated and if I could pick up on their manual of operations on the fly, I was sure these guys could.

"No, I'm in the lead." I motioned to the Copperell bridge crew, standing behind us, their weapons at least pointed in a safe direction. "Keep one of your people in the rear, keep an eye on the pilots. We lose them, we lose this ship."

"Gus, you ride drag," Gray ordered. A sigh was the only response, but a tall, skinny figure ambled to the back of the line.

"Offset file," I told them, motioning everyone straight behind me. "No mines, no tripwires, no grenades so no wedge formation and no need for a three-meter separation. Better we're able to concentrate fire."

I wouldn't have bothered explaining that to any of the others, but I had an idea of how American infantry trained and even if these guys were super-special secret squirrels, they'd still be using similar movements and want to know why I wasn't. If Gray disagreed with my reasoning, he didn't argue about it, and they fell into formation behind me as we went up the ramp.

I really wish we had one of those drones Chuck's team had used back in DC because going over the hump of that ramp was about as nervous as I'd been in the last two years. It wouldn't have worked, of course, since the things were propeller-driven and there was no air in this section of the ship, but maybe they could rig something up on an RC car…

Next time.

That was the kind of thing I wanted from the alliance I'd proposed to the President, the sort of ideas I hadn't been around to see developed while I was gone, the ingenuity of the last three decades applied to Creator technology. I'd had all the right ideas, just a day late and a dollar short. Without a technological solution to the problem, I handled it the old-fashioned way and charged over the top, fighting an instinct to yell at the top of my lungs. No one would hear it.

I expected a hail of gunfire to meet my charge, but instead, I got nothing but an empty passageway and closed hatches. The crew didn't wear space suits on duty. They had to have taken shelter in one of the airtight compartments, or behind an emergency door. Or maybe I was just kidding myself, but the bridge was a quarter of a mile away and I didn't have time to be paranoid. I ran.

"You have to know this isn't going to work, Commander Travers."

Zan-Tar's voice in my headphones nearly sent me diving for cover, *did* make me miss a step, stumble into a crouch, the butt of my rifle coming up into my shoulder as I searched for the source. But I knew the source. He'd bounced the signal through the Vanguard's comms.

"You're on this ship, huh?" I asked, getting back to my feet and advancing at a fast walk, acting as if I was undaunted by the thought that Zan-Tar was watching us. In truth, I was very daunted but didn't have time to show it. "I didn't think you'd come after me yourself, being a general and all. I thought you might have sent one of your stooges to handle it…expendable."

"No bloodline of the Empire is expendable." The words

should have sounded outraged, righteously indignant, but instead they were only mildly offended, and I laughed.

"Oh, come on, General. How do you think I got on board the *Nova Eclipse*? How do you think I killed Mok-Lan?" My pace increased as I spoke, on a roll now, believing the act I was putting on. "One of your people betrayed the Empire because it was in their individual interest to do it. I think that's why you've had so much success conquering the rest of the galaxy. *They* all have honor, loyalty, so they can't understand it when a society like you comes along that doesn't. Well, I have news for you, you've come to the *home* of backstabbing and deceit. You've met your match here and the best thing you and your gang of intergalactic scavengers can do is load up everything you can carry and get the hell out while the getting's good."

"We're sealed inside the bridge behind an impenetrable emergency barrier," Zan-Tar snapped, and I could tell I'd finally gotten him angry, which seemed like an accomplishment. "I can see that you didn't bring along any plasma projectors, which means nothing you're carrying can burn through. This ship is going to be the one that destroys your precious *Liberator* and all you've accomplished is to give yourself a front-row seat. And just in case you think you can go back to your fighter and escape…I've raised the defense shield over the hangar bay. Try to fly out and it will rip you apart."

"Dani," I said, switching frequencies, "are you listening to this?"

"Not just listening to it," she confirmed grimly. "Living it. He's not lying. The energy field rose behind us just a few seconds ago. I've never tried to fly through one, so I don't know if he's telling the truth about what'll happen, but the instruments show it's there."

"I assume you've checked whether I speak the truth," Zan-Tar went on as if he'd been listening into our conversation. "So you know what will happen next. After I destroy the ship and your friends along with it, you'll be forced to surrender unless you wish to die once your suits run out of air. And once you've blacked out from lack of oxygen, we'll repressurize the ship and take you prisoner anyway. You'll be taken back to our imperial headquarters on Copperell, where you trespassed once before, and questioned. And you *will* talk. One of you will. We'll find out where you've been hiding your ships and your leadership, the place our prisoners have referred to as Sanctuary." Zan-Tar was snarling now, all pretense of being a reasonable man among the unreasonable gone, as if rejecting his offer and fighting back had been a personal insult. "And when we find it, we still won't kill you, Charlie Travers. You'll be kept alive…barely. Long enough to watch us lay waste to your base, slaughter everyone who's pledged allegiance to you. And maybe then, only then, will you realize how great your mistake was in turning down my terms."

I said nothing, letting him ramble, hoping it would give him a false sense of security. And I didn't stop, picking the pace back up to a quick jog. Only minutes had passed, but we only *had* minutes. The bridge entrance should have been just fifty yards ahead. I'd seen it before, in person and in mock-ups during simulations on the *Liberator* and the images were engrained deep in my memory…but this wasn't in those memories. The emergency seal was thick and imposing, and I'd seen those before, though not here. I'd burned through them on the *Nova Eclipse* with the plasma projector Zan-Tar had spoken of and if I'd known this was going to happen, I would have told the Delta team to pack some of them.

Unfortunately, this whole thing had occurred to me a little late in the game for that and when it had, I'd been hampered by the fact that the Delta crew wouldn't have any experience with a plasma gun, and it was a lot more problematic to use than a pulse rifle. And like the Anguilar, all our troops were down on the surface. Luckily for me and not for Zan-Tar, we had those cracking pods. As long as they worked.

"Gray," I said, trying to remember what I knew about the emergency doors, "get on the left. You three…" I pointed at the Copperell. "Get behind them. When this thing moves, Gray, so do you. Bridge crew, stay here and if anything gets by us, shoot the hell out of it. Do *not* shoot us." I looked across the reflective visors, unable to see their eyes. "Everyone ready?"

"Hoo-ah, sir," Gray said, still just as calm as though this was just another security detail.

"I see you there, Charlie," Zan-Tar taunted. "Do you think I'll let you in if you ask nicely? Those pulse rifles could fire for a year and not cut through the door."

"Keep talking," I murmured, putting the cracking pod against the security panel and pushing the button.

The light on the face of the device blinked yellow way too many times before it turned green. The door moved and so did I.

30

It raised more slowly than I'd remembered, and when I hit the floor, the rifle at my shoulder, it was only seven or eight inches off the deck, just enough for me to get a view of the inside of the bridge. Not as many Anguilar as I'd thought, no more than two dozen crammed into the compartment, all of them in space suits, colored the same as their dress uniforms, all of them armed with pulse rifles or pistols.

They hadn't expected the door to move, that was clear by how slowly they responded to its rise, turning away from monitors. What was on the monitors, stretched across the main screen, nearly made me freeze as well. The ship had been boosting while we made our way to the bridge and on that screen, the *Liberator* lumbered naked and vulnerable across the empty space between the Earth and the Moon, painfully slow. Around her, hell raged, the naked white arc light of particle cannons ripping at the fabric of reality, their blinding crescendo undercut by the accompaniment of angry red pulse fire. The Vanguards zoomed in and out between the ships, careful, much more cautious than Gib would have been if I'd given him the green light, taking shots and backing off.

I should have told him to do whatever he had to in order to save the *Liberator*, should have let him cut loose, but we'd already had two of the fighters destroyed in the last battle and we just couldn't afford to lose any of the things since they weren't making them anymore. Another mistake, like the plasma guns, because one of the cruisers had slipped the cordon of the fighters while they were tied up with the other three, was heading straight for the *Liberator*.

I pulled the trigger. I barely had to aim, as packed as the bridge was with crew, but I did anyway, going for the pilot first. The navigator, the helmsman, whatever the Anguilar called them, the ones who actually flew the ship, was always in the same place, the same station, and he was one of the few who didn't have a gun in his hand, wasn't looking at the emergency barrier. After my first shot, he wasn't looking at anything, slumping over his controls.

As if the shot had flipped a switch, the entire gathered mass opened fire my way, though too high, sparks and heat flashing off the door three feet above me and I ducked below the barrage. If I'd been alone, that would have been that, but Gray and his people, though they might have been new to pulse rifles and combat in a vacuum, weren't new to gunfights.

But the Anguilar on the bridge were. They'd been packed together, and not for some tactical reason of massed fire but more because they wanted the comfort of other people to calm their nerves. They were used to shooting at targets *outside* their ship, and not getting shot back at for the most part. Short, controlled bursts tore into them, left to right, and the Delta boys had taken to heart my speech about not hitting any vital equipment because not a round missed. Not one of *ours* anyway.

Once the fire from the Delta team drew the attention away from me, I added my own gun to the mix and worked from right to left. It wasn't slow and it wasn't clean, and they could have offered to surrender but none did. One of ours went down and I couldn't even tell who, just that it was one of the Delta soldiers and that they weren't getting up. Even if we'd been close enough to get the man to treatment on the *Liberator*, the hole in his chest wasn't the thing that would kill him…that was the vacuum the hole let in.

The other two operators didn't let up on their fire, but the Copperell pilots ran up and grabbed the wounded man, dragged him back, and then he was out of my peripheral vision and I couldn't afford to look away from the Anguilar. The ones in back, maybe half a dozen of them, tried to use the ones in front for cover, and when those fell, they tried to squeeze behind the acceleration couches, but they didn't give up for all that, firing blindly, barely looking over their cover.

I didn't want to take the chance of anyone hitting the control panels while they were trying to take out the last few.

"Cease fire! Cease fire!" I yelled, scrambling to my feet and sprinting forward, letting my rifle drop away on its sling while I pulled my heavy pulse pistol from its holster.

This was more like it. Everything else we'd done, all the spying and politics and speeches, it had been a nightmare and I'd felt like the kid I was, but this was what I'd been doing for two years and it all finally seemed real to me. Pulse gun fire streamed over my head, and I dropped into a slide as it tracked lower, like heading into third base on a steal.

The slide took me off to the side of the control panels, and the last of the defenders turned with me, barrels swinging around, still spitting fire. Not fast enough. I fired without aiming, pointing the gun like it was an extension of my arm. Short bursts, two or three rounds each, but it was sufficient since they weren't wearing armor. Two, then three, jerking away like they'd touched a live wire, and when the last three lurched out from behind the chairs, trying desperately to get away from me, the Delta soldiers cut them down and for a long second, all was silent.

I spared the dead a glance, wondering which of them was General Zan-Tar, but there was no time to figure it out now.

"Pilots, get this damned thing ready to fight!" I ordered. "Hurry, now!"

I holstered my handgun and pulled bodies away from the stations. Blood had frozen to crystals and, through intact visors, the faces already appeared mummified. My stomach turned and I thought about the casualty, but there wasn't time to check on him and I barely remembered to switch frequencies.

"Val, we have the bridge. Tell me Engineering is secured."

"Done, Charlie," Val replied. "There'as about ten of them down here, and it was bad. Lost two of your soldiers and one of the Peboktan, Charri, but the other two have control of the compartment."

"Get the ship sealed up and repressurized," I told him. "And make sure the energy field over the hangar bay is down!"

The Copperell were good at their jobs and already in position at navigation, weapons, and sensors, bringing us in toward the enemy cruisers. I fought to remember the pilot's name.

"Candon," I found it just before I was about to call him by his station, "open fire on the lead cruiser the second we're in range! Give him everything you've got! Gray."

I wasn't sure if the man was still alive, but one of the two soldiers huddled over the body of the third looked up at me and I caught a glimpse of his features through the visor.

"I'm going back to my fighter. I can do more out there. Keep a watch on the bridge and make sure they didn't leave us any surprises."

"Copy that, sir."

I wanted to tell him I was sorry about his friend, but I still had another call to make before Dani saw that shield fall and took off without me.

"Dani," I said, panting with exertion as I sprinted back the way I'd come, the aches and pains and bruises starting to make their way through the surge of adrenaline. "We've got control. I'm coming back to the fighter. Get her ready for launch."

Nothing. What the hell?

"Dani, do you copy?" Was there some problem with the comms now? Maybe the energy field had done something to them…

The intersection rushed up at me and I nearly tumbled head-first down the ramp, barely able to control my descent, arms flailing. Urgency broiled in my gut and I knew I had to get to the bay, not just because they needed me out there but because something wasn't right.

"Dani," I repeated, reaching the ruined section of passageway where our particle cannon shots had hit home. "Dammit, answer me!"

The fighter, I saw with a measure of relief, was still there. That had been my biggest fear on the race from the bridge, that she'd just taken off without me and I'd be stuck here while the battle raged outside and someone else fought it. The hatch was closed and secured and didn't open at my approach, which made no sense. I'd left the bird depressurized and Dani wouldn't have had any reason to seal it up again since she knew I'd be coming back.

But something was different. It took me two full seconds to realize what it was. The intact Anguilar lander was gone. A lone figure lay sprawled where it had been, their armored space suit dark against the gray deck, and as fast I'd sprinted back to the hangar bay, I made it to that space suit even faster, as quick as I'd run since high school.

I knew who it was, recognized the suit even face down, and I prayed that I was wrong, prayed to a God that surely had His hands full with an entire universe of intelligent life that I wouldn't find what I knew was waiting when I turned the suit over. The hole burned through the chest plate mocked my prayers, sneered and told me my God wasn't listening.

Through the visor of the helmet, Dani Campling's unseeing eyes stared back at me.

31

A SOB RACKED my shoulders and tears that I couldn't wipe away blurred my vision.

Like the Delta Force soldier on the bridge, there was no hope she could yet be saved, even with the almost magic medical tech of the Creators. The shot had been fatal enough, without the intense cold that had leached its way into her suit through the breach, crystalized her blood. The vitreous humor in her eyes glittered through her faceplate like the facets of a diamond.

I forced myself to look away from the statue-still features and the hideous wound through her armor and instead, examine her hands. Her right hand was clenched, her trigger finger extended, like she'd been holding a gun when she died and someone had pried it out of her grasp.

An Anguilar had done this. One we missed, who'd snuck back behind us and somehow, drawn her out of her fighter, and I couldn't figure how. She'd been smart enough to lock the hatch behind her, though, and whoever it was hadn't been able to get past the security, so he'd taken the shuttle. It had only been minutes.

I stood, choking down a sob. I couldn't do anything for Dani…but maybe I could still catch the son of a bitch who'd killed her.

The security plate on the side of the Vanguard yielded to the code I fed it, though it hadn't given way to the scorched, blackened scar where the killer had tried to blast it with a pulse pistol. The Kamerians built better than that, yet I cursed them for how slowly the hatch opened and squeezed through before it was all the way down.

Stash the pulse rifle, run startup sequence for the engines, strap in, it all went by rote, my thoughts far away, disconnected from where I was and what I was doing. All I could think of was how I was going to tell Gib, thinking of the two of them together and how happy he'd been. What would happen when he found out.

The belly jets rumbled, the weight coming off the landing gear, and I twisted the steering yoke to turn the fighter around on maneuvering jets until the nose faced into the blackness again. Gritting my teeth, I pushed the throttle forward and blasted out of the bay, ignoring the swathe of glowing destruction I left behind me.

The sensor screen was a collage painted in fire, hard to separate out anything from the coruscating energy of an exploding Anguilar cruiser. Gib had finally nibbled away at the ship's defenses and brought one of them down, which left three, the one racing straight at the *Liberator*, the one still engaged with the Vanguard squadron…and one making a break for minimum jump distance. And rocketing to intersect the cruiser was a single Anguilar shuttle.

The ship we'd taken over roared past me, a lion pouncing on a wounded gazelle, firing already at extreme range, and the twin horns of light gored through the midsection of the Anguilar who'd been zeroing in on the *Liberator*. The enemy cruiser glowed and shuddered, but I let the battle slip out of my perceptions as it slipped out of my front screen.

My entire universe was that one shuttle, my purpose for being to cut it off before it reached the fleeing cruiser. Acceleration lunged past the inertial dampeners, punching me in the face, and I welcomed the pain, a reminder of what I had planned for whoever was inside that shuttle. That Dani had been a combatant, a soldier, a legitimate target for the enemy, made not a single bit of difference. I was going to kill them.

"I'm sorry, Commander Travers."

It was Zan-Tar, coming over the comms again, though his tone differed greatly from the one he'd been using to taunt me while we'd advanced on the bridge. He sounded as if he meant it.

"Sorry for how I spoke to you," he amended. "You must understand, I didn't expect your gambit to board my flagship. It's typical of you, and perhaps I should have seen it coming, but this was a probing mission to test the defenses of this world and you weren't supposed to be here at all."

I said nothing, no longer interested in either his mind games or his self-conscious sense of noble superiority. He was likely on the cruiser, and I didn't care if he escaped, didn't care about his dire promises of future invasions. I just wanted to kill one man.

"And I'm sorry about your copilot," he went on, and my blood froze. "You must understand, I couldn't be captured by you once it became clear you'd actually take the ship. That was the purpose of my ungentlemanly behavior, of course, to keep you and your force focused on the bridge, not searching for a single Anguilar officer sneaking back to the hangar bay. At that point, it was fairly simple to lure your copilot out of her fighter. Ideally, I wanted to take the Vanguard and present it as a prize to the Emperor to turn this into some sort of triumph rather than a bloody nose, but the woman was smart enough to secure the hatch behind her. Your females are much more capable than ours, apparently. I had no choice but to kill her from ambush. I'm sure you would have done the same thing."

General Zan-Tar was in that shuttle. He'd been on the cruiser, hadn't been one of those bodies on the bridge. Somehow, I'd known that, known that someone who'd risen that high in the Anguilar military wouldn't have been interested in any heroic last stands. Those were for lesser beings, not bloodline-blessed Anguilar.

The red line signifying the maximum range for the fighter's particle cannon chased the shuttle, kissing the rear of its engine plume, teasing me. I gave into impatience and fired, but the beam guttered out just shy of the fleeing bird. He was still taunting me, in his way, I realized.

"I'm afraid we'll have to continue this conversation at another time," he went on, the shuttle sailing into the hangar bay of the cruiser as she slowed down to receive it. "You must know I shall return."

The cruiser swallowed up Zan-Tar's shuttle and was gone in a polychromatic flare, retreating into hyperspace, where I couldn't touch them. My mouth had gone dry, my brain numb. He'd gotten away. I'd failed her.

Lost in a haze, I might have been a passenger in the fighter watching some other man turn the Vanguard into a braking burn, heading back for Earth orbit. I couldn't remember checking the scanners, yet I knew that the last two Anguilar cruisers were glowing clouds of debris spread between the Earth and the Moon. The IFF told a story to that other, more observant pilot that Gib's squadron was intact and waiting for someone to give them an order, something that other guy couldn't do.

Something only I could do.

"Second..." The word came out as a hoarse croak and I cleared my throat, tried again. "Second squadron, follow me in. We're going to help First clear out the rest of the Starblades and provide air support for the ground forces." And I doubt I could have even managed that much if I hadn't known Laranna was down there, depending on me. "Candon," I said to the pilot aboard the captured Anguilar cruiser, "escort the *Liberator* into high orbit and maintain relative position until you hear from me. Lenny, get a lander over to the Anguilar ship with a relief engineering crew and tell the pilot to transport the Delta team back to DC."

I didn't wait for acknowledgement of any of the orders, just shoved the controls forward, breaking orbit, heading into the atmosphere. If I let myself talk to Gib, I'd have to tell him what happened.

I didn't want to do that until he was on the ground.

I DIDN'T LIKE FLYING the Vanguard in an atmosphere.

Out in space, it was easy to pretend this was a high-end video game from some rich kid's arcade, that none of it was real and if I died, I could just pop in another quarter and try again. Down in the soup, as the more experienced pilots liked to call it, every shake and shimmy, every sway and shudder felt like the one that would throw me into an out-of-control spin and smash the bird into the ground at supersonic speed.

Somehow, it hadn't been so frightening when Dani was in the gunner's seat, ready to tease me mercilessly if I showed any sign of fear or hesitation. Now, the silence in the cockpit amplified the creaking metal and the roar of the jets to a deafening background noise and I tried the comms again just to hear a human voice, even if it was just my own.

"Laranna, do you copy?"

She might not. I'd entered the atmosphere on the opposite side of the planet from her, not from any intention, just to descend as quickly as possible, and I was currently twenty thousand feet over the Great Plains. No problem for a radio wave but our intership secure comms worked on some other principle, lasers maybe, and required either line of sight or a ship in orbit to relay the signal. I had neither, apparently. It was ridiculous. The fighters could transmit and receive regular microwaves but not to *each other* because of some stupid security protocol put in place by a paranoid Kamerian centuries ago, and Lenny claimed he couldn't bypass it without totally reprogramming each fighter's on-board computer.

Cursing under my breath, I opened the throttle just a *little* more and my reward was an immediate increase in turbulence, something not all the gravity-resist or inertial dampeners in the universe could do away with. Mach six. I could go faster but doing it at this altitude would shake me like a smoothie in a blender, even with all this Kamerian technology. Ten minutes to DC.

"Charlie, you copy?"

Shit. It was Gib. He and his squadron were stretched out in a V with me at the point, but he hadn't tried calling me until now and I'd dared to hope he wouldn't. I paused as long as I could get away with, wondering if he'd just give up if I didn't answer.

"Charlie, it's Giblet. Do you copy?"

So much for that.

"Yeah, Gib," I replied morosely. "I read you."

"I can't get through to Dani's personal comm line." His tone was plaintive rather than worried. Just a technical problem. Nothing to worry about.

I could have lied, told him that just to keep him calm, but Gib was a friend and I owed him the truth. I opened my mouth to give that truth to him and damn the consequences, but I was saved by one of those unsecure microwave transmissions, staticky and fading in my earphones.

"Unknown rider, unknown rider, this is the United States Air Force. Identify yourself immediately. Squawk 1214 and identify."

And according to the sensors, yes it was. One of those new jets I'd seen on the internet, the F-22. Sleek and futuristic, but not as futuristic as mine. A flight of four, approaching from our front, maybe two hundred miles away. I touched a control on the comm panel to match his frequency.

"US Air Force, this is...*Commander* Charlie Travers of the resistance Vanguard Wing," I replied. "We're proceeding to the DC area to provide air support against the Anguilar."

Nothing for a second, and I imagined the pilot, who sounded old enough to be at least a major, was passing the information on to his base and from there to the next level up and so on.

"Umm..." the man stuttered, which was, I suppose, some indication of how strange this all was, since I'd always heard fighter pilots were known for their steel nerves and ice-water blood and absolute certainty. "...Vanguard Wing commander, roger that. My superiors request you follow us down and confer with them in person."

I made sure I hit the mute button before I sighed. The guy was just doing his job.

"Negative," I told him. "The fight is in DC and that's where we're needed. You can feel free to try and stop us, but I imagine those heat-seeking missiles you're carrying cost a lot of taxpayer money and you'll waste every single one of them without even scratching our paint. Not that you can keep up, anyway."

Not waiting for a reply, I gave the throttle just another little nudge. Mach seven. The others followed and if the fuselage shook like a wet dog, it was worth it to think of the looks on the faces of the pilots when we shrieked past them faster than any of them had ever flown.

DC might have been ten minutes away, but the fight wasn't. The sensor lit up with warnings of bogies and the IFF transponders flashed blue somewhere over Indiana…or maybe Ohio. It was hard to tell from up here.

"First squadron, do you copy?" I transmitted. "This is Charlie, someone answer me, dammit!"

"What the hell took you so long?" Laranna asked, just as a Starblade shot past us with a Vanguard riding hard on its ass. "Were you doing an inventory of the Anguilar cruiser's liquor supplies for your private stash?"

I was about to pull around into a sharp turn to follow her, but the particle cannon cut apart the morning sky with cloud-to-cloud lightning and the Starblade disappeared, burning fairy dust now, falling out of the sky for a waiting child to make a wish and start flying.

"The cruisers are toast except one that escaped," I told her. "What's the situation here?"

"We're still mopping up the last ten Starblades," Laranna said, as casual and calm as that Air Force fighter jock *should* have been. "We can handle them, but the ground forces are barely holding off the Anguilar infantry. The Strada need your help."

"Right. Heading there now." I swallowed hard, knowing I

shouldn't say it now, that it was unprofessional, but needing to very badly. "I love you."

"Love you, too...*Commander*." The grin traveled through the transmission, carried on her voice, and then she was gone, arcing back around into the fight.

She'd saved me from having to answer Gib. Now it was my turn to save Chuck and the Strada. And the US government, of course.

Couldn't forget about them.

32

I'd never seen Washington DC from the air before. Never flown into Dulles, and during the chopper flight from the South Lawn to Arlington, the shades had been closed, robbing me of the chance to rubberneck.

I certainly hadn't expected that the first time I saw it, it would be on fire.

Not the whole city, obviously, and not even the White House or the Capitol Building. No, what burned were the old office buildings lined up along Pennsylvania Avenue, landmarks all, I'm sure, but I couldn't recall the name of a single one of them as I flew low above the raging battle. Things were laid out for me like a sand table, the distribution of friendly and enemy troops obvious...not least because the destruction was a clear line of demarcation.

Dozens of Anguilar armored vehicles stabbed down the street

like a spear aimed directly for the White House and I wondered how they knew it was their primary target. I didn't doubt it had to be defended, though. With dozens of Starblade fighters in the air, there was zero possibility that they'd taken the chance of trying to fly the President out in Marine One, which meant he was down in that same bunker they'd brought us to after the attack by the Russians. Not exactly huddled in darkness since the place had been pretty luxurious, but probably scared shitless.

He had reason to be. The sides of the street weren't just a graveyard for old buildings, they were the graveyard for tanks and armored personnel carriers…and the soldiers who'd manned them. Flame consumed the vehicles, those that hadn't already burned out, and I winced at the thought of the men trapped inside them. Not just ground troops, either. The wreckage of crashed aircraft littered the blocks around the main drive, spreading the fires laterally into the rest of the city, the parts where people lived and worked. No fire engines would be responding to those fires until the fighting stopped.

The Army troops had been slaughtered, but they'd accomplished one thing—they'd blocked off the side streets with the burning hulks of their vehicles, keeping the Anguilar troops from spreading like the flames to destroy more of the city. The only thing blocking the enemy's path to the White House was Chuck's company of Strada warriors and their own armor…though not much of it.

Chuck might have been light infantry, but he'd arranged the armored assault vehicles into a classic defense in depth, and the success of his strategy was evidenced by the smoking husks of the

Anguilar's front rank. They couldn't hold out forever, though, not with at least a battalion of Anguilar facing them.

Eventually, more conventional military forces would have overwhelmed them, but probably not before they burned their way through to the presidential bunker and, at the very least, threw the entire nation into chaos by decapitating the government. At the worst, they could hold him hostage and stall for time until reinforcements arrived. If not for Chuck. If not for us.

"Chuck," I called, having neglected to give him any official callsign and not worried about being overheard, "this is Charlie. Have your people pull back, button up and keep their heads down. We're making a gun run."

I switched freqs to Gib and his squadron, not having the time to wait for Chuck's reply.

"Follow me around, Second. Burn these bastards down."

They fired at us as we arced around, passing over the White House, but the scattered bursts from the heavy pulse cannon mounted on the Anguilar vehicles couldn't penetrate our shields, couldn't do more than light our birds up with the fiery halo of avenging angels. Still, we didn't fire back yet, just continued the turn. The SAM emplacements on the White House roof tracked us, the launchers spinning to match our trajectory but not bothering to launch, either because they knew we were friendlies or maybe because they'd already tried the weapons against the Starblades and seen how useless they were.

The second the Strada defensive position disappeared under the nose of my Vanguard, I opened fire. This would have been a great time to have Dani on the pulse turret, pouring a constant stream of fire into the enemy while I punctuated the lighter weapon with the particle cannon, but she was gone and I was alone. The only tool I had was a hammer and the Anguilar became the nails.

Mushroom clouds of red and white blossomed off the street as blasts from the particle cannon ripped into the pavement and turned it and the Anguilar atop it into burning vapor. The others swooped in behind me and matched the intensity of my fire, the atomic inferno swallowing up the length of Pennsylvania Avenue from curb to curb. Vehicles and the Anguilar troops inside them disappeared in blinding flares of white energy, and it wasn't until the first dozen double ranks had ceased to exist that the troops at the end thought to abandon their vehicles.

Pulse fire from Gib's squadron chased after them, cutting the armored troopers down, but I ignored them, concentrating on the vehicles. I slowed the Vanguard to a hover, the drive pods angled downward, atmospheric jets screaming with effort, and smashed the Anguilar battalion like a spoiled child breaking unwanted toys. With every pull of the trigger, I saw Dani's lifeless face, in every explosion of flame, the glint of the hangar bay lights off her frozen eyes. These troops hadn't killed her and killing them wouldn't bring her back. They probably weren't even Anguilar, most likely Krill or other subject peoples, and I just didn't care.

"I think we got 'em all, Charlie," Gib transmitted, gentle reproof in his voice.

As if a veil had been lifted from my eyes, I blinked and saw that there was nothing left of the Anguilar column, black smoke enshrouding the entire road for a good mile. Nothing moved, nothing lived.

"Have your planes scout the area for runners," I told Gib, my voice dry and raspy. "I'm going to land and coordinate with the ground forces."

In truth, I was going to land because the trembling in my hands had spread to my shoulders, my stomach, and I wasn't sure how much longer I could keep the Vanguard in the air. The utter destruction on this side of the Strada position forced me to circle back behind them, touching down not twenty feet from the metal fence in front of the White House.

No tourists watched from the other side of that fence, no Secret Service agents or police observed my Vanguard thumping in a harder landing than I would usually have made. The ones on duty had either gone to the bunker with President Louis or lined up beside the Army troops and died with them.

I paused in the hatchway and pulled off my helmet. Sweat had dried beneath it, matted my hair, but what bothered me were the salty tracks on my cheeks where the tears had dried. I pulled off my gloves, scraped the rheum out of my eyes and off my face with the back of my hand before I walked down the steps, steadying myself against the side of the plane so I wouldn't stumble. My legs had no strength left in them. Everything, every ounce of energy I'd tapped, had faded along with that last shot.

A Strada armored vehicle had broken away from the defensive positions and rumbled to within twenty yards of me before it stopped and Chuck Barnaby hopped out, his visor up, a pulse rifle held in the crook of his arm.

"That was a good formation," I told him, nodding toward the main body of his troops. Strada climbed out of their vehicles, staring at the glow from the destruction, unsure what to do. "I have Second Squadron hunting for any Anguilar dismounts. Detail a couple of your APCs to follow their directions and go in on the ground if they need it."

"Right," he said, turning back to the others, speaking softly into his helmet mic.

Chuck had stepped up. None of this seemed to faze him, though I could have thought of a lot of young officers who would have been in shock from the battle. He looked at home in our armor, fighting at the head of the Strada, and I wondered if he wanted a job.

I also wondered when someone was going to come out of the White House and want to talk about all this. It had better be soon because I wasn't certain how much longer I could stay on my feet. I was seriously thinking about sitting on the ground beside the fence line when the second Vanguard descended on pillars of fire only a few hundred feet away. Heat pounded at the exposed skin of my face, the scream of the landing jets battering my ears, but I didn't move, didn't flinch. I knew who this was. I knew what he wanted.

The landing was a rough one for Giblet, and the side hatch dropped open even before the Vanguard's belly gear had settled into their hydraulic housings. Gib tossed his helmet aside with a curse and jumped down from the hatch, ignoring the steps. He ran at me so violently I was sure he'd throw a punch, but I didn't lift a hand to defend myself, just waited. He came up short, but not by much, standing nose to nose with me.

"Where is she?" Giblet demanded, not bothering to look inside my fighter. "She wasn't firing the turret. I saw. Where is she?"

"She's back on the cruiser," I said, my voice breaking at the last word. I tried to tell him the rest but the look on his face, the utter, bleak devastation stopped me, and only tightly clenched teeth kept me from collapsing to my knees. A veil of tears blurred my vision, and I couldn't speak through the sobs. But I had to. I owed that to him, and I was able to choke out the words. "She didn't make it."

I expected Gib to scream, to rage, to hit me. I wanted it, wanted *someone* to punish me for letting her die. The whole thing had been my idea and I'd known the risks and done it anyway. Selfishly, I'd figured that the likeliest one to die would be me, and I hadn't prepared myself at all for the possibility that I'd have to live with the consequences of my decision.

But Gib didn't yell, didn't take a swing at me. Instead, he wrapped me in his arms and pulled me into a hug, saying nothing.

"I'm sorry, Gib." The words were broken glass ripping at my throat. "I'm sorry. I left her in the fighter to watch the hangar bay. I thought she would be safe…"

"None of us is safe," he told me, his tone cold enough that I pulled away, looking him in the eye. No anger flared behind his gaze, just icy detachment. "Look at this place." He waved around at the destruction. "The people here didn't even know there were any other intelligent life forms besides them." He sneered, a little of the old Gib making its way through the chill mask. "For certain definitions of intelligence, anyway. They were living their lives, obsessed with their own problems, their petty little differences, their worst-case scenario probably that some Earth government they didn't like would have more power than they did. They thought everything out there…" His eyes traveled upward. "…was far away, meaningless. Not worth considering. They thought they were safe, until the Anguilar just decided that they needed more slaves, more tribute, more resources they didn't have to work for."

The static crackle and boom of distant pulse fire echoed off the burning buildings. Somewhere, the Strada had killed a fleeing enemy soldier. Gib shook his head.

"No one in this galaxy will ever be safe until every one of these Anguilar bastards is dead." He turned abruptly, drawing his sidearm and striding purposefully down the ruined street.

"Where are you going?" I called after him.

"They're still out there," he said, not turning around, pistol held at the ready. "Trying to run."

I rushed up to him, putting a hand on his shoulder.

"Gib, the Strada can handle it."

He smiled at me, but there was nothing pleasant in the expression.

"I'm gonna be honest with you, Charlie. I've never thought of this as *my* war. My people are scattered, we have no homeworld, everyone hates us, most of them would kill us all if they had the chance. I've stayed with the resistance because you're my friend and I know you'd die for me. Which is something I never had before. And then, Dani…" Pain spasmed across his face before it hardened again. "Something else I never had before. But now…" He shook his head. "Now it *is* my war. The Anguilar did that. And they're going to regret it."

Giblet walked toward the sound of distant gunfire. I let him go.

33

I STARED AT THE PHOTO. I'd been looking at it for a half an hour, unable to tear my eyes away, and when the phone timed out and the screen went dark, I'd tap it to bring it back to life.

Dani was young, her hair longer, tied into a ponytail, her face dusted with freckles and split into a grin as she straddled the dirt bike. It looked new and, knowing Dani, I was willing to bet she'd bought it herself. Off to the side was a blond woman in her late thirties or early forties, good looking in a rough-hewn sort of way, her blue-jean and T-shirt style similar to teenage Dani's. Her mother. She'd passed away while Dani was in college. On the other side of the photo, leaning against the back of the bike's seat was a younger teen, close enough in looks to Dani and her mom that he had to be the younger brother she'd told me about. He wore a ratty concert T-shirt for some band I'd never heard of and his blond hair was longer than his sister's. No tats or piercings yet…he was too young for that. But Dani had told me they came later, after their mother had died. Around the time Pete had gotten into drugs.

"I wonder if I should try to find him," I murmured.

Laranna sighed and took Dani's phone from me, sticking it into her jacket pocket, replacing it with her hand, her fingers tightening around mine. She stood, as if unable to settle down, burdened with nervous energy, while I'd given into inertia and hadn't stirred from the leather-bound antique sofa since the Secret Service escort had deposited us here in the President's private offices nearly an hour earlier.

"She told us that her brother was in a bad way," Laranna reminded me. "He might not be in any condition to receive the news of her…passing."

"But he's the only family she has left," I argued, though without much enthusiasm. Not because I particularly wanted to be the one to break it to the kid, drug addict or not, but because I felt like I owed it to her.

"No," Laranna said, bending down to kiss the top of my head. "*We're* her family. We need to make sure she'll be remembered. That her sacrifice wasn't in vain."

"Was it a sacrifice?" I asked, bitterness a sour taste in my mouth. "Or was it just my screw-up? I shouldn't have left her alone there."

"Who would you have left with her?" Laranna crouched beside me, taking my face between her hands and forcing me to meet her eyes. "This is a war, Charlie. You've known that since Strada. We love the people who stand beside us to fight it, and we lose the people we love. Was war ever different for you, here?"

I thought of Poppa Chuck's stories of the brothers-in-arms he'd lost on bombing missions in World War Two and shook my head. And I remembered what I'd said to Congress.

"Oh, thus be it ever when free men shall stand," I quoted, "between their loved homes and the war's desolation."

The door to the office burst open and I sprang to my feet instinctively as a pair of Secret Service agents preceded President Louis into the room. The man looked worn and haggard, and I wondered if he'd gotten any sleep in the three days since the Anguilar attack. Tagging along behind him were General Gavin, National Security Advisor Donovan, Secretary of Defense Mattheis, and the Secretary of State, Madison Barrett. It was a regular staff meeting and I wondered why we weren't in the Situation Room.

None of them said a word until Louis fell tiredly into his seat on the other side of the desk and the Secret Service agent closed the door behind us.

"Congress has passed a resolution authorizing the use of military force against the Anguilar," Donovan told us.

"And it was still too damned close," Louis said.

"There are those on both sides of the aisle," Barrett explained, taking a seat beside me on the sofa, "who still blame this on your presence here. We've told them that the Anguilar weren't even aware of your visit, that if you hadn't been here, they would have wiped us out, but people tend not to believe what the government tells them anymore."

"With good reason," General Gavin muttered, earning a glare from the President.

"But it passed," Donovan went on, undaunted, leaning against the president's desk in a familiar way that Louis didn't look askance at. "In an emergency session. And so did funding for the new weapons programs."

"I'm sure it didn't hurt," Gavin added, "that you guaranteed us that the cruiser you captured would remain in the system and be partially crewed by US servicemembers. Not to mention the technicians you're leaving to help us in salvaging the crashed vessel. I understand a surprising portion of that ship is still intact."

"If you're in this war," I said, unable to muster a spark of enthusiasm for their news, "then you're in it all the way. They're coming back. Their general, Zan-Tar, told me as much. It won't be immediately, but when they do, it'll be with overwhelming force. Not a dozen ships, but a hundred. Brigades of ground troops, thousands of fighters. *If* we give them the chance to build up that large of a force. If we don't make sure they're too busy someplace else."

"You made your point, Mr. Travers," President Louis sighed.

"*Commander* Travers," I corrected him softly, and Louis finally did smile.

"Commander Travers," he amended. "And that's the other decision that *I've* made as Commander in Chief. Once the new weapons systems are in place and initial training has been completed, we'll be putting our troops on your ships for strikes against the Anguilar Empire."

"Congress isn't going to like putting US troops under the command of a foreign government," Gavin warned, and I thought maybe he meant he wouldn't like it, either.

"Is it?" Louis asked and Gavin and I both looked at him curiously. "Is the resistance a government?" he elaborated. The President sat back in his chair and motioned toward me and Laranna. "You have no elected officials. You have no bureaucracy other than the intelligence network you told us about. Hell, your military doesn't even have an official ranking system or any means of promotion other than someone above you getting *killed*, if I understand correctly."

I winced, suddenly self-conscious. I'd thought about that, but there always seemed to be something more important happening than working on officious nonsense like ranks and promotion systems.

"We didn't have much of a military until about a year ago," I tried to explain. "We started with a bunch of refugees with no training and spent months trying to get them drilled to the point where they could be an organized infantry, but that was kind of a side project because most of our training emphasis was on engineering and bridge crews. Then we got ten thousand Strada volunteers, but they're from a warrior society and already have their own hierarchy so we just left that to them…" I shut up, realizing I was starting to sound like a whiny excuse-maker.

"So, no organized government," Louis said, nodding as if he'd made his point. "Ergo, you're *not* a foreign military. Particularly since you're an American citizen, Charlie, even if you've been living abroad."

"*Very* abroad," General Gavin commented dryly. "But what are you suggesting, Mr. President?"

"There's the age problem," Louis mused, staring at me intently, as if he hadn't heard the Chairman of the Joint Chiefs speak. Twenty-five is too young…" His face brightened, eyes widening. "But according to your birth certificate, you're *not* twenty-five. You're *sixty*!"

"Sir, I'm afraid I'm lost," I admitted, shaking my head. "What does my age have to do with…"

"The last time you were on this planet, son," Louis interrupted, and it seemed he was finally getting to the point, "you were a commissioned officer in the United States Army, and you never received a discharge, honorable or otherwise. I wonder if all of our worries about trusting our military forces to a foreign guerilla might not be assuaged if you were to be formally recalled to active duty." He shrugged. "We'd have to promote you, of course. There are regulations to be gotten around, but if the President can't do it, who can? Colonel, I'm thinking, unless you're married to the whole *commander* thing." Louis grinned. "We'll just have to make sure not to put anyone higher than colonel out in the field, so you can still be in command."

I realized my mouth was hanging open, so I shut it before anything had the chance to fly in, but I still didn't say anything, too flabbergasted for words.

"Think about it for a while," Louis encouraged. "It'll probably take a few days to get all the red tape taken care of, anyway. I can't force you..." He chuckled, folded his hands. "Well, *legally* I could force you, but you have starships and fighters and weapons that can destroy a city, so really, no, I can't force you. But I'd like you to consider it. It would be a much easier sell if I could tell the American people that the effort to defeat the evil alien empire was being led by an American military hero."

"Charlie," Laranna said frostily, her eyes boring into Louis without the slightest bit of deference, "*is* an American military hero. Not to mention a hero to all the resistance."

I examined the floor closely, ears going hot.

"Of course," President Louis agreed, spreading his hands in a conciliatory gesture. "And we all believe that. But we're not talking about those of us in this room drinking a toast to Charlie. We're talking about convincing three hundred *million* people to send billions of tax dollars and our young men and women into harm's way."

"A *colonel*?" General Gavin repeated, disbelief heavy in the word. "Sir, all the military experience Mr. Travers has is thirty-five years old!"

"Which is why he's going to need a liaison," Louis agreed. "Someone he trusts who can act as a go-between with us. Someone who knows how the American military works...perhaps better than most, given his heritage." The President leaned over a speaker set in his desk and pressed a button. "Send him in."

The door swung open and Chuck Barnaby walked through, a

bemused expression on his face and major's oak leaves on the epaulets of his dress uniform.

"Mr. President!" he said, stiffening to attention and saluting.

"At ease, son," Louis waved the courtesy away. "Come on in and have a seat." Chuck gave me a doubtful look but sat down on the edge of a chair, feet flat on the floor like he might need to get away quick. "I know you had your heart set on being a Ranger company commander, but how would you like to go with our boys to the stars, instead?" He eyed the younger man sidelong. "That's a trick question, by the way…that promotion came with a catch. Go pack your bags, son. You're going for a little trip."

"I'm sorry about your friend."

I looked around at Lenny entering the gym and sighed, grabbing a towel from the weight rack. I'd been looking forward to getting off the planet for the simple reason that I was tired of talking to generals and politicians and, worst of all, the media. I'd been forced to give a press conference and of all the horrible experiences of my life, that had to rank right up there among the worst.

Up here on the *Liberator*, I hadn't even had to talk to most of my friends. The Vanguard squadrons were out on patrol, Mallarna and the Peboktan engineers were split between the USS *Dani Campling*—I'd insisted on that as a condition of turning her over to the American Space Force—and the cruiser that had crashed in the desert. Just outside St. George, Utah as it had turned out. Laranna and the Strada were still downstairs, coordinating with Chuck and Gray to institute a training program for Army and Marine infantry with the new weapons and armor and me…well, I'd used some lame excuse to get back up here so I wouldn't have to talk to anyone for a couple days. So I wouldn't have to hear them tell me how sorry they were about Dani.

That included Lenny, but how do you say no to a seven-foot-tall robot?

"Thanks," I told him, wiping away sweat. I hadn't been able to hit the weights for over a week and the time off was making this workout twice as hard as usual. "What's up?" I asked pointedly, hoping he'd take the hint.

"This incursion by the Anguilar was most unwise, I think," he said, rolling across the rubber-matted floor to gaze at his reflection in the mirrored wall. "They sent too large a force for a scouting expedition and too small of one to accomplish their mission if they faced any real opposition." No, he wasn't looking at his own reflection, I thought, he was looking at mine, as if watching me for a reaction.

"Yeah, we were damn lucky they didn't realize we'd be there," I admitted, not knowing what he wanted from me. "And, I guess, that they didn't just send a small transport to make a run by the planet. We probably wouldn't have detected them and wouldn't have been here when they came back."

"That isn't the only reason we were lucky." He turned, facing me. "I monitored the progress of your attempts to convince the American government to join us. If it hadn't been for the attack by the Anguilar force, I doubt you would have been able to come to an agreement in time to protect the planet from occupation."

A chill went up my spine despite the sweat, as if the air conditioning had just been adjusted downward.

"Yeah, I suppose so," I said carefully. "What's your point, Lenny?"

"Only this," he said, rumbling across the rubber mat, his massive form wobbling slightly as he passed over an irregularity in the material. "We may not be so lucky next time. You keep asking if you're really in command, Charlie Travers. But I would ask you something as well. If you are truly in command… perhaps you would do well not to bounce from one crisis to another, acting as your instincts tell you. Perhaps you should begin to think in the long term. You will not always be able to salvage the situation by the seat of your pants. And neither will I."

I stared at him after he left, trying to convince myself I was paranoid. He was just pissed I'd gotten his ship damaged, that I'd been hasty and headstrong about this entire operation. He *wasn't* saying what I thought he was saying, that Lenny had arranged somehow for the Anguilar attack in order to make the US government cooperate with us.

That would be crazy.

I laid back on the bench and lifted the barbell off the brackets and tried not to think.

Amazon won't always tell you about the next release. To stay updated on this series, be sure to sign up for our spam-free email list at jnchaney.com.

Charlie and the rest of the crew return in ROAD of VENGEANCE, available on Amazon.

CONNECT WITH J.N. CHANEY

Don't miss out on these exclusive perks:

- Instant access to free short stories from series like *Backyard Starship*, *Sentenced to War*, and more.
- Receive email updates for new releases and other news.
- Get notified when we run special deals on books and audiobooks.

So, what are you waiting for? Enter your email address at the link below to stay in the loop.

https://www.jnchaney.com/taken-to-the-stars-subscribe

CONNECT WITH RICK PARTLOW

Check out his website

https://rickpartlow.com

Connect on Facebook

https://www.facebook.com/DutyHonorPlanet

Follow him on Amazon

https://www.amazon.com/Rick-Partlow/e/B00B1GNL4E/

ABOUT THE AUTHORS

J. N. Chaney is a USA Today Bestselling author and has a Master's of Fine Arts in Creative Writing. He fancies himself quite the Super Mario Bros. fan. When he isn't writing or gaming, you can find him online at **jnchaney.com**.

He migrates often, but was last seen in Las Vegas, NV. Any sightings should be reported, as they are rare.

Rick Partlow is that rarest of species, a native Floridian. Born in Tampa, he attended Florida Southern College and graduated with a degree in History and a commission in the US Army as an Infantry officer.

He has written over 40 books in a dozen different series, and his short stories have been included in twelve different anthologies. Visit his website at **rickpartlow.com** for more.

Printed in Great Britain
by Amazon

49537562R00235